Scandalous Duke

League of Dukes Book Five

By
Scarlett Scott

Scandalous Duke
League of Dukes Book Five

All rights reserved.
Copyright © 2020 by Scarlett Scott
Published by Happily Ever After Books, LLC
Print Edition

ISBN: 979-8-602290-60-8

Edited by Grace Bradley
Cover Design by Wicked Smart Designs

This book or any portion thereof may not be reproduced or used in any manner whatsoever without the express written permission of the publisher except for the use of brief quotations in a book review.

The unauthorized reproduction or distribution of this copyrighted work is illegal. No part of this book may be scanned, uploaded, or distributed via the Internet or any other means, electronic or print, without the publisher's permission. Criminal copyright infringement, including infringement without monetary gain, is punishable by law.

This book is a work of fiction and any resemblance to persons, living or dead, or places, events, or locales, is purely coincidental. The characters are productions of the author's imagination and used fictitiously.

For more information, contact author Scarlett Scott.
www.scarlettscottauthor.com

Felix Markham, Duke of Winchelsea, has devoted his life to being the perfect statesman and raising his daughter after his beloved wife's death. But when devastating bombings on the railway leave London in an uproar, he is determined to bring the mastermind of the attacks to justice. He will lure the fox from his den by any means.

In her youth, Johanna McKenna donned a French accent and stage name to escape the clutches of her violent father and became the darling of the New York City stage as Rose Beaumont. Her past comes calling when her brother's reappearance in her life leads her into a dangerous web of deceit. She finds herself hopelessly trapped until she receives an offer she cannot refuse from London's most famous theater.

Felix's plan is clear: bring the famed Rose of New York to London, secure her as his mistress, and drive his quarry to English shores. But the more time he spends in Johanna's company, the more he realizes nothing is as it seems, least of all the woman who feels as if she were made to be in his arms. When he finally learns the truth, it may be too late to save both his city and the enigmatic lady who has stolen his heart.

Dedication

For Dad. You're right. It all started with *Trapping in Canada* by John P. Elag. Thank you for the chicken soup during deadline week to fight off my cold, and for telling everyone you meet to read my books.

Prologue

New York City, 1882

"JOHANNA."

The voice was unmistakable, though the name, almost, was not.

No one called her Johanna any longer. To everyone who thought they knew her, she was Rose. Mademoiselle Beaumont. The Rose of New York. Any of those would do.

She had not been Johanna to anyone other than herself in years.

She stiffened, a dull throb of foreboding blossoming to life in her gut at the familiar face and form before her. Unexpected and yet as recognizable as the back of her own hand, despite the intervening years.

"What are you doing in my hotel room?" she demanded, her voice trembling, betraying her.

She was confident in her talent as an actress, but some fear was far too real to be disguised. He looked much older now, his blond hair thinning. More like their father than she could have imagined.

He smiled, as if this were a pleasant visit. As if he were a welcome guest. "I have my ways."

Of course he did. Drummond McKenna was a powerful man, as Michael McKenna had been. Leader of the Emerald Club. Scion of great wealth and great misery. The mere sight of her brother was enough to remind her of the stinging lashes she had endured for her disobedience.

"How did you know where to find me?" she asked.

"The Rose of New York?" He sauntered toward her, and she realized he was holding a framed picture in his hands. "Your face is everywhere, Jojo. Handbills, the papers, hell, nearly every *carte de visite* in the city has you on it."

"Do not call me Jojo," she bit out, eying the picture he held once more. She recognized the frame, for it had cost her a small fortune. But the price she had paid to buy it was no comparison to the picture it held.

That picture, the only one she possessed of Pearl, was priceless.

"Why not?" He glanced down at the burled walnut frame he held. "It is your name, sister."

The hated pet name from her childhood reminded her of everything she had spent all the years since trying to forget. "I am Rose Beaumont."

Rose Beaumont hailed from Paris.

She was fashionable. Sought after. An enigma. Rose Beaumont was the woman Johanna wished she were. A chimera, it was true. Another role she played.

"You will always be Johanna McKenna to me," Drummond told her. "Just as you will always share my blood."

"Tainted blood," she dismissed. "I have no wish to claim it. I have done everything in my power to take myself as far from the man who sired me as possible."

Her mother was an innocent. Siobhan McKenna had died shortly after bringing Johanna into the world, leaving two children behind to face the tyrannical wrath of a man who had drowned his grief in whisky.

"Hate Father as you must, but I am your brother, Jojo, and I need your help." Drummond paused, then held up the picture. "She looks like you when you were a wee wisp, you know."

She closed her eyes for a moment, as a rush of profound grief hit her. "She did."

He inclined his head, studying her, expressing no hint of compassion. His face was, in fact, cold as stone. "She is dead."

Three stark words. Unfathomable and yet true all at once. Unlike the lashes on her back from so long ago, however, Pearl's death was a wound that would never heal.

Johanna flinched. "Yes."

"This picture is precious to you, then," Drummond said, still holding it in his hands.

"It is the only picture I have of her," she admitted, before she could think better of the confession. But her mind and heart were one, desperate for him to give it back to her. "Please, Drummond. Do not—"

He dropped it onto the floor. The crack of the glass was like a dagger piercing her heart. She cried out and rushed forward, dropping to her knees, uncaring about the glass, whether she cut her fingers. She was single-minded in her need to rescue that photograph, to keep it from further damage or harm.

That one last memory of Pearl. The one that could never fade.

Her brother's booted foot pressed down on the frame, trapping it beneath his weight. More glass crunched beneath his sole.

"No," she cried out, the denial torn from the depths of her. "Remove your foot. This is the only image of her I have. My sole remembrance."

"At last the mask slips," he drawled from above her, his tone unconcerned. "You are not as immovable as you pretend. If only everyone could see the famed Rose of New York thus, on her knees, crying over some broken glass and an old photograph."

"I am not crying," she denied. But her eyes were welling and desperation was setting in. She wanted his foot removed before he did further damage. She wanted Pearl's picture back. "Take your boot off, Drummond."

He chuckled, but there was no levity in his tone. "Yes, you are, sister. And no, I will not. Not until you give me something in return."

Everything inside her froze. "What do you want?"

She would give him anything in that moment, in return for the photograph trapped beneath his merciless boot. She would accept lashes. Torture. Any punishment for the way she had fled the McKenna family.

"Good of you to ask, sister dearest." Though his tone was cheerful, she had no doubt the intent behind his words was decidedly the opposite.

"What is it?" she demanded, her patience snapping.

How had she imagined she was free of this? She had feared, as her name had become well-known and as her likeness was spread so prolifically, that she would be recognized. But the years had gone on, and no one had ever come for her. The silence had lulled her into the foolish belief she was finally free.

But she was a McKenna, was she not?

She would never truly be free of the shackles of misery which had been hers since birth.

"How do you think your adoring public would see you if they knew you were a liar?" he asked, giving the picture another grind beneath his boot. "Do you think they would be understanding of the manner in which you have deceived them, pretending to be a French *émigrée*? Changing your name. Changing everything about yourself. Why, it is almost as if you have been playing a role, Jojo."

Most actresses took stage names; it was commonplace. Not all, however, assumed nationalities as she had. Most did not affect an accent. But she had been young at the time she had begun her career, so very young. And she had not contemplated the ramifications of her decisions.

She tilted her head back to study her brother, aware her hands were in shards of broken glass, as were her knees. She did not care. "Are you threatening me, Drummond?"

"*Threatening* is such a painful word," he said slowly. "Hardly apt in this instance. I am your brother, delighted to have found you after so many unnecessary years spent apart. Naturally, I require your assistance in a few small matters. If you cannot aid me, I will, regretfully, be compelled to share your real name and true heritage with the public who adores you."

Her patience was gone. Her hands were on his boot now, cut and bloodied from the broken glass she had found her way through. Blood smeared over the leather, but she did not care. Desperation clawed at her.

She had to have Pearl's photograph, just as she had to protect the persona she had created in Rose Beaumont. She had worked all her life, fought and fumbled, played hundreds of roles, memorized thousands of lines, studied great actors and actresses. She had done everything she could to find success. To make something of herself. To become Rose.

She could not risk having the truth revealed. Could not bear for the public to realize Rose Beaumont was a fiction, that she was not French at all but rather an Irish immigrant who had run away from home at the age of fifteen and found her way to a traveling company. If she did not have the stage, she had nothing left at all. No means of supporting herself, no hope for the future. Death would be a preferable option, for at least then she could join Pearl.

But though she tried with all her might, her brother was taller and stronger than she was. Hands slippery with blood and made painful by glass splinters proved unsuccessful at removing his boot-shod foot.

"What do you want me to do?" she asked desperately, resigned to her fate.

She could only run from the past for so long until it caught her.

Chapter One

London, 1883

FROM THE MOMENT he first saw Rose Beaumont grace the stage that evening, Felix had known why she was the most celebrated actress in New York City. He also knew why Drummond McKenna, the Fenian mastermind behind the explosions on the London railway, would want her in his bed. And he knew he was going to do his damnedest to use the beauty to lure McKenna to the justice awaiting him.

But for now, he would settle for champagne.

He took a sip, watching his quarry from across Theo Saville's sumptuous ballroom where the company of *The Tempest* and the city's most elite patrons of the arts had gathered to fête the Rose of New York. Trust Theo to throw a party lavish enough for an emperor. The servants were aplenty, the food was French, the champagne likely cost a small fortune, and the company was elegantly dissolute.

As a duke from a line that descended practically to the days of William the Conqueror, wealth and ostentation did not impress Felix. As a man who had lost the only woman he had ever loved, women did not ordinarily impress him either.

Rose Beaumont, however, did.

In the light of the gas lamps, she was a sight to behold. Dressed in an evening gown of rich claret, her golden hair worked into an elaborate Grecian braid, there was no doubt she commanded the eye of every gentleman in the chamber. Rubies and gold glinted from her creamy throat, her lush bosom and cinched waist on full display.

And though he observed her to hone his strategy, he could not deny he was as helplessly in awe of her as the rest of the sorry chaps gaping at her beauty. He had watched her perform, so mesmerized by her portrayal of Miranda, he had forgotten he was attending the theater to further his goal. For a brief beat, he forgot it anew as she tilted her head toward Theo and laughed at something droll he had no doubt said.

Theo looked pleased, and well he should, for though he had brought Rose Beaumont to his stage as a favor to Felix, there had been so much fanfare surrounding the arrival of the famed Rose of New York, that his already much-lauded theater was enjoying an unprecedented amount of attention. But he was also favoring Mademoiselle Beaumont with his rascal's grin, the one Felix had seen lead many a woman straight to his bed.

Felix had not painstakingly crafted his plan just so Theo could ruin it with his insatiable desire to get beneath a lady's skirts. No, indeed. Felix finished his champagne, deposited his empty glass upon a servant's tray, and then closed the distance between himself and his prey.

As he reached them, he realized, much to his irritation, that Rose Beaumont was lovelier than she had been from afar. Her eyes were a startling shade of blue, so cool, they verged on gray. Her lips were a full, pink pout. Her nose was charmingly retroussé. Hers was an ideal beauty, juxtaposed with the lush potency of a female who knew her power over the opposite sex.

Their gazes clashed, and he felt something deep inside him, an answering awareness he had not expected, like a jolt of sheer electricity to his senses. There was something visceral and potent in that exchange of glances. A current blazed down his spine, and his cock twitched to life.

She smelled of rose petals. Rose had been the scent Hattie favored. The realization and recognition made an unwanted stirring of memory wash over him. He banished the remembrance, for he could not bear to think of Hattie when he stood opposite a woman who had shared the bed of a monster like Drummond McKenna.

"Winchelsea," Theo greeted him warmly. "May I present to you Miss Rose Beaumont, lately of New York, the newest and loveliest addition to the Crown and Thorn?"

Her stare was still upon him. He looked at her and tried to feel revolted. But the disgust he had summoned for her when she had been nothing more than a name on paper refused to return. Her beauty was blinding, and he told himself that was the reason for his sudden, unaccountable vulnerability. That and the scent of her. Not just rose, he discovered, but an undercurrent of citrus. Distinctly different from Hattie's scent after all.

He offered a courtly bow. Though he no longer chased women, he recalled all too well how to woo, and he reminded himself now that this was a duty. One in a line of many he had spent in all his years as a devoted servant of Her Majesty.

"Mademoiselle Beaumont," he said when he straightened to his full height. "My most sincere compliments on your performance tonight. You were brilliant."

"Thank you," she said, her gaze inscrutable as it flitted over his face. "You are too kind."

Her husky voice reached inside him, formed a knot of desire he did not want to feel. Why did she have to be so damn beautiful? He cast a meaningful glance toward Theo, who had been his friend for many years. And who knew what was required of him in this instance.

"If you will excuse me," Theo said smoothly, "I must check in with my chef. The fellow is French and quite temperamental. Mademoiselle Beaumont, Winchelsea."

Theo departed with the sleek grace of a panther, leaving Felix alone with Mademoiselle Beaumont. His friend's defection occurred so abruptly, Felix found himself unprepared.

"That was badly done of him," Mademoiselle Beaumont said in the same voice that had brought the audience to their knees earlier that evening. It bore the trace of a French accent, one which had been notably absent from her earlier performance.

"I beg your pardon, Mademoiselle Beaumont?" he asked, perhaps in a sharper tone than he had intended.

He was out of his depths, and he knew it. He had procured mistresses before. He had been a statesman for all his life. He had been involved in complex investigations, harrowing danger, the aftermath of brutal violence. He had witnessed, firsthand, the wreckage of the rail carriages in the wake of the bombs, which had recently exploded.

But he had never attempted to make a Fenian's mistress *his* mistress.

"Mr. Saville," Mademoiselle Beaumont elaborated. "He was giving you the opportunity to speak with me, was he not?"

"I cannot say I am capable of speaking for Mr. Saville's motivations," he evaded.

The statement was a blatant prevarication, for Felix did know precisely what spurred his friend in every occasion: money and cunny with a love of the arts thrown in for good measure.

"Forgive me, but I have already forgotten your name," she said. "Was it Wintersby?"

"Winchelsea," he gritted, though she did not fool him.

He had seen the light of feminine interest in her gaze. She felt the attraction between them—base animal lust though it may be—as surely as he did. Some time may have passed since he had last engaged in the dance of procuring himself a bed partner, but it had not been that long, *by God*. And some things a man was not capable of erasing from his memory.

"Of course." She smiled, but it did not reach her eyes. "Winchelsea. I am not a naïve young girl. I know what you want."

His heart beat faster, and a chill trilled down his spine. She could not know who he was or what his true intentions were. Surely not. "Oh? I pray you enlighten me, Mademoiselle Beaumont. What is it I want?"

She stepped closer to him, her red silk swaying against his trousers. "You want me."

She did not elaborate. Nor did she need to.

Her proclamation was the immediate source of both relief and anticipation. Here was a game he could play. He lowered his head toward hers, not near enough to kiss but near enough to tempt himself to close the distance and seal their mouths. Her lips were so full. Her eyes so wide. He did not think the luminous sheen in them could be feigned, though her fluency as an actress was undeniable. How shameful that such a creature should belong to a soulless villain.

"And if I do want you, Mademoiselle Beaumont?" he dared to ask, allowing his gaze to devour her face. Part of his task would be easy. His desire for her was inexplicable, yet real. "What would you say?"

Those inviting lips curved higher. Her smile was intoxicating. "I would say though you flatter me, you cannot have me."

Damnation.

He ought to have known getting the Rose of New York to fall into his arms would not be an easy feat. But determination was a river that had run through him all his life, and it had yet to run dry. The evidence suggesting the gorgeous viper before him was privy to a great deal of invaluable information concerning her lover was far too strong to deny.

"You speak with such conviction, my dear lady," he told her smoothly, playing the part of lover as he knew he must. This mission was too delicate. Too important. "But I am a man who cannot resist a challenge."

"Some challenges are better resisted," she returned, and though she denied him, she did not make an effort to put any distance between them.

Felix did not disagree.

"Better for whom?" he wondered.

Her smile faded. There was a world-weariness in her eyes he had not noted before, but he saw it now. "Better for you, of course."

What could have caused the sadness haunting her husky voice? The strange urge to discover it, to learn her secrets, hit him. Not because of the task ahead of him, but because there was something about her that affected him. He knew better than to allow it. Better than to think of her as a woman.

And yet, he could feel the warmth emanating from her. Though they were in the midst of a ballroom filled with others, it was as if the two of them were alone. Another surge of awareness licked through him, languorous and hot and laden with sensual promise. He had not been this attracted to a woman in as long as he could recall.

Damn it.

He had not expected to want her, not with everything he knew about her and her ties to McKenna. He had believed himself beyond the throes of lust. He was so inundated with his work for the Home Office and Verity, he had not bothered to acquire a new mistress after his last affair had ended. That was the reason for this unwanted desire coursing through him now, he was sure of it.

"I shall be the judge of that, Mademoiselle Beaumont," he said at last. "Perhaps we could find somewhere more private to speak and better acquaint ourselves with each other."

He was at home in Theo's house. And as a sybarite, Theo knew the importance of comfortable, private rooms in abundance. There was a red salon just down the hall Felix could put to good use.

And put his plan into action. Because there was one reason he was pursuing Rose Beaumont, and it was not her fair face or form, nor was it the mysteries of her past, and it most certainly was not the hunger she had awakened within him.

He needed to find out everything she knew about Drummond McKenna and use her to sink the bastard's ship before he could do any more harm to innocents.

JOHANNA OUGHT TO have denied the duke, and she recognized her mistake the moment he escorted her from the ballroom. Before that, in fact. When she had placed her hand in the crook of his arm. Touching him had been unwise. Because he made her feel the same restless stirrings that had once caused her so much pain.

But that had been years ago, and she was far too world-weary now. Johanna had been known as Rose Beaumont for so many years, the name had become a part of her. It was the role she played best of all. One she was constantly honing. She liked to think of Rose as her shield. A mantle she donned to protect her from everything and everyone she wanted to forget.

The Duke of Winchelsea was shattering that role. Stripping her of the shield. For a brief, mad moment, when he had suggested they retire to another chamber together, she had forgotten to be Rose. She had allowed herself to be Johanna. Her guard had dropped.

He had kind eyes.

A serious countenance.

One had but to look upon him to see he shouldered great responsibility.

But none of that mattered now, for he was dangerous. She had recognized the frank admiration in his gaze, the carnal hunger, the blatant sensuality. She had seen it all before, in the eyes and the countenances of hundreds of men.

She had never, however, been tempted by it with such ease. Nor had she been so thoroughly bound by secrets and lies. The documents and dynamite secreted inside a trunk in her hotel were a burning coal of guilt, searing her from the inside out. She knew what she must do with them, but the knowledge was heavy.

The duke said nothing as he guided them into a low-lit chamber decorated entirely in shades of scarlet. The door closed behind them, drowning out the strains of the orchestra in the ballroom and the gay din of the revelers a few doors down.

She recognized the recklessness of her acquiescence. She never should have agreed to speak to him alone. But the truth was, she was weary after her journey across the Atlantic, followed by days of rehearsals. Weary from worrying over her brother, fearing she could never truly escape him. The ballroom had been an overwhelming swirl of faces and the urge to escape, to find some quiet, had been preeminent.

"Here we are," he said then, three simple words she felt in

her core.

Was it his clipped, patrician accent? The deep rumble of his baritone? His masculine scent of sandalwood and amber? She had been alone with many men, desired by them. Powerful and wealthy men had chased after her, and she had denied them all. Nobility no longer awed her as it once had.

For some reason, being alone with the Duke of Winchelsea left her feeling shy. She released her hold on his arm and stepped away from him.

Johanna forced herself to remember who she was, the sought-after Rose of New York. Her pictures were produced by the thousands. Every man who saw her wanted her. None of them could have her.

She faced him, stealing herself against the potent magnetism he exuded. "If you think to make me your lover, Your Grace, I must disabuse you of such fancy."

"You are jaded, Mademoiselle," he observed mildly. "I have yet to make my intentions clear."

She inclined her head. "You need not have; they are transparent enough. I have been an actress for many years. This is not the first time I have been propositioned. Nor, I suspect, will it be the last. And yet, my answer will always remain the same."

A small smile flirted with his sensual lips. He was seemingly unconcerned by her assertion. "Would you care for some brandy, Mademoiselle Beaumont?"

He strode past her to a sideboard she had not noticed. It was clear he was familiar with Mr. Saville's home. She wondered if he made a habit of wooing actresses here, and then she wondered why the thought made her stomach tighten. Why the thought of him with another should nettle.

He was nothing to her. A stranger. Why, she would likely never see him again after tonight. Besides, she had matters of far greater import to concern her. She could not afford to become involved with any man, let alone a handsome nobleman who would never accept her as his equal.

But he was awaiting her response now, watching her with a hooded gaze she felt like a caress. Wondering if she wanted brandy.

"Yes, please," she said, watching as he poured equal measures into two snifters.

Perhaps some spirits would calm her. Or at the very least cure her of this strange affliction. This affinity for a self-assured duke she should not want. She had promised herself long ago she would no longer make foolish mistakes.

London was her chance to be free of the chains of New York City. She had left all the ghosts, all the pain, behind. And she could not give in to the charms of a handsome duke who had never known a speck of the suffering she had weathered in her life.

He sauntered back to her, holding out an offering. "Truce, Mademoiselle. I believe we began in rather the wrong fashion, and I seek to make amends."

She accepted the snifter, their fingers brushing as she did so. An arrow of pure need shot straight through her with such ferocity, she bobbled the glass. Some of the liquid spilled over the lip, onto her hand and his.

Heat flared to her cheeks, a seeming impossibility for a woman who had not flushed unless it was on command for years. "Forgive me my clumsiness, Your Grace."

Her fine gloves were stained, as were his.

"There is nothing to forgive," he said mildly, removing the snifter from her hand. "Allow me to assist."

She watched helplessly as he placed both their glasses upon a table, then removed his gloves. The sight of his hands, large and long-fingered, elegant, dusted with a fine smattering of hairs, should not affect her. She had seen men's hands before. Had been touched by them on stage almost every night. Men's hands were nothing new. Nothing unfamiliar.

Why this man's hands made longing flare to life deep within her, she could not say.

"That is hardly necessary," she protested. "My gloves will dry."

"Nonsense." He withdrew a monogrammed handkerchief and took her hand, deftly plucking away her glove.

She thought she had been moved before, but the touch of his bare skin upon hers was a revelation. Desire simmered to life. Her nipples puckered beneath the stiff constraint of her corset. She inhaled against a rush of sensation she did not want.

But through the maelstrom assaulting her, he remained calm and firm, dabbing at her fingers with the silken square of fabric. Quite as though he were accustomed to tending to others. Which was silly, for she was sure he could not be.

He was a duke. He must have a legion of servants at his command.

And yet he was fretting over the ruined silk of her gloves, the liquid coating her fingers. His head was bowed, his handsome face a study in concentration as he applied himself to his ministrations.

"Thank you, Your Grace," she said, irritated by the breathless tone of her voice.

Completely unfeigned.

She needed to calm herself. To keep her mask firmly in place.

"I am afraid I owe you a pair of gloves," he said, holding her hand in his as he glanced up.

His verdant eyes were the precise color of spring grass. They trapped her for a heady moment.

"You owe me nothing," she denied, not about to accept a gift from him or from any other man. "I am certain the stain can be removed. But if I should require a replacement, I possess more than enough coin."

He tucked the ruined glove inside his coat, and then he stole her other glove as well, his movements so swift and efficient, she did not realize what he was about until it was too late to stop him. And then both her hands were in his, and he was lifting them to his lips.

His mouth glanced over her flesh so lightly, it may have been the gossamer touch of a butterfly's wings except for the fire it sparked inside her. "Give me your address, and I will see them sent 'round."

She swallowed. There was something about revealing where she was staying to the Duke of Winchelsea that seemed intimate. Far too intimate. "There is no need for you to thieve my gloves."

"I fancy the notion of keeping a little piece of you, Mademoiselle." He gave her hands a gentle squeeze before relinquishing them.

His words and his nearness sent a frisson down her spine. "I am not giving you my direction, sir."

"A small matter," he said, sounding unconcerned. "I will discover it with little trouble."

"I will not accept your gift," she countered.

"It is not a gift, Mademoiselle Beaumont, but a replacement. An apology for my injudicious spilling of brandy upon you."

She was the one who had caused the glass to move, and they both knew it. But if she further pursued the matter, perhaps he would probe into the reason why. Her unwanted reaction to him.

A reaction she could neither deny nor shake.

Where was the brandy when she needed it?

"You wished for an audience with me, Your Grace," she reminded both of them. "What was it you wanted to discuss? The hour grows late."

Perhaps the crush of the ballroom would have been a better place to remain after all. Mindless distraction was preferable to dangerous distraction.

"Of course." He retrieved the brandy, offering the snifter to her once more. "How thoughtless of me to keep you here to myself, away from your many admirers."

He misunderstood her. So much of her life had been spent with eyes upon her—audiences, the public, the men who wanted more from her than she was willing to give, her brother—that following the conclusion of a performance, all she wanted to do was return to the privacy of her hotel. Enjoy a warm bath.

She had only been in attendance this evening because Mr. Saville had required it of her. He was paying her a small fortune, and a handful of social appearances were part of her contract. It was a wise display of the man's business acumen, for her presence drew much attention to both himself and his theater. And she needed this money and her reputation both in order to make her bid for freedom at the end of her stay in London.

But she said none of that as she accepted the brandy and lifted it to her lips for a bracing sip. "I am afraid Mr. Saville may take note of my absence."

"Do not fret about Mr. Saville," he assured her, his watchful gaze studying her. "With performances as masterful as yours, I daresay he will not give a damn what you do or whom you do it with."

There was a subtle suggestion in his words, an underlying hint of the wicked.

She heard it, and a part of her she had thought long gone resurfaced. The reckless part of her. The part of her that thrived on passion and impetuousness. She took another sip of her brandy, seeking to drown it beneath the alcohol's impending glow.

"Do you visit the theater often?" she asked Winchelsea, in lieu of the question she truly wished to ask.

Do you make a habit of seducing actresses?

"Whenever I am able," he said solemnly. "Not nearly as often as I would prefer."

She had no notion of what might keep a duke busy. She had once been courted by a German prince, but he had been a vainglorious man who occupied all his time with the procuring of new bed partners. He had offered her a veritable king's ransom for one night with him and her fellow actress Fanny Carlton. She had declined, of course.

But Winchelsea did not seem the sort for such libidinousness.

"Why not?" she asked, the brandy making her bold.

Making her forget she ought to be seeking an end to their dialogue and time alone rather than prolonging it.

He lifted his snifter to her in salute. "Duty, Mademoiselle."

She had been correct in sensing the weight of responsibility upon him, then. For a man she judged to be in his mid-thirties, he did not possess any of the laugh lines one would expect of a man his age. No grooves bracketing his mouth, but there was evidence of a frown crease on his forehead.

"Duty," she repeated, wondering what kept him from smiling more. From laughing. "You strike me as a very solemn man. One who would benefit from more lightness in his life."

His sculpted lips twisted. "Life is dark, my dear. After all the tragedies you have acted in, surely you know it just as well as I."

Oh, she did. But no drama could compare to the tragedy she lived.

"Of course," she agreed simply, drinking more of her brandy, for nothing could induce her to put the unspeakable pain of her past into words.

Especially not to a man she had just met this evening.

A man who was her social superior.

A man who wanted her in his bed just like all the others before him had.

He was no different, she told herself. She had far weightier matters to concern her.

"But I am willing to divert myself from it," he said then, "with the proper inducement."

His gaze settled upon her mouth.

She felt the effect of that bold stare all through her traitorous body. "I am afraid you will have to look elsewhere, Your Grace. My stay in London will be a short one, and I have no interest in dalliance."

He finished his brandy, cradling the snifter in his long fingers as he watched her, assessing. "You were correct, you know."

She frowned at him, trying to follow the direction of his conversation and failing. "I beg your pardon?"

"I do want you, Mademoiselle Beaumont," he said, as calmly as if they were speaking of the weather.

With a nonchalance that struck her, chipping at her veneer. Once more, she was Johanna, just for a flash, before the indomitable Rose returned.

Her chin went up. "Of course you do. But that does not mean you shall have me."

But his admission shook her, all the same. Part of her longed to accept the promise of pleasure he offered.

"Would you care to make a wager?" he asked.

"No." She finished her brandy as well, but it did nothing to calm her wildly racing heart. "I would not."

He moved toward her again, and this time, a small smile curved his lips.

She liked that smile.

She wanted more of it.

"Five thousand pounds says I will have you in my bed within the next sennight," he said.

She would deny him. Tell him no, quite firmly. Leave the red salon and the Duke of Winchelsea behind.

But the wickedness inside her was clamoring to life.

"I accept your wager," said her foolish, foolish lips.

She did not think she imagined the flash of triumph over his handsome features. But all too quickly, it was gone, leaving her wondering.

He bowed before her. "Until we meet again, Mademoiselle Beaumont. Tomorrow is day one."

Chapter Two

OF ALL THE mutton-headed things he could have done, making a bet about bedding her was surely the worst. That had been Felix's first thought when he had risen earlier this morning, and it had continued to dog him with the persistence of a canine who wanted his dinner in all the hours since.

It plagued him now, as he was seated in his study with Verity across from him, her sweet little round face so much a precise replica of Hattie's that looking upon her never failed to make the old ache rise in his chest. An ache of four-and-a-half years and counting.

"Do you not think so, Papa?" she asked suddenly.

Her voice, too, was another source of sadness, for it was undeniably a sweeter, smaller rendition of Hattie's. So many pieces of his wife remained, long after she was gone, each one a painful gift.

Christ. He pressed his fingers into his throbbing temples and realized he had not been listening to a word his daughter had spoken for the last half hour. What the devil was the matter with him?

"Of course I think so, poppet," he told her.

"I am relieved you think reading is a waste of my day as well," she said, grinning at him impishly. "Shall you tell Simmonds my time should be devoted to something far more suiting, like going to the aquarium or the waxworks instead, or shall I?"

He frowned, for he should have known better than to agree with anything his daughter said. "Verity, you know very well I will do nothing of the sort. Reading is important for a young lady these days. Your mother would have wanted you to study it vigorously and broaden your mind."

It was the wrong thing to say.

Again.

He could afford to lose far more than the five thousand pounds in a wager, but he could not afford to go about things the wrong way with his daughter. He was dreadful at communicating with the fairer sex, and that much was apparent.

Verity's chin tipped up. "But my mother is not here, Papa."

"No," he acknowledged on a sigh. "She is not."

Most days, he buried himself so deeply in his daily obligations—Home Office, Special League, Verity, estates, Markham's, his other business interests, and the list went on—he scarcely had the time to reflect upon the gaping absence of Hattie in his and Verity's lives. The years since he had lost her had taught him distraction was a blessing, though not a panacea.

"You still speak of her as if she is," Verity accused.

Did he? He stopped attempting to assuage the ache in his temples, surrendering to the headache which would eventually consume him, and raked a hand through his hair. He did not think so.

"I speak of what she would have wanted for you," he corrected gently, "because she loved you desperately, poppet. I do not want either of us to forget her."

"I never knew her," Verity countered, a stubborn edge

entering her voice.

She was older than her five years. Perhaps the fault was his. Perhaps being motherless was the culprit. Regardless of the cause, his daughter had been growing markedly more stubborn of late.

"You *did* know her," he argued. "She held you in her arms when you were a babe. You know her now. When you look in the glass, you can see her face reflected back at you. When you speak, it is her voice. Deep inside your heart, her love lives on."

But oh, how hollow and empty his words sounded as he spoke them. Hattie's death would forever haunt Felix and Verity both. He suspected he would never think of her without the inevitable sensation in his gut, rather like a dagger twisting, to think she was forever lost to him.

Why her, he had cried out to a God who had seemingly forsaken him in the dark days following Hattie's death. *Why not me?*

He still did not have his answer. The meaning of some pains in life, he had discovered, were not to be found.

"I love you, Papa," Verity told him. "All I have to remember my mother is her pictures."

"And her gloves," he reminded his daughter. "Her locket. Her hair."

"Things," his daughter sneered. "I do not want them from a mother I cannot recall."

The throbbing in his temples reached a dramatic crescendo. "You are not permitted to speak of your mother with such disrespect, my lady," he warned.

"I do not want to read," she said then, pouting. "You cannot make me. Simmonds cannot make me."

He wondered if her aversion to reading stemmed from the fact that her mother had loved it and would have wanted more than anything for her daughter to be well-read, or if she was truly struggling with learning it. He pressed his fingers into his temples again, desperate for relief. "I can and will, and so does Simmonds. You must take your studies seriously, Verity. Your mother—"

"Would have wished it," she interrupted.

Her green eyes, so like his, stared at him with unrelenting defiance. She was, at once, the most adorable and beloved creature he had ever beheld, but also the fiercest. Perhaps she was right, and perhaps he did rely too much upon Hattie.

"You may have the rest of the afternoon to do as you wish," he allowed. "I will inform Simmonds."

The smile Verity gave him was another arrow directly to his heart, because it was Hattie's too. "Thank you, Papa. I knew you would see reason."

He passed a hand over his face, feeling overwhelmed. It was no easy task to raise a small child, grieve a wife, and take upon an ever-increasing list of responsibilities from the Home Office. "You are welcome. Now run along, Verity dearest. I have a great deal of work to which I must attend."

She rose and performed an excellent curtsy. He watched her go, her glossy curls flying behind her as she sailed across his study with far too much enthusiasm for decorum. And then he stalked to his sideboard and poured himself some whisky before settling back into his desk to pore over reports from his American agents who had been tasked with watching New York Fenians.

Inevitably, his mind returned to Rose Beaumont and the daring cut of her red silk dress. In just a few, short hours, he should see her again.

And though it should not, the prospect filled him with anticipation.

Far better than grief, he supposed. The whisky would dull

his aching head, and the papers before him would remind him of what he must do and why.

JOHANNA SUPPOSED SHE ought not to have been surprised to find Winchelsea awaiting her that evening in her dressing room. But somehow, she was. She had just finished another night as Miranda, and the heightened emotions that always roared through her during a performance remained with her as she crossed the threshold and saw him there.

Saville's theater was new and well-appointed. The audience tonight had been abuzz with anticipation and eagerness. The Rose of New York was taking London as she imagined a conqueror would. Gratification was exactly what she needed, a welcome distraction from the painful course ahead of her. And she felt, in that moment, incredibly powerful.

She felt as if she were capable of anything. As if she astounded even herself.

Until she saw *him*, and he sucked all the breath from her lungs. The door snapped closed behind her back, but she remained where she was, staring. Though the room was a fair size compared to most dressing areas in theaters she had experienced over the years, the duke dominated the space, making it—and her—seem hopelessly small.

"Your Grace," she said. "How did you get in here?"

"Mr. Saville was kind enough to assist me." The low purr of his voice slid over her senses like fine silk as he prowled forward in a self-assured manner.

He was every bit the duke, exuding an aura of command. As if he could snap his fingers and make all the world do his bidding. Including her.

But she was not the same naïve girl she had once been,

and she forced herself to remain stern and unaffected. "Perhaps there is a different question I ought to have asked. *Why* are you here?"

With a slight smile, he extracted a pair of gloves from his coat and held them out to her. "If you will recall, I owed you these, and since you were not obliging enough to provide me with your direction, I was left with no choice but to call upon you here."

She stared at the gloves, refusing to take them although she could see how fine they were. They looked soft, adorned with delicate embroidery. A single rosebud, she realized.

"I already told you the gloves are an unnecessary gift," she said. "One I cannot accept."

No matter how beautiful or expensive they were. Winchelsea had made his intentions clear. He wanted her in his bed. And she was determined she would not make herself his conquest. Besides, she could make excellent use of his five thousand pounds in her new life abroad.

"And I told you they are no gift." His response was smooth, the gloves outstretched between them, dangling from his long, elegant fingers. "Consider these remuneration for the damage I inflicted upon your other pair."

She pressed her lips together, refusing to be swayed. It did not matter how lovely the gloves were, or that it seemed he had specifically commissioned them for her, with the red rose emblazoned upon them. "I consider them what they are, Your Grace. An attempt to win my favor so you can find yourself in my bed. But I remain firm on both the gloves and the vow I will not take you as a lover."

"You do not like the gloves?" he asked, dragging the empty fingertips of the glove over the palm of his left hand.

"They are lovely," she admitted, briefly following the motion of the empty gloves, rather like a caress.

For one wild moment, she wondered what his palms would feel like beneath her own seeking fingers. The hand was such an intimate part of the body, capable of bringing great pleasure. When he had taken hers in his yesterday, she had felt only the suggestion of warmth and strength. What would a more leisurely exploration discover? She supposed a duke's palm would bear no calluses. Rather, it would likely be softer than hers.

Almost as if he were privy to her thoughts, he stilled. "You do not like *me* then, Mademoiselle?"

"I do not know if I like you or not," she informed him, and that much was true. "I am not acquainted with you well enough to decide."

That last was a desperate lie. For she already knew part of her liked him far too much. The weakest part of her.

"I can remedy that." He grinned, slowly. A rakish forelock fell over his brow.

His hair had a curl to it, and he wore it rather long on top, natural and without the heaviness of pomade or hair grease. When he smiled, she could not deny the desire pooling in her belly. Lower still. Between her thighs.

But she had not come to London to fall into a duke's bed. She had come here to finally free herself from the last ties to her past. To free herself from Drummond and the hold he had over her.

She realized, belatedly, she still wore the grease paint, wig, and gown to remind herself of the latest role she played. One of many.

"I need to change from my costume, Your Grace," she told him. "I have not the time to get acquainted, for I am weary after my performance."

"Of course." He was still watching her with that green cat's gaze, moving the gloves slowly over his palm, the action unbearably erotic.

She imagined him trailing those wisps of satin over her naked flesh. Over her nipples. And beneath her corset, the peaks of her breasts pebbled and ached. If his eyes were cat's eyes, she was the mouse. Somehow, she did not think she would mind if this big, powerful man played with her.

The acknowledgment filled her with a renewed sense of purpose. She must get him to go. To leave this space. To leave her in peace. Too much was at stake for her, and she could not risk more ruinous complications.

"If you will excuse me, the hour grows late, and I must remove all traces of Miranda," she prodded, irritated at herself for the breathiness of her voice, a perpetual problem in his presence.

"I can assist," he offered, the intensity of his regard making a jolt go straight through her.

"I have someone who aids me," she forced herself to say, wondering, quite belatedly, where Jenny was. "Thank you, Your Grace, but I must decline."

"Ah," he said slowly, drawing out the word, as if he had just reached a tremendous realization. "You do not trust yourself in my presence. I should have realized. Forgive me."

Her lips tightened. Precisely what was he suggesting? She was not so weak she was unable to succumb to his handsome, ducal face. "You have it wrong, Your Grace. It is you whom I do not trust."

Removing Miranda's dress was not terribly difficult—tapes in the back, to facilitate removal between scenes. And like most theater garb, it had been repurposed at least a dozen times by a seamstress with a deft hand, which meant it was loose and free-flowing. Beneath it, she wore her corset, chemise, drawers, and a petticoat.

She had been seen wearing far less by dozens of others. In

her early days of theater, before she had built the clout she now possessed, before she had been The Rose of New York, she had been forced into innumerable situations in-between scenes which had necessitated a lack of inhibition.

"I assure you, I am perfectly capable of offering you aid without ravishing you," he told her then, a smile working at his lips.

His mouth was beautifully sculpted, she noted, the lower lip full and lush. The bow firm and quite masculine. A delightful dichotomy. She liked that small smile of his. The urge to see it deepen, to watch it bloom, hit her with sudden force. Along with the desire to be the reason for it.

She dashed such ridiculous notions away, for they would only hinder her purpose.

"Nevertheless, I must insist you go now," she told him, pleased with how firm her voice sounded.

"Very well, Mademoiselle Beaumont." He offered her the most elegant bow she had ever received. "I shall tell Mr. Saville to find your woman. Forgive me for mistaking your boldness for daring."

Johanna stiffened. She prided herself upon her daring, her mettle, her consequence. These few, precious traits, aside from her ability to become whomever she wished, whenever she wanted, were her only sources of vanity. Indeed, they were all she had left. And she was grasping them with both hands in a life that had left her with precious little beyond the belongings she had packed into a trunk and two valises back in New York.

"Wait," she ordered him when he made to leave.

He stopped, his expression questioning. "Mademoiselle?"

"You may assist me." The capitulation left her before she could think better of it.

Her vanity was speaking for her, but her vanity was not

what she fretted over. All the rest of her was. The dangerous tasks before her were. It would be best, she knew, to keep herself from everyone. She had no wish to embroil anyone else in her misery.

"Splendid." He moved swiftly back to her, tucking the gloves inside his coat before eying her sternly. "Turn."

His terse directive took her by surprise. For a moment, she could do nothing but stare at him, drowning in his fathomless gaze. "Turn?"

"Turn," he repeated. "Your tapes are at the back, are they not?"

"Yes," she agreed, swallowing against a rush of unwanted sensation this abrupt suggestion of intimacy brought with it. "They are."

And then some small part of her wondered, once more, how and why he knew so much about an actress's costume. She was almost certainly not the first, though why the thought should disturb her so, she could not say.

"Then aid me in aiding you, if you please," he said, his voice low.

She felt the gruff timbre of his voice in every part of her. Every instinct she possessed warned her to flee. To run. To never let this dangerously handsome duke with a voice of sin assist her in disrobing.

But her pride was stronger than her common sense. Perhaps it always had been. And so, she turned, presenting him with her back. "How is this, Your Grace?"

"Excellent." He stood so near, the heat of his breath fanned her nape.

A shiver went through her that only deepened when his fingers brushed against her skin. She could not be certain if it was her imagination or if he lingered there. But it seemed an eternity passed between the first brush of his fingertips on her flesh and the subsequent gaping of the back of her gown.

As each tape came undone, it loosened more and more until he was drawing her dress over her shoulders. And here, thank heavens, her chemise kept his bare hand from her weak flesh. He peeled the twain ends of her costume down her body until it pooled about her feet.

And then, his hands settled upon her waist, spinning her about so she faced him.

"Your slippers," he said.

She was acutely aware of her state, clad in only her undergarments before him, her every curve on display. The corset she had worn to fit into Miranda's gown had been laced tighter than she ordinarily preferred. So much so that her bosom was pressed high, crowding over the edge, spilling over the décolletage of her chemise.

And he was speaking to her of slippers. For a wild beat, she could not fathom why.

"I beg Your Grace's pardon," she managed, gratified her voice did not sound entirely dazzled and breathless.

For this was dangerous territory she had entered indeed.

"Your slippers," he said again. "I assume you are exchanging them for something sturdier in the streets, yes? It was raining quite a torrent when I arrived, and I should think these little scraps would be of little use to you in a deluge."

Of course. The slippers she had worn on stage were thin and unsuitable for wearing out of doors. They were excellent for gliding across a stage. But hardly acceptable for a grim, rainy London evening.

Then, something else occurred to her. He had been concerned about her welfare. He had thought about her comfort. She could not recall when anyone else ever had. But she ruthlessly squelched the small flare of appreciation. He was watching her, awaiting her response.

"Yes, you are right. These slippers are made for the stage and not for the business of traveling about London." Her cheeks were hot. In fact, her entire body felt flushed. Overheated. She tingled. It was insufferably warm in here. Dressing rooms of theaters had notoriously poor ventilation, after all, and this one, while one of the better she had experienced, was little different.

Surely that was the reason for her discomfit.

He sank to his knees before she could stay him. And if she had been warm before, she felt as if she were being scorched by the blazing heat of a July sun now. The duke extended a hand, looking up at her with a calmness which irked.

"May I, Mademoiselle?" he asked.

How dare he be so cool and unaffected when he had set off such a riotous tumult within her? She did not think she had ever been so aware of a man before. She was attuned to his every movement. His breaths. The subtle changes in the way he clenched his jaw, the darkness of his pupils which had flared when her costume had first fallen to the floor.

He wanted to help her to remove her slippers. She could have told him she did not need his aid. After years on the stage, she was quite nimble and flexible, and she could manage anything on her own, even in a tight-laced corset.

But the thought of him tending to her, touching her ankles…it held undeniable appeal. "You may," she allowed.

He grasped her ankle in a delicate but firm touch, his long fingers wrapping around it. "Lift your foot, if you please."

She obeyed, doing her utmost to maintain her poise. One tremble, one sway, and he would recognize the effect he had upon her. She watched him, his dark head bent, his handsome profile visible to her, and held still as he gently pulled the slipper from her foot.

She let out a sigh when the slipper was gone, for in truth,

it had been rather tight across the fleshy top of her foot. The removal after several hours of wearing it brought welcome relief.

He grasped her foot in both hands, kneading the sole. "You spend much time on your feet. They must ache."

Dear Lord. The duke was massaging her foot, his thumb digging into muscles that had been drawn tight, knowing just where to touch and how. She bit her lip to hold back an appreciative moan threatening to burst forth from her.

"I am accustomed to it," she said. "There is no need for you to—"

"Hush, Mademoiselle Beaumont," he interrupted. "There is every need. Those blasted shoes were clearly too tight. I will tell Saville to acquire new ones more suited to your size."

His concern struck her. Made a queer sensation unfurl. She refused to acknowledge it. "That is quite unnecessary, Your Grace. The slippers are fine. Most theaters require the actors and actresses to provide their own costuming, so I do not dare complain."

"The Rose of New York deserves painless feet," he told her, a frown creasing his countenance.

Here was the expression he wore most often, she felt certain, one of concern.

Somehow, that knowledge touched her. Burrowed its way into a crack in her heart and settled in. But she was stronger than her heart. She always had been. And one show of tenderness from a man was not enough to make her tear down the protective walls she had built around herself.

The Rose of New York did not possess feelings off the stage.

"Thank you for your distress on my behalf, Your Grace. But the slippers will do. I have experienced far worse over my tenure as an actress." She thought of the first role she had ever played, remembering how ill-fitting her gown had been, and unlaundered, smelling of the stale sweat of dozens of players before her.

His thumb found a particularly sensitive place. "Do not be a martyr, Mademoiselle. If Saville will not grant you the slippers, I will buy you some myself."

This time, she could not suppress the sigh of contentment his ministrations caused. "You must not make a habit of buying things for me, Your Grace. I have already told you, I do not want your gifts."

He placed her foot back on the floor and moved to the other. "Lift."

She did as he asked, eager, in spite of herself, for the same treatment. The slippers *were* tight, and her feet *did* ache. She had spent a great deal of time walking in the park earlier that afternoon, determined to clear her mind with some fresh air in preparation for her role that night. However, the air had been murky with fog, and she had been unable to shake the thoughts of a handsome duke with whom she had struck a most unwise bet.

The same duke who was now removing her other slipper and giving this aching foot, too, a slow and knowing massage. How good it felt to have a man's hands upon her. Hands that were gentle and comforting rather than harsh and angry and painful.

Johanna realized then that she must not allow him to continue. "Thank you, Your Grace," she said, relinquishing her foot and moving swiftly away from him.

To the opposite end of the small chamber. Which was not far, unfortunately. Only a handful of steps. She took a deep, steadying breath, attempting to garner control over her vacillating emotions. To tamp down the part of her that wanted to give in to the promise of pleasure in this man's arms, in his bed. To indulge in a respite, however brief, from what she must do.

To forfeit five thousand pounds she could ill afford to lose.

To take him as her lover although she had to hold firm to her decision to remain an island in this vast sea of London. Indeed, in this vast sea of life.

"Where are your boots?" he asked, just over her shoulder.

He had followed her. Of course, he had. Like any predator stalking his prey, he sensed her growing weakness.

She turned about. "I can manage the rest myself, Your Grace."

When she found Jenny, she was going to give the woman a harangue. If she had been within Johanna's dressing room as she was meant to be, Johanna would not be alone and at the seductive mercy of the Duke of Winchelsea.

"Of course you can manage," he said, and still there was that calm in his voice. In his expression. "But that does not mean you must deny me. You were managing with aching feet as well, were you not?"

Oh, how awful of him to make sense.

"Yes, I was," she acknowledged.

"But now they feel better, yes?" he pressed, remaining where he was, not encroaching upon her any further.

He did not need to, and they both knew it.

"They do." She paused, her wits scrambled, as she attempted to find the means of convincing him—and herself—that he must go away and not come back. "But I have been suffering through tight shoes, sore feet, and all manner of discomforts and pains my entire life. I am accustomed to it."

"If a man grows accustomed to the rain, that does not mean he does not also long for the sun," the duke quipped. "I want to take away all your discomforts and pains."

"You cannot possibly do that," she said, and of this she had no doubt. "No one can."

Because no matter how far she traveled or how much she overcame, the sins of her past were never far from her heels.

"Let me try, Rose." His low voice was an invitation. To sin. To indulgence. To pleasure.

He had called her Rose. And though it was the name she answered to, for some reason, hearing it in his decadent baritone felt wrong.

"Why?" she asked, though she knew she should not. "Do you make a habit of chasing after actresses?"

"No," he said simply.

"You are familiar with Mr. Saville," she pointed out, mistrusting him and his motivations.

"He is my friend."

"You are proficient at removing costumes."

A half smile quirked his well-molded lips. "I confess, you are not the first lady I have ever helped to disrobe. You are not shocked by such a revelation, I hope."

Of course she was not. Everything about this man was masterful. Measured. He knew how to woo a woman. There was seduction in his every gaze, in his deep voice, in his touch.

"Nothing shocks me," she told him honestly. "I have been an actress for almost half my life. I believe I have seen, heard, or done everything anyone can possibly fathom."

A muscle tensed in his jaw, his gaze going hooded. "Then one man assisting you in your toilette can hardly be cause for alarm."

He was right. She stared at him, at a stalemate. If she insisted he go, she was revealing more of herself than she wanted. It would be an admission of how greatly he affected her. How badly the wickedest part of her wanted him and all the unspoken pleasures he promised.

"I am hardly alarmed, Your Grace," she denied, reminding herself she must be Rose, always, and never Johanna. Rose was bold. Daring. She flashed him Rose's coquette's smile. "Continue aiding me if it pleases you. My boots are just over there beside the chair, and my button hook is on the table."

"It pleases me greatly," he said, and there, once more, was the intensity in his countenance she could not define.

Could not look away from.

How odd it was to order about an aristocrat. To tell the duke he could fetch her boots, as if he were a lowly servant rather than her social superior in every way. Before she could say anything else, he turned and acted upon her directions, gathering her boots and the button hook before returning to her.

Once more, he sank to his knees. This time, he did not linger over her feet, however, and she had to admit she mourned the lack of attention he paid them. One by one, he slid them into her boots and fastened the buttons.

He stood, his gaze devouring her, lingering over her breasts, which still swelled over her corset, perhaps more so now because of her agitation "Where is your gown?" he asked.

"In the wardrobe," she said, once more marveling at the strangeness of the moment.

The man.

She felt at once as if she had known him forever, as if she had known him always. An abrupt rush of familiarity swept over her. It was as if she had dreamt this moment, this day when she stood in a London dressing room after performing in *The Tempest* and a handsome, enigmatic duke played lady's maid for her.

He turned away from her, crossing to the wardrobe with even, measured strides. And she admired the breadth of his back as he went, the long leanness of his form. He even moved with great command.

When he returned, he drew it over her head. She busied herself with settling the fall of her skirts and drawing on her sleeves before presenting him with her back. He fastened the buttons lining her bodice with effortless ease, as though he had been born to the task.

He reached the last button, his fingers brushing her nape. "Ride with me in the park tomorrow."

She froze, the combination of his touch and his words almost too much. "I cannot."

"Why?" His hands settled back on her waist, gently spinning her until she faced him. "Is there another?"

"That is none of your concern," she told him. "Especially since you will never be my lover."

The half smile flitting with his lips widened. "I have six days following this one to prove you wrong, Rose."

She wanted to remain impervious to him, truly she did. But his persistence was battering her already-weakened defenses. "You will need far more than six, Your Grace."

His smile at last reached his eyes. "I will send a carriage 'round to fetch you for dinner following your performance."

"I have not agreed to dinner." She raised a brow at him, trying to ignore the way he held her waist. To forget about how much she liked the feeling of his hands on her.

"You cannot deny me twice in one day," he countered. "It is against the rules of the game."

"I was not aware we were playing a game." Though her tone was wry, she could not deny, at least inwardly, that she found this man and his banter intriguing.

That she wanted more of both. What was wrong with her? A dalliance with him was an impossibility.

"You are correct, Mademoiselle." His levity faded, those

green eyes of his searing into hers. "This is far from a game. But I have never wanted to win anything more."

Her heart thudded. And though she was fully dressed once more, she felt more vulnerable than she had earlier. More exposed. Because she wanted him, too.

And it terrified her.

"Dinner," she found herself saying.

What would be the harm? One dinner with a handsome duke. Just one. Nothing more.

He smiled, but this time it did not reach his eyes. "Until then, Mademoiselle."

Abruptly, he released her, stepping away before offering her a bow. She wondered at the hint of sadness she had seen in his gaze. Any why he had not pressed his advantage. Why he had not at least attempted to kiss her.

But then she told herself she should be grateful he had not. That she did not want his kiss.

"Until then," she said, feeling the loss of his touch despite her determination to remain aloof and unaffected.

She watched him go, the door closing quietly on his departing back. It was only after he had gone that she discovered the gloves, with their beautifully embroidered roses, laid out on the table. She had not seen him place them there.

Against her better judgment, she slipped them into her reticule, telling herself she would return them to him tomorrow.

Chapter Three

𝒥OHANNA ARRIVED AT a handsome townhouse late the next evening. True to Winchelsea's word, a sleek black carriage had awaited her at the theater following her performance. Part of her had expected him to be within, but the conveyance had been mercifully empty.

She was not certain how she could withstand such proximity to him. In a confined space. With his handsome face and intense gaze and his deliciously masculine scent.

The ride to her destination had not been long. But she had fretted the entire way.

Wondering what she was doing.

Knowing she should never have accepted Winchelsea's invitation.

As she descended from the vehicle, she took in her surroundings. The edifice was not nearly as large as she would have expected for a duke. At home in New York City, the mansions of the wealthiest were immense, taking up entire city blocks. More like castles than homes.

The coachman aided her down, and she noted he wore livery. Even the duke's servants were impeccably dressed. She thanked him and went up the walk, a new bout of nerves assailing her as she lifted the brass knocker bearing a lion's head and rapped.

An august-looking gentleman—the butler, she supposed—opened the door, greeting her with perfectly polite formality. "Good evening, Mademoiselle Beaumont."

It was a reminder that she was expected.

But then, of course, she was. She had known that. Still, for some reason, the *aide-mémoire* nettled just a bit. The duke had been certain of her acquiescence. She allowed the butler to take her wrap, hat, and reticule, the knot inside her drawing up tighter with each passing second. A sense of excitement, along with a matching foreboding, had settled within her.

Accepting this invitation to dinner had been unwise and reckless. She had enough to worry her without adding a lover to the mix. Without adding a man who looked at her in the way Winchelsea did. A powerful man.

An enigmatic man who still remained so much a mystery.

The wall coverings were vibrant, she noted, shades of deep, bold emerald damask. A smattering of pictures adorned the hall in equally bold colors. There was an expensive-looking vase, and the heels of her boots clicked on the marble floor as the butler escorted her to the blue salon, where he informed her His Grace awaited her.

The butler announced her formally before bowing and taking his leave, closing the door behind him. The duke had been pacing the length of the chamber when she entered, and he moved toward her now in slow, purposeful strides.

"Mademoiselle," he said softly, taking her hand in his and raising it to his lips. "You are enchanting this evening."

His elegant beauty struck her in the chest. Her pulse leapt. And the heat of his mouth, even through her gloves—not the embroidered gift he had given her, but her own serviceable pair—sent matching warmth to pool low in her belly.

"Your Grace," she acknowledged. "Thank you for sending the carriage."

"I promised I would." A brief frown creased his forehead. "I would have accompanied the carriage, but I was detained. I hope you will forgive me?"

She wondered what had detained him, and realized just how little she knew of this man who was charming her with such ease. "There is nothing to forgive. I was pleased to pass the journey here in silence after another exhausting performance."

The whirlwind of the stage never failed to amaze and delight her. No matter how many times she claimed the stage and took on a role, she was still in awe. The cast of players, the audience, the lights, the raw emotions a drama required an actress to harness and then bring to life, it was heady stuff. But taxing.

He lowered her hand but did not release it. "You must be quite tired after three performances in a row. It is fortunate you have a day of rest tomorrow evening."

Yes, she did. And she did not bother to ask him how he had arrived at his information. Though she supposed it was common enough knowledge that her understudy would be playing Miranda in the evening's play while Johanna only needed to attend morning rehearsal.

"It is," she agreed, attempting to turn her mind to what she would do with that free time.

Anything to distract her from how handsome the duke looked in his evening finery. Black coat, charcoal waistcoat, with a white shirt beneath and black trousers. With his tousled dark curls, he looked like a gothic hero torn from the pages of a romance.

"Would you care for a glass of wine before we dine?" he asked solicitously, releasing her hand and stepping away from her at last.

She felt at once a great mixture of relief and consternation at the distance he had placed between them. "Wine would be most welcome," she agreed.

Perhaps it would help to settle the riot within her. Perhaps it would dull the attraction she felt for him, one she could not seem to shake.

He moved to a sideboard and poured two glasses of wine as she watched, wondering what it was about him that made her heart hammer so fast in her breast. She had seen handsome men before. Wealthy men. Powerful men. Heavens, she had been courted by a prince.

Why should the Duke of Winchelsea stand out in a sea of so many? Why should he call to her in a different way, in a way no other before him had? It seemed dreadfully unfair, particularly given the tragedy which had become her own life.

He returned with the wine, offering the glass to her in a disquieting echo of the night they had met. Had it only been a mere two nights ago? How did it feel as if it had been much longer? This time, however, she took great care not to tilt the glass as she grasped the stem, accepting it from him.

He raised his goblet. "A toast is in order, I should think. To The Rose of New York. Long may she reign over the stage and the hearts of men."

She raised her glass by rote, but the wine tasted less than sweet on her tongue. For she had never reigned over the heart of any man, and no one knew that better than she did.

Talk of hearts inevitably made her think of Pearl, and when she did, her own heart gave a pang. She took a long sip from her glass, hoping the wine would numb her pain though she knew it would not. Nothing ever did.

"You are frowning," the duke observed.

Instantly, she smoothed her expression. Her years as an actress had given her great awareness of her countenance. Ordinarily, she was able to keep her features a mask of indifference. The true emotion was reserved for plays.

It disturbed her to know her mask had slipped.

That he had seen beneath it, if just for a moment.

"I never frown," she countered, taking care to enhance the French accent she had long-ago adopted as part of her persona as Rose Beaumont. "Life is filled with too much color and joy."

A lie, as it happened. Perhaps the lives of others were. But never hers.

From the moment she had been born, it had been nothing but sorrow. Her father blamed her for her mother's death. He had been a cold and unforgiving man by nature, but the whisky had changed him. He had become consumed by it. And then, the violence had begun.

Thank God she had escaped.

"Nevertheless, you were frowning now," Winchelsea observed. "I do hope I am not the source of your distress."

No, he was not, but she would not think of Drummond now. Rather, she would focus upon the five thousand pounds she needed to win. She would think of her freedom, of doing what she must, regardless of how much it cost her. Of being far beyond her brother's reach forever.

You are Rose Beaumont, she reminded herself.

The darling of the stage.

She took another sip of her wine, feeling its warmth suffuse her, and recalled this, too, was a role she played.

She smiled. "You could never be the source of my distress, Your Grace. You have been far too solicitous and charming to me. I shall be spoiled."

"Have you not already been spoiled by others?" he asked, an edge creeping into his tone.

No, she had not. She had loved. Too much, too hard. She had lost as well. Those parts of her could never be regained or restored.

"I have never met a gentleman like you, I think," she said carefully, realizing it was true.

She could not quite discern what it was about him that made him different, but he was. He was different and she was drawn to him. And being drawn to any man was dangerous indeed.

Five thousand pounds, she thought again, a litany. *Your freedom. Think of never again looking over your shoulder. Never again knowing the sick taste of dread, the grip of fear in your gut. Think of all the good that will be done when Drummond no longer has the capacity to hurt anyone.*

Those funds could aid her in the future she sought. From London, she would go to Paris. And from there, Berlin. Drummond would never chase her that far if he somehow escaped prison, and if he did, she would outrun him. Five thousand pounds could hide her quite well, and she must not lose sight of that unexpected windfall.

"I am not certain if I should consider that a compliment or an insult," the duke said wryly, watching her with a twist to his lips she could not help but to find irresistible.

"Perhaps both." Her own smile deepened, and it was not feigned. He amused her. Intrigued her.

This was not good.

How would she manage to resist him through the next hour? The next five days? Ever?

"I can honestly say the same of you, Mademoiselle," he told her.

Their gazes held. "But surely you know a great deal of other actresses."

There it was again, the knife's edge of jealousy creeping into her heart. She did not know why the notion of him seducing others before her should bother her so.

"I have known others," he agreed mildly. "But there is only one Rose of New York."

She wondered, then, if he was attracted to her because of her notoriety. Some men had sought her out and attempted to woo her for just that reason. They wanted Rose Beaumont on their arms. Rose Beaumont warming their beds. They wanted to parade her before their friends and cronies as if she were a prized stag.

"You were familiar with me, then, before my performance?" she pressed.

"I had seen your photograph," he said carefully.

Ah.

She did not know what to make of his words. Her stomach tightened. But there was an undeniable burst of pleasure inside her too. "You arranged with Mr. Saville to meet me."

It was not a question but rather a statement, for she knew the answer already.

"I did," he acknowledged, before taking a sip of his wine.

This man wanted her. She had known it from the first moment his vibrant emerald eyes had burned into hers. Had felt it, deep within her. He had made it apparent. But she knew his kind, she was sure.

"You wanted me because the notion of a famed actress on your arm appeals to your manly sensibilities," she guessed.

"If I have manly sensibilities, no one has made me aware of them." He drained his glass and placed it upon the sideboard before sauntering toward her. "They sound dreadfully boring and terrifically unctuous."

She had not expected levity. He was smiling now. And she could not shake the impression it was a true smile. She drank more of her wine because she did not know what to say.

He was watching her, and his smile made him seem younger than his years. Almost boyish. An answering ache she did not want to feel flared to life at the sight of those lips curved. The urge to feel them against hers was strong.

But foolish.

She would not give in.

"You are making light of me, Your Grace" she observed at last, because she had finished her wine, and because it seemed he was waiting for her to speak.

It had been her turn, after all.

Why did he make her feel so off-kilter? The same way she had after traveling on the steamer from New York. For days after her arrival, she had still felt as if she were swaying on the rolling tides of the sea. It had been most disconcerting.

"I would never make light of you, Mademoiselle." Neatly, he plucked the empty glass from her fingers. "Dinner should be ready by now. Are you hungry, my dear?"

As if on cue, her stomach gave a rather aggressive rumble as response. Her ears went hot as she flattened her palm over it. "Forgive me, Your Grace. I am hungry, yes. Between rehearsals and the performance, I do not believe I consumed more than tea and bread all day."

"Tea and bread?" His smile vanished, replaced by a scowl. "Is Saville working you into the grave? Surely there was time for more of a repast."

There had been, but she had spent the afternoon soaking in a hot bath and attempting to calm herself. She had sworn, for a moment that morning, when she had returned to her hotel, that she had spied her brother. Though the man had been swallowed up by the crowd of the street and she had not seen his face, she was sure by now it had been her imagination. Drummond would not have followed her here, to where he was most in danger.

She hoped.

It was one of the chief reasons she had booked her passage

and escaped New York City, bringing along the documents and funds he had requested. She had done so knowing she could be arrested herself should her connection to The Emerald Club and her brother be discovered and should the incriminating evidence be found in her belongings. The risk had been worth the reward, and she had grown daring enough to take the gamble, given the sudden offer from the Crown and Thorn. It had seemed almost too good to be true, the chance to free herself at last.

Still, the realization her brother could have followed her here had filled her with a grim sense of foreboding she had found difficult to shake. But shake it she had, and shake it she would continue to do so, for the duke was awaiting her response.

"The bread and tea were all I managed today, but the fault was not Mr. Saville's," she explained. "He is a remarkably forward-thinking theater owner, and it is my privilege to be upon his stage."

Over the years, she had endured all manner of theaters, managers, owners, fellow actors and actresses...nothing would surprise her any longer.

"You must take time for more," Winchelsea said, frowning at her. "Fortunately, I am here to feed you."

Yes, he was. And yesterday, he had been there to rub her aching feet. To worry about her tight slippers.

Warmth she did not want to feel suffused her. No one had worried about her in years. The last man who had claimed to do so was long gone from her life. Nothing but a memory best forgotten.

Her stomach growled again, and she could not stifle her own horrified laugh.

He winked at her, then offered her his arm. "And not a moment too soon."

BY THE TIME dinner reached its conclusion and the dessert course arrived, Felix was faced with a disconcerting and wholly unwanted realization.

Part of him *liked* Rose Beaumont.

And it wasn't just his cock, he was ashamed to admit. He was not merely physically attracted to her beauty and undeniable allure. Not only carrying out a duty. Somehow as the dinner had progressed and the wine had begun to flow—enabled by his assiduous servants—he had somehow forgotten the reason he was seated across from her at the table.

But he forced himself to remember now. She was a dangerous woman. Deeply involved with Drummond McKenna. Suspected of colluding with the most violent faction of the American Fenians. She had information he needed. She was the most potent lure he could use against McKenna to bring him to English shores.

One day, in the coming weeks, it was possible he would have to see her arrested.

But despite the endless litany of why he must not allow himself to soften toward her, he did. She was clever and sleek and mysterious. He wanted her for all the wrong reasons.

He wanted her in spite of the villain she had taken to her bed, in spite of the deeds she herself may have committed. As he watched her consume her plum tartlet, he had to wonder how she could bear the touch of such a man. She was an intelligent woman—he had discerned as much with ease from the first moment they had met. Surely she had to abhor the evil McKenna was about. How could she take part in it?

Duty and obligation, those twin bugbears, returned. He reminded himself the reason for this dinner was to attempt to uncover information. To glean more facts. Anything to bring him closer to finding McKenna and bringing the villain to justice. He had to use Rose Beaumont however he must.

She was but a pawn in this deadly game he played.

"How long is your stay in London?" he asked, determined to continue on the course he had agreed upon in the wake of the bombings on the London underground.

Two massive explosions, tearing rail cars into twisted metal and shattered glass, as if they were nothing more than children's toys. McKenna had been responsible. The puppeteer pulling the strings from afar. Felix needed to clip those strings.

"I will be here for six weeks, and then I am on to Paris," Rose told him. "From there, Berlin. And from there, wherever I may roam and find my way upon the stage."

"What of New York City?" he asked, for the itinerary she mentioned was news to him. "When do you plan to return? Surely, the Rose cannot be without her city for too long, or the city without its Rose?"

Something in her expression changed. There was a subtle tensing of her lips, her jaw. Her gaze flitted down to the table. Her smile faded. "I have no plans of returning."

What the devil?

No plans of returning to New York City? This news, like her itinerary, was unexpected. The Special League double agents stationed in New York had reported seeing her in the company of McKenna the day before she had boarded a passenger ship bound for Liverpool.

But he must not allow his surprise or confusion to show. Mademoiselle Beaumont had a particular manner of studying his expression, as if she were mining beneath the surface for some greater treasure. Undoubtedly, it was down to her undeniable talent as an actress.

"You have no plans of returning ever?" he asked nonchalantly.

"No." She met his gaze, and for a moment, the haunted expression on her face, the desolation in her eyes, was undeniable. But it was gone in a flash, so quickly he doubted he had ever witnessed it. "I have a number of offers from theaters throughout the Continent. I will travel. See the world."

"But surely you have someone awaiting you in New York," he pressed.

He did not miss the tremble in her hand as she lifted her wine glass to her lips for a lengthy sip. "There is no one."

He could not allow the pronouncement to go unquestioned.

"No family?" Felix asked.

In truth, for as famed as she was, with hundreds of articles written about her, her likeness everywhere, there was almost no information to be had concerning Rose Beaumont herself. Endless accolades about her performances, gossip about her lovers, descriptions of her dresses, her hair. But her origins were murky. Some stories suggested she had been born in Paris, others in the French countryside.

"No family," she said quietly.

But there was a tenseness in her voice that was unmistakable.

"No lover?" he prodded, reasoning such a query, though invasive and unspeakably rude, may be the sort of question a man determined to make her his mistress would pose.

In truth, he wanted to gauge her reaction. It was possible she had thrown Drummond McKenna over. Or he could have done the same, given her impending travels. The time apart was long. But he found it difficult to believe McKenna would relinquish the opportunity to have yet another person he could control within London. Yet another soldier hiding in plain sight.

Felix needed to uncover the truth of the matter, and with all haste. Because if she was no longer McKenna's mistress, that meant using her as a weapon against McKenna may not prove as potent a lure as he had originally supposed.

"There is no one," she repeated, her gaze steady upon him.

He wondered then if he could believe her. It was entirely possible she was lying to protect McKenna. Perhaps even that she suspected Felix or his connection to the Home Office. This development was something he would need to take to the Special League. The League leaders would relay the information to their double agents in America, who could determine the veracity of her claims.

Together, they would retool their plans for McKenna's ultimate capture, however they must. Too much was at stake.

"That news bodes well for me," he said then, his gaze melding with hers.

She smiled at him sadly. "There is a reason I do not have a lover. I do not have one, and neither will I take one."

That was certainly a lie.

She had one, and he was a cold-hearted bastard who orchestrated bomb explosions on the railway. Who sent his villains to do his bidding, laying dynamite everywhere innocent civilians could be hurt or killed.

He reminded himself of who Rose Beaumont was, and how she had come to be here. What manner of man she allowed to share her bed. And his heart hardened. "Yet you are here, Mademoiselle Beaumont. One cannot help but wonder why, if you are so set against taking a lover."

She finished the last bite of her tartlet, and damn him, but even the way she consumed her dessert was seductive. An art form. "Your Grace all but coerced me into settling upon this dinner, if you will recall."

"How different our memories are." He paused, studying her. "I extended an invitation, and you accepted. Because you find my manly sensibilities irresistible, no doubt."

She bit her lower lip to stifle her smile. "On the contrary, I accepted because you were insistent, and I grew weary of arguing with you."

He had noted she was not a woman given to lightness. Her mien was often grave, and there were shadows in her extraordinary eyes. She wore sadness like a cloak, wrapped all about her.

The ridiculous urge to hear her laughter surged inside him. To win her smiles. To ease the weight she seemed to hold heavy on her shoulders.

He banished the unwanted desire. For he was not meant to like her. Indeed, he was not meant to think of her as a person at all. She was a means of aiding his quest to bring Drummond McKenna and all those within his web to justice. Perhaps herself included. He did not dare trust her.

"I shall consider myself fortunate you were weary, then," he said, before deciding to change the subject. There was a table between him and his quarry, and while they had shared an enjoyable repast, he had still managed to wrangle precious little information from her. "Would you care to withdraw to the salon, Mademoiselle?"

Her eyes widened, and he did not think he imagined the flare of awareness within them. The understanding an audience alone with him, unattended by servants producing an endless barrage of courses, was forthcoming. That it would be the prelude to something more.

"While I thank you for the invitation, the hour grows late," she said. "I have a morning rehearsal, and I should probably be on my way."

He could not let her go so easily. His days with her were limited, and he needed to pounce upon the information only she possessed while he could. He knew how to goad her into getting what he wanted.

"I understand," he told her. "You are afraid."

"I am not afraid." Her shoulders stiffened, her spine going straight, chin tipping up in defiance.

"You are," he pressed. "You are afraid to be alone with me. You do not trust yourself, do you?"

"Of course I trust myself." She stood then, with all the bearing and dignity of a queen. "I am going to win our wager, Your Grace."

He stood as well, the grin kicking up his lips real, much to his dismay. He was not supposed to be enjoying this skirmish with her, this battle to get her into his bed. *Christ*, he was not supposed to bed her. But there was something about Rose Beaumont that was so very alluring.

She intrigued him. He wanted to learn her mysteries—all of them.

"Fair warning, my dear," he drawled, rounding the table and offering her his arm in gentlemanly fashion. "I adore a challenge."

She took his arm, allowing him to escort her from the dining room. "I am not challenging you. I am merely stating a fact."

Her scent hit him, and he knew a brief wave of memories. Hattie on his arm. Hattie laughing at a dinner party at some sally he had made. His wife had possessed the loveliest smile. The aching sear of grief hit him in the chest, just as it always did. He missed her every day.

"Your Grace?"

The lilting, accented voice of Rose Beaumont intruded upon his grim musings, returning him to his surroundings.

He realized they had entered the blue salon that had been studiously decorated by his last paramour with an eye to comfort and pleasure. The use of the townhome had been hers for the duration of their six-month affair, and it had been where he had brought Rose for dinner because taking her to his true home, where Verity was, had been an impossibility.

But he was standing there now, frozen, trapped in the murk of the past.

The reminders of everything he had lost.

He swallowed down a knot of despair. "Forgive me for woolgathering, Mademoiselle."

His voice sounded hoarse. Troubled, even to his own ears. He had found comfort in the arms of other women following Hattie's death. It had taken him years to manage it, but he had. Still, none of them had been her. None of them could compare.

He did not think it was the woman on his arm who brought with her the surging sea of his past, but rather his reaction to her. He had been attracted to other women before, but it had never been as visceral as his reaction to Rose.

"There was a sadness in your eyes just now," she observed, the hand still resting lightly in the crook of his elbow moving to stroke his forearm in a gesture of surprising tenderness. "Something is troubling you."

"A matter of the past," he dismissed. "Nothing more."

He would not discuss his wife with the actress at his side, a woman he scarcely knew. A woman he dared not trust. A woman who was here with him for reasons he must not lose sight of or forget.

"The past stays with us always, does it not?" She cocked her head at him, studying him, a small, sad smile flitting over her lips. "No matter how far we travel, no matter how much time passes, we cannot outrun ourselves, all the hurts and pains we have known. They follow us everywhere, locked inside little valises in our hearts."

What a strange creature she was, insightful and rare. He could not shake the wild thought that Hattie would have liked her. That *he* could like her, were their situation not so dire. Had she not shared the bed of a despicable villain like Drummond McKenna.

"The past is never far from the present," he agreed solemnly. It was the only concession he would make. The only one he could. "What is it you seek to outrun, Mademoiselle Beaumont? Or may I call you Rose?"

Her gaze shuttered, and she released her grasp on his arm, stepping away from him. "There is nothing I seek to outrun. I am looking for a new beginning. Closing one book to begin another."

Interesting. Was she suggesting she had indeed broken off with McKenna? He had to dig deeper. To find out more.

He followed her as she wandered across the plush carpet, taking in the chamber with a curious stare. "There must be a reason for you to be closing the book, as you say."

She made her way to the piano dominating a corner of the room—this, too, had been a relic from his last lover, a famed German opera singer. "May I play, Your Grace?"

He watched as she trailed her fingers over the smooth ivory keys, not exerting enough pressure to make a sound. How lovingly she caressed them. The wicked beast within him imagined, just for a beat, her trailing her touch over his body in the same fashion. And his cock went hard.

He cleared his throat, willing the desire to abate. "You may, Rose."

She raised a brow and cast an arch look in his direction. "I did not give you leave to call me that yet."

Yet, she said. As though she planned to.

This was promising.

"I decided the time to ask for permission is at an end between us," he said as she seated herself on the bench.

"How autocratic of you, Your Grace," she returned, but there was neither heat nor censure in her voice. "Do you have a request?"

He studied her, thinking she looked at home, not just behind the piano, but in this salon. For a moment, he could almost fool himself into the belief they were lovers, that there was nothing but desire and attraction binding them to each other. But that was a dangerous fantasy indeed, one he could ill afford to entertain.

"Sing whatever pleases you most," he told her.

She cast him a small smile, and then her fingers began moving over the keys, producing a haunting melody that paled when her lovely voice filled the air. "My life is like the summer rose," she sang, "that opens to the morning sky."

Felix could do nothing more than watch her, completely in her thrall. Her tone was melodious and clear, tinged with a poignant note of melancholy which could not be feigned. It was as if she felt the emotion of the song, as if she lived and breathed it much as she did the roles she played on the stage.

"My life is like the autumn leaf," she crooned on, "that trembles in the moon's pale ray."

The evocative lyrics of the song settled over him, until gooseflesh pebbled on his skin. She was not just beautiful as she sat there serenading him. She was magnificent. The melody wound around him as she reached the final crescendo.

"On that lone shore loud moans the sea," sang Rose, "But none, alas, shall mourn for me."

As the last key hung in the air, Felix could not fight the powerful rush of attraction hitting him. Every instinct within him screamed to go to her and claim her mouth as his. He wanted her so badly, he did not dare move, lest his restraint snap and he snatched her off the piano bench like a marauding beast.

"That was lovely," he forced past the lump in his throat, the need pumping through him in a frenzy he had never before known.

Was it the song? The words? Rose's voice? Or was it merely Rose Beaumont herself, seated before him like one of the Muses?

"Thank you, Your Grace." She smiled at him, and it was genuine, filled with radiance. "It has been quite some time since I have sung for anyone, aside from the stage. It has always been one of my small pleasures."

He felt the force of that smile to the soles of his bloody feet. "You have a voice to rival the angels'."

A pretty pink flush crept on her cheeks. She stood, fussing with her skirts and refusing to meet his gaze. "It is passable, I suppose. You need not flatter me."

Could it be that he had rendered the famed Rose of New York shy with his praise? The prospect was astounding, but he could not help but to think it true. And he could not keep himself from going to her then. He skirted the piano, stopping when he stood before her.

She glanced up at him at last, and their gazes met and held. So much passed between them in that moment. He felt as if he were seeing her for the first time, and as if she were seeing him too. All his good intentions fell away, crumbling beneath the pressure of the need for her that had become a fire in his blood.

A lone wisp of golden hair had come free of her coiffure, resting upon her cheek, and he could not resist sweeping it gently to the side. "I am not flattering you, my dear. I am being truthful. You possess a rare talent to inhabit the song, as if you are feeling all the emotions yourself as you sing them. I have never heard another sing with such vulnerability, such honesty."

Her flush deepened, but she did not step away. "It is merely because I have always excelled at playing roles. That is what I do best. I don a mask, a character. I become someone else for a few minutes, a few hours. I forget who I am. I make the audience forget, too. That is the gift of every good actress."

Now that he had touched her, he could not seem to stop. He traced the backs of his fingers over her cheek, admiring the warm smoothness of her skin. "What role are you playing now, Rose? I confess, I cannot help but to wonder."

Her lips parted, and he did not miss the hitch in her breath or the way her pupils expanded. "I am playing the role of the woman who wants to win five thousand pounds from a duke who thinks he will lure me into his bed."

He should have expected as much in her reply. But in truth, the breathiness of her voice gave lie to her words. She was every bit as attracted to him as he was to her. But she was fighting it. Fighting him.

"I think you lie, Rose," he told her softly. "I think you are playing the role of the woman who does not want me to kiss her. Because in truth, I think you want me to kiss you very badly right now."

She swallowed. "You are as sure of yourself as ever, Your Grace."

"Felix," he countered, and he was not sure why, but the moment the invitation left him, he knew it was right. He told himself it would foster a greater connection between them. Lull her into a false sense of comfort. Help her to reveal everything she knew about McKenna. "Call me Felix when we are alone, Rose."

But he could admit that he also wanted to hear his name on her lips. Whispered in that husky voice. Better if it were on a cry of passion.

She raised a hand to his face in a fleeting touch. "I cannot call you that, just as I cannot be alone with you again. Thank you for dinner, Your Grace. But now, if you will excuse me, the hour grows late and I truly must go."

At last, she stepped away from him, and he allowed her to go, not pressing his advantage. Instead, he offered her a bow. "I will have my carriage deliver you to your hotel as you wish."

She looked startled, as if she had expected him to argue. But while there was nothing he wanted more than to kiss her, he knew he did not dare trust himself. His hunger for her was too great. He needed the night to clear his head and remind himself of the responsibilities he bore.

He needed to recall the true reason for wooing Rose Beaumont.

He needed distance and distraction and, very likely, the use of his hand.

She stopped on the threshold of the salon and looked back at him, a golden goddess in the gaslights. "I have not enjoyed myself this much in as long as I can recall. For that, I am in your debt."

And then, in a swish of silken skirts, she was gone.

Chapter Four

SHE HAD ALMOST allowed the Duke of Winchelsea to kiss her. The thought had chased her all the way back to her hotel the night before in his carriage. It kept her from sleep until the faint strains of dawn had painted the London sky. During her morning rehearsal, she had forgotten her lines and missed her cue twice.

Twice.

Rose Beaumont did not forget her lines or her cues. *Ever.*

Thoroughly disgusted with herself, she left the theater near noon, only to find the same gleaming black carriage awaiting her. This time, the door opened and the man who had been invading her thoughts ever since last night—ever since she had met him, if she were honest—stepped down. He was dressed informally, but the sight of him in a coat and top hat, his sensual lips curved in a welcoming smile that was just for her, made her heart beat faster than the wings of a hummingbird.

"Mademoiselle Beaumont," he greeted.

"Your Grace." She dipped into a semblance of a curtsy, as she supposed was only proper. "What are you doing here?"

"Making certain you have something more to eat than bread and tea today," he said, extending his arm.

He was a caretaker. She had come to understand that about him. He fretted over her feet, her stomach, her comfort.

Over *her*. It was disconcerting and yet also strangely heartening. That a duke, a nobleman of such elegance and stature, would show such consideration for an actress, spoke a great deal of his character.

He wants you in his bed, reminded a cynical voice inside her. *That is the reason for his kindness. His shows of compassion. He wants to keep his five thousand pounds, to show you off on his arm.*

But as she stared at him in the midst of the bustling city, just outside Mr. Saville's West End theater, she did not want to believe the jaded part of her. She wanted, instead, to allow herself to believe in the fiction that Winchelsea cared. Because she was a woman who had reached the unlikely age of twenty-six without ever having been truly cared for by anyone.

What is the harm, asked a different voice inside her, *in indulging just once? In forgetting about Drummond and what you must soon do?*

She listened to the latter voice and accepted his arm although she knew she should not. "Feeding me will not make me any more inclined to change my mind," she informed him. "I am still every bit as determined to win."

"And I am every bit as determined you shall lose," he returned, his smile deepening until it reflected in his eyes and a tiny set of grooves bracketed those vibrant emerald orbs. "You have no notion of the lunch I have in store for you."

Yesterday's dinner had been a veritable feast. The endless procession of courses had been more food than she had ever dreamt of consuming in one sitting. But for a woman who recalled all too well the sharp pangs of a hungry belly, it had been pleasing.

"We shall see," she told him primly, allowing him to escort her to the carriage and hand her up neatly.

She settled on the well-upholstered bench and expected

him to sit opposite her. But he did not. Instead, he climbed inside—and even this action, he achieved with flawless elegance—and settled his long, strong body at her side. His thigh brushed her skirts. His delicious sandalwood scent hit her.

And so did a wave of longing.

She supposed it was inevitable. One could not remain in the presence of a man as devastatingly handsome as the Duke of Winchelsea and continue to be unaffected by him.

Felix, said the second voice inside her.

The wicked one.

But no, she must not think of him so familiarly. Nor allow his nearness to undo her resolve. She had far more important matters to occupy her mind than a man. Except he was crowding her. His coat was a soft temptation brushing against hers. Even his elbow seemed somehow sinful as it jostled hers.

She inhaled at the contact, and he took note, mistaking her reaction.

"Forgive me my lack of grace," he said in his perfectly clipped patrician accent as the carriage swayed into motion.

It occurred to her she ought to ask him about their destination. How trusting she was, merely following him. Going wherever he chose to take her. Acting the part of the kept woman. And of all the roles she had played in her life, kept woman was one she had never played. She was no man's mistress.

Falling into this ease and familiarity with the duke so quickly was dangerous in so many ways. Foolhardy. Stupid, even, given what lay ahead of her. She was, at this moment, a drowning woman after her ship had sunk, watching the last lifeboat sail into the horizon.

"You are forgiven, Your Grace," she said, acutely aware of

his regard. "But I wonder if you might not be more comfortable on the opposite squab."

"No," he said, his voice a low and decadent rumble she felt everywhere. "I am most comfortable right here."

Of course he was. And so was she, which was entirely the problem.

She liked the way he touched her, the way his warmth and his scent invaded her senses, no matter how much she knew she must not. "Where are you taking me? I think I should have asked before, instead of allowing you to abscond with me."

"If I were to truly abscond with you, my dear Rose, I would not be taking you somewhere to satiate your stomach," he said, his voice taking on the tone of a growl. "I would take you to my bed."

Somehow, the word *bed* on Felix's lips held untold possibility. Such a tempting capacity for sin. It made her pulse leap and heat flare to life in her core.

But she must not think of that.

And neither must she think of him as Felix.

He was the Duke of Winchelsea. A stranger. A man who would never bed her. Never satiate other needs. *Good heavens*, a man she must keep her distance from if her reaction to him grew one bit stronger…

"I suppose I must consider myself fortunate, then, that you are not in the absconding mood today," she quipped, disturbed to realize how familiar he felt to her. How right such banter seemed. How natural.

"For you, dearest Rose, I am always in the absconding mood." His regard was intense.

She felt it in her core, in an answering ache and blossom of desire. For some absurd reason, she had to stifle the urge to beg him to abscond with her now. What was getting into her?

She had worked far too hard to get to where she was, to build her reputation as Rose Beaumont. To become an actress who was not only esteemed but in demand. To free herself from the chains of her past. To escape her brother. To make a new life for herself.

She was the phoenix, rising from the ashes. She was the Rose of New York, and she must not allow herself to lose sight of that. Not for the handsome duke at her side. Not for anyone.

"You would find it difficult indeed to abscond with a woman who is unwilling," she told him then. "I would beat down the walls of the carriage. Holler from the window for everyone to hear."

His lips twitched with mirth. "Somehow, I do not believe you would be that unwilling, Rose. But I will not test you today. Today, I merely want to feed you."

The warmth in his regard and in his tone settled deep inside her. "I did not expect to find you here today."

"If I had warned you, you would have been prepared with your arsenal of weapons. You would have told me *no*, I have no doubt." He paused and raised a brow at her, maddeningly handsome. "I could not risk you denying me. However, I had a strong suspicion that if I arrived when you were hungry, my chances of your acquiescence would be exponentially increased."

She could not suppress her laughter at his admission. "Quite sly of you, Your Grace. I would applaud your cunning, but I have a feeling that would only encourage you."

"Come now," he said softly, "you must give me a fair chance to win the wager. How can I win it if I do not see you?"

"Perhaps I should go into hiding," she suggested thoughtfully. "I could tell Mr. Saville I am dreadfully ill for the next few days. Leave for Paris early."

He pressed a hand to his chest. "And leave me here nursing a wounded heart?"

She sent him a sidelong glance. "I hardly think your heart would be wounded. You have known me a scant handful of days."

"Long enough to know I admire you greatly."

She tried to steel herself against the delicious rumble of his baritone. But how could she not feel those words in her core? How could they not affect her, especially when coming from this elegant, beautiful man?

She flushed and looked away, turning her attention to the window and the passing panorama of the London cityscape instead. If she looked at him for one moment more, she was going to give in to temptation, she was sure of it. And she could not do that. Must not do that.

"How can you admire me when you do not know me?" she asked against her better judgment. "You admire the idea of me, Your Grace. The notion of the Rose of New York on your arm. In your bed. Do not think you are the first, and nor shall you be the last."

"Rose."

There was a note of urgency in his voice, but she kept her gaze averted. For if she looked at him, met his gaze, listened to any more of his silver-tongued words, she was not sure she could trust herself to remain impervious. She had believed she possessed a hardened heart, but he was fast proving her wrong.

"Rose, look at me."

Still, she did not look.

"Please."

In the end, it was the beseeching tone in his voice as much as the entreaty that chipped away at her resistance. She glanced back toward him once more. A mistake.

The hunger in his gaze was undeniable.

It filled her with a want all her own, and she knew her need was reflected back at him. She was an actress, yes, but this moment, the connection between the two of them was as compelling and real as it was nettling. She could not always hide herself behind a mask.

"I admire you," he said. "Just as you are. Not the Rose of New York. *You.*"

Everything inside her froze at his words, and she knew a sudden, knife-like pang inside her breast that she was deceiving him. After she had taken the stage name Rose Beaumont and invented her French background to lend herself an aura of mystery, she had only ever admitted the truth to one other man. With others, she had never wanted to; the delineation was always there.

The separation had been clear. She had never felt truly drawn to anyone, and after the last time, she had vowed she would never allow herself to lower her guard and feel it again. But for some reason, she almost blurted the truth to him.

My name is Johanna McKenna.

It was there. On her tongue. In her heart.

The carriage stopped.

He gave her a lingering look. "We have arrived at our destination."

She inhaled, giving him a jerky nod, preserving her secret as she knew she must. Thank heavens they had reached wherever they were headed when they had. But a minute more, and she would have revealed far too much of herself to him. Then she would have been well and truly vulnerable.

"The timing is perfect," she said brightly, slipping back into Rose Beaumont once more. "I am famished."

"As am I," he said, his voice low and gruff.

And she knew he was not speaking about food.

But then, neither was she.

FOR THE SECOND time in as many days, Felix was seated opposite Rose Beaumont as they dined together. And this time, no less than the first, he was once more in sensual agony perpetuated by her nearness. They were ensconced at his customary private rooms at the sumptuous hotel on Regent Street he had owned before he had unexpectedly inherited the title and all its burdens from his cousin. He still owned Markham's, in fact, though he employed others with its daily management and operation and went to great cares to keep his ownership to himself.

She cast him a glance from beneath lowered lashes. "You have not eaten a bite of your luncheon, Your Grace."

He stared down at his *vol-au-vent* and *oeufs au bouillon*, realizing belatedly she was correct. He had not been hungry. Strike that, he *was* hungry. But it was not for the damned food, even if the French chef on staff was one of the finest in London. And even if the hunger in question was altogether wrong.

Base and shameful. A violation of everything he held sacred.

He cleared his throat, feeling suddenly as transparent as a window. And as lost as a ship being tossed about on a stormy sea. "I was momentarily distracted," he said, and this, at least, was true. "Is the fare to your liking, my dear?"

With each moment he spent in her maddening presence, he had to remind himself with an increasing amount of sternness that he was not meant to be enjoying this.

He was performing a duty.

A task.

Rose Beaumont meant nothing to him. She was the enemy. A woman he could not trust. Every American agent he had in New York had reported she was colluding with the Fenians.

Except, those words he had spoken to her earlier in the carriage? They were true. He *did* admire her talent, her beauty. Somehow, half of him felt what the other half could not bear. *Good Christ.* This was madness. The woman was connected to one of the worst villains of the century, and she was probably every bit as guilty as he was.

"The fare is delicious," she said then in her sweet, pleasing tones, and once more, that husky voice wrapped around him like an embrace.

He could not help but to notice a lilt in her words, dancing beneath the French accent. Some hint of another land entirely. Ireland, it seemed, but there was no mention of that in any of the stories of her history which he had read. If it were true, it would certainly make sense.

"I am pleased you enjoy the meal." He took a bite of the *vol-au-vent*, the earthy flavor of truffles and the richness of pastry and chicken briefly distracting him.

His chef was fine, damn it. Exceedingly talented. The man had fashioned cookery into an art form. Little wonder the guests of Markham's were so well-pleased, its recommendation clear in all the best London guidebooks being printed.

"You come here often, do you not?" she asked, eying him curiously. "The staff seem very acquainted with you."

There was almost an edge to her words, to her query. Jealousy? Though he was certain she felt the spark between them—like electricity coursing through wires whenever they were in each other's presence—she was McKenna's mistress. Or she had been recently enough for it to matter.

He could lie to her about the hotel, but why? Revealing

this small part of himself—the first true part of himself that he had conceded to her at all, really—could do him no harm, he reasoned.

"I own it," he admitted casually, before taking a sip of wine.

She frowned at him. "I beg your pardon, Your Grace?"

And still, she would not call him Felix. He did not know why her refusal should irk him so, but it did. He told himself it was because the oversight indicated his lack of success with his duties.

"I own it," he repeated. "The hotel. *This* hotel. It is mine."

"You own this hotel." It was her turn to take a drink of wine. "Why did you not say so?"

He flashed her a wry smile, once again forgetting everything between them was a lie for just an instant. Enjoying himself. Finding pleasure in these moments spent with her, in their banter. "Was I to have announced it to you?"

"No." Her lips formed a perfect pout he wanted to kiss. "But you may have mentioned it in passing. Did you bring me here so you would impress me with your wealth? If so, I must caution you, it will do you no good. I have been wooed by wealthy men before."

Of course she had. This should come as no surprise to him. She was beautiful and sought after. She had been the mistress of another man up until very recently, if she was being truthful with him.

Yet somehow, the notion of other men wooing her stung. Some strange and base part of him wanted her to be his. Alone. Although he knew it could never be.

"I did not bring you here to impress you with my wealth," he countered calmly, casting away all other unwanted thoughts but the need to answer her. "I brought you here because I knew we could dine comfortably in private and enjoy an excellent meal. My chef here at Markham's is one of the best in England."

"He is talented," she agreed, relenting as she forked up another bite of food from her plate. "I cannot imagine why I allowed myself to exist on bread and tea when I could have enjoyed such sumptuousness."

"Now you know what is awaiting you, if you but ask, seek, or allow me to spirit you away," he said. "I propose luncheon every day. And dinner as well, following your performances."

In truth, he was greedy when it came to her. He wanted all her time. All her smiles. Her lips, her curves, her bare skin beneath him—*God, yes*, he wanted that, too.

"Surely Your Grace's time would be better served in far more important matters," she suggested.

Yes, his time would indeed be better served than engaging in fantasies about a woman who was altogether wrong for him. And forbidden. He was wooing her, it was true, but not to win her. Merely to use her. He must not allow that important fact to go forgotten.

"There is no other manner in which I would spend my time," he said.

He *had* to spend his time with her, he reminded himself. He needed to find a way to strip her of any and all information she possessed concerning McKenna. If she was no longer the man's mistress, that meant parading her all over London on his arm would not accomplish the effect he had hoped.

"I do not dare accept your offer." She paused, then offered him a sad smile. "I need your five thousand pounds far too much."

He drank his wine, watching her closely. "Why, Rose?

Surely Saville is paying you handsomely for your stint at the Crown and Thorn."

"He is indeed," she agreed mildly. "But I need all the funds I can manage if I want to travel the world. I am an actress in high demand now and can command an excellent wage for myself, but it was not always thus. And I do not fool myself. It will not always be this way. Another Rose of New York will take my place one day."

It was a stark view of life, of her future. Against his will, Felix felt an answering pang in the vicinity of his heart. A place Rose Beaumont had no place being anywhere near.

"You are young and talented," he said. "You have many years ahead of you."

Her lips compressed, and this time, the bleakness of her expression was undeniable. "Perhaps, and perhaps not."

"That is certainly a grim view," he observed, even as he told himself he should leave well enough alone. He should not pry further into the matter. Her future did not concern him. Only her present and his ability to use her to imprison Drummond McKenna did.

"A pragmatic view." There was an undeniable sadness in her eyes, raw and real. "I have learned life can be fleeting. One day, it can seem certain, and the next, it is gone, like a candle flame sputtering into darkness."

She spoke like someone who knew the keen agony of loss and grief. And because he lived each day with the blade of despair lodged in his chest where happiness and contentedness had once dwelled, her reaction drew him. Though he tried to recall she was an actress, seasoned and well-trained, unparalleled on the stage, he could not shake the feeling this reaction, this pain inside her, was real.

"Life can indeed be fleeting," he agreed, thinking of Hattie. Of how vibrant and filled with life she had been, until the day she had breathed her last breath and she had been but a shell of herself. "I have experienced this myself."

"I had a daughter," she told him softly.

The revelation shocked him to his core. He had known nothing—there had been nothing to suggest she had a child. But then, he realized the tense she used. The direction of their conversation.

His gut clenched on a wave of sympathy. Losing Hattie had been like losing a part of himself. But Verity…he could not fathom the loss of his daughter. Could not bear to imagine it.

"You need not explain yourself," he hastened to say, feeling like a cad for sitting here with her, manipulating her, deceiving her, when she was a mother who had lost her child.

No amount of information he could glean from her was worth hurting her or forcing her to relive the agony of her loss.

"Her name was Pearl," she said, almost as if she had not heard him. "She was nine months old, the light of my world. I was young then, so very young, and the woman I left her with while I worked and rehearsed could not wake her from her nap. When I returned from rehearsals that day, she was already an angel."

God, the pain in her voice, in her expression. She looked, suddenly, so fragile. As if a touch would break her. As if she were fashioned of the finest crystal, and one kind word would make her shatter.

He stood, not thinking about his mission. Not thinking about his duty. Not thinking about her connections to the Fenians or his need to prod information from her. All he thought about in that moment was her.

Rose Beaumont had lost her daughter. And though the wound was an old one, he knew from experience that grief was a scar upon the heart that never truly healed. One false move, and it tore open again, bleeding everywhere.

"Rose," he said, all he could manage as he skirted the table. "I am sorry."

He did not need to say more. Could not if he tried. But it did not matter, because she was in his arms, and he was embracing her. The sweet, familiar scent of rose petals hit him, and he could not deny the rightness of her in his arms, her soft heat melded to his rigid planes.

Her arms wound around him, and she pressed her cheek above his heart, as if she found comfort in the steady thumps, the affirmation of life. "I have not spoken of her in a long time. It was eight years ago, but I have not forgotten."

"You will never forget," he said, his hands traveling up and down her spine in soothing strokes. Against his better judgment, he buried his face in the fragrant golden upsweep of her hair. "And nor should you. We carry the ones we loved in our hearts and our memories always."

There was no mistaking the trembling shaking her. She was sobbing. A cynical part of him recalled how great an actress she was, capable of a vast portrayal of emotions. That part of him said this, too, could be an act.

But somehow, he did not believe that.

"Who have you lost that you loved?" she asked, her voice muffled by his waistcoat, but the sadness within it could not be feigned.

"My wife," he admitted.

How strange it seemed to be discussing the woman he loved with another woman. A woman who was his enemy. A woman he could not trust. A woman he was bound to betray.

She stiffened. "You had a wife?"

"Yes." Felix searched for words, an explanation. How to give voice to the best years of his life? He had been besotted with Hattie from the moment he had met her.

Her father had earned his fortune in the mills he owned. He had believed in educating his daughters. Hattie had been intelligent, opinionated, and unique, mirth always dancing in her eyes. She had been the brightest star in the night sky. She had been the only star in the sky.

And then, she had burned out.

And now, here he stood, alone in a private room at Markham's with a woman he was destined to betray, taking comfort in her embrace.

"I am so sorry, Felix," Rose said.

The genuine compassion in her voice, it could not be feigned. He had no doubt.

Just as the sympathy he felt for her was real. Despite the situation, the obligations weighing heavily upon him, the facts he knew about her, the doubts he had… On this, their mutual grief, they were united. The rest did not matter. They were two people who had lost, who grieved, who understood each other on a level that surpassed all else.

He was still holding her, his hands stroking her back, her scent enveloping him, when he realized she had called him Felix. And she had tipped her head back, her bright-blue gaze holding him captive.

"I am sorry for your loss, Rose," he said thickly. "That you lost your daughter. I, too, have a daughter. If I lost her… I cannot imagine the pain you endure, the anguish."

"You have a daughter?" she asked, her eyes searching his. "You never said so before. Why not?"

Because Verity had no place between them. She was all he had left of Hattie. All he had, aside from his duties, his fortune he had acquired prior to inheriting the dukedom. Verity was precious. Special. Mentioning her to Rose Beaumont seemed wrong. A sacrilege. A betrayal of his wife.

Rose's face shuttered then. "I understand." Her tone was tinged with bitterness and, unless he was mistaken, hurt.

She attempted to extricate herself from his embrace, but he held fast, not wanting to put an end to their connection just yet. And not in this fashion, her feeling betrayed and foolish. For some reason, he could not bear that.

"It is difficult for me to speak of her," he said, the words forced from him. "Difficult, even, for me to be her father. For me to look at her. She reminds me so very much of her mother... It is not her fault, of course. The blame is mine. Verity is but a child."

It was more than he had intended to divulge. More, even, than he had ever revealed to another.

Rose stilled, her gaze hard upon his, searching. "Verity is her name."

"Yes." He released the breath he had not realized he had been holding.

"How old is she?"

"She is but five years old," he said, once again saying more than he wished.

"She must be lovely," Rose said, her sad smile once more in place. "I am sure your wife would have been beautiful."

"Verity is," he agreed. "And Hattie was."

"I almost wish you had not told me, that you had not taken me in your arms and let me weep." Her smile faded.

"Rose," he began.

"But you did," she interrupted quickly. "And you cannot take it back. Nor can I. My name is Johanna, Felix. If we are to carry on with whatever this is, I would hear you call me by my true name rather than the name I chose for the stage. You have shared a part of yourself with me, and I am offering this part of myself in return."

Johanna.

He stared at her, shock filtering through him, even as he supposed it should not. Actresses and actors were well known to assume names for the stage. Her words struck him. *I am offering this part of myself in return.*

"Johanna," he found himself repeating, trying the name on his tongue.

He liked it. Johanna suited her far more than Rose. It was lovely and mellifluous, just as her voice.

"Yes." She frowned then. "Please do not tell anyone else, however. It is imperative that my true name be kept a secret from the public."

More secrets.

How intriguing. And revealing.

He wondered what else she was hiding. What she was hiding from. Or perhaps, *who* she was hiding from.

"Your secret is safe with me, my dear," he assured her.

But he knew the stinging blade of shame as the words left him. For he would have to take this information, this admission of hers, and see what else he might uncover. He withdrew from her, acutely aware of the tangled web in which he now found himself.

"Thank you, Felix," she told him, mustering up another of her melancholy smiles.

"Shall we finish our luncheon?" he suggested.

How he wished she had not called him Felix. And how he wished he did not have to lie to her.

"Of course," she agreed, flushing. "Forgive me my tears."

"There is nothing to forgive," he assured her, the words hollow to his own ears. Because there was *everything* to forgive. And the truth was no longer as concise and clear as it had once seemed.

Chapter Five

*T*HE MESSAGE JOHANNA had been waiting for had arrived.

A note, seemingly innocent enough, instructing her to arrive at the Royal Aquarium at half past one that afternoon, signed by Mrs. Harriet Wilson. The past, never far from her frantically fleeing heels, had finally come calling. And it had happened just as Drummond had promised her it would.

With a stoic sense of acceptance, Johanna finished her breakfast before sending a note to the Crown and Thorn indicating she would be missing the morning's rehearsal because of a stomach ailment. Although the aquarium in Westminster was not a far jaunt from the theater, she knew her mind would not be able to concentrate on her lines with the afternoon meeting looming.

Moreover, she had a suspicion Felix's carriage would be awaiting her.

Felix.

Johanna's heart lurched at the thought of him as she returned to her hotel room and secured the door behind her. Somehow, during the course of their luncheon yesterday, something had shifted between them. Their shared revelations of grief and loss had connected them in a deeper sense than mere attraction ever could.

She could no longer think of him as Winchelsea. He was

far more than that to her now. But she must not think of him at all, for she had other matters to attend. Matters that made her heart pound and her palms go damp as she crossed the sumptuous carpet of the suite and made her way to the trunk she had left carefully locked and packed following her arrival.

The time had come to see to its contents.

Reaching into a hidden pocket in the lining of her valise, she plucked out a key. She dropped to her knees, fitted the small key into the lock, and opened it. Her hands shook as she removed the lock and opened the lid of the trunk.

The contents were as Drummond had promised: three biscuit boxes tucked into sawdust, a sealed brown packet lying atop both. Hands shaking, she retrieved the packet, then brushed the sawdust from it. She ought to have opened the trunk earlier, she knew, but she had been dreading this moment. Dreading the discovery she would make.

The certain knowledge that she had transported dynamite to England in her own personal trunk. If she were to be discovered in possession of such incriminating documents and materials, she would be arrested. She had no doubt. And Drummond had been quite clear on the potential repercussions.

She could still hear his voice warning her.

If you fail me, I will see you killed. Prison will be the least of your worries.

And though she was in London now, she knew the strength of his power was no different than it had been in New York City. His ability to harm her was every bit as real. He had Fenian followers stationed throughout England under various disguises. No one was truly safe from his wrath, including her.

His men knew where she was staying. They knew her name. She was meeting one of them at half past one, and he was certainly not Mrs. Harriet Wilson. The first order Drummond had given her was to deliver the packet of communications upon receipt of a note to meet at a predetermined location from Mrs. Wilson.

She closed the lid on the trunk, locked it, and carried the packet to the writing desk stationed by the window. He had also been adamant she was not to break the seal of the packet. But if she was ever going to free herself of him, she had no choice.

Johanna seated herself at the desk, staring down at the packet. When the offer from the Crown and Thorn had arrived, she had been so relieved at the prospect of life across the sea, far away from her brother's influences. Until she had been forced to tell him she was leaving, and he had decided to use her travel plans as an opportunity to secret lignin dynamite and communications into England.

But she had not given up her dream of freeing herself from him.

Instead, she had formulated a plan of her own. It would not be easy. Indeed, it was terribly dangerous. If she managed to carry it out, however, she would finally be able to sever the ties that had been binding her to Drummond after a year of fear.

It all began now.

She picked up a letter opener and carefully used the thin edge of its silver blade to slice through the adhesive. Johanna held her breath as she went, praying she would not tear the paper. If she did, it would be instantly detected by the man she was to deliver the packet to.

Ever so slowly, the envelope opened, until she reached the final corner. One more slide of her opener, and it was done. She reached inside and extracted the papers contained within, careful to keep them in order. A cursory examination of them revealed a list of future targets, an ingredients list and instructions, addresses and names, and a letter.

Taken separately, they were not particularly damning. But along with the biscuit boxes cemented closed in the trunk, there was no doubt what she was looking at. On a deep breath, Johanna took out pen and paper, and then she began to painstakingly copy each document.

When she had completed her task, she returned the documents to the envelope and applied a new layer of glue, taking care to smooth out every crease. She returned the copies she had made to the locked trunk.

And only then did she breathe easier.

The first step of her plan was done, but there were many more to come. If she did everything right, she would be able to deliver the trunk and its contents to London police just before she left for Paris. Drummond would be arrested, and even if he incriminated her or revealed her true identity to the world, she would be safe from him forever. She could not live beneath his thumb, fearing his wrath, any longer. Even if her freedom came at the cost of losing everything she had built, it would be worth it.

But if she made one wrong move, her brother would have her killed.

Either way, she would be free.

FROM HIS VANTAGE point in an unmarked carriage, Felix watched as Rose—strike that, *Johanna*—descended from a hired hack before the massive red brick building housing the Royal Aquarium. Though she wore a concealing hat and had dressed in rather nondescript fashion, he would recognize her anywhere.

When she had cried off rehearsals that morning, Theo had sent him a note.

And Felix was deuced thankful he had.

His meeting with Special League leaders and the Criminal Investigation Department of Scotland Yard had ended just in time for him to arrive at Johanna's hotel as she left. Acting on instinct, he had followed her here, to the massive glass-topped building which, contrary to its name, housed a poor showing of fish. It was better known for its summer and winter gardens and a plethora of other entertainments which had little to do with the aquatic.

All in all, an excellent place to blend in with a crowd. Or perhaps to conduct a meeting with someone, unobserved in the milling throng of entertainment seekers. The knowledge made an edge of something decidedly like jealousy knife through him.

Who would she be meeting? And why?

It was his duty to determine that. Felix told himself it was duty *only* as he descended from his carriage and asked his driver to await him before crossing the street and entering through the same doors Johanna had. Once inside, he proceeded through the hall with care, moving with the crowd whilst looking for her.

As if his eyes knew instinctively where to travel, he found her, standing in the sunlight in the midst of the gardens, near a massive statue of a man mounting a horse. He found a place beneath a large, leafy plant whose name escaped him. It was the perfect vantage point.

He watched as she waited by the statuary, glancing about in agitated fashion, as if she were searching for someone. Part of him prayed she was not, but part of him knew—oh, how it knew, she was. His gaze scoured her figure, noting the way her gloved fingers grasped her skirts, gripping into the folds of the nondescript fabric.

How different she seemed in this moment from the golden-haired siren who owned the stage and made her audiences sigh and weep at her command. Her beauty was still undeniable, but the tense manner in which she held herself gave her away. Her dress was plain. She had left her large hat in the coat room, but curiously, she wore her dolman draped over the crook of one arm.

Almost like a shield.

Or as if she were using it to hide something.

Suspicion once more took root, branching into his heart and constricting. He realized he did not want to believe the worst of her. Yesterday, over luncheon, when she had been in his arms and revealing part of herself to him, they had bonded.

Unless she had been playing a role—and for an actress of her skill, it was entirely possible—something had changed between them. It was as if they had crossed a bridge together. He felt, quite inexplicably, closer to her. She had shared her given name with him, the story of her daughter. He had told her about Hattie, about Verity.

Had shared the shattered pieces of himself with someone for the first time.

Felix did not want to be wrong about their connection the day before. He did not want to believe she had come to the aquarium for a nefarious purpose. Instead, he wanted to believe she had been honest. That her grief had been real and not some weapon she had chosen to wield against him, the one most certain to puncture his wounded heart and render him vulnerable.

As he watched, a man, tall and thin, approached her. They exchanged a few words. Felix was too far away to attempt to read their lips and discover what they were saying.

Johanna did not look comfortable with the man, however. They circled the horse statue slowly. Johanna cast a few glances about her, as if she were looking for someone.

And then, she withdrew a large packet from beneath her draped dolman, extending it to the man. The man took it, said a few more words, and turned to disappear into the crowd.

Heart hammering in his chest, Felix followed the man, determined to find out who he was and what was within the packet. Dreading both answers.

For suspicion was a heavy weight upon his chest, and he feared he already knew.

WHEN JOHANNA LEFT the Crown and Thorn that night, it was once again raining. And once again, Felix's carriage awaited her. This time, however, he was not within it. Stifling a surge of disappointment, she settled herself on the plush squab and closed her eyes as the conveyance swayed into motion.

Tonight had been yet another performance as Miranda. For the next few days, she would immerse herself in rehearsals for the next role she would play, Katherine in *The Taming of the Shrew*. Her six-week tour in London comprised three, two-week runs of Shakespeare plays, and each was no less demanding than the last.

But her impending roles were not the reason for her weariness now.

No, indeed. The weariness was thanks to her afternoon sojourn to the Royal Aquarium.

She had done it. She had passed off the packet as Drummond had required. The man had not appeared to notice the envelope had been opened and then resealed. But only time would tell whether or not her deception was discovered. He had been terse, simply approaching her as she had been told he would.

"I believe we have a mutual acquaintance," he had said. "A Mrs. Wilson?"

And she had responded as she had been instructed. "Mrs. Harriet Wilson?"

He had asked her if she was alone or accompanied then, and she had informed him she was by herself. The man had been soft-spoken and mild-mannered. He had possessed the slight brogue she had come to know from fellow Irish who had emigrated to America. In time, their accents were smoothed down like pebbles worn by the waters of a stream.

But he had not frightened her in the way Drummond did. Perhaps because unlike Drummond, she did not know what the mysterious man she had met was capable of. With her brother, she was certain. She had experienced his abuse herself.

He was not just heartless, but soulless as well. Just as their father had been before him. Just as ready to inflict brutal harm upon anyone who stood in the way of what he wanted or anyone who defied him.

She shuddered in her seat as she thought of Drummond. There had been a reason she had spent half her life running from him. But in her foolish bid to flee her past, she had succeeded far too well. When her life had finally become comfortable—when her roles had become leading roles and when the public adored her, when she had food aplenty upon the table and fine clothing on her back, that was when he had found her.

And he had struck.

Not physical blows at first, but emotional ones.

The physical blows had come later. Small, at first. A slap,

pulled hair. Rages where he had destroyed every stick of furniture in her hotel room and she had been forced to leave and pay for replacements. Then worse. A broken finger. Punches to the ribs, where no one would see the bruising.

The unwanted memories had her hands shaking. She gripped her skirts to calm herself and took a deep breath. *He did not follow you here*, she told herself. *No one will hurt you here. You are safe from him.*

If her plan unfolded accordingly, she would be safe from him forever. His reign of terror upon her and the people of London both would be over within weeks. The next step awaiting her was to alert the police about the trunk Drummond had sent with her from New York and to provide them with the copies she had made of the correspondences within the packet she had delivered earlier today.

But that would wait—*had* to wait—until her London performances were complete. She hoped this afternoon's summons had bought her the time she needed to secure her freedom.

As the carriage rocked to a halt, she peered out the window and realized they had arrived, once more, at the townhouse where she had previously dined. In the hours since his revelation about having a daughter, it had occurred to her she had seen no sign of a child in the home. Not a ball, not a nursemaid, not books.

The driver opened the door to the chilled night, and a gust of wind sent a torrent of rain spraying into the carriage, coating her.

"Begging your pardon, Mademoiselle Beaumont," said the man tugging at the brim of his hat as he held an umbrella aloft. "The weather is growing worse. If these winds and rains keep up, no one will be going anywhere tonight."

Suspicion lit within her—was it something the duke had

instructed his man to say? An excuse to persuade her to stay the evening? To spend a night in his bed as he had wanted all along?

But a fresh gale of wind gave lie to that fear as it turned the umbrella inside out and tore it from the driver's grasp. A wall of cold rain pelted her as it blew into the interior of the vehicle.

"Blast!" the drive swore. "Stay here if you please, Mademoiselle."

The door slammed closed, and she was treated to the sound of more muffled cursing from beyond as he presumably searched for a replacement umbrella. Meanwhile, the wind continued to howl around them, one sudden burst so violent, the entire carriage shook. The unmistakable jingling of tack beyond proved the horses were not particularly pleased by the weather either.

Perhaps it had not been planned, then.

The door swung open once more, revealing the driver's triumphant grin and the production of a replacement umbrella. "If you do not mind making haste, Mademoiselle? I fear this umbrella will soon meet the same fate."

Another burst of wind made the edges curl, making her realize she must go or suffer the lashing torrents of rain without shelter. She rose from the bench and exited the carriage with the aid of the driver. Another rush of wind sent raindrops into her face as they made their way up the front walk.

"This is not His Grace's primary residence, is it?" she managed to ask as they drew near to the door with its lion head knocker.

"Of course not," said her guide as he led her through a fresh torrent of rain. "This is where he keeps his... This is one of his other residences, Mademoiselle."

Ah. Just as she had suspected. Thankfully, the brewing storm had disarmed her driver enough that he had almost divulged the complete truth. This small, though elegantly appointed townhome, was not the duke's residence at all. It was, instead, where he kept what she could only assume was his mistress.

Another burst of wind slapped rain into her face as the driver rapped on the portal, adding to her inner misery. She was the sort of woman he would not invite to his home. She was not his social equal. What had she been thinking, imagining they had somehow grown closer at yesterday's luncheon? Thinking she knew him?

Calling him Felix?

Her ears went hot, and shame curled in her belly, turning her empty stomach into a sick sea. Of course she was not worthy of dining in his true home. She was an actress. He was a nobleman. She had birthed a child out of wedlock. He was a duke.

It should not make her feel ill, and yet, it did.

The realization felt like a betrayal. How dare he reveal such private and painful details about himself to her? How dare he hold her in his arms as if he cared? How dare he pursue her as he had, and then relegate her to the home where he had brought other women to his bed? And not just other women, she reminded herself. Paramours.

The door opened to reveal the butler. "Mademoiselle Beaumont, good evening. You are expected."

Of course she was. Grimly, she wondered how many *other* ladies had been expected, in just the same fashion.

She thanked her driver and stepped inside, nonetheless, because another burst of wind had assailed them and turned his second umbrella inside out. It would be horribly rude to avail herself of the man's courtesy and then require him to make the journey to her hotel in this deluge.

The door closed upon the storm, and she handed off her pelisse and hat before following in the butler's wake as he led her through the entryway and down the main hall. He stopped at the threshold of the salon where Felix—no, Winchelsea—had taken her following dinner. The room with the piano.

Another woman's piano?

How many others had sung to him from it?

But why should she care? She had no claim on him and had no wish to find herself in his bed. She was leaving London in a matter of weeks, and with the terrible plague of Drummond following her, she could not allow herself to be distracted from her course. The repercussions were far too dangerous.

She swallowed the knot in her throat as the butler announced her. Forced herself to push all hurts and doubts aside. And swept past the butler with a *thank you* and a sweet smile.

Rose Beaumont was firmly in place as she made her way into the room. Johanna might as well have been as far away as New York City in this moment: an entire, vast sea. The duke was on the opposite end of the room, his expression almost severe as he bowed to her. She was dimly aware of the butler excusing himself and the door to the salon clicking gently closed in his wake.

"Good evening, Johanna," the duke said in his low, delicious baritone.

Her true name spoken in his voice seemed somehow a betrayal after what she had just uncovered. She wished she had not told him she was called Johanna instead of Rose. Wished she had not allowed herself to entertain the foolish weakness she felt for him.

But she would face him calmly, she vowed, and with her head held high. "Good evening, Your Grace."

She had not intended to place an emphasis upon his title, but she did. Even to her own ears, her words held an almost mocking tone. She swept into a deep curtsy, keeping her face deliberately expressionless.

If he wanted to do nothing more than bed her, he would be sorely disappointed. For she had never been the sort of woman to engage in *affaires*. She was, instead, the sort of woman who shared nothing of herself with anyone. That she had lowered her defenses, and that she had been wrong to do so, stung.

His countenance was as grim as she felt, but his eyes were vibrant and intense, searing her. "Yesterday, you called me Felix. I was hoping we may have reached an understanding."

Though he said the words with ease, she could not shake the sense that they did not ring true. Something about him was different tonight. He was somber. Intense in a different fashion than before. As an actress, she was more attuned to those around her than most people. Acting relied upon reading the emotions of one's fellow players, taking that energy and harnessing it in turn.

"There is no understanding to be reached between us," she said, "other than that I will soon be five thousand pounds richer."

She needed that money. She needed to steel herself against his handsome charm, which was suddenly so much more compelling now that she was alone with him in the room. His lips drew her attention, and for a brief, mad moment, she wondered what it would be like to feel them against her own.

She chased the unwanted thought from her mind.

"I propose we change our wager." He closed the distance between them, stopping when he was near enough to touch.

"Change it how?" she asked, painfully aware of his sandalwood scent hitting her.

"We eliminate it." His gaze held hers. "You have demonstrated an estimable determination to win. I, on the other hand, am being kept from what I want most. Unless I am mistaken, we have found ourselves at a stalemate."

Kept from what he wanted most.

Her.

It had been so long since she had been touched. Since a man had held her gently in his arms in truth rather than in the course of a drama being enacted on the stage. A great pang of want hit her before she could stay it. And not just for the mere act of any man's tender touch, either. But specifically for his.

This man's.

Why was it so impossible to cling to her resolve when he was in such tempting proximity?

"I do not want to win," she countered. "I must."

That was true, as much for the additional funds as it was for her ability to cling to her own sense of honor.

He was unsmiling. "Forget the wager. I will give you the five thousand pounds."

She froze. "Give me the five thousand pounds, Your Grace? What are the terms of such a benevolent gift?"

"You."

She swallowed. "I beg your pardon?"

"I will give you the funds and concede the wager to you. In return, you will give me yourself." He watched her in that intense manner he possessed.

As if he could see inside her, to all the parts of herself she kept hidden from the rest of the world. To the parts of her she had kept locked away. The parts of herself she did not know existed.

Everything inside her wanted to say yes. She needed the

funds. She wanted the duke. But she had never sold herself, and she never would.

Her chin lifted. "I believe you are mistaken about me, Your Grace. I am not for sale. Nor have I ever been. And while five thousand pounds would make my future much easier, I am not prepared to barter my body in order to attain it."

"I am not buying you, Johanna, but compensating you. Showing you my appreciation." He paused, his gaze flitting to her lips. "It is a common enough understanding."

"One you have reached many times before, no doubt," she snapped. "This is where you bring your women, is it not?"

His full lips compressed into a tight line as he watched her. "It is the residence I procured for my last mistress."

Anger burst open inside her. She lifted her hand and slapped his cheek. "How dare you?"

Pink blossomed instantly on his skin, and he rubbed the place where she had done him violence. "I meant you no insult."

He had paid her one, nonetheless.

But part of the ire burning within her right now was aimed at herself as much as it was him. Because she was tempted. His proposition would give her everything she wanted, but her pride would not allow it.

"I will not be your kept woman," she told him. "I cannot be bought. I *will* not be bought. And neither will I be insulted by remaining here with you a single moment more."

She turned away, but he caught her arm in a grip that was gentle, yet firm. And when she turned back to him, the regret on his handsome face did something to her. She softened. Her resolve melted under the blazing heat of desire.

They had been dancing around each other for days, but the attraction sparking between them was undeniable. She felt it now, more poignantly than ever, luring her back to him. Keeping her here. Making her want him in spite of all the reasons why she should not.

"I am sorry, Johanna."

Of all the things she had expected him to say, an apology was not one of them.

"Your Grace," she began, only to be interrupted by him.

"Stay," he said softly. "Please."

Chapter Six

ONCE AGAIN, FELIX had bungled things.
Badly.

"Do not go," he entreated when she said nothing, staring at him with such raw hurt in her expression he did not believe even an actress of her caliber could affect it.

For all her secrets and all his suspicions of her, he wanted this woman more than he had wanted another in as long as he could remember. His emotions were warring within him, a confused tumult of need and want and anger.

And frustration.

When he had followed her earlier in the day and seen her meeting with a man, his suspicions had been raised. Felix had attempted to pursue the man, but he had disappeared into the throng of diversion-seekers. Which left him, once again, with more questions than he had answers when it came to her.

He did not want to believe she was involved with the Fenians. Did not want to believe she was doing anything nefarious. But what he had seen earlier, coupled with the knowledge he had of her in New York City from the League's double agents, painted a bloody damning picture.

He resented her for making him feel things he had no right to feel. For making him so torn between duty and his incomprehensible attraction to her that he had decided, as he awaited her arrival that night, there was only one way to put an end to all this madness.

To stop courting her. Put an end to the wager.

And so he had offered her the five thousand pounds in exchange for her body. Her reaction had not been what he had anticipated. But he could admit he had deserved that slap. He had never before propositioned a woman with such a crude offer. He had merely allowed his frustrations to sink their talons into him too deeply.

"Why should I stay?" she asked quietly.

The emotions he had been attempting to keep at bay teemed inside him. Hunger was a beast, rampaging through him, making him weak. Making him forget all the reasons why he must not do what he was about to do.

He pulled her toward him with one swift motion, and she was flush against his chest, her breasts full, round temptations, the maddening scent of rose petals making a new surge of lust pound in his ballocks. Her hands flitted to his shoulders. Her mouth was an offering he could not resist.

He told himself he was obeying his duty.

"Because of this," he rasped, and then, his lips were on hers.

Nothing could have prepared him for the initial contact, her mouth beneath his. Their lips fit together perfectly, hers supple and warm and smooth. She made a kittenish sound of need, her arms linking around his neck, and stepped into his body. They were pressed together, from thigh to mouth, the crush of her silken skirts billowing around his trousers. Her scent was everywhere, and he had the brief, incredulous thought it would stay with him forever now. That her lush perfume of rose and citrus, like the seduction of her kiss, would be imprinted upon him always.

Felix forgot everything in that moment but the woman in his arms. He kissed her furiously, ravaging her mouth with his. Kissed her because he had to. Kissed her because he wanted her to experience the same need careening down his spine, the white-hot desire to be possessed by him in the very same way he wanted to possess her.

God, yes, he wanted to possess *her*. This rare, enigmatic creature. This woman of secrets and mystery. He wanted her beneath him. Wanted all her bare skin burning into his, her golden hair unbound on his pillow, wrapped around his fist. Wanted to sink inside her wet heat and make her scream.

His desire for her was beyond his capacity to control it. Beyond duty and honor. He was mindless, helpless, thoughtless. She was everything, all around him, making him weak. Making him hers.

On a groan of painful pleasure, he coaxed her mouth to open. Her tongue met his, and the kiss turned decadently carnal. It was primal, a mating. Her fingers were in his hair, tunneling through the strands, grasping handfuls. She rose on her toes, pressing her mouth into his harder.

He had not been wrong about the passion flaring between them. She felt it, too. He would stake his life upon it. This was not the kiss of an actress but the raw, real kiss of a woman. A woman who wanted him every bit as much as he wanted her.

His instincts took over, and he guided them across the salon toward the piano where she had sung for him two nights earlier. Alone, in the darkness of the night, he had imagined having her here. He had thought of her sitting on the bench with her skirts raised, her legs spread to reveal the sweet pink flesh hidden between them. He had thought of sinking to his knees before her like a supplicant at the altar of a goddess. Of licking her, sinking his tongue inside her. Tasting her.

The animal within wanted that now. But he was not certain he could go slowly. A leisurely seduction would not be possible. The raging erection in his trousers was demanding to be freed. He was almost delirious with lust.

So delirious, he missed his aim. Instead of guiding her to the piano bench, he guided her into the keys. The dissonant sound produced by her skirts brushing against the ivory echoed through the chamber, momentarily breaking the thrall in which she held him.

He tore his mouth from hers, his breathing harsh. Her back was to the piano, and her eyes were hooded, almost drowsy. The vibrant blue hit him. The obsidian discs of her pupils were wide. She looked as if she had been drugged. Her lips were full and dark, puffy from his kisses. Her breathing was as ragged as his.

He had never wanted her more.

"I will not accept five thousand pounds," she told him.

He was so startled by the husky sound of her voice, it took him a moment to focus upon what she had said. They were back to his ill-advised offer of money in exchange for bedding her.

She was turning down his proposition once more. As she should.

Disappointment lanced him, and yet, her persistent refusal buoyed his spirits.

"Please forgive me for the insult I paid you," he said, thinking again of her stinging slap, the outrage on her countenance.

Either she was playing the grandest role of her life, or she was being honest with him. As honest as she had been yesterday at luncheon when she had revealed some of the details of her past with him.

"No money," she repeated. "I will not be bought."

"Of course not," he agreed, reluctant to loosen his hold on her and allow her to slip from his embrace.

He liked having her in his arms.

"I will give myself to you freely if and when I choose." Her gaze searched his. "But I still intend to hold you to the wager. You have three more days to attempt to defeat me and fail."

She was certain of herself, especially after the kisses they had just shared. After he had almost ravished her on the piano bench. After she had turned to flame in his arms.

He would have said as much had not a rapping at the door intruded. Felix released Johanna and stepped away from her, putting some much-needed distance between them once more. Needed for his sanity, anyway.

"Enter," he called, wondering why the devil his butler would dare disrupt their tête-à-tête.

But when the door swung open and he saw the servant's expression, he feared he knew. He braced himself, anticipating the worst.

"There has been an explosion at Halford House, Your Grace," said the butler. "I have received word the Fire Brigade has been sent to douse the flames."

Everything inside him shriveled, and an incapacitating rush of fear walloped him.

He could only think of one thing.

"Verity," he ground out. "Is she safe?"

"She had not yet been found when word was sent, Your Grace."

Dear God. His daughter. He could not lose her. Would not lose her. He had to go, to find her, to make certain she was safe. She was all he could think about, fear lashing his heart so tightly he could scarcely breathe.

"Carriage?" he clipped.

"It is being readied," the butler reassured him. "It will be here within moments."

He nodded, the dread rising within him along with the fear. It was the same sickening churn of emotions that had consumed him when Hattie had passed. She had been ill for days, ravaged by a cough, delirious with fever, and he had known on the final day. That sense of loss was just as vivid now. Just as choking. As mocking. As terrible.

He scarcely took note of the domestic excusing himself so he could see to the sudden preparations for travel. Raking a shaking hand through his hair, he attempted to bring air into his lungs, but it would not come. His chest ached. His heart galloped. He broke into a cold sweat, his fingertips tingling.

Not now, he denied inwardly, railing against himself for this weakness.

He could not afford to suffer one of his fits now, not when Verity needed him. They no longer happened nearly as often as they had in the days after Hattie's death. By now, he only suffered them every few months.

But one was taking him, and though he tried to gulp breaths, he could not. Could not move. Could not speak.

Verity. His sweet little girl with her round cherub's face and sparkling green eyes and her undeniable resemblance to Hattie. She was all he had left. God, what if something had happened to her? What if she was trapped somewhere now, alone, flames coming for her?

Through the haze of panic attacking him, a calm, familiar voice comforted. Arms came around him. A hand passed over his back in soothing strokes.

"You will find her," promised the husky voice of an angel. "As soon as the carriage is ready, you will go to her, and you will find her, and she will be safe."

Only, the angel was no angel at all. She was the last woman he could trust.

None of that mattered when she took him in her rose-scented embrace and wrapped her arms around him. The terror clawing at him from the inside out lessened. His heart slowed down.

"Breathe, Felix," she said. "I am here. Your daughter will be safe. Just breathe."

And somehow, he was holding her back in a tight embrace, this woman of so many faces and roles, this stranger, and his face was buried in the silken cloud of her hair. He inhaled slowly, then exhaled, hoping she was right.

The panic slowly subsided to a dull ebb.

By the time his butler returned to announce the carriage awaited him, he was calmed sufficiently enough that he could function. But though he could not explain why, he knew he still needed Johanna at his side. He wanted her there. He clasped her hand in his.

"Come with me," he said, the words an anguished plea, but he did not care. There was no room for pride in this moment, and he needed to stay strong for his daughter's sake.

Johanna did not hesitate. She gave a single nod. "Let's go."

JOHANNA SAT BY Felix's side in his carriage, just as they had the day before. But unlike their luncheon ride to Markham's Hotel, there was no levity or passion between them. There was only desperation and fear. She had never seen a man look graver than the Duke of Winchelsea did as the carriage swayed through the howling wind and battering rains, rumbling over slick roads as they made their way toward his home.

His true home, a place he had never invited her to.

But she would not dwell upon that distinction now.

Because his daughter was in grave danger. And if they did

not find her before it was too late…

No. She would not allow herself to entertain such an unthinkable notion.

"You will find her," she reassured him, the words spoken as much for his benefit as for hers.

The change that had come over him earlier had been terrifying, as if he had been struck a fatal blow as he struggled for breath. The shock of the news had rattled him badly, and understandably so. He had already lost a wife. He could not bear to lose a daughter as well.

Once more, they were drawn together by the commonality—they were both parents, both people who had loved and lost. And she wanted with all her heart for his daughter to be safe.

He squeezed her fingers, his grip almost painful. "Thank you."

"Everything will be well. Have faith, Felix."

Of course, having faith in the face of life and death was not always effortless, particularly when death could come so easily. So suddenly. But if there was any way she could bring him peace, help to calm him as they bolted through the night to find his daughter, she would gladly do it.

"If anything happens to her…"

"Nothing will," she insisted, though she, too, battled the rising fear within.

The butler had said there had been an explosion. Likely, it would have been caused by a faulty gas line. However, the word had triggered a reaction in Johanna as well. For she knew what her brother had been planning in London. She had the evidence of it hiding in a trunk back at her hotel.

In the time since the initial revelation, she had been able to shake the fear Drummond would have somehow been responsible for such an egregious crime. He was aiming for large public gatherings and symbolic buildings, not personal residences. She had yet to betray him, so he could not have laid a bomb in some sort of retaliatory measure if he had someone following her.

He had told her he would, that his eyes and ears were everywhere.

And while she had not seen anyone tracking her movements, she believed Drummond. She knew him. She feared him. It was one of the reasons she had not sought out authorities immediately upon her arrival in London. She was terrified he would watch her every movement and take action before she had a chance to defend herself.

But there was nothing for him to fear from her being wooed by a duke. She had shown her brother he could trust her from afar by delivering the documents as he had asked. She stopped, however, at the dynamite. Before she handed the trunk over to anyone, she would be delivering it to Scotland Yard, along with all her knowledge of her brother. Then, she would flee to Paris before anyone was the wiser.

"I should not have been away from her tonight," Felix was saying, breaking into her troubled musings. The guilt weighing down his voice cut into her heart. "I should have been there. If I had been, this never would have happened. She would have been safe."

"The Fire Brigade and this horrible deluge of rain will go a long way toward putting out the flames," she soothed. "You must not blame yourself for this. Even if you had been at home, there is nothing to say you would have been any more capable of rushing her to safety than others. Perhaps you would have been injured or trapped yourself."

"Ah, Johanna." He slid an arm around her shoulders and hauled her into his side in a crushing embrace. "I do not know what I would do if you were not here. You have helped me to battle my demons, to remain as calm as possible, and you have my endless gratitude for that."

She did not know what to say to his raw expression of thanks. So she held him back, every bit as tightly as he held her. Held him as she wished someone had her after Pearl's death, when she had been so devastated that every breath she had taken had threatened to break her. But there had been no one for her then, and it was why, she thought, she wanted to be here for the Duke of Winchelsea now.

If, God forbid, something had happened to his daughter Verity, Johanna would hold him just like this. She would hold him all through the night, and the next day as well if need be. She would cry with him. Rage with him. Chase away the pain as best as she could.

She hoped, oh how she hoped, she would not need to do so.

The carriage came to a halt after what seemed the most interminable ride ever. It had felt like years, but it must have only been minutes. Felix jerked away from her and threw the carriage door open. The acrid scent of charred beams and plaster hit her as she struggled to follow in his wake. The street lights were lit, but the tremendous downpour of rain and dampness in the air rendered their effect lackluster.

Smoke filled the air, curling around her as she raced down the street toward the imposing edifice, making it more difficult to see. Fire brigade members were scattered about, along with an assemblage of people she could only assume were the duke's servants. The downpour refused to relent, and her skirts were heavy and sodden by the time she reached the gathering.

The duke was speaking to a woman who was sobbing wretchedly.

"Simmonds, please tell me you have found her," he was

begging, his voice breaking.

"I am so sorry, Your Grace. I looked for her everywhere until the smoke was too thick, and I had to flee," the woman said. "No one has seen her. No one knows where Lady Verity went."

An inhuman cry of sheer agony tore from him.

Johanna pressed a hand to her lips to stifle her own cry of pain on his behalf. She had hoped and prayed ever since first learning of this disaster that Felix's daughter would have been found by the time they arrived. That all his worry and fear would have been for naught.

He turned away before she could call out to him, and she knew, instinctively, he was going to go inside the home to search for his daughter. She also knew she could not allow him to undertake such a task alone. If his daughter were indeed within, and something had happened to her, Felix would be destroyed. Summoning all her strength, she gathered her soaked, heavy skirts in her hands, and ran after him.

Shouts erupted in their wake, and one of them was the chief of the Fire Brigade, she was sure, alerting them to the dangers within. Felix threw open the front door, and she followed, slipping on the slick marble floor as she did so. The combination of the darkness, the rain, and the smoke outside had made it impossible for her to tell which area of the home had been affected by the damage the most.

"Felix," she called, feeling as if she must be the voice of reason. "Wait for me! You must take care, or you will injure yourself, and then you will be of no use to Verity."

But there was no reasoning with a desperate man, and she recognized the futility of her attempts as he refused to pause. Onward he stalked, a man determined. And after she chased, terrified for him. For his daughter. Equally unwavering in her need to help in whatever manner she was able.

Thankfully, the fire had not reached much of the house, it would seem, for lights were still lit deeper within the main hall. Though smoke hung in thick clouds, Johanna could at least see where she was going. Could see Felix's broad back and long legs disappearing as he headed for a grand staircase up ahead.

She grabbed her skirts in her fists, raised them high, and ran after him. Halfway up them, he snarled over his shoulder, "Johanna, you should not be here. Go back to where you are safe. I will find her myself."

"No," she denied, every bit as vehement. "I am not allowing you to do this alone."

Because if his daughter had indeed been claimed by the smoke and flames, he could not face that agony on his own. She would not let him. Could not bear to contemplate such a nightmare.

"Verity!" he began calling. "Papa is here! Verity!"

There was no answer save the echo of his voice, laden with desperation.

"Here now, we have only just gotten the flames out here below," called a male voice from the floor. "You should not go up there. It may not be safe."

"I don't give a damn if it is or if it isn't," Felix growled. "Nothing is going to keep me from searching for my daughter."

"Madam, if you would please come down, at least," entreated the voice, presumably speaking to Johanna.

"No," was all she said, getting quite breathless now from the exertion of chasing after the duke.

She did not care. She followed resolutely in Felix's wake, adding her voice to the calls. He did not bother to convince her to leave. Instead, he told her to peruse the rooms on the right of the hall while he checked those on the left.

They worked in concert, traveling in and out of rooms, opening doors, searching beneath tables and chairs, seeking out every darkened corner. But it was all to no avail. By the time they reached the end of the hall, they had still not uncovered a sign of her. But they were both coughing, and Johanna suspected the smoke was burning Felix's lungs every bit as much as it was burning hers.

"Where is the nursery?" she asked. "It is possible she is still there."

"Her governess said she searched for her." Felix began taking the next flight of stairs two at once.

"Do you trust her?" Johanna asked, trailing in his wake, for it was a question which needed to be posed.

They could not afford to dally, for each minute they spent in fruitless search was one minute more during which Verity could succumb to the thick smoke afflicting the home.

"I did," he bit out. "But perhaps you are right. We will go there next."

On the next floor, the smoke was not nearly as thick, perhaps not having had the time to rise as high just yet. Johanna thought it a good sign as she and Felix ran into the nursery, both of them calling out to Verity as they went. There were no lights lit in the chamber, and they had to rely upon the gaslights burning in the hall to see through the shadows.

"Papa?" croaked a terrified little voice from somewhere within the murk.

"Verity?" The relief in Felix's voice set off a similar burst within Johanna's heart.

"Is that you, Papa?" asked the girl, a sob in her words.

"Of course it is me," he said. "Are you hurt, my darling? Can you come to Papa?"

"I'm not hurt." She coughed then. "But everyone was

running away, and yelling. Someone said there was a fire. I tried to follow Simmonds, but then I lost her. So I came back here."

Johanna could discern faint movement through the shadows at the far end of the chamber. And then, there was a small figure running forward, arms outstretched. In the next moment, Felix was hoisting her in his arms and holding her tight, burying his face in her hair.

"Verity, thank God," he breathed. "I prayed I would find you, the entire way here. I cannot lose you."

"I was afraid, Papa." The girl's arms were wrapped around Felix's neck every bit as tightly. She sobbed. "I was so scared without you."

"I am here now," he assured her. "I am here."

Johanna watched the tearful union through a sheen of her own tears and through her own silent prayer of gratitude.

HOURS LATER, AFTER the Fire Brigade had inspected the damage to Felix's townhome and after they had been certain the flames had all been doused, and after the servants had been accounted for and arrangements for them to spend the evening in a myriad of other places had been arranged, Johanna found herself once more inside Felix's carriage. This time, there was a slumbering, smoke-scented girl tucked between them.

His devotion to seeing his staff safely settled for the night had impressed her. Especially given the undeniable fact that they had all escaped unscathed whilst leaving a terrified little girl behind. But he was a fair man, and she had seen evidence of that tonight, along with evidence of just how much he loved his daughter.

He was an excellent father, Johanna thought, casting him a sidelong glance now. And his daughter's love for him had been evident in the way she had clung to him as if she were a vine twisting about a tree. As if she feared he would disappear if she let go of him. The sight had made Johanna's heart swell and yet ache all at once.

"Please, Johanna," he said suddenly, reaching out to her. "Stay the night with us. I promise nothing untoward will happen. You will have your own chamber. My daughter will be beneath the same roof. It will be entirely proper."

She looked down at the sleeping girl who was nestled so trustingly against her, soot streaking her cheeks. Not for the first time, she wondered what Pearl would have looked like, had she lived. What she would have sounded like.

Something inside her shifted, her heart warming. She felt a connection to this child, though she knew she should not. That she had no right to, in fact. But in this moment, the rain lashing the world beyond, and the three of them safe within the dry, warm cocoon of Felix's carriage, she recognized a kinship with Verity.

Johanna was a mother without a daughter.

Verity was a daughter without a mother.

"She will need a bath when we arrive," Johanna found herself saying, her mind switching, with such ease, into the maternal. As if it had never left her.

When she had been a mother, her every day had revolved around Pearl. What she would eat, when she would sleep, who would look after her. For a long time after her daughter had died, Johanna had still sworn she heard Pearl's cry in the small flat they had shared. She had gone to answer it, only to find emptiness where her crib had been.

Sometimes, she heard it in her dreams.

Less now than she once had.

But seeing Verity, holding the little girl in her arms, had brought it all back.

"She smells of smoke and is covered in soot," Felix observed, passing a loving hand over his daughter's head. "I expect you are right. But without Simmonds, I fear I am lost."

He was asking her, without forming the question, to bathe his daughter. After the upheaval of the night, she knew just how much of a concession this was for him. He was entrusting her with his beloved daughter, the one person he loved more than any other in the world.

"Not lost, surely," she said. "You are a commendable father. But I can well understand there are certain matters to which a man will necessarily look to a female. I can assist her if you like."

"I sacked Simmonds," he said, shocking her with the admission. He passed a hand over his face. "She left Verity behind. Never bothered to look for her. I cannot keep a woman in my employ who only cares for herself and not for her charge."

"I do not blame you," she said softly. "I would have done the same, were I in your position."

He took her hand in his suddenly, raising it to his lips for a kiss, his stare intense. "Thank you, Johanna."

"For being truthful?" The smile she sent him was rueful, for she was thinking she had not been entirely honest with him from the start. Indeed, there remained facts she was still hiding. "You need not thank me for that."

"No." He shook his head slowly, his gaze never wavering, and she could not miss the sparkle of admiration there. "For being you. For staying by my side and snatching me from my demons when I needed it most. For following me into danger. For helping me to find her. For staying with her whilst I attempted to sort out this horrid mess. For everything. I know if Hattie were here now, she would be every bit as appreciative of you as I am."

The mentioning of his dead wife—for surely that was who *Hattie* was—caught her off guard. It seemed, at once, an insult and a compliment. A reminder of who she was in his life, a woman so insignificant he had not brought her to his true home until a fire had nearly burned it down. And yet also an encomium, coming from this man, who had clearly loved his wife so.

So she grasped his hand in return, and she said the only thing she could. "You do not need to thank me for any of that, either, Felix."

Chapter Seven

*D*YNAMITE.
Fenians.
Bomb.

The words churned in his mind, a sea of unwanted knowledge he could not escape as Felix's carriage carried him away from Scotland Yard. The fire at Halford House had been no accident. The explosion which had sparked the blaze in the entry hall and front salon had not, as he had hoped and assumed, been caused by a faulty gas line. But rather, lignin dynamite.

Colonel Olden, the Home Office Chief Inspector of Explosives, had broken the news to him first thing that morning when he had answered the summons taking him away from his home. The summons which had left Verity behind in Johanna Beaumont's care.

"There was a box," Olden had said. "Partially exploded, though not entirely. And along the perimeter of Halford House, another box was discovered. There is lignin dynamite within."

Lignin dynamite was uniquely American.

A calling card, of sorts.

American, just like Johanna Beaumont, the mistress of Drummond McKenna. Felix's hands closed into impotent fists as the carriage swayed through London. How had he allowed himself to believe her story of moving on to the Continent, of never returning to New York City? How had he let her cast her spell upon him, until he could think of nothing more than her talents as an actress, her gentle beauty, her sad past? How had he believed they had bonded?

Christ, how stupid was he? How naïve?

She was an actress, and a bloody talented one at that. Everything she had told him had probably been a lie, one cleverly planned to manipulate him. And oh, how she had succeeded. Even after he had witnessed her meeting with a man at the Royal Aquarium, he had somehow allowed his desire for her to convince him she was not as guilty as she seemed. That her refusal of his five thousand pounds in exchange for bedding her had meant she possessed a modicum of integrity and honor.

In truth, all it likely meant was that she was loyal to her protector. He could see it all so clearly now, and it left him sickened. The gratitude he had felt for Johanna's steadfast presence at his side the night before had vanished, and in its place seethed a horrible fury. *Good God*, if she dared to harm Verity, he would murder her with his own bare hands.

Yes, it made horrible, disgusting sense, the more he thought upon it all. Johanna—if that was her true name—had known he would be away from his home. Perhaps the business with the strange man at the aquarium earlier had been a part of it. A means of arranging the entire affair.

Bombs had been laid at his home.

Where his innocent daughter lived, where she slept.

And now, he had left Verity with *her*. With the last woman he ought to have trusted, it would seem.

How had he been so blinded by desire? By his own sense of self-importance? *By God*, he had almost lost Verity. The only part of Hattie he had left. And Good Christ, had he actually been so blinded in his relief last night at finding his daughter safe that he had actually told Johanna Hattie would have been appreciative of her?

He scrubbed a hand over his face, his self-hatred greater than it had ever been.

What would his wife say if she could see him now, chasing after a woman who was involved with one of the most dangerous criminals of the age? He had kissed her yesterday. He had almost made love to her on a piano bench.

What a stupid bastard he was.

The carriage came to a halt after what seemed like a century. He did not bother to wait for the door to open. He threw it open himself and leapt to the street. Anger and bile rising in his throat in equal measures, he stalked up the front walk and threw open the door.

His butler was there in a trice, looking alarmed.

"Where the devil is my daughter?" he demanded.

"Your Grace," the butler said, "Mademoiselle Beaumont and Lady Verity are in the salon, I believe. Is something amiss?"

Everything was amiss. He was amiss. The terror and panic from last night were fresh once more, clamoring up his throat.

But he could not give voice to the roiling emotions warring within him. *Christ*, he was not certain he could speak past the relief washing over him. The servants knew where his daughter was. No further harm had come to her. He would whisk her away from Mademoiselle Beaumont forthwith.

"Thank you," he told the domestic, already stalking toward the salon. "Nothing is amiss. That will be all."

As he neared the door, which was partially ajar, the sound of music hit him. It was Johanna's melodious voice, singing, the piano accompanying her. But the song was…

Quite unrecognizable.

He stopped.

"I once stepped in a puddle and found myself in a muddle," Johanna sang.

"I went to see the fishes and made a lot of wishes," came Verity's voice next, singing as well.

"Excellent rhyme," Johanna commended, the strains of a simple ditty still pounding out on the piano. "Oh, I have one! I stopped to read a book but scarcely gave it a look when in came a grumpy ogre who took it away."

Verity giggled.

His chest tightened, his heart seizing. *Dear God*, when had he last heard his daughter laugh? Had he ever? He suddenly could not recall. But that sound, that sweet, haunting sound, was the most beautiful music he had ever heard.

He hesitated to interrupt, lingering there in the hall. Eavesdropping, as it were, upon his daughter and a woman he could not dare to trust. A woman who had him more confused than he had ever been. Because what manner of woman would arrange for bombs to be laid outside an innocent child's home and then sing silly rhymes with her the very next morning?

Bloody hell.

"I walked beneath a ladder, and felt quite a splatter," Verity sang, "from a finch flying overhead."

Johanna laughed delightedly. "How grotesque, my lady. I do like the way you think. Now I shall have to match... I danced with a man from St. Eyre who passed an odorous cloud on the stair."

At that, both Johanna and Verity collapsed into giggles.

"A cloud!" Verity said, giggling wildly. "A cloud of pure rot!"

He could not tarry another moment more in the hall,

listening. He coerced his legs to move across the threshold, forced his arm to open the door. And there they sat, his daughter and Johanna, one golden head and one set of ebony curls, bent together, their faces wreathed in smiles.

The moment Verity spotted him, she sobered, rising from the piano bench. She dipped into a curtsy. "Papa."

Johanna stood as well, a charming flush in her cheeks as she also dipped in deference. "Your Grace. Do forgive us our silliness. I hope you did not overhear. We were inventing some new songs."

"Rhyming songs," his daughter added, smiling once more. "Mademoiselle Beaumont is lovely, Papa! We have been having such fun all morning."

"Fun," he repeated grimly. He was reasonably certain the child before him had been consumed with levity over a ditty about a fart, of all things.

How was he to deal with such a conundrum? It seemed altogether impossible, the situation untenable.

"I am sorry, Your Grace," Johanna added, her flush deepening. "I hope I did not teach Lady Verity anything too terribly untoward. I have found lightheartedness in the heaviest moments can sometimes help to ease one through them."

He allowed his gaze to linger upon her, and he was torn between the urge to kiss her and the urge to shake her and demand the truth from her beautiful lips. His paternal rage had dimmed as he had stood in the hall, listening to their silly songs. Listening to his daughter giggle.

What a priceless sound, his daughter's happiness.

If this woman could make Verity laugh again, part of him did not give a damn if she was colluding with every Fenian in the world, as long as she would promise to keep his daughter safe. But that was foolish thinking and selfish, too. Entirely unworthy of a man who had been entrusted with the safety of the nation.

"Lightheartedness," he began, only to be interrupted by another peal of Verity's laughter.

She clapped a hand over her mouth, her eyebrows raising to comical effect.

Johanna placed a protective arm around her shoulders and drew Verity nearer, into the billowing silk of her skirts. "Silliness," she said again. "We meant no harm, Your Grace."

Good God, she was comforting his daughter, much as she had in the carriage the night before, when Verity had been safely bundled between them. What was he to say to this? What could he say? Something inside him was shifting. Breaking open. He was an egg, raw, which had just been cracked.

"I know I should not have been so unladylike, Papa," Verity added, her tone contrite even as the mirth dancing in her eyes suggested she was not entirely sorry.

It occurred to him that he had spoken a grand sum of two words since interrupting their lively ditty. He was about to ask his daughter to go see Simmonds, his standard means of dismissing her, when he realized he could not do so. Simmonds was seeking other employment without a reference.

His daughter had survived the fire unscathed, no thanks to her, and he would be damned before he would give the woman a recommendation. Verity had confided in him that she had arisen in the commotion, to find her governess already gone. The woman had never bothered to fetch her, but had simply fled, fearing only for her own safety.

But he could not dwell upon the horrid events of the previous night for too long, or risk bringing on one of his fits once more.

Felix cleared his throat. "Verity, perhaps you might return

to your chamber for a nap."

"Where is Simmonds?" his daughter asked, instead of obeying him.

"Simmonds is no longer your governess," he bit out, trying to stifle his ill will toward the woman and failing miserably.

If anything had happened to Verity…

If the smoke had reached her chamber…

He shuddered, for he could not entertain any more such thoughts.

"I never did like her," his daughter said, looking rather smug. "Does this mean I do not have to read, Papa?"

"Of course you must read," interjected Johanna before he could offer a single word. "Reading is a great gift. One that takes your mind on journeys you could never otherwise embark upon."

Her words were true, and yet Felix could not help but to be irritated at the encroachment. And what was he to do about her? Here was a woman he did not dare believe to be what she presented herself as, a great actress, and yet every part of her—every look, word, and deed—made him want her more. Even as his rational mind knew how skillful she was at applying her trade, he could not make the rest of him discount what he had just overheard.

What he now saw.

She was still rubbing his daughter's slim shoulder, almost absentmindedly. It was the first time he had ever seen another female showing her tenderness, and the sight hit him in the gut. So, too, the manner in which his daughter responded, like a kitten looking to receive affection.

"Do you like to read, Mademoiselle Beaumont?" Verity was asking now, gazing adoringly up at the woman who so consternated him.

"Of course I do," said Johanna, giving his daughter a radiant smile. "I must do so, for I am an actress. I need to read scripts in order to be able to portray a character. Being able to read is very important for every lady, you will find."

"It is?" asked his daughter, her tone skeptical.

Felix could say nothing. All he could do was watch the scene unfold, in such stark opposition to the meeting he had so recently had with his daughter, during which she had challenged him on the same matter.

"Of course it is," Johanna assured her. "Reading is how you learn, and when you are learned, no one may look down his nose at you, my lady. You will command the respect of everyone in your presence."

"But I have not entirely understood it," Verity admitted, with eyes only for Johanna. "Simmonds would grow tired of my confusion and bark at me. Sometimes, she slapped my hands and made me stand in the corner."

The devil she had.

Felix strode forward, almost as if Simmonds were standing before him. Which she decidedly was not. Still, he glowered down at his daughter.

"Simmonds did what?" he demanded, for the woman had been imbued with no such power from him.

He would never have countenanced allowing his daughter to stand in a corner, or to be slapped. But then, a rising tide of shame walloped him, for he realized he had never truly bothered himself to ask or to investigate the manner in which Simmonds was instructing his daughter. He had simply been existing. He had been happy to have aid. Pleased his daughter seemed well enough.

Verity flinched at the tone of his voice, clutching at Johanna's skirts and somehow burrowing into them until there was scarcely anything left of her. A pale face, glossy curls, and bright eyes were all that remained.

He forced himself to gentle his tone, for his anger was not directed at his daughter, but rather at the woman he had already sacked. He would sack her all over again if he could. "Why did you not tell me, poppet?"

"Simmonds told me I mustn't," his daughter admitted, her green eyes—his sole contribution to her features, it would seem—wide and swimming with tears.

Something akin to a fist connecting with his gut hit him. Protectiveness toward his daughter. Despair he had let her down. Anger toward Simmonds. A renewed sense of helplessness. Confusion about the woman who was, even now, comforting his daughter in a way he could not.

The panic was pushing forward, dark and murky and terrifying.

His heart was beginning to pound.

But he could not—must not—allow himself to succumb.

Felix sank to his knees, meeting his daughter eye to eye. She looked like Hattie more than ever, a reminder of all he had lost. A reminder of what he must protect, unflinchingly and always.

"You must tell me if someone is unkind to you," he told her softly. "From this moment forward, you will not listen to your governess first, but to me. If anyone raises a hand to you, I must know. If anyone is cruel to you, I will be the one to cut her down. Do you understand, poppet?"

She nodded. "Yes, Papa."

"Come now, Verity." He opened his arms to her, hoping she would embrace him. The gesture was rusty with disuse, and he knew he must practice it more often. That he must hug his daughter as often as he had the chance.

When had he become so buried in his work that he had forgotten to hold his beloved daughter in his arms? He hated himself for it.

Verity at last ceased clinging to Johanna's skirts and launched herself at him. Her little arms entwined around his neck, and she pressed her cheek to his. Her hair smelled of roses, and he supposed Johanna must have used her shampoo and soap upon Verity last night in the bath. There was no trace of smoke. No lingering remembrance of the hell they had been through together the evening before.

Except for the fresh scars upon his heart.

"Do you promise Simmonds is never coming back, Papa?" Verity asked, still clinging tightly to him.

"Yes," he managed past a sudden thickness in his throat. "I promise.

He was keenly aware of Johanna's gaze upon him. Aware too of the prick of tears in his eyes. The rushing tide of emotion that threatened to carry him away, much like the waters of a ravaging flood. What he read in her countenance almost knocked him on his arse.

There was a sheen in her blue gaze, a melancholy twist to her smile. He wondered if she was thinking of her own daughter, remembering her. But there was also something else present. Something he could only describe in one fashion: tenderness. Such tenderness, the magnitude of which he had not seen directed toward himself in as long as he could recall. That he had not seen directed toward Verity in what seemed an aeon. Not since...

Hattie.

His wife's name and her memory were like a needle jabbing unexpectedly into his flesh. A visceral reproach. He must not allow Johanna Beaumont to further distort his feelings. To creep beneath his armor. To tear down all his defenses. He reminded himself that the tenderness she exhibited now emerged from a woman who had carefully honed her craft.

Except, it did not feel feigned as his gaze meshed with hers. It felt heart-stoppingly real. *Good God*, what was the matter with him? Why was he so weak when it came to this woman he dared not trust? This woman who had shared her body with his enemy?

It made no sense, and he needed to get to the bottom of the matter.

He cleared his throat once more. "Verity, darling, run along to the chamber you were given last night. You may play with your doll until I come and find you."

He kissed the sweet-scented crown of her head, reluctant to open his arms and let her go. He could feel her heart beating fast against his chest. She was so precious to him. So very beloved, small and fragile in his arms.

But he let her go, because he knew he must. He needed to address matters with Johanna. Needed to see if he could sift through what she had told him and what he had witnessed, what he knew of her, and separate the chaff from the wheat, the lies from the truth.

In short, he needed to discover whether or not she was a dangerous, deceptive viper or she was the victim of one.

JOHANNA WATCHED FELIX'S daughter skipping from the salon in an exuberant burst of girlish spirits.

"Do walk like the lady you are, Verity," he reminded her sternly.

"Yes, Papa," his daughter called, curtsying once more, before she was gone.

The moment the door closed upon her, the atmosphere in the room changed. When he turned back to Johanna, Felix's demeanor had settled into a rigid mask. Even his green eyes, ordinarily so vibrant and warm, were cold and hard. She wondered where he had gone so early this morning, and whether that trip was the reason for his coolness.

Something had made him unhappy. His guard, which had dropped during Verity's revelations about her governess, was firmly in place. The love he plainly had for his daughter had melted her heart. His affection had vibrated in his voice, had been raw and real in his expression. He had appeared, in the moment when he had taken Verity into his arms, more man than duke.

But every part of him as he faced her now was the regal duke once more.

"I should be leaving," she said, reminded she did not belong here. "I hope you do not mind that I waited until you returned. Lady Verity did not want to be alone, and it did not feel right to leave her in the care of the servants."

His jaw clenched. "Thank you for remaining here with her. For entertaining her."

Still, he was so cool. His tone frosty.

She felt uncertain. Perhaps the childishness of her song had displeased him.

"I am sorry for the song," she said, clasping her hands before her to keep them from twisting in the skirts of her gown. It was the same one she had worn yesterday, and she was keenly aware of how she must appear, wearing the previous night's rumpled gown. Her hem had been sodden and muddied, and she had done her best to clean it by hand before draping it on a chair before the fire in her chamber to dry.

He, by comparison, was austere and debonair. He was dressed immaculately in a black waistcoat, coat, and trousers, with a white neck cloth and shirt. He was unfairly handsome this morning, as always.

"The song, Mademoiselle Beaumont?" he asked.

Ah, so she had once more reverted to Mademoiselle Beaumont. The formality was as telling as it was troubling. She must have vexed him a great deal.

"The odorous cloud in particular," she elaborated, and then felt the tips of her ears burn as a mad flush overcame her. "I find children like to sing songs, and the more inane the better. Forgive me. I know Lady Verity is the daughter of a duke. I should not have presumed to lead her in such frivolity."

He swallowed, drawing her gaze to the prominence of his Adam's apple, the strength of his corded neck. The wide angle of his jaw, kissed with the shadow of whiskers. He had not shaved this morning in his press to leave the house, it would seem.

For a brief, fanciful moment, she wondered what those whiskers would feel like beneath her seeking fingers. Rasping against her cheek, her throat. Her breasts.

He moved toward her slowly, almost as if he were drawn against his will. "You sing with children a great deal, do you, Mademoiselle?"

"There is an orphanage in New York City I visit from time to time," she said, thinking of the children she had oft visited there, missing them. "Many of them were of an age with your daughter. They all liked to sing with me."

"I cannot imagine a single soul who would not like to sing with you," he said, stroking his jaw with his long, elegant fingers, watching her in an almost predatory manner. "You do have a way of enthralling everyone you meet. Keeping everyone beneath your spell. How do you do it?"

He was nearer now, and she could have asked the same question of him. For he had held her in his thrall from the evening they had first met at Mr. Saville's fête. And there it was again, the scent of sandalwood seeping into her senses. Surrounding her. Making her yearn for him in ways she ought not.

"How do you do it, Mademoiselle?" he persisted, his voice low and dark. Not cold any longer, but not warm either. "You did not answer me."

She fought the urge to retreat, to put more distance between them, for there seemed something undeniably dangerous about him now. But she held her ground, remaining by the piano where she had stood upon his entrance.

"I was not aware I held such powers, Your Grace," she said. "I am just an ordinary woman, after all."

"There is nothing ordinary about you, Johanna Beaumont." He reached out, touching a curl that had escaped the chignon she had twisted her unruly hair into that morning. "Not one single, blessed thing."

She forced herself to smile, affecting Rose's airs. Rose's aura. "I am gratified you think so."

"I do not think so." He continued to toy with that lone curl, not touching her anywhere else. But his gaze had dropped, lingering upon her lips. "I know so. There are secrets in your eyes, you know. Shadows."

What a fanciful thing to say. Strange, too.

She thought of the trunk awaiting her in her hotel. Of Drummond. And then she banished both equally unwanted thoughts.

"We all have secrets and shadows, do we not?" she asked, trying and failing to keep the breathlessness from her voice.

What this man did to her—the power he held over her—was frightening. She had gone from laughing with a child, singing an inane song, to longing for him with a rush of desperation that was as troubling as it was undeniable.

"Something tells me you have more than most, Johanna," he said.

And then he touched her. One idle stroke of his forefinger down her jaw.

She felt that touch in her core. She had to bite her lip to keep from crying out, from asking for more.

"Why are you so concerned about the secrets I bear, Felix?" She mimicked him in the retreat from formality, using his given name once again.

"Do you know what caused the fire at my home last night?" he asked instead of answering her question.

His shift in subject took her by surprise. "No, I cannot imagine. What was it?"

"A bomb," he said succinctly. "Two bombs, to be precise. One of them did not detonate, thank God, or the fire and damage would have been far worse."

A bomb.

Good, sweet God.

All the heat that had been burning inside her was doused by that one word. Indeed, she felt as if all the warmth had been stolen from her entire being. Icy tendrils of dread wrapped themselves around her heart.

Surely it could not be... But as she told herself those words, she knew them to be a lie. Her brother was capable of anything, including ordering someone to lay bombs outside a residence. Perhaps he had done so in an effort to frighten her. To show her he was watching and his power extended across the sea.

She knew what she had to do.

Even if it meant her career as an actress would come careening to a halt, she had to seek out the police now. To give them all the evidence she had against her brother. She could not afford to wait lest anyone else get hurt. If something had happened to Verity, she would have never been able to forgive herself.

She took a deep breath before making her revelation complete. "My name is not Johanna Beaumont. It is Johanna McKenna."

Chapter Eight

M<small>CKENNA</small>.
Johanna *McKenna*.

Not Rose Beaumont. Not even Johanna Beaumont. But *Johanna McKenna*.

The French accent was gone, and in its place was only the faint trace of a lilting Irish brogue. She stood before him, stripped of every artifice. Herself for the first time since he had first met her.

Felix stared down at the woman who had been driving him mad from the moment he had first seen her, his mind staggering about like a drunkard as he attempted to make sense of what she had just told him.

Good Christ. Surely she was not that bastard's *wife*?

"Please." She reached out to him, gripping his forearm, her pallor stark as her expression. "I need your help, Felix. It is a matter of life and death. For me, for others. Will you help me?"

Life and death.

She wanted *his* help?

How rich. He ought to haul her to the nearest prison for being married to such a swine. For pretending to be someone she was not. Anger replaced the confusion, roaring through him like an inferno.

"I cannot promise you anything, madam," he bit out.

"What could you possibly need from me?"

Her grip on him went tighter. "I need your help finding the proper authorities to speak to about my brother. He is a dangerous man. I have great reason to fear him, to fear that he will harm either myself or others... Indeed, I believe he may have been responsible for the bombs laid at your residence last night."

One word sank into him. Brother.

Brother.

Drummond McKenna was her brother? Could it be true? His mind grappled with this new revelation. Did he dare trust her? Dare believe she was telling him the truth? He did not know. Everything inside him was a swirling sea of confusion and turmoil, of emotions. Rage, despair, relief, agony.

"Your brother," he forced out. "What manner of man is he, to be laying bombs?"

"He is a Fenian," she whispered, releasing him at last to press a hand over her mouth. Undisguised upset glimmered in her brilliant eyes. "Please, Felix. You must help me. I have evidence against him at my hotel. A great deal of it. I have been planning to turn it over to the police before I leave for Paris, but I am too afraid of what he will do. I cannot wait."

She had evidence against Drummond McKenna? That seemed too good to be true. Coupled with her sudden revelations, it made his suspicions of her increase tenfold. It was possible she was lying now. That her confession was but one more act in a series of so many. For a seasoned actress such as her, it would be an easy performance.

This could all be one elaborate ruse created in the event he grew suspicious of her.

But that gave him pause. She had not known of his suspicions. He thought once more of the shock on her countenance, how pale she had grown, and he did not think it had been counterfeit. It had seemed real. Just as real as Johanna Beaumont—nay, *McKenna* seemed.

His mind quickly worked through the details, the possibilities. If Johanna was indeed Drummond McKenna's sister, that would certainly explain the closeness of their relationship in New York City. She had claimed she was afraid of him, which could also explain a great deal.

One thing was clear: he could not yet be sure if he could trust her, but he needed to investigate her claims. He needed more time. More evidence.

He took Johanna's arm in a gentle but firm hold and led her to a settee. "Come and have a seat, my dear. You will need to tell me everything if I am to help you. And you must begin at the beginning."

She nodded, her sorrow almost palpable. A sob fled her lips. "Oh, Felix. I am so very sorry for drawing you and Verity into such danger. If I had possessed an inkling that Drummond might do such a thing, I would have warned you. I would have stayed as far away from you as possible."

God, he wanted to believe her. Wanted it so badly he could taste it. Wanted to believe the tenderness she had shown his daughter was real. That she was as terrified of her bastard of a brother as she claimed. That she possessed evidence against him that would lead to the capture of more Fenians here in London.

And more than anything, he wanted to believe everything that had passed between them was honest and true. But he must not think of that now. There was far too much at stake.

"Do not worry, Johanna," he urged as he helped her to sit and then forced himself to sit opposite her, giving them some necessary distance. "I will do everything in my power to help you."

She took a deep, shuddering breath, then dashed at the

tears on her cheeks. "Thank you, Felix."

He knew a searing shame at her gratitude, for it was spoken with such sincerity. And if she was being truthful with him right now and he was deceiving her, surely he would go to hell for such a sin. Still, to protect his daughter and the other innocents of London from further danger, he would do what he must.

Anything.

"You must tell me what you know," he urged Johanna.

She cast him a tremulous smile. "My father was a violent man, ruled by his need for drink. Often, when he was so consumed by the bottle, he...beat me. As I got older, he ordered my brother to do it, and he did. He...seemed to take pleasure in hurting me. When I was fifteen, I ran away and joined an acting company. I changed my name to Rose Beaumont in the hopes they would never find me. But over the years, my reputation built. Suddenly, I was sought after, my pictures being passed about on handbills and *cartes de visite* and in the papers. A year ago, my brother found me."

His gut clenched at the broken revelations. Either she was putting on the best act of her life, or every word she was relaying to him was true. "What did your brother do when he found you?"

"One day, I returned home from rehearsals to find him waiting for me," Johanna continued, and the undisguised fear in her voice was like a dagger to his heart. "I had but one picture of Pearl, and he destroyed it. Ground it beneath his boot heel and then poured a vase full of water all over it. He told me if I did not help him as he wished, he would reveal my true name to the papers. Being an actress is all I have left, the only means I have of supporting myself. And though I have done well and am able to live in comfort, if the public were to turn against me, I would be left with nothing in short order."

Felix realized his hands had balled into fists. "He destroyed the only picture you had of your daughter?"

She bit her lip, obviously trying to stave off another wave of tears. "Yes. I attempted to salvage it after he had gone, but the damage was severe. I—I still have it, because it is all I have left, aside from the tiny lock of her hair I kept."

He would hunt down Drummond McKenna like the vile miscreant he was and hang him from the nearest gallows with his own two hands for that crime alone. He could not fathom the sort of man who would willfully ruin a mother's only picture of her dead babe. And when that mother was his own flesh and blood, his sister...

"I am going to kill him for that," he vowed before he could think better of the words.

"It is my fault for being so weak," she whispered. "I should have fought back. I should have clawed at him, done anything I could to save it. Instead, I watched as he ruined it, and then I did everything he asked of me."

"You were terrified of the man," Felix said, and before he knew what he was about, he had gotten up from his seat. He could not remain where he was, watching her relive what had happened to her, watching her tremble, and not seek to offer her comfort.

He slid his arm around her, drawing her protectively into his side. The doubts he harbored about her were slowly falling away in the face of the truth she was willingly surrendering to him. Such an intricate tale could not be fiction.

"I should have been stronger," Johanna insisted, leaning into him. "For the last year, I have been living in fear of him, doing as he asks. He has become, like our father before him was, obsessed with the notion of Irish Home Rule. My family is from County Cork, you see. We immigrated to New York when I was a child. Drummond, my brother, is running a vast network of Fenian sympathizers. They are in New York, and they are here, in England. He was responsible for the bombings here in the London Underground. I am certain of it."

His blood went cold at her words. "Johanna, if you knew this to be true, why did you not do something to put an end to this?"

"It is what I am attempting to do now," she said, her expression stricken. "Drummond never admitted his guilt to me, but he has been using me to pass information amongst his men in New York. He is convinced there are people watching him, English agents. Spies of some sort. He is trying to keep his ties as quiet as possible and using others to make it appear as though he is not involved. One of the reasons I came here to London was to escape him, and another reason was that I knew I would have the best chance of turning incriminating information in to the police here."

If that were true, she was more daring and worthy of his admiration than he had previously thought.

"In what manner has he been using you, Johanna?" he asked next, recalling he must keep his emotions at bay.

He had to collect as much information as possible. To attempt to investigate everything she was saying, to remain rational and emotionless. Regardless of how much he longed to draw her into his arms in this moment and promise her he would always protect her.

She took another shuddering breath. "He gave me a locked trunk containing dynamite and correspondence."

Dynamite?

Bloody hell. This was getting more convoluted—and dangerous—by the moment.

If she was found in possession of dynamite, she could be

arrested. And now that he was reasonably certain of her innocence in the matter, and harboring these unwanted feelings toward her as he did, he could not allow that to happen. His instincts were telling him the woman before him was every bit as much of a victim of Drummond McKenna as hundreds of others who had been affected by his wrath.

He thought then of the correspondence she had mentioned, and recalled all too well the sight of her handing over a packet to the man in the Royal Aquarium.

"Do you still have the trunk?" he asked.

She nodded. "Yes, I do. It is in my hotel. I made copies of all the correspondence within it and when one of his men contacted me to arrange a meeting so he could receive it, I gave him the originals. I fear that is where I made a mistake. They must have realized I had broken the envelope seal. Perhaps they were watching me. I believe I am the reason bombs were laid at your home, Felix. I am so very sorry. Had I any inkling something like this would have happened, I would have gone to the police the moment I arrived in London. I never dreamt Drummond would attempt to cause harm to your daughter. I hope you believe me."

He stared into her bright-blue eyes, still shimmering with tears, and he read all too clearly the anguish in their crystalline depths. He took her hand in his, giving it a reassuring squeeze. "I believe you, Johanna. I do not believe you have the capacity to harm others in the way you have described your brother does. And I do not blame you. There is no way you could have known what would happen. Why were you waiting to bring this information to the police?"

"It is selfish of me." She closed her eyes. "I was desperate to give myself enough time to free myself, to be certain I could go somewhere he could not reach me. I wanted to finish my stay here at the Crown and Thorn, to deliver the trunk to the police, and then leave for Paris. Drummond promised me he would have me killed if I was either arrested or if I betrayed him. And after seeing what he has done, laying bombs at your home, I can see I was right to fear what he is capable of here."

It made sense. She was a woman alone, and the need to protect herself, to get herself as far away from her brother as possible, seemed all too plausible. He had to make a decision.

He hesitated for only a beat before forging onward. "I will do everything in my power to help you, Johanna, but you must promise me one thing."

Her eyes fluttered open. "What promise would you have me make?"

"Stay here with me," he said, knowing the invitation was a risk and taking it anyway. "I will contact Scotland Yard on your behalf. They will go to your hotel, remove the trunk. I expect they will also want to interview you."

Panic washed over her features. "Will they arrest me?"

Not if he had anything to say about it.

"I do not believe so," he told her carefully. "There is always the possibility. You have willingly smuggled dynamite into this country at the behest of criminals. By law, you can be imprisoned, but I will do my best to protect you. You could be Queen's Evidence against your brother and anyone you met here with ties to Fenians. That you are a woman, and that you have been living in fear of your brother and were coerced into undertaking these dangerous deeds, will benefit you."

She clung to his hand. "You owe me nothing. I have brought danger into your life. I do not expect you to aid me. It is asking far too much of you. Besides, you have Verity to worry about. Your first concern must be keeping her safe."

His heart warmed, and more of the lingering doubts he held about her were chased away by her concern for his daughter. "This is the best way to keep her safe. Your brother must be stopped, Johanna, before he has the opportunity to hurt more innocents."

Johanna nodded. "Yes, he must be. Violence is not the way to achieve political victories, and history has taught us that over and over. But I fear very much, where Drummond is concerned, that he enjoys inflicting pain upon others. This quest is not so much about Ireland as it is his desire to control others and to watch them suffer."

Irish Home Rule was not an unworthy cause. Felix himself understood and agreed with it. What he did not agree with, however, was the Fenians' attempts to strong-arm the government into getting what they wanted by putting innocents in danger.

"Are you prepared for what will come, after I contact Scotland Yard?" he pressed gently, for he could feel her trembling.

She took a deep breath. "I will do whatever I must. I have known, all along, that when the time came for me to go against Drummond, it would not be easy. But it is what is right."

Felix did not dare reveal his connections to Scotland Yard, the Home Office, and the Special League with her. He was not yet certain he could trust her. Time would tell. For now, he had the information he needed from her. It was a beginning.

"You are a brave woman," he told her, and this, at least, was truth.

Going against her brother's edict and breaking the seal on the correspondence he had given her to make copies of the documents had been bold. Perhaps even foolhardy. And it was all the more reason why her remaining here with him was so imperative. When McKenna learned his sister had gone to Scotland Yard, he would be in a murderous rage, Felix had no doubt. If he wanted to keep such a valuable witness safe, he would have to see to her welfare himself.

Yes, that was the only reason he wanted her beneath his roof, he told himself.

Liar, accused a voice within him.

A voice he promptly ignored.

"I am not brave," she denied, tears studding her lashes as she met his gaze. Her distress was palpable. "If I was, I would have taken a stand against him that first day. I would never have allowed him to control me."

He thought of the girl she must have been, terrified and young, running from a father who beat her. Changing her name. Finding her own path. *Christ*, he could not fathom it.

An overwhelming surge of emotion hit him then, right in the chest. In the heart.

He didn't think. He lowered his head. Kissed those tears. Stole them with his lips. Licked up their salty misery. He wanted to take away her pain. To thieve her fears. To hold her in his arms and keep her safe from her brother. Safe from all the world, from anyone who would do her harm or bring her sadness. To chase away her grief.

To keep her here with him.

Always.

That was a dangerous want. A ridiculous need. It made no sense.

But it was there, beating inside him. He pulled her closer, his arm still around the soft curve of her waist. She felt so right. Johanna fit against him perfectly. As if she belonged. As if she had always been meant to be tucked into him, right there at his side.

"Felix," she whispered.

His name, that was all.

His undoing, that was everything.

He could not exist for another second without claiming her lips as his. When their mouths met, it was different from their last kisses. This kiss was gentle and soothing, two people lost in a maelstrom, seeking shelter and solace. Seeking each other. He went slowly, not opening his lips at first. Just pressing their mouths together, absorbing the silken heat of her, breathing in her breaths.

He ran his nose along hers, and somehow, his hand had come free of hers and found its way to her face. He caressed her cheek, where she was smoother, her skin as luxurious as velvet and every bit as soft. She made a helpless sound of need, and it sent him over the edge.

His restraint shattered. So, too, his control.

His fingers sank into her hair. Pins rained on the settee around them. He did not care. His mouth opened over hers with an almost savage insistence, but she answered him with a sigh. She opened for him, her tongue sliding against his. She tasted sweet, like the cocoa biscuits that were Verity's favorite. He had requested them for breakfast that morning, hoping it would cheer her after all she had endured the night before.

But *God*, he did not think he would ever be able to consume one bite of them himself without thinking of Johanna. Without his cock going rigid in his trousers as it was now. One sip from her lips was all he required, it seemed, to become a ravening beast.

Because now, he could not stop. She was kissing him back with a desperation to match his. Her arms twined around his neck. And she was pressing nearer to him, her body wrapped around his until she was almost in his lap. The thought of her in his lap was enough to make him more rigid. His ballocks drew tight.

He wanted to haul her atop him, her thighs bracketing his so she was open to him. He wondered if her cunny would be as soft as the rest of her, if it would be wet, if she would taste just as sweet. And somehow, he knew she would. He imagined her skirts pooled around them on the bench of the settee, opening the fall of his trousers so he could slide into her hot sheath.

But he could not do something so depraved.

Could he?

No, said his rational mind.

Yes, said the rest of him.

The base animal within him, the one who had wanted to consume Johanna whole from the moment he had first laid eyes on her when she had commanded the stage at the Crown and Thorn, overtook him. And he was helpless to stop.

He pulled her into his lap in truth, never breaking their kiss. She went willingly. Easily. And she knew what he wanted, it seemed, because she wanted it, too. She straddled him on the settee, her skirts trapped between them. In his fantasy, he had not realized how voluminous they were, how the layers of her petticoats and silk and satin would become an impediment with which he needed to wrestle. But wrestle with them he did, until they were no longer a mountain pinned against him but a great, billowing waterfall.

One of his hands sank deeper into her luxurious golden curls, grabbing a handful in a gentle grip to angle her better for his kisses. The other went beneath her skirts. He skimmed over the warm curve of her hip, denied her flesh by her lacy drawers.

Until he reached the split.

Nothing could have prepared him for that first touch. He ran his fingers over her slick seam, parting her folds. She was wet, so damn wet. He groaned, wanting to taste her there, to slide his cock home. Not yet. For now, this was all he dared take. All he wanted her to give.

He found the plump bud of her sex and circled it with his forefinger. Johanna cried out, thrusting herself into his hand, grinding against him as if she could not get enough. He circled her again, then worked over her with firm, quick strokes. All the while, he continued to kiss her, swallowing her broken cries as the pleasure he gave her made her increasingly mindless.

She rocked against his hand, thrusting as if they were making love.

He broke the kiss at last, and urged her head back, wanting to watch her face. He slicked her dew back down to her opening, abandoning the greedy flesh he had been torturing. Holding her gaze with his, he slid a finger inside her.

Damn.

Her channel gripped him, and he was engulfed in tight heat. He moved his finger in and out of her in a slow, delicious rhythm, gratified when she moaned and clamped down on him, drawing him deeper. Her eyes were half closed, her breath coming in short pants.

Her mouth was red and swollen from his kisses, the tender skin around her lips pink from the stubble of the whiskers he had yet to shave. She had never been more beautiful than she was now, wearing his marks, lost in the pleasure he was giving her.

He added another finger and fucked her deeper, finding a place that made her jerk and cry. She was so wet now that the sounds of him sliding in and out of her echoed erotically through the salon. He grazed over her pearl with his thumb as he moved.

She bit her lip. Her fingers were in his hair now, clasping fistfuls, tugging on him. And she was riding him, her body undulating along with the rhythm he had begun. What he wanted more than anything in that moment was to sink home inside her with his cock. But it was too soon, and he knew it. He would settle for this, for her dew dripping down his fingers, for the tight clamp of her. For watching her take her pleasure. The desire rolling over her features.

She was getting closer now.

Her body was tensing and her movements were increasingly jerky. The desperate little sounds she made drove him to the brink, but it was worth it just to watch her spend. He was a man with a purpose. He would not stop until she came, until she reached her pinnacle and shattered into a thousand little shards in his arms.

"I want you to spend for me," he told her, moving faster, curling his finger slightly to reach that magical place inside her once more. "I want to watch you when you come."

He had never in his life uttered such wicked words to another woman before. They were torn from him now. Edged with desperation. With a desire so potent and frenzied, he could not control it or himself.

But the words did not shock her. Instead, they seemed to push her over the edge. Her back bowed and she clamped down on his fingers, shuddering around him as she threw back her head. A low, lusty moan escaped her. He stayed with her, thrusting in and out until the last spasm rippled through her.

He withdrew from her, his heart hammering in his chest, his cock so hard he swore he was going to explode if she so much as shifted on his lap. But as desire thundered through him, he knew he could not finish what they had begun.

Indeed, he had never intended for things between them to progress so far.

Reality seemed to intrude upon Johanna's bliss as well. She released her hold on him and scrambled from his lap, clapping a hand over her mouth.

"Johanna," he began, "I am sorry. I had no intention of—

"

"Nor did I," she interrupted, flushing from head to toe as she shook out her skirts.

It was the same gown she had worn yesterday evening, and after a night running through the rain and a fire-damaged townhome, it had already been worse for wear. Being crumpled in his lap had not helped matters.

He stood, a throbbing, unfulfilled ache in his groin he did his best to ignore. "Forgive me, Johanna. I only meant to offer you comfort, not ravish you."

Her color deepened, her fingers twisting in her skirts. "The fault is mine, Felix. I thank you for your kind offer of protection and for extending me your hospitality, but I think it best if I return to my hotel."

With a curtsy, she turned and fled the salon before he could stop her.

Still rocked by what had just happened, he watched her flee.

And then, he could resist temptation no more. He raised his fingers to his lips and tasted her at last.

He had his answer.

She wasn't just as sweet. She was sweeter.

And he had not a chance of resisting her.

JOHANNA FLED.

It was her first reaction. Her instinct.

Over the threshold of the salon, down the hall to the main entrance. Out the front door. It was not until she reached the bustling street that she realized she had left behind her gloves, hat, and coat. The air was chilled, and one glance down at her bedraggled state, and she knew she looked a fright. Her thoughts were a reckless, rushing jumble, every bit as disheveled as her outward appearance.

She had no notion of what time it was.

No way of getting back to her hotel.

She was likely missing her rehearsals for the second straight day.

The Duke of Winchelsea's fingers had been inside her.

At the last thought, another aching surge of pleasure throbbed between her thighs. The delicious languor of her spend was still licking through her body, still humming in her veins. No man had ever brought her to such a searing, delicious crescendo with nothing more than his fingers and his words.

His words.

Dear God, his words.

I want to watch you when you come.

And he had watched her. And she had come. The pleasure had been terrifically intense. Mind-numbing.

What had she done? She had entrusted all her secrets to a man she scarcely knew. And then she had entrusted herself to him as well.

She paced on the front walk, her hair wild and half-unbound around her shoulders, her mind an utter mess. Back and forth until she was dizzy with it. Carriages and hacks moved on the street with disinterest. The sounds were familiar: jangling tack, the distant dissonance of voices and wheels rumbling over the road. Last night's deluge had given way to the morning's fog.

What was she going to do now? She did not have her reticule, she realized. That, too had been left behind within the duke's home. She was too prideful to make a return in her crazed state. She had just run as if fleeing a house aflame.

And for the wisdom of her actions, she may as well have

been.

Once, long ago, she had entrusted herself to a man. He had been charming and handsome as well. He had kissed her and courted her. Patrick had been another actor in the first company she had ever toured with. And she had believed he had loved her. Had allowed him to pressure her into giving him her body. He had left in the night when he had discovered she was pregnant, and she had been alone to raise Pearl, as a girl of seventeen.

In all the years since, she had not allowed another man to touch her, unless it had been within the bonds of a scene. Acting was permissible. Trusting another man was not. Nine years had passed, and yet it would seem she was as foolish as she had ever been. She had not known the Duke of Winchelsea for two weeks, and already she had allowed him not just kisses but far, far more.

And allowing him anything at all was dangerous.

Reckless.

Stupid.

Because her heart—her wild, foolhardy heart—already felt things for him. Things she did not want to feel. That she had no right to feel. She was leaving soon. She would never see him again. And he was a duke, a man who had not invited her to his home until it had been burning down.

What was wrong with her?

She was making another pass of the walk when a man walking on the opposite side of the street caught her attention. It was a combination of his height and the way he moved that struck her as painfully familiar. He wore a hat pulled low, and his face was averted. But she paused, mid-stride, watching him.

For the second time in the last half hour, her heart was pounding frantically, but this time not because of desire but for another reason entirely.

Fear.

Raw, blistering, fear.

She was imagining things, she told herself. Drummond was not here in London. He would not be here, where he could be arrested at any moment. Where the police wanted to throw him into prison for life. He would never put himself at such risk.

And yet, she could not stop watching the man. He turned toward her slightly, as he walked, and their gazes met. Shock washed over her, making her mouth go dry. She was rooted to the spot, unable to move.

Good, sweet, Lord.

It was…

"Johanna!"

At the sound of Felix's voice calling her, she turned instinctively to find him stalking down the walk after her, his expression clouded with worry. "Come back inside before you catch a chill. You don't have your wrap."

She wrenched her gaze back to the street, still robbed of speech, but the man was gone. Had it truly been Drummond? Her mind refused to believe it. How? And why?

Felix was behind her now, his hand on her shoulder as he gently turned her back to him. He was frowning, his gaze searching. "What is the matter, Johanna? You look as if you have seen a ghost."

And she felt almost as if she had.

She shuddered, inhaling slowly and forcing her racing heart to calm before attempting to explain. "I thought I saw my brother," she managed. "In the street just now. But when I turned back, he was gone. I am certain it was my worried imagination, but it gave me a fright."

Felix drew her into his side, his arm a comforting band

around her waist. "Come back inside with me now. Whether or not it was your brother you saw, I promise you I will do my utmost to keep you safe, from this moment forward."

"I cannot let you do that." Sadness crept over her, the shame at her recklessness returning. She had given in to her weakness for him twice. She must not do so a third time. "I will look after myself, just as I always have."

Because she had learned her lesson a long time ago, that no man could be trusted.

Including this one.

No matter how much she wanted to.

She gazed up at him, reminding herself this man, this duke, was not for her. He could not be. She was a danger to him and his daughter both. And there was no future for them together. She was leaving for Paris. He belonged here in London. She was an actress. He was a nobleman.

He was still frowning down at her, every inch the aristocrat. "You can let me, and you will, Johanna. If the man you saw in the streets just now is your brother, then you must allow me to help you."

"Felix," she began to protest.

"Johanna," he interrupted. "You promised me."

"I did not." But part of her was vacillating now. Part of her wanted to accept the Duke of Winchelsea's offer to keep her safe. To accept his every offer, and all his kisses, his every touch, too. To spend every night between now and the day she left for France in his bed.

But that was the old part of her. The careless girl she had once been. The one who still longed and hoped and dreamed. The one she must do everything in her power to ignore.

"Come inside with me now, Johanna," he urged. "Do not be stubborn, I beg of you. You need my help, and I am more than willing to give it."

"Why?" she bit out, her emotions careening wildly inside her as she stared up at his handsome face. "Why do you want to help me? Why would you do such a thing, put yourself in jeopardy, for a woman you scarcely know?"

It could not merely be because he wanted to bed her.

She knew men found her attractive, but she did not fool herself that her wiles were so strong.

His bright-green gaze plumbed the depths of hers. For a beat, he said nothing, simply held her in his thrall with his magnetic intensity. The energy crackling from him was like live electric wires.

"Because I care about you," he said at last, his voice rough and low. Almost a growl. "I want to see you safe because I cannot bear the thought of more harm coming to you. When I think of how you have already suffered, what you have lost, and yet the way you have continued on, holding your head high, building a name for yourself, forging a career from the dust…I am in awe of you, Johanna McKenna. I have been from the moment I first saw you. And I want to be the man who keeps you safe rather than the man who makes you fear."

His words reached inside her to a place she had not known she possessed. And although a gust of wind picked up, whipping at her skirts and making her shiver, she was somehow warmed. Warmed from the inside out. No one had ever said something like that to her before.

No soliloquy in the finest play could compare.

She was softening, yielding. She knew it. But still, she had to try. For his sake as well as Verity's and for Johanna's sake too. If Drummond was indeed in London, it meant no one was safe. And Johanna was determined to never open her heart again. To never trust another man.

"I have never feared you," she said softly. Sadly. Desperately. "You have only been kind and good to me, Felix, and for that I must thank you. But please do not take this on. This is my battle to fight, my war to wage."

"Our battle to fight," he insisted. "Our war to wage."

"No." Tears sprang to her eyes anew. "It cannot be. You must stay out of this."

"I won't," he vowed, his tone determined, his voice strong. "You cannot keep me from your side. If that vicious bastard is out there somewhere, I will tear him apart with my own bare hands before I allow him to hurt you. Do you understand? He is not going to hurt you, or anyone else, ever again if I can help it."

He was so vehement, so determined, so fierce.

But he was a duke, not a warrior. He was elegant and refined. He did not have a network of men at his disposal, ready to do his bidding.

"You cannot save me," she said. "I am already lost."

"You are not lost." He searched her face. "You are here, with me. Exactly where you belong."

She wanted him to be right. Oh, how she did. But deep in her heart, she knew he was wrong. Still, she allowed him to lead her back inside.

She told herself it was because she needed her reticule, pelisse, and hat.

But it wasn't the first lie she had ever told herself, and she had a feeling it would not be the last.

Chapter Nine

*F*ELIX WAS IN the devil of a muddle.

"Tell me this again," commanded Lucien, Duke of Arden and leader of the Special League. "I am sure I must have misheard you, because it sounded as if you just told me the actress Rose Beaumont is Drummond McKenna's sister, that she has a trunk full of dynamite hidden in her hotel room, and that she is currently staying at the townhome where you keep your mistresses, along with your daughter. Surely none of that is what you said just now."

They were seated in Lucien's study, accompanied by his duchess, the former co-leader of the Special League who was taking a step back from her duties since she was now with child. Once a Pinkerton agent, the duchess had been hired several months ago by Felix himself to aid Arden in his task. Using a ruse, she had infiltrated McKenna's inner circle in New York City, posing as a servant.

That, more than anything, was the reason Felix had made the duke and duchess his first stop after seeing to the addition of guards at his townhome to ensure Verity—and Johanna too—were safe. He trusted the duchess implicitly and respected her greatly. Her case history spoke for itself. No one had been closer to McKenna than she had.

Except, it would seem, for the woman he was now harboring beneath his own roof.

Therein lay the muddle.

Because he believed Johanna. Everything within him wanted what she had revealed to him to be true. Needed it to be true. Because his feelings for Johanna McKenna were murky. He had been intimate with her. Kissed her. He desired her.

Bloody, sodding hell.

"I believe you heard Winchelsea correctly, Arden," the duchess said, fixing Felix with a solemn but searching look. "Winchelsea, have you gone to Scotland Yard with this information yet, or to the rest of the Home Office?"

"I have not," he admitted. "It is a breach of protocol not to inform them, I know. But given the sensitive nature of my relationship with the lady in question, I deemed it best."

The Home Office was aware of his plan to obtain information from Johanna, but as far as they were concerned, she was Rose Beaumont, mistress to Drummond McKenna. Not Johanna, sister to the devil, woman who had smuggled lignin dynamite into London.

Ye Gods.

That bitter fact still sent a knife of fear twisting into his gut.

"I never saw Mademoiselle Beaumont in the Emerald Club during my covert operations there," the duchess said then.

Her words chased the fear with a burst of relief. He was aware, of course that "Rose Beaumont" had been seen in McKenna's presence on innumerable occasions about New York City. That she had interacted with known Fenians within McKenna's circle on a regular basis. But it stood to reason that if she had not been within the club, what she had told him about her brother using her as a courier of sorts made sense.

"Miss *McKenna*," he corrected softly. "I am inclined to believe her when she tells me she is McKenna's sister. I do not believe she had a reason to dissemble. Not about that, anyway."

Of course, she had every reason to deceive him about an endless list of things. If she had any hope of saving herself and remaining free from prison, she would have to win his trust. But he was still determined to rely upon his instincts.

For if he could not, then he had kissed a viper and taken her beneath his roof. She was sleeping three doors down the hall from his own daughter. Such folly did not merit contemplation.

"Good God, Winchelsea," Arden interrupted then. "There is dynamite at this female's hotel. In her trunk? Lignin, you say?"

"Yes." He sighed, for that was the most damning fact of all in Johanna's entire, convoluted tale. "Although, to be precise, there *was* dynamite at her hotel. I have since had it moved to another location, lest McKenna discover that his sister will be turning Queen's Evidence against him."

He had arranged for the trunk to be brought to his townhome, fearing McKenna's men would catch wind of what was afoot and attempt to confiscate it. It would seem they were already aware of Johanna's connection to him, hence the bombs which had been laid at Halford House. Either that, or they had merely targeted him because of his work with the Home Office, the Special League, and Scotland Yard. The investigation was in its infancy, and it was far too early to tell.

"Christ, now you are telling me you are harboring dynamite?" Arden demanded. "Have you lost your bloody mind, man?"

"I have not," he denied calmly, even as part of him inwardly suspected he had. For he had certainly never gone to such great lengths for a female before. "I am keeping the evidence safe. I need to arrange for the colonel to confiscate it and conduct tests. He will be able to determine the veracity of Miss McKenna's claims in regard to the lignin. It will be important to take note of whether or not the material has come from the same source. He should be able to use the samples he retained from other bombs as comparison."

"Why did you not go to the colonel first?" Arden asked, his expression a mask of implacability.

Felix was acutely aware of how easily their fortunes had changed. Months ago, he had come down upon Arden with ruthless precision for a lapse in his judgment as leader of the Special League, forcing him to take on a partner. And now, it would appear—to outside observers, at least—that Felix himself had made the gravest error of all.

"Because I am concerned about the manner in which Miss McKenna will be treated," he answered honestly, aware of how it sounded.

As if he had tender feelings for her. As if he wanted her in his bed. And much to his shame, both of those things were true. Truer by the day, the hour, the minute, the second.

"You want to make certain Miss McKenna is treated fairly," the duchess observed.

"Of course I do," he said. "It is our duty to treat everyone with whom our paths cross with fairness. The Crown has imbued us with such an obligation."

"But there is more," she noted, her countenance softening. "You care about her, do you not? You began all this with the notion that you would bring McKenna to heel by using his mistress against him, but you have fallen for the mistress yourself along the way."

"She is not his mistress," he said before he could stay the words.

How foolish he sounded. How like a man who was being held helplessly in the thrall of one Johanna McKenna. Because he was. Yes, indeed. He was.

"So says the lady in question," Arden added. "A woman who is an actress by trade."

Yes, this too, was damning, and he knew it. Johanna was incredibly skilled at her trade. Easily the most compelling actress he had ever watched on stage. Her command of her art was unparalleled. But he had also, he thought, come to know the woman beneath the great Rose Beaumont's façade. That woman had a heart, a past, pains and hurts and scars.

That woman was the one he kissed. The one toward whom he possessed tender feelings.

He sighed. "I understand your skepticism, Arden. Indeed, I am battling against my own inner cynic. Johanna is undeniably a skilled actress. But I have reason to believe everything she has revealed to me thus far."

Arden's expression was one of undeniable disgust. "Forgive me, Winchelsea, but it seems to me that you are thinking with your..." His words trailed off as he sent a glance in the direction of the duchess, as though belatedly realizing he had been about to say something he ought not in the presence of a lady.

Even if the lady was his wife and had likely heard far worse.

And, since the lady and duchess in question was formerly the famed H.E. Montgomery, Felix could only presume she had.

"You were going to say something inexcusable to Winchelsea," the duchess accused Arden before turning back to Felix. "I think what my husband is trying to convey is that you must take care to separate the way you feel about Mademoiselle Beaumont—er, Miss McKenna—from the duties facing you. We must all take care and proceed with great caution, while we determine the lies from the truth. In the meantime, given the recent explosion at your townhome, it is paramount that we do everything in our power to see you and your daughter safe and to see McKenna caught once and for all."

"Ever my better half," Arden said on a sigh, sending his duchess a besotted look.

Felix cleared his throat, feeling suddenly ill at ease. His neck cloth had perhaps been tied too tightly that morning. For the strangest sensation struck him as he watched the ease and undeniable love between the Duke and Duchess of Arden. Surely it could not possibly be envy.

He was pleased with his life exactly as it was. He had no desire to marry another woman. Hattie was the wife of his heart, the wife of his soul. No other could take her place or compare.

"We will divert some guards to your current residence," the duchess said.

"I have already taken the measure of moving some myself," he said, relieved that husband and wife had realized they were not alone in the chamber once more. "But if you have more to spare, I would gladly accept them. I want Verity safe. And Miss McKenna as well. I think it would be best if the League and Scotland Yard together confer to obtain the trunk. But that brings me to another matter."

Scotland Yard. While Felix was often the binding thread between Scotland Yard and the Special League, the police force had recently developed a new counter-Fenian division that was working in concert with the League. And the number of arrests of suspected Fenian sympathizers had tripled since then.

"I cannot promise you Miss McKenna will be safe from

charges, Winchelsea," Arden said then. "You know as well as I that such a thing is impossible."

"The devil you cannot," he argued. "You are working closely with the head of the Criminal Investigation Department."

"She could be guilty as sin," Arden returned flatly. "As I said before, your judgment is clouded by the way you feel about the lady. Regardless of what her story is, she is a known associate of one of the most dangerous blackguards of our times. Even if she is truly the man's sister, she could still be taking her orders from him. Has it not occurred to you that she could be using her wiles for her brother's nefarious gain?"

Of course it had, but it also made precious little sense.

"If that were indeed the case, she would have come to me immediately, rather than the other way around. And there would have been no need to reveal her true identity. She came to me in good faith and provided her knowledge of evidence against McKenna that I believe will prove invaluable to our efforts to see him apprehended." He paused, warming to his cause. "But Miss McKenna will only provide the evidence if she is given the assurance that no charges will be laid against her."

The last was pure fiction on his part. Johanna had made no such stipulation, but the Duke of Arden's reaction to Felix's revelations concerned him. For he knew that Arden's suspicions would only be magnified by Ravenhurst, the inspector leading Scotland Yard's newest counter-Fenian division.

Ravenhurst was a stickler. Suspicious of everyone. A cold-hearted bastard.

And there was no way Felix was throwing Johanna upon the mercy of such a man. Not without some reassurance. Since Arden had been working closely with Ravenhurst, he was just the man to obtain that reassurance.

"That is very wise of Miss McKenna," said the duchess then, pinning Felix with a frank look that said she knew precisely what he was about.

The damned woman was too intelligent for her own good, but that was part of what had made her such a tremendous asset to the Special League.

"I agree," he said to the duchess, meeting her gaze unflinchingly. "She is already taking a great personal risk in providing us with the evidence. Her brother has threatened her life should she speak against him or turn over the trunk in her possession."

"If she is innocent as you believe," the duchess prodded thoughtfully, "why did she not volunteer this information sooner? Immediately upon her arrival in London, for instance? Instead, she harbored the dynamite and the documents. She also met with one of the Fenians."

It was a fair question, and one that had also troubled him. But as he searched inside himself now, he could honestly say, his previous concerns had dissipated. Perhaps it was the tender ease she had with Verity. Perhaps it was something more. Whatever the reason, she had won him over.

"She was buying herself time," he replied. "Miss McKenna has been abused, controlled, and threatened by her brother for the last year. Coming to London was to be her means of escaping him at last. However, she also was keenly aware of the dangerous reach her brother has. She was hoping to wait until the end of her six-week turn on the stage to contact police, so she could then carry on to Paris and not have to remain in a city where her brother has so many foot soldiers willing to carry out his evil for him."

This, too, made sense. His doubts about Johanna were falling away, one by one, like leaves dropping from an autumn tree. Soon, there would be none remaining. There would be only the other emotions he felt for her. Emotions he would not examine now. Perhaps not ever.

"I must admit, that, too sounds plausible," the duchess said slowly, casting a glance back at Arden. "I have seen many cases in my past where a family member—a wife, a sister, a daughter—had been too fearful to speak out against someone they knew had committed a crime."

"I will speak with Ravenhurst," Arden relented. "If the situation is as you say, and McKenna does indeed have a history of terrorizing his sister, I have no doubt he will be amenable to avoiding laying charges against Miss McKenna."

"Thank you." He felt as if a weight had been lifted from his chest. "All I ask is for Miss McKenna to be treated with respect and fairness, and to be kept safe."

"I make no promises," the duke warned. "But I will try. God knows you have been responsible for aiding me more times than I can count. And since you helped to save my wife's life, I am eternally indebted to you."

Arden referred to when the duchess had been held prisoner by some of McKenna's men within a London warehouse. By the time their contingent of Special League and Scotland Yard forces had arrived, the Fenians had detonated bombs and set off a roaring fire. Arden, the Duke of Strathmore, and the duchess had just narrowly escaped with their lives.

It was a chilling reminder of just how deadly the men working for McKenna were. Just how great their potential for savagery. They would stop at nothing to gain what they wanted, but he would be damned before anyone else paid in blood.

He rose and bowed. "Thank you, Arden. Duchess. Come to me when you have Ravenhurst's reassurance, and the investigation can proceed."

Johanna's belongings had arrived from the hotel. All of them, that was, save one trunk.

She stared at the valises and trunk now, sitting end to end in the chamber where she would be spending the next few nights. A few and no more, she reminded herself firmly. She must not get accustomed to this. Even if the chamber was large and sumptuous, the room decorated in stunning style.

"Would you have me unpack them for you, ma'am?" asked the maid who was tentatively hovering alongside the trunks in question. "It would be my pleasure to see you settled."

The domestic—Owens, as she had introduced herself—was kind and eager to be of assistance. But Johanna felt odd accepting the assistance. Indeed, as she stood in the center of this beautiful chamber, a chamber which had likely once belonged to Felix's former mistress, she could not help but to feel that she did not belong.

She had never before had a servant attend her.

Nor had she ever had a room as elegant and finely appointed as this one.

But along with her awe at the luxurious surroundings was the heavy weight of dread. For she was running from Drummond, and she had never in all her years been able to run so far or so fast he had not been able to eventually catch her. The last time, it had taken several years. This time, there was no telling.

She suppressed a shiver at the thought, tamped down her fear.

"I will see to the unpacking myself, Owens," she forced herself to say.

"It is no trouble, Miss McKenna. His Grace has tasked

me with seeing to you," the maid said. "Direct me as you like, and I will see everything tucked away nice and neat, just where you want it."

Miss McKenna.

How odd it was to be addressed by her true name after so many years. But Felix had informed the staff, and even his daughter had taken to referring to her as Miss McKenna now. She could not deny it left her feeling as if she were in a strange state of vulnerability. But most vulnerable of all, given everything that had happened, was her heart.

An unwanted thought occurred to her then.

"Owens, you were not employed by the last…resident of this home, were you?" she asked, hoping Felix had not also given her his former mistress's maid.

"Oh no, Miss McKenna." Owens smiled tentatively. "I am new to this position. Being a lady's maid has always been a dream of mine."

The domestic's admission sent a spear of guilt through her.

"Forgive me for being churlish, Owens," she hastened to say. "Of course you must do what you like. I merely did not want to cause you extra work or trouble."

"Nonsense." Owens opened the first trunk. "Do you have a preference as to where your undergarments shall go, ma'am?"

Johanna wanted to tell the maid not to unpack all the luggage entirely, for she had no intention of remaining here long. But she did not want to see any further shadows of disappointment darken the maid's expression. And a voice inside, she refused to acknowledge, suggested perhaps she would stay here longer than she supposed.

That she would *want* to.

Felix's face rose in her mind, handsome and concerned.

Tugging at her tender heart in ways she could not afford to allow.

She cast a glance about the room once more, taking in the sleekly polished wardrobe, the large bed with its intricately carved headboard and posts. Oh, how she wished the chamber had not once housed a former lover of his. She had no right to feel envious or jealous of a paramour from his past, and she knew it. She had no hold on him. No right to him, and she never would.

And yet…

Some part of her felt, quite foolishly, as though she did.

"Ma'am," prompted Owens. "Shall I sort everything for you and then inform you of their location when I am finished?"

Bless the woman for seeing how overwhelmed she felt by everything that had happened in the last few days.

"Yes," she agreed, summoning up a smile. "That would be wonderful, Owens, thank you. I believe I will go in search of Lady Verity while you work. Excuse me."

She left the chamber behind and did not have far to roam. She descended one floor and was instantly treated to the sound of delighted girlish giggles, followed by hastily approaching footsteps.

Two sets, unless she missed her guess. One large, one small.

She rounded a bend in time to find Verity being chased down the hall by the Duke of Winchelsea, her curls fluttering about her angelic face. Father and daughter were both smiling.

"You will never catch me!" vowed his daughter.

"I shall catch you if it is the last action I take," he called in a mock stern voice.

Johanna froze, mesmerized by the sight of father and daughter at play. Of the so oft serious and elegant Duke of

Winchelsea racing down the hall after his daughter. Of the matching smiles they wore. The laughter.

Their lightheartedness and the moment itself melted the ice in her heart.

Emotion slammed into her with such force she almost lost her balance and toppled over. As it was, she scarcely had time to prepare herself when Verity made her way to Johanna and launched her little body unexpectedly into her arms.

"Save me from the evil Papa dragon," cried the little girl, giggling.

Johanna clutched Verity to her tightly, relishing the embrace. How much she had missed when she had lost Pearl. The thought left her feeling the same old ache, along with something else. Something new.

"I will save you, fair maiden," she promised, playing along with the game past the lump in her throat as Felix reached them.

He stopped, near enough to touch. So near the scent of sandalwood wafted over her. His countenance changed as their gazes met and held.

"Miss McKenna," he greeted her formally.

For his daughter's benefit, she guessed, clinging to that same indifference. Trying to forget the way he had kissed her and touched her. The way he had brought her such pleasure.

But, *dear Lord*, how could she ever forget that? It was a sheer impossibility.

"Your Grace," she returned, making her best attempt at a curtsy while she held his still-giggling daughter in her arms. "I had not realized you had returned."

The moment she said the words, she wished she could take them back, for she was making a revelation she had no wish to make: that she had noted his absence. That she had been wondering where he had gone and when he would return.

Which of course, she had.

In spite of her every instinct to keep her distance from him and not to allow herself to become emotionally attached to him in any way, she could not deny the feelings he incited deep within her. Hated feelings. Unwanted feelings.

Lingering beneath the surface of every moment.

"I was seeing to some matters of mutual concern," he told her then, his tone somber. All the levity had leached from his handsome face.

And she knew the reason for it. Knew, too, what he spoke of. Her heart clenched painfully. He had spoken with Scotland Yard on her behalf, it would seem. She had no notion of whether the news was good or grim from his expression.

"I appreciate your attentiveness to such concerns," she said quietly before lowering Lady Verity to the floor.

Verity clung to her, seemingly unwilling to let her go, and Johanna did not blame her, for she was hit with a similar sensation. Seeing Felix's daughter smiling, her green eyes dancing with merriment, lightened Johanna's heart. After the trauma of the evening before, it was a relief as well. The little girl was so full of life, so precious. Johanna could not help but to feel a maternal pang whenever she looked upon her, a reminder of what she had lost.

"Miss McKenna, I beg of you, do not lower me or the Papa dragon will catch me!" cried Verity, still lost in the vivid world of her imagination.

Johanna wondered if this was a game Felix played often with his daughter. It certainly held an air of familiarity. Here was another side of him she had not seen. Yet another side she liked. He was a good father to Verity, a loving father. She felt, as she stood there, a dreadful interloper in their family.

She was acutely aware of the fact that she did not belong here. And indeed, that by the mere virtue of her presence, she could be putting the both of them in very real danger. She could not bear for anything else to befall either of them. She must go as soon as she was able to find other lodgings.

"Do stop attempting to climb Miss McKenna as if she is a tree, poppet," Felix told his daughter then, though there was no bite to his words.

The fond smile on his lips made Johanna's insides turn to liquid.

Verity dutifully released her, but the moment the girl's feet touched the carpeted hall, she cried out, throwing an arm over her forehead in a dramatic gesture. "Oh, woe is me. I have fallen into the moat."

She pretended to swoon then, collapsing into a heap of frilled skirts.

Johanna could not help but to laugh at the girl's antics. Felix was no better able to contain his mirth. His deep, husky laughter rang through the hall again, and she could not stay the wave of warmth it sent crashing over her this time.

He had a beautiful laugh.

But of course he did. Everything about the Duke of Winchelsea was gorgeous and elegant and far too perfect. He was not of her world.

"It would seem you are not the only one beneath this roof with a flair for drama, Miss McKenna," he observed, his gaze locked with hers once more.

His words reminded her, quite belatedly, that she had missed her rehearsals for today. And not only that, but depending upon the time, she would likely miss the entire evening's play altogether. Dread struck her.

"I must get to the Crown and Thorn immediately," she said. "In all the commotion, I have completely forgotten to attend rehearsals. Mr. Saville will be very displeased with me, and I cannot blame him. Do you have the time, Your Grace?"

"Do not worry about the time," Felix said, his laughter gone now.

She mourned the loss. He looked like a man who needed more lightheartedness in his life. She did not have the time to worry over it, however, because she was going to be late for *The Tempest*.

"But I must," she argued. "I need to hire a hack to take me to the Crown and Thorn at once."

"I sent a note 'round to Mr. Saville on your behalf earlier today," he told her, surprising her. "I informed him you would not be attending the theater at all today."

"But I cannot miss a performance," she argued. "I have never, in all my years as an actress, missed a show."

"You are going to miss this one," he said, his tone grim. "You cannot believe after what you have told me that I will send you off to the theater on your own this evening."

And there he was, taking care of her again. Fretting over her once more.

She must not allow it.

She frowned. "The choice is not yours to make, Your Grace. I have a contract with Mr. Saville, and I am obligated to perform, regardless of the circumstances."

"Help me," Verity called from the floor then, interrupting the sudden tenseness of the moment. "Someone rescue me from the moat, oh please!"

Jolted from the heaviness of her thoughts, Johanna bent without thinking and scooped the girl into her arms once more. It was not until she stood to find Felix's gaze pinned to her that she realized she was taking liberties that were not hers to take.

"Forgive me, fair maiden," she said, reverting to what she

did best—playing a role. "I fear I must flee, for another quest awaits me. I have to surrender you to the Papa dragon after all."

With that, she shifted Verity in her arms so that Felix could take his daughter from her. He did, though the girl attempted to cling to Johanna's neck.

"Do not go, Miss McKenna," she begged, pouting from her father's arms. "I was having such fun. Papa has never played princess and dragon with me before."

There was the answer to her question, then. Just as she had supposed, Felix did not have much room for levity or lightheartedness in his life. What, she wondered, had changed? What had made this fearsome, staid duke come undone enough to laugh with his daughter? To pretend to be a dragon?

She did not dare suppose it had been her influence. That her silly song had shaken him enough to make him realize his daughter needed laughter the way plants needed sun.

"I am afraid I must go," she told the girl.

"You must stay," Felix insisted. "Theo already knows you will not be in attendance this evening and has made other provisions."

How tempting the notion was. To remain here, with Felix and Verity, to bask in their presence while she could. But that was not just foolish, it was reckless. If she was to continue supporting herself abroad with her work as an actress, she could not simply fail to appear.

"I told you, Your Grace," she said, "I do not miss my shows."

"Please, Miss McKenna," Verity chimed in. "Papa is excellent at playing dragon and princess, but I doubt he can sing the way you can."

She felt her resistance sliding. Just this once. What would

be the harm?

"You see?" Felix flashed her a quick, tender smile that did strange things to her heart. "We are, the both of us, depending upon you."

The fight left her. What could she say to Felix and Verity, this father and daughter who had somehow fallen into her life and filled her with emotions she had no longer thought she possessed?

There was only one answer that felt right.

"Very well," she allowed. "I will stay."

Chapter Ten

JOHANNA MCKENNA HAD worked some change over him, and Felix could not deny it any longer as he sat with her in the salon following dinner. Verity had been tucked into bed some time ago, yawning and smiling. When she had thrown her arms around his neck and pressed a kiss to his cheek, his heart had seemed to swell to thrice its original size.

And it was all the doing of the alluring woman seated alongside him.

He had not realized just how potent an elixir his daughter's happiness could be until he had heard her laughing with Johanna McKenna. Nor had he realized how much Verity longed for his attention and affection.

When he had returned from his meeting with the Duke and Duchess of Arden, he had felt as if he carried the weight of a dozen worlds upon his shoulders. But then, he had seen Verity's sweetly cherubic face, and he had known such a rush of gratitude for her. Thankfulness that she was alive, that she had not been injured or worse in the fire at Halford House. Humbled that she was his.

She had asked him, very seriously, if he wanted to play dragon and princess with her. And so he had. And he had chased her down the hall, laughing with her as if he were no more than a lad himself.

It had been nothing short of miraculous. Nothing short of

wonderful.

"Thank you," he told her.

She slanted a startled look in his direction. "What are you thanking me for, Your Grace?"

Now that they were alone, out of the listening ears of his daughter, he did not want the formality between them.

"When we are alone, I would prefer if you continue to call me Felix," he said.

A charming tint of pink colored her cheeks. "As you wish, Felix, but you have nothing to thank me for. I have brought nothing but danger to your door, which is the last thing I would wish for you."

The danger would have found him inevitably anyway. The Fenians were growing bolder in their plotting and their targets by the day. But she did not know the depths of his involvement with such matters. He had kept his work at the Home Office a secret from her out of necessity.

"I do not want to think about the danger now. We are safe here, and you have my word on that. As I see it, however, I have much to thank you for. You have brought happiness back into my daughter's life." He paused, struggling to find the proper words for what he wanted to convey. "I have not heard her laughter as many times in the last five years of her life as I have today."

"Lady Verity is a lovely girl," Johanna said softly, her wistful smile once more in place.

The one that told him she was thinking of her own daughter. She must have been an excellent mother. Watching her with Verity filled his chest with an odd tightness he could not explain. With a longing.

He supposed it made him wonder how Hattie would have been with his daughter, how their little family would have grown together, had they had the chance. Much as Johanna must look upon Verity and wonder how her life would have differed had her daughter lived.

"She is my saving grace," he said honestly of Verity. "In the early days, after losing her mother, I do not think I could have survived without Verity."

"You loved your wife very much," Johanna observed.

"Yes," he answered honestly. "I did. When she died, a part of me died along with her."

At least, that was what he had thought, how he had felt. But now, he could not help but to wonder if that was not entirely true. If instead, he had believed a part of himself dead which had not truly died at all. If that part of him had merely been lying dormant, waiting for the right moment to come back to life.

Or waiting for the right person.

Waiting for Johanna McKenna. The last woman for whom his heart should long. And yet, the only one for whom it did.

"She was a fortunate woman, to have been so loved by you," Johanna said.

There was no jealousy in her voice, only raw candor.

"I was the fortunate one." His voice was rough with emotion now as he recalled Hattie, his charmed marriage with her. From the moment they had begun courting, she had stolen his heart. He had never had a hope of defense against her. "I wish Verity could have known her. But Hattie died when she was so young. She has no memories. All she knows of Hattie is what I tell her."

That still broke his heart every time he thought about it.

He knew that much would never change, regardless of how much time passed and how much healing he was able to do.

"I am sorry, Felix," Johanna said, touching his hand.

"That must be so incredibly difficult for you. My heart aches for both you and Verity."

The unexpected contact warmed him. When she would have withdrawn, he moved quickly, taking her hand in his, lacing their fingers together. How good this connection felt. How necessary. As necessary as his beating heart, as his next breath.

Her compassion moved him.

"We are fortunate," he said, "though I think I did not realize just how fortunate until I saw Verity in the nursery, until I heard her voice, until I held her in my arms and realized she was still alive. We have each other, which is more than some."

More than Johanna herself, but he did not say that.

He sensed her stiffening at his side, and he knew she heard the unspoken words. Though he longed to learn her story, he would not force her. There would come a day, he hoped, when she would willingly share the details of her past with him.

"I think of her," she said, taking him by surprise. "My daughter, Pearl. I think of her every day. There will never come a time when I do not feel her absence in my life. When I do not remember her and wish she were still here with me."

The sadness in her voice hit him directly in his heart. Without thought, he slid his arm around her, drawing her into his side. And though she felt right, tucked against him, her curves pressing into him in all the right ways, his gesture was not about desire but about comfort. A silent acknowledgment of her pain, of what she had endured.

He noted, not for the first time, that she did not speak of Pearl's father. Since her name was Johanna McKenna, he could only assume she had never wed the man. He found himself curious about what sort of man could capture Johanna

McKenna's heart and win her. But he said nothing, for he did not dare pry.

"There is no cure for grief, I have found," he said instead, speaking honestly and from his own experience. "Years dull the pain in incremental measures, but still, some days are worse than others. Some days, it is a flood, over your head. Other days, you can swim just long and hard enough to keep from drowning in it."

He was afraid she might move away from him, might seek to put some distance between them. But instead, she wrapped an arm around his waist in return, her hold tight. As if she were taking comfort from him every bit as much as he was taking it from her.

"It has been nine years since I lost her," she said quietly.

"Nine?" He stared down at her in surprise. "You must have been nothing more than a babe yourself then."

"Seventeen." Her voice was sad. "I was seventeen when I became a mother. I scarcely knew how to look after myself then. It was far too soon. I blame myself for what happened, of course. If I had been older, wiser, wealthier, if she had a father in her life who could have provided for us, she would have lived."

He stroked down her spine calmly, caressing, but inside him, irritation flared to life at the man who had taken advantage of a young girl on her own in the world. "You need not speak of it, Johanna."

"I want to." She glanced up at him from beneath lowered lashes. "I am not embarrassed by my past. Others would be, I know, but I have always reasoned that Pearl was the very best part of me. I will not have her memory as nothing more than a shameful secret."

He nodded, because he understood. In polite society, an unwed young mother was a source of shame for her family, ostracized by all who knew her. She would either be forced to give up her baby or to hide herself in the country or on the Continent.

"Tell me whatever you wish, my dear," he said, still caressing her back.

He admired her strength. He did not think he had ever met another who had endured as much as she had and who still found the fortitude to carry on. A woman who could care for and laugh with a child she scarcely knew.

"Her father was another actor in the traveling company I joined when I ran away from my father," she said slowly. "He was older than I was, thirty to my fifteen, and I thought of him as a brother. I had been with the company for a few months when everything changed. He often performed the largest roles in our plays. He told me he would help me get bigger roles, better roles."

Dread curdled in his gut as she paused, letting out a bitter laugh. He knew where her tale was going, and it was beginning to make him ill. That a thirty-year-old man would take advantage of a girl of fifteen made him want to do the bastard violence. But he ground his molars and forced himself to remain silent.

"I was in awe of him, I suppose," she continued, staring into the floor at a memory only she could see. "I allowed him to persuade me to do things I would not have otherwise done. Not long after I discovered I was going to have Pearl, he left in the night. He moved on to a rival company, and I never saw him again."

"The bastard should be hung from the gallows for what he did to you," he growled, unable to hold his tongue a second more. The vitriol inside him was at high tide, spewing forth. "You were a child, Johanna. He was a man grown."

She glanced back at him. "I do not regret it, for it gave me

Pearl, and those months with her, being her mother…they were the best months of my life."

Unshed tears glittered in her eyes, and he felt an answering prickle in his own, and then his vision blurred. His cheeks were wet. He was crying. Crying for the woman he held so securely to his side. Crying for the girl she had once been. Crying for Pearl, the baby she had lost.

"I am sorry," he told her again, finding his voice, knowing it was trite, but unable to find other words to match the way he felt.

"What is this?" she asked, her tone awed as she reached up and skimmed the soft pads of her fingertips over his cheeks, collecting his tears the same way he had once stolen hers. "Do not cry for me, Felix. I do not deserve it."

He caught her wrist in a gentle grasp, holding her hand still when she would have removed it, and pressed a kiss to her fingers. The wetness of his own sorrow painted his lips. And then he kissed the center of her palm before lifting his head and meeting her gaze.

"You, Johanna McKenna, are the strongest, bravest woman I know," he said, meaning every word. "I admire your resilience, your determination, the ferocity of the love in your heart."

"Oh, Felix," she whispered, her hand going to his cheek in a soft caress. "You should not say such things to me."

"Why not?" he asked, pushing her.

This moment between them was a bridge. They could cross over it together, or they could retreat to their separate sides. He sensed it, and he knew what he wanted. He had only ever felt this depth of emotion and passion once before in his life, and it had been with Hattie.

It seemed the greatest irony of all that he should find it again now with a woman who was the epitome of everything he should not want. She was an actress with a scandalous past and undeniable ties to one of the most volatile Fenian plotters in America.

"Because it makes me want to kiss you," she said then, disrupting his every thought.

Sending his ability to think or act rationally fleeing.

She had just taken his hand and started halfway across the bridge. And damn it all, he was going to lead them the rest of the way.

"Then perhaps you should," he dared.

FELIX'S WORDS LANDED in Johanna's heart.

He wanted her to kiss him.

Her past had not chased him away. He did not now look upon her as if she must pin a scarlet letter to her breast and hang her head in shame. He wanted her in spite of who she was, what she had done, and all the danger surrounding her.

And he had wept for her. For Pearl.

For that alone, she could fall in love with him.

Perhaps she already had.

She knew that kissing him now would mean more than it had before. The hour was late. She was spending the evening at his home. Everything between them had changed. Though she had not lain with a man since she had been sixteen, she had spent all the years since deflecting the overtures of men. She was not an innocent. She was wise and weary.

But she was also longing. Longing for this man. For the taste of his lips. For his arms around her. Longing for the way he could replace old memories with new. Now was her chance, she reminded herself as she stared at him, helplessly in his thrall. She would have to leave tomorrow so that he and

Verity would be safe and Drummond's men would divert their dangerous attacks elsewhere.

Indeed, now was her *only* chance.

She wrapped her arms around his neck and drew his head toward her, stopping when there was a scant inch separating their lips. "Are you sure you want a woman like me? You are a nobleman, and I am anything but noble."

The arm banded about her waist tightened, and his other hand cupped her cheek as his verdant gaze seemed to devour her. "You are the noblest woman I know."

What could she do then, but kiss him? There was no other response she could possibly fathom. The Duke of Winchelsea, so handsome and austere, so elegant and poised, thought her noble. And he was looking at her in a way that made her melt.

She was not certain which of them was the first to move.

All she knew was that in the next breath, their lips were fused. And this kiss, it was different from the others they had shared. It was infused with emotion that had been absent before. She moved her mouth slowly over his, suddenly acutely aware of her every sense: the decadent scent of him, the abrasion of his whiskers beneath her palms, the supple smoothness of his lips, the way he tasted of sweet wine and the raspberry fool that had been their dessert at dinner, the low sound in his throat.

Her fingers sank into his hair. The kiss deepened. Their tongues slid languorously against each other. She sucked on his. Desire pooled low in her belly, and lower too. Between her thighs, she throbbed. She was wet and aching.

It was as if no time had passed between their ravenous interlude earlier that day and now. Yet, everything had changed. Her feelings for him had deepened in ways she could not have fathomed hours ago.

"Johanna," he groaned against her lips.

It felt so very right to hear her true name spoken in his delicious, patrician voice. The desire inside her was building to a crashing crescendo. All the emotion surging within her was overwhelming.

She forgot to care about tomorrow.

Forgot to worry.

Forgot about all the pain and heartache she had been dealt.

In this moment, she was powerful, and she was wanted. And the man in her arms was good, so very good. He was a nobleman, it was true, but he was noble in the truest sense, from the heart. He had been doing nothing but looking after her and taking care of her, worrying over the tightness of her shoes and whether or not she ate, wanting to see her safe, bringing her here to his home, doing his best to protect her from everything and everyone.

She had never met another man like him, and she knew, instinctively, she never would. Just as she knew if she did not give herself to him this night, she would regret it forever.

The time was now.

The man was in her arms.

Felix. Duke of Winchelsea.

But truly, when she kissed him, and in his protective embrace, he felt like so much more than a name and a title. He felt like the other half of her heart, the part of her she had not realized was missing until the moment he had brought it back to her. It had been there, on the tears running down his cheeks. Tears for her, tears for Pearl.

She wanted to worship him. To do everything she could for him. A new, almost crazed need overtook her. Still kissing him, she kept one hand firmly in his hair while the other grasped a handful of her skirts. She hiked them. And then, she straddled him.

Just as she had earlier. But this time, she was not going to run. This time, she wanted more than just the pleasure he could give her.

She wanted all of him. And she wanted to give him pleasure in return. He had given her so much already, and she had only taken.

One of his hands settled on her waist. The other went beneath her skirts, skimming over her calf before igniting a trail of fire all the way to her hip.

He jerked his head backward suddenly, breaking the seal of their lips. His breathing was harsh, nothing more than ragged pants flitting humidly over her lips. Their gazes locked and held.

"This is not what I intended," he said. "After everything you have shared with me, I cannot—"

She silenced him with a kiss. A long and lengthy and delicious one. Her tongue slipped past his lips, and he made a sweet sound of surrender, kissing her back. This was what she wanted, what she needed now. Desire. Felix.

She did not want his sympathy or his sadness. She wanted *him*.

And she told him. With her lips and tongue. With the desire burning white-hot inside her. With her hand, which she slid between their bodies until she found his cock, long and thick and hard. He seemed to burn into her palm through the barrier of his trousers. She palmed him, gratified at how he seemed to swell beneath her caress.

He broke the kiss once more. His expression was as dazed as she felt. He looked almost as if he were drunk, and she was sure she looked the same. She had never known desire so strong, so overwhelming.

She was sure she had never known desire at all until Felix.

Had never before understood how one man could make her body come to life.

"Johanna," he bit out, his voice low. "This is not why I invited you to stay here with me."

She knew that, of course. Nor was it the reason she had accepted his offer.

"Felix," she countered, lost in his eyes. "I want you. And you want me."

"God yes, I do," he admitted.

He need not have said the words, because the evidence was still hard beneath her hand. But she liked the way he sounded, almost desperate. As if he had to have her. As if he was helpless to fight the way she made him feel.

This time, she answered him with deed.

She took his mouth. Kissed him long and slow and deep. Kissed him with intent, letting him know with her lips and tongue just how much she longed for him.

A growl of sensual promise sounded deep in his throat.

At last, his hand moved, skimming over the fabric of her drawers. Unerringly, he found the split between her legs. The first touch of his fingers to the bud of her sex was electric. He teased it with slow and deliberate strokes, circling it. A surge of ecstasy went down her spine. Their tongues tangled.

She was ready, so ready for him.

Perhaps it was because she already knew the pleasure he could bring her. Their bodies seemed unusually attuned to each other. It did not require much for him to work her into a frenzy.

She was already clamoring for more.

Her body was on fire.

At her core, she pulsed and ached and wanted and needed.

His nimble, knowing fingers continued to play over her.

And her fingers found the buttons at the fall of his trousers. She undid them. And then, her hand slipped past the barrier of fine fabric to hot, delicious flesh.

Until his hand slid from between her legs and he stayed her with a gentle clutch of her wrist.

He tore his lips from hers. "Not here. Not like this."

Her cheeks went hot. "Forgive me. I do not know what came over me."

But when she attempted to scramble from his lap, he held her fast, his gaze intense upon hers.

"When I make love to you for the first time, I want it to be in a bed, Johanna," he said, his voice a low and decadent rumble, sliding over her like velvet.

For the first time.

She must tell him this would be the only time. But seated as she was, their limbs entangled, her blood coursing with fire, her mouth swollen from his kiss, she recognized such a statement for the inevitable lie it would be.

How could she ever make love to this man just once?

Once would never, ever be enough.

She swallowed, then took a steadying breath. "This was not my intention."

"Nor was it mine." He closed the distance between them and kissed her sweetly, chastely on the lips before pressing his forehead to hers. "Go to your chamber, and I will follow as soon as I am able."

A thrill swept over her, chasing any of the lingering shame. There was only one word she could manage to offer. "Yes."

With his aid, she stood, shaking out her crushed skirts.

"Johanna?"

The question in his voice had her glancing back up at him. He looked so unlike his ordinary, elegant self in that moment: disheveled and wild, his dark hair mussed, his lips darkened, his green cat's gaze burning into her.

"What is it, Felix?" she asked softly, her body still humming with awareness, still aflame with thwarted desire.

"If you change your mind before I arrive, I will understand," he told her, belatedly unfolding his tall, lean form into a standing position.

She held his gaze. "I will not change my mind. Not for you. Not ever."

Johanna had never meant words she had spoken more than these. It was a confession, an admission. An acknowledgment of how much he meant to her, how greatly he affected her. And it was more than she had ever given another.

Acutely aware of that fact, she gave him one last look before turning to flee the chamber. His words chased her out the door, sweetly rumbled revelations.

"Nor I, Johanna."

But as she made her way to the chamber where she would be spending the night, she wondered at the strange undercurrent edging his voice. Something far too close to regret.

Chapter Eleven

FELIX HAD NO excuse to ameliorate the guilt rising within him as he stood in the hall outside Johanna McKenna's bedchamber. Plenty of time had passed since she had swished out of the salon earlier in a seductive swirl of silk and satin skirts, leaving him behind with a cock that was hard as marble. He could not blame his decision upon the grip of lust.

And he could not blame it upon duty, for somehow, over the course of the time since he had first met her, his sense of obligation had slowly and more surely come to rest upon her rather than upon his work for the Home Office.

He could not say he had fallen prey to her maddening kisses. Or to her knowing touch. Though, *bloody hell*, when she had undone the fall of his trousers earlier and touched him, it had required all the control he possessed to keep from driving mindlessly into her.

Later, he would not be able to say she had ensnared him or lured him. He would not be able to blame his decision upon the disaster the day before. He could not blame the sudden reminder of how precious and precarious life was.

No, indeed.

Because one fact was as undeniable as it was irrefutable: he wanted Johanna with a ferocity that nearly tore him apart. He wanted her because he was selfish and greedy, because she reminded him he was alive, because she made him remember how good life could be. She made him remember how a woman's touch could undo him. She reminded him of what happiness felt like.

He wanted her.

Desperately.

It was elemental, and yet it was also more. He could not yet decipher what. All he could say was that despite his every reason to distrust her, despite her Fenian connections, despite all the ruinous ramifications bedding her could potentially cause for him, there was no other place he could spend this night.

No other woman with whom he would spend it.

He rapped softly. Twice.

Before he could attempt a third, the door opened.

Johanna wore a dressing gown belted at the waist, the soft glow of the gaslight illuminating her burnished curls, which she wore unbound and trailing over her shoulders, across the fullness of her breasts. Her gaze met his, and she took a step back.

"Come in," she invited.

He did not hesitate. In one heartbeat, he was over the threshold and the door was closing behind him. The scent of roses and citrus hit him. Her eyes were wide pools of blue to rival the sky. Laden with mysteries he wanted to unlock.

"You are beautiful," he said, a vast and despicable understatement.

For in truth, words could not convey the way she looked, like some goddess come to life. He had seen her in a state of dishabille before, of course, on the day he had gone to her at the Crown and Thorn. But tonight, for the emotions roiling through him, she was more beautiful than she had ever been. Because she had revealed the depths of her heart to him—her grief, her pain—and because he had seen the goodness in her heart.

For as long as he lived, he would never forget the sound of her glorious voice singing silly ditties with his daughter.

The memory of it made him want to kiss her again.

But he did not, not yet, for he was keenly aware of the time that had passed between their reckless kisses in the salon and now.

"And you are the most handsome and elegant man I have ever seen," she told him, fiddling with her curls, almost as if she were nervous.

"I hope I am not presumptuous in coming here." Unable to resist, and drawn to her as if a magnetic pull existed between them, he moved forward until he could catch the hand twisting her curls in his. "I hope you have not changed your mind."

"Never," she whispered, threading her fingers through his so that their palms kissed. "I already told you, I will not change my mind when it comes to you, Felix. I care for you far too much for that."

She cared for him.

His gut clenched.

But somehow, and much to his surprise, being with her thus did not feel like a betrayal of Hattie's memory or the love they had shared. And neither did it feel like a deception when Johanna said the words. It felt, instead, incredibly real.

And powerful.

He drew her into his body by their linked hands. He, too, was wearing a dressing gown. The lack of layers separating them meant that all her soft, warm curves spilled against him in the most pleasing fashion.

"Johanna McKenna," he said softly, his gaze roaming her face, committing it to memory. "You are a special woman.

Your gift is not just your beauty or your talent as an actress, but your heart as well."

He splayed his other, free hand over her chest atop her thumping life-source. Her heart was beating fast. But so was his. Every interaction between them had led to this moment. To this breath. To this touch.

He wanted her so much, he ached with it. Need was a ravaging beast inside him, pulsing through his blood. His cock was hard and he had not kissed her yet.

"Do not say things like that to me," she returned, squeezing their interlaced fingers. "You will make me fall for you even more, and I already know what is happening between us is not meant to be. It will make the inevitable end so much more difficult."

Everything within him railed against the notion of an end for them.

Inevitable?

He thought not.

But then, he remembered all the obstacles in their path. The dynamite she had smuggled into England, the connection to Fenians, his duty to the Home Office, the untenable position in which he now found himself, falling beneath the spell of the woman he had been meant to use. And he could not deny what she had said.

"You cannot fall for me any more than I have already fallen for you," he said instead, the admission torn from him.

Her heart was still beating a rapid staccato against his palm.

Her lips parted as she stared up at him. "You are falling for me? A duke, falling for an actress? Surely such a thing is not done in your society, Felix. Do not give me cause to hope when I cannot. I am not ignorant of the ways of the world. I can warm your bed, but I can never warm your heart."

"You can," he insisted, "because you already have."

"Felix," she murmured, a protestation.

"Johanna, I want you more than I have ever wanted another woman since my wife." He stopped and swallowed against the knot of a rising tide of emotions he could not bear to face.

She stared at him, searching his face and his gaze for he knew not what. But whatever she wanted, whatever she needed to know, it was there and it was true. He had meant every word he had spoken.

Tonight had nothing to do with duty or obligation, not with the Home Office, not with Fenians or Drummond McKenna, not a bloody thing to do with dynamite or danger or fear. It was, entirely, about a man and a woman. Felix and Johanna.

And that was all.

"Kiss me," she demanded.

"With pleasure," he growled, yanking her the rest of the way into his body.

His lips were on hers as the last syllable left him. She made a sweet sound low in her throat, and then somehow, her hands were in his hair and his were in hers. Heavy, silken strands teased his fingers as he tunneled through her golden curls. His tongue was in her mouth. Hers was writhing against his.

Desire licked through him, running down his spine, settling in his groin. His ballocks were drawn tight, need a steady throb pulsing to life more and more with each kiss, each caress.

Their kiss deepened until it was less an act of wooing and more an act of sinful carnality. They were well-matched in their desperation, their mouths moving as one. Harder. More insistently. Open and hungry. He bit into the lush fullness of her lower lip. She nipped him back.

Their hands were traveling, exploring. He found the loosely tied knot on the belt of her dressing gown, and she seemed to discover his at the same moment. He felt his robe loosening, then gaping as the twain ends of her dressing gown went slack. Needing to see her, he broke the kiss, then watched with awe as he slid the fabric from her shoulders.

It fell away, pooling on the floor.

She was not wearing a nightdress beneath it.

Which meant...

Good Lord. A wave of desire so forceful it almost dragged him to his knees washed over him. She was a miracle of creamy curves. Her breasts were high and full, tipped with hard, pink nipples. Her hips were lush, her legs deliciously bare, bereft of stockings or garters. Golden curls shielded her mound from his view at the apex of her thighs, but he recalled the slick heat of her on his fingers, her sweet taste, and he wanted more.

She had prepared for him, he realized.

She had stripped herself of every piece of her attire save the dressing gown.

And she was glorious. Even more beautiful than he could have imagined—though imagined he had, every night since the first day they had crossed paths. He did not know which part of her he wanted to worship first. She had a mole, a tantalizing beauty mark, perfectly round, on her right breast. It mesmerized him, and he thought he might begin there.

"Johanna." Her name was all he could manage to say at first as desire pounded through his veins, hardening his cock. But that was not enough, and it would not do, so he forced more words to come. "You steal my breath."

Her smile was shy. "Then we are well-matched, for you steal mine as well."

He shrugged out of his dressing gown, scarcely taking note of it falling to the carpet. All he could think about was her. She wound her arms around his neck and pressed her tempting body flush against his. And then they were kissing once more.

But this kiss was different than all the others.

It was wild and furious. Hot and bold. This kiss was an acknowledgment. A promise.

They were moving together, their lips clinging, bodies in tandem toward the bed. They fell onto it together, Felix positioning them so that Johanna lay on her back and he was atop her. Her legs parted for him, and he broke the kiss at last to trail his mouth down her throat.

Her skin was so soft and silken. He lingered over her frantically beating pulse, the evidence she was affected by him every bit as much as he was moved by her. And somehow, the knowledge she should be forbidden to him, that he should not be here now, naked with her in her bed, about to make love to her, only heightened his desire.

He could not get enough of her. His lips traveled over the elegant protrusion of her collarbone and then to the rounded slope of her shoulder. Lower, down the curve of one breast. He placed a kiss on the peak and then whorled his tongue in a circle around her nipple before flicking over it.

She made a throaty sound of approval. He sucked her nipple, running his hand over the dip of her waist, down her hips. Her legs fell open, and his fingers found her wet heat as he traced her seam to the plump bud of her pearl. She was as blissfully responsive there as ever. He teased her with slow, lingering strokes as he sucked on her nipple.

Her body bowed from the bed as he increased the pressure with his fingers and moved to her other breast. He lingered over that tempting beauty mark, kissing it first and then lapping over it with his tongue.

But that was not enough. He had to have more. He kissed down her belly, his palms gliding over her inner thighs to spread them wider. The sight of pink, glistening folds held him riveted. An arrow of heat shot straight to his loins.

"Felix," she protested, her voice shy.

"Hush," he soothed, pressing a kiss to each of her inner thighs. "Let me worship you."

He wanted her surrender. Her bliss. And he was not going to stop until he had both. Because everything in him knew, then and there, that this woman had always been meant to be his.

NOTHING COULD HAVE prepared Johanna for the sensation of Felix's mouth upon her.

There.

On her most intimate flesh.

He found the center of all her longing with his tongue. She cried out, her fingers finding purchase in the rumpled bedclothes. She grabbed fistfuls and forgot to be ashamed. Forgot to be embarrassed. Forgot anything but this man, his strong hands splayed on her thighs, holding her open for his sensual torture, his mouth moving over her, devouring her…

He fluttered light licks over her pearl. Her hips jerked from the bed. She wanted more. She was on fire, writhing beneath him, unable to keep herself still. She was thrusting, urging him on. Desperate.

And then that wicked tongue of his licked into her. Filled her. *Dear God*, it was too much. The desire burning inside her heightened. She became aware of every new sensation. The abrasion of his whiskers on her tender flesh. The steady thrust of his tongue inside her again and again. The vibration of his moan of appreciation, which she felt everywhere, all at once.

Just when she thought she could not withstand more, he moved back to the bud of her sex, drawing it into his mouth and sucking upon it as he had done to her nipples. And then he sank one long finger inside her. As he had before, he worked in and out of her, but this time it was more.

This time, the pleasure was almost violent.

Because he was alternating between suckling her and lashing her pearl with his tongue. Long, pulsing licks. The electric nip of his teeth. He added a second finger, and when he curled them within her, he found that special place once more, that place she had not known existed.

And everything splintered.

She came undone. The pleasure inside her was so intense, she could not stifle her cry. Her body trembled beneath the rush of her release. He continued the wicked drive of his fingers and the relentless licks of his tongue as the last shudder subsided.

She was boneless. Weightless. Mindless, too.

He rose over her, and she took a moment to admire his virile masculinity. He was bold and beautiful, his chest broad and firm, his abdomen spare and banded with muscle, his flanks strong. From between his legs jutted his cock, long and thick.

She had scarcely glanced over it earlier before he had put an end to their frenzied embrace in the salon. She wanted to feel him again now. To take him in her hand.

So she did.

He was hot and smooth and firm. She stroked over his flesh, gratified when he jerked into her hand and a moan tore from him.

"Put me inside you," he told her, his voice low.

The decadent order sent a new frisson of desire straight through her, ending in a steady ache between her thighs. An ache that could only be assuaged in one way. She parted her legs more and guided him to the place where she wanted him most. The first touch of his tip to her entrance was incredible.

They moved together, and in the next breath, he was filling her. One thrust. Hard and delicious. She hummed her satisfaction. He guided her legs around his waist. The sensation was intense. He changed the angle of their bodies and slid deeper inside her.

His handsome face a study in intense restraint, he began moving. Her hands traveled every inch of him. Everywhere she could reach. The taut plane of his abdomen, the walled muscle of his chest, his shoulders, his biceps.

The rhythm he began was slow and exquisite.

Torturous.

"You feel so good," he told her, wonder lacing his voice.

And she could understand that wonder, because it was unraveling inside her, all around her. Changing her.

She had thought she had experienced lovemaking in her past. But that had been nothing. Felix did not just take, he gave. He claimed her body as if he found her magnificent, as if he paid homage to her, as if her pleasure was the greatest gift.

"You feel wonderful," she told him past the relentless pounding of her heart, past the increasingly ragged bursts of her breaths as they left her.

"Shall I go slow, darling?" he asked softly.

Darling. He had called her darling. Though it was but a common term of endearment, it crept inside her heart, and there it remained.

"Faster," she said, raking her nails lightly over his upper arms. "More."

"Bloody hell, you'll be the death of me," he said.

But then he obliged, quickening his pace, moving in and out of her in hard, frenzied strokes. It was good. So good. The pleasure was building inside her again, desire burning to a feverish crescendo.

She moved against him, angling, wanting all of him she could take. He was large, his cock filling her. Stretching her. She was flying then, soaring high. Bursts of pleasure shook her as she spent, arching her back and crying out his name.

Through it all, he kept thrusting. Tremors shook her, her sheath clamped on him, and still he moved, in and out, deeper, harder. He was almost slamming into her now, the ferocity of his thrusts electric. Everywhere they touched, she was on fire. He lowered his head and sucked a nipple into his mouth, and then he bit it.

"Come for me again, Johanna," he ordered against the curve of her breast. "I want to feel you tighten on my cock. I want to watch you lose yourself."

His wicked words had a tremendous effect upon her.

She moaned, feeling herself get slicker, the evidence of her desire pooling beneath her on the bed. The wet sounds of their lovemaking echoed in the quiet of the chamber. She was close, so close, to reaching her pinnacle once more.

She bit her lip, transfixed by the sight of him making love to her. His body was a thing of beauty. It seemed a travesty to her that he was forced to hide it daily beneath so many layers of disguising cloth. She did not think she had ever seen a more beautiful man.

"You are close, aren't you?" he asked, his baritone a decadent rumble.

He licked her nipple. His fingers found their way between them, to the place where they joined, and then he was working her pearl once more. Stimulating her, circling the painfully sensitive nub.

She was closer than close. Another torturous circle of his fingers over her greedy flesh, and she was lost. She was not just flying. She was shattering. Shattering into a thousand pieces of glittering light. She came so hard she saw stars. She shook beneath him, shook as mindless pleasure overtook her.

"God, Johanna," he said, his voice tight as he continued to thrust in and out of her. "You are so beautiful. So perfect. I wish I could stay inside your cunny all night."

And on those wicked words, he withdrew suddenly from her body, grasping his cock as he spent into the bedclothes at her side.

Chapter Twelve

FELIX WOKE TO find himself in an unfamiliar chamber for the second night in a row. But this morning, unlike the last, he awoke to a warm, lush body curved against his. To the sweet, musky scent of lovemaking mingling with rose petals and orange. To Johanna McKenna, the woman who should have been his enemy. Formerly Rose Beaumont. Keeper of secrets. Golden-haired siren. Legend of the stage.

His.

For now, taunted a voice deep inside him.

She had burrowed near to him in the midst of the night, probably sometime after their second round of lovemaking. He had not left after the first time, reluctant to leave her side. And he had been heartily glad for his decision when she had woken him with a kiss.

One kiss had led to another, and then another, until they had both collapsed, sweaty and sated upon the bed, and neither one of them had been of a mind to move.

He had never before slept in the beds beneath this roof. This home had been for the slaking of mutual pleasure, nothing more. He had taken mistresses because he had possessed no interest in obtaining a new wife. Hattie had been the wife of his heart, and he could not bear the thought of tethering himself to another woman in the same way.

He had Verity to look after. Though he had the burden of

his title and the need for a male heir, he had spent all the years since his period of mourning had officially come to an end—*officially*, for it had never stopped, in his heart—avoiding matrimony. No other woman could have compared.

No other woman could have matched the way Hattie had made him feel.

But then, Johanna had come along. And she had changed everything. She had made him aware, so keenly aware, of everything he was missing. She had brought him back to life in a way he had not imagined possible.

She was a complication he had never expected.

The last woman he should have allowed into his fragile heart after losing Hattie. Everything about her was wrong: her past, her brother, her future. What place could they have in each other's lives? She was an American fleeing a desperate situation, an actress who earned her bread on the stage, one who intended to carry on to Paris and Lord knew where else after her time in London.

She would be gone then.

Out of reach. Nothing but a memory.

Something deep inside him railed against the thought of Johanna McKenna ever leaving his side.

And because she was here now, he could not resist kissing the top of her head, and then the tip of her nose. From there, he could not stop. He had to have her lips as well. And he did, kissing her awake.

She made a soft murmur and her arms wrapped around his neck.

Their tongues slid together in a slow, lusty rhythm.

His cock was instantly hard and ready. The night before had done nothing to slake his hunger for her. If anything, it had only made it grow stronger. He could not stop himself from rolling his hips into her, letting her feel the effect she had upon him.

She broke the kiss, tipping her head back to look at him.

What a sight she was, her golden curls a riot around her beautiful face, naked and sleepy and flushed.

"Good morning," he murmured.

"Good morning," she said, smiling sweetly. "I thought I dreamt you."

"I am all too real."

She shifted against him, her eyes going wide, lips parting. "I feel that."

She referred to his erection, which was painfully hard and ready for her, aching to be deep inside her once more. She moved against him, bringing him into contact with her hot cunny.

He reached between them, his fingers sliding over her folds. *Bloody hell*, she was already wet for him. He had not intended to stay the whole night. Nor had he intended to wake like this in the morning, voracious for her. But he had, and he was.

And unless he was mistaken, she felt the same.

"The hour is early," he said, teasing her pearl. "Everyone else is likely still abed. Shall I go?"

She licked her lips, her pupils dilating wide. "I think…perhaps you should stay a bit."

"Just for a bit?" he asked, tracing her seam before sinking one finger inside her.

"Oh," she breathed, gripping him tight with her sheath, pulling him deeper. "Yes, you definitely must stay. But longer, I think. I am not sure a bit will be enough."

Nothing would ever be enough when it came to her. He knew that much instinctively.

"Last night was…" He paused as he struggled to find words.

There were none.

"It was," she agreed softly.

He had not just allowed this woman into his heart. She had made her home there.

He was in love with her.

Realization hit him in a blinding moment of clarity, so strong and undeniable, so shocking, he could do nothing. He stilled, staring at her. Losing himself in her eyes. Probably, he had fallen in love with her the moment he had heard her singing with Verity.

"Felix?" Johanna's brow furrowed. "Is something amiss?"

Yes.

He was not meant to fall in love with her. Not with anyone. Indeed, he had not imagined such an emotion would be possible for him ever again. Not after losing Hattie as he had.

And now, he had fallen in love with the sister of his enemy. A woman who was connected to the Fenians he was sworn to defend his country against.

"Everything is well," he forced himself to say. For in a sense, it was.

He had not felt such a sense of rightness in his chest since the day he had asked Hattie to be his bride. It seemed a lifetime ago now. He had been much younger. Not yet a duke. Not a father. The world had seemed so much simpler, the weight of responsibility so much less heavy.

"You are frowning," she observed, glancing her fingers lightly over the grooves which had undoubtedly settled in his forehead.

That gentle touch was his undoing.

He nudged her fingertips with his nose, and then he kissed them, and then he withdrew his finger from her sheath, painting some of her dew lazily over her clitoris. She responded instantly, her body moving against his.

"I do not frown," he told her slowly. "Not when a beautiful American is naked in my arms."

"You are attempting to distract me," she accused without heat.

He grinned, playing with her some more. "Is it working?"

"You know it is, you wicked man."

"I am very wicked," he agreed.

And he was, because he was going to make love to her again. And again. And he loved her, he knew her story, but he had yet to tell her his. He had yet to tell her the truth.

But he would not think upon that now, because Johanna's hand had closed over his cock, and she was stroking him slowly. He thought he might die from the pleasure. Besides, they had time, yet, to plan a course of action. For the truth to be fully revealed between them.

"Bloody hell, woman, you are going to have me spending in your hand."

Their lips met, and the kiss was long and deep, laden with promise.

She tipped her head back, breaking the kiss, her gazing meeting his. "I want you inside me, Felix."

Those words from her lips.

God.

He was lost.

His cock was rigid and ready.

"Ride me," he told her.

Her expression changed instantly to one of adorable befuddlement. She truly was an innocent, Miss Johanna McKenna. He would enjoy every moment of debauching her. He kissed her again, and then rolled onto his back.

"I will show you," he said, the words emerging from him as a growl.

He positioned her over him, her hair a sweet-scented

curtain of billowing golden curls. Her breasts were such pretty temptations, full and tipped with hard nipples he could not wait to suck. Gripping his cock with one hand, he guided her with the other.

She sank down on him, gripping him with her slick heat.

They sighed in unison at the pure bliss of it.

He was ballocks-deep inside her, and nothing had ever felt better. Until she began to move. She undulated slowly, and he helped her to find a rhythm. His hips were thrusting beneath her.

"Oh," she moaned, arching her back.

He leaned up and caught her nipple in his mouth, suckling hard. She cried out and pumped against him wildly. Her breasts were as sensitive as her cunny. He liked that about her. In truth, he liked everything about her. The way she tasted. The way she drenched his cock whenever he said naughty things to her. The way she looked as she rode him.

She was uninhibited in her passion, and he liked that about her too.

He moved to her other breast, losing himself in the rhythm, in the delicious friction. Losing himself in her. Her rump was moving in swift, sensual strokes as she took him deep and then slid back up, almost freeing his cock before sinking back down on him again.

Harder. Faster. Their rhythm was wild. He felt her tightening on him and knew she was near to spending. The sight of her fucking him alone was enough to make him come. But he could not release his seed inside her. He knew he must not. He could control himself. Prolong this delicious moment between them for as long as he could.

But then she lowered herself on him once more, and when she did, she came, clenching on his cock with so much force that he could not hold back the torrent of his own release. His restraint snapped. He spent inside her, coming with such ferocity that his vision went white around the edges. He emptied himself as the spasms of her own pleasure rocked her.

And though he knew it had been wrong, he could not summon up even a modicum of regret.

Mine, he thought to himself. *Not just for now.*

For forever.

Somehow, he had to make it so. Because he could not shake the feeling he had found the second chance he had sworn did not exist. Not a replacement for Hattie—no, never that. But someone he could love every bit as much.

Someone who might, he hoped, love him back.

JOHANNA WOKE ONCE more to find herself in an unfamiliar room, in an unfamiliar bed. As an actress, she had become well accustomed to changing beds, rooms, cities, states, countries. Nothing was permanent. She had never truly had a home, not since she had been fifteen, and the brick edifice she had inhabited along with her father and brother had hardly qualified as a home in the true sense.

She stretched, arching her back. The bed was more luxurious than she was accustomed to. So too the linens covering it. She felt as if she were enrobed in luxury. But she also felt deliciously languorous. All through her body was the steady pulse of sated desire.

Belatedly, she became aware of where she was: in Felix's home. Of what she was wearing: not a blessed stitch. Of what she had done with him the night before. And in the midst of the night when the moon had been high over London. And again early this morning, when the sun had just been beginning its ascent.

She ached in strange places.

But she felt so strangely, wonderfully alive. As if the world around her had taken on a new, vibrant color. As if everything had changed.

Of course, that was silliness.

For nothing had changed except her determination to cling to her honor. She was still plain old Johanna McKenna, masquerading as Rose Beaumont, still a woman who needed to earn her wages at the Crown and Thorn tonight. Still the sort of woman the Duke of Winchelsea would never wed. The sort of woman he would make his mistress.

And take to his bed.

Just as he had.

Still, she could not regret what had passed between them. He was a risk she would willingly take. Whatever it was that burned whenever they were together was too hot, too magnetic, to be ignored. She could not help but to want more of it.

He was a generous lover, she had discovered, with a wicked side. Those beautifully molded aristocratic lips liked to say the filthiest things. And she loved it.

Because she loved *him*.

Johanna sat up in bed, clutching the bedclothes to her as the knowledge hit her with the force of a blow. Somehow, along the way, she had done the most foolish thing she could have possibly done. More foolish than giving her body to a duke she was bound to leave.

She had lost her heart to him.

She had fallen in love with such ease, she had not realized it was happening until it was too late to stop her feelings. But of course she had. He had done nothing but care for her and fret over her from the first. He was a wonderful father.

Watching him with Verity had opened her eyes to a new, previously unseen facet of his personality.

She could not pinpoint now, as she sat there in the rumpled bed that still smelled of him and their lovemaking, when it had happened. Perhaps the fall had been gradual, a natural progression beginning from the day he had swept her from the ballroom at Mr. Saville's and had proposed his wager with her. Certainly, it had been finalized the moment she had watched him chasing after his daughter, laughing with her.

And she loved his daughter too.

She saw in Verity not the daughter she had lost but a sweet girl with her father's eyes. A young lady with an impish smile and a clever mind, but who was desperate to have a mother in her life. Johanna knew the feeling, because she was desperate to be a mother. Desperate for the only role she had never been fortunate enough to play twice.

She blinked back tears and threw the covers away from her, only belatedly recalling she was nude when cool morning air hit her. The fire which had been stoked the night before was nothing but a gentle glow on the opposite end of the room. She looked about for her dressing gown and found it with some difficulty, for it was not where she had discarded it in her mad rush to make love with Felix.

Johanna took a deep breath and shoved her arms through the sleeves of her robe with shaking hands. She could not dwell upon these unwanted emotions roiling through her. She did not belong here. Not beneath this roof, not in Felix and Verity's gilded world, not even in this city, this country.

And every minute she tarried put the people she loved at risk of Drummond's wrath.

Resolutely, she walked to the dresser where a basin and pitcher sat. She poured some cool water into the bowl and splashed it on her face, seeking to calm her rioting emotions.

The first splash was a jolt to her senses. The second was almost calming. The third was necessary to stave off a rush of tears.

She closed her eyes, hunched over, her face dripping, the sleeves of her dressing gown damp reproaches against her wrists. She would have to leave this morning. Say goodbye to the little family she had just come to know and love. Goodbye to Felix and Verity.

But she had loved and lost before.

She could survive this, she told herself. Because she *had* to survive it. For Felix's and Verity's sakes.

Besides, even if she lingered, there was no future for her here. She would not be the secret he kept tucked away in this home, waiting until he replaced her with another. She had meant what she had told him what seemed a lifetime ago now. She would not be a kept woman. Not anyone's, but most especially not his.

"THE NEWS IS not good, I am afraid," the Duke of Arden told Felix the moment he had entered the townhome's small library later that morning, his expression grave.

"You have spoken with Ravenhurst," Felix guessed.

Arden nodded. "He is refusing to make a concession for Miss McKenna."

Raking a shaking hand through his hair, he paced away from Arden. *Bloody hell*, this was not what he wanted to hear. Not what he needed to hear, especially after last night.

"Why not?" he demanded, turning back to the duke.

Waking to Johanna in his arms had been nothing short of miraculous. He could still feel the sweet warmth of her curves, her bare skin pressing against his. For the first time in years, he had felt a connection with a woman that was deeper than desire. It was real and true, pounding through him.

He had vowed to protect her, and protect her he would. Because she was the woman he loved.

"Ravenhurst's division has been watching her since her arrival in Liverpool," Arden explained, his voice somber.

"I know all that," Felix said dismissively. "I am the one who alerted the department of her impending arrival. I am the one who arranged the whole damned thing."

And he felt sick over it now.

He felt as if he had betrayed her. Which was impossible, because he had not known her then. But he knew her now. As intimately as a man could know a woman.

"Ravenhurst tells me they saw her exchanging a parcel with another known Fenian they have been surveilling," Arden continued then.

Fear knifed into him, along with the icy claws of dread. *Damnation*, the meeting he had witnessed that day in the Royal Aquarium. He had not seen any signs of her having been followed. But if the man she had met with was being watched, it stood to reason she would have been seen as well.

"She did meet with a Fenian," he agreed slowly, "but this, too, was at her brother's behest. She copied the entire contents of the package before turning the parcel over to the man."

"Christ, I was hoping you would tell me Ravenhurst was bluffing." Arden scrubbed his hand along his jaw in agitation. "This is not good, Winchelsea. Not good at all."

He could see, of course, where Arden was coming from. *Hell*, he could see where Ravenhurst was coming from. It all must look quite damning.

But it was not.

He knew it was not.

"I have the copies of the documents within the package in my possession," he said. "Johanna intended to turn it over to

Scotland Yard along with the dynamite."

"So she says," Arden pointed out, his mien more grim than it had been before. "You must understand how it appears to Ravenhurst. This female is entangled with Fenians. She smuggled dynamite into England—"

"At the behest of her brother, a villain who has perpetuated a reign of terror upon her," Felix interrupted. "Damn it, Arden, she is an innocent in all this."

"It hardly looks as if she is innocent," Arden said. "If she were truly innocent, she would not have smuggled the dynamite and the correspondence to begin with. She would have refused her brother's demands."

"And have him beat her or worse?" Felix's ire was fast getting the better of him, blood pumping through his veins, and he needed to move once more. To walk, to pace, to keep from smashing his fist through something.

Like the Duke of Arden's face.

Because his quarrel was not with the Duke of Arden. Nor was it with Ravenhurst, who was only doing his duty as the chief of his division. Rather, it was with Drummond McKenna, just as it had always been.

"Do you have proof he beat her?" Arden asked softly.

Of course he did not, aside from the fear he had witnessed in Johanna's eyes. The terror in her voice. The tears she had cried. Tears which he had tasted.

He turned and stalked back down the length of the library. "I have her word," he said, his voice trembling with the conviction and the rage burning within him. "That is enough for me."

"The word of an actress who has surrounded herself with Fenians," Arden concluded.

"Bloody hell! I do not give a damn that she is an actress. Her profession does not render her any less capable of telling the truth than anyone else," he bit out.

"Perhaps not her profession," Arden said, "but her connections to Fenians certainly do. I want to believe she is innocent as much as you do, Winchelsea, truly I do. But you are too involved in this case, in this woman. You must try to take a step back from it all and view the facts as presented in a calm, objective fashion."

"Forgive me," he returned bitterly, "but this soliloquy is rather an irony coming from you, Arden. Tell me, have you ever been capable of viewing your wife in a calm, objective fashion? Were you calm and objective when you ran into a burning warehouse to save her?"

Arden had risen as well, and now he stiffened, almost as if he had been delivered a blow. "She is my duchess. The woman I love. Miss McKenna is a veritable stranger to you, and one you would do well to be skeptical of."

But Johanna was not a stranger. He loved her. He had spent inside her. *Good God*, he could have gotten her with child this morning in his mad lust. He had only just found her. He could not lose her. Not now. Not ever.

"I care about her, Arden," he managed past the lump in his throat. The fear clogging his lungs. "I care deeply. I would run into a burning building to save her, without a thought for myself."

"This is worse than I feared," Arden said.

Determination had him moving, crossing the chamber. "What are you saying, Arden? Just tell me and have done with it."

"Ravenhurst intends to have her arrested when Scotland Yard arrives to take command of the trunk." Arden sighed. "They are going to use the witness who saw her delivering a package to the Fenian, a man they have already arrested this morning and are holding on charges of possessing an infernal machine. Ravenhurst intends to offer that man an incentive to testify against Miss McKenna."

All the air seemed to flee from his lungs.

So, too, the capacity to speak.

The thought of Johanna imprisoned was enough to make his entire body go cold. Ravenhurst was calculating enough to do such a thing. Determined enough to use whomever he must in his quest to be the one who put an end to all the Fenian uprisings.

"I will not allow it," he growled, denial coursing through him. "I will do everything in my power to see that they cannot arrest her."

Arden's gaze was searching. "What do you have in mind?"

"First, I am going to marry her," he said. "And then, I am going to lure her bastard of a brother here once and for all so he can pay for his sins."

If this was the burning building, he was running inside. And he was not emerging until she was safe in his arms.

Chapter Thirteen

JOHANNA SAT IN the small salon following breakfast, Verity at her side on the piano bench. Felix had been inexplicably absent from breakfast, leaving behind a note that he would shortly return. Following everything they had shared, coupled with her realization that she must fast put some time and distance between them, Johanna found his desertion disquieting indeed.

Fortunately, his daughter was there to lift her spirits. They had spent breakfast trading silly tales they invented, each trying to outdo the other, until the both of them were giggling helplessly, wiping tears of mirth from their eyes. She had to admit that not much breakfast had been consumed. But Johanna had been grateful for the distraction from the heaviness of her thoughts and the looming prospect of what she must do.

Just as she was thankful for it now, as her fingers traveled over the ivory keys of the piano in a familiar melody. They were back to their foolishness again, which seemed the order of the day. She had a scant few hours to spare in which she would be forced to say goodbye to the precious child at her side—and her equally precious father—and if Johanna lingered on the reminder too long, she would weep.

Far better to laugh.

It was an old trick she had learned in life. One which had

always stood her in good stead.

"Your turn, Miss McKenna," said Verity gleefully. "You must begin, and I shall sing the next verse."

"You remember the rules of the game well, my lady," she told the girl with a smile.

Verity smiled back at her, and Johanna's heart seemed to clench. "Go now, Miss McKenna. Come up with something suitable for me to rhyme with, if you please."

Johanna changed the melody and began a new song with ease, clearing her throat. "Very well, I shall. In a moment. Or perhaps two…oh dear, I cannot think of a single word to sing. Perhaps you ought to have your turn first, my lady."

Verity giggled, seeing through the ploy and enjoying it just the same. "No, no, you cannot talk through the song, or else it is not a song, Miss McKenna. You must invent a verse."

"I must?" She raised her brows. "Are you certain? I thought you said it was your turn to sing the first verse."

"No!" Verity squealed with delight. "I said it must be you."

Johanna pretended to ponder, all the while keeping her fingers moving over the keys. "Oh, I understand now. It must be you who sings first, correct?"

"Incorrect, Miss McKenna," Verity said, laughing so hard, it was difficult to make sense of her words. "You must be the one who sings first."

"Yes," she teased, continuing to play. "You shall be the one who sings first. Go on, I am waiting."

"Miss McKenna!" Felix's daughter could not seem to manage a coherent word as she collapsed into another fit of giggles.

"Yes?" Johanna said, pretending to frown. "I have already told you I understand everything clearly. The first verse of the song will be sung by you. I only hope you will choose a verse that is an easy rhyme."

"No," Verity countered, still laughing uproariously. "That is not what I said."

"I beg your pardon?" Johanna shouted as she pounded on the keys harder, filling the room with sound. "I cannot hear a word you are saying, my lady."

"Stop!" Verity hollered at the exact moment Johanna ceased playing.

"Yes," she said in an agreeable tone, as if she had not heard the girl at all. "I will begin playing once more while you contemplate the perfect verse. Do take your time."

When she held her hands poised dramatically over the keys as if she were about to play again, Verity grabbed them, laughing.

"No, Miss McKenna! You are a silly goose, deliberately misunderstanding me."

"Must I be a goose?' she teased. "I would far rather prefer to be a different sort of bird. A duck, for instance. Or perhaps a swan."

Verity's giggles were interrupted by the salon door opening. There, at last, stood Felix on the threshold. The mere sight of him alone was enough to send a jolt of awareness straight through her, landing between her thighs where she still ached from all the times he had claimed her body.

"Papa!" Verity cried with delight, shooting from the piano bench and dipping into a perfect curtsy.

Remembering herself belatedly, Johanna stood as well, curtseying to Felix, which felt strange indeed given the closeness they had just shared. After waking skin to skin, formality between them seemed not just odd but almost painful.

Still, she reminded herself she must grow accustomed to it. Her time here was limited. Growing shorter with each tick of the mantel clock.

"Lady Verity," he greeted, bowing formally as his gaze traveled to Johanna's. "Miss McKenna."

Their stares met and held. A jolt passed through her. A current she could not deny. Her heart was breaking, then and there, to know what she must do.

She swallowed against a rush of emotion. "Your Grace."

He stared at her for a beat longer than necessary, and she could not help but to wonder what he was thinking. Had he regretted their passion together? Where had he gone this morning? What could have been the reason for his absence?

But then, none of that mattered, did it?

"Where have you been, Papa?" Verity asked, giving voice to Johanna's inner turmoil in her innocent way. "Miss McKenna and I were just about to sing a silly song. Would you care to join us?"

"No silly songs today, poppet," he said. "But I do understand Mrs. Cuthbert has made some cocoa biscuits just now. Why do you not run along and have a taste of them, see if they are as good as the ones Monsieur Favreau makes?"

"But Papa," Verity protested. "I would rather sing with Miss McKenna than eat biscuits."

"Off with you, poppet," he told her, his voice firm, though tender. "There will be plenty more opportunities for you to sing your ditties with Miss McKenna."

Verity cast a glance in Johanna's direction.

No, there will not be, Johanna wanted to cry out.

But her heart was still breaking, and she could not seem to find the strength within her to say a single word. And so she smiled reassuringly at Felix's daughter instead.

"I shall go," Verity decided, "but only because Papa demands it. I am certain no one can compete with Monsieur's biscuits."

Felix was only halfway across the chamber from her now, drawing nearer. And she could feel her inner resolve weakening accordingly. There were the lips she had kissed, just this morning. There was the body that had been so strong and powerful beneath hers. His cat's eyes were fathomless this morning.

How she wished she knew what he was thinking.

"Go on now, poppet," he instructed Verity.

Verity curtseyed, and then she flounced from the room.

Felix watched her go before turning back to Johanna and closing the last of the distance between them. His gaze searched her face. "Good morning, Johanna. You are well?"

She knew what he was asking, and her cheeks went hot. "Quite well, Your Grace."

"Verity is likely halfway to the kitchens," he countered, his voice low. "You need not resort to formality with me now."

"I am afraid I must," she said. "What happened between us, it was wonderful, Felix, and I shall hold the memories in my heart forever. But what we need most—what you and Lady Verity need right now—is to be safe. You will not be safe for as long as I remain beneath your roof."

"You belong here," he argued, reaching for her hands.

She clutched him back, much to her shame, linking her fingers through his. Because she could not resist. One last touch. One last time...

"I do not belong anywhere," she corrected him gently. "I never have."

"Perhaps not before, but you belong here now." He pulled her gently into his chest. "You cannot imagine I will let you go, Johanna."

"You must," she insisted. "The danger is far too great. If something were to happen to you or to Lady Verity, I could never forgive myself."

"I understand how you feel, because I feel exactly the same." His gaze was tender. "I want to protect you. I *will* protect you."

She wanted to look away, but she could not. This man had become her greatest weakness. Every part of her longed for him. Her body, her heart, her mind.

But it was not meant to be.

"This is not your battle to fight, Felix," she told him. "I alone am to blame for the untenable position in which I now find myself. I must face this on my own."

"You will face it at my side." He withdrew his hand from hers and cupped her face. "As my wife. Marry me, Johanna."

She stared, certain she had misheard him. Foolish, foolish heart to invent fictions. Stupid, wild imagination. Fleeting, nonsensical fancy. Or perhaps she had fallen asleep, and this was nothing but a dream.

She blinked, and the Duke of Winchelsea still stood before her, wearing the same earnest expression upon his handsome face. Looking as serious and somber as he ever had. He seemed to be awaiting an answer from her, which was entirely silly. But it was apparent that he was all too real, and she was not, in fact asleep. Still touching her face as gently as if she were fashioned from the finest porcelain.

She had to say something.

"I beg your pardon?" she asked him. "I must have misheard you."

He lowered his lips to hers then for a long, slow kiss.

When he pulled back at last, she almost forgot all her objections.

Almost.

"If you heard me asking you to marry me," he said, "then you did not mishear at all. You would do me the greatest honor, Johanna McKenna, if you would agree to become my wife. My duchess."

His words were so fantastical, so unexpected, that for a moment she could do nothing more than gape at him, wondering if he had somehow gone mad in the course of the hours since she had seen him last. He appeared quite serious, however. Quite sane.

Except for the words he had uttered.

"You cannot wish to marry me," she said. "I am not at all the sort of woman a duke would take to wife. Indeed, I am no lady. I am a woman who has always treasured her independence. I am an actress. I have committed scandalous sins in my past. I was an unwed mother. And beyond all that, I am the sister of a Fenian."

"Everything you have said is true," he observed calmly. "With the exception of three of your statements, I shall not offer any arguments. However, I must point out that I do wish to marry you, you are just the sort of woman this duke would take to wife, and you are, indeed, a lady of the finest mettle. As for treasuring your independence, I can see and admire that in you, and I would never seek to encroach upon yours when we are wed. You are one of the most talented actresses of our age. You were taken advantage of by a much older man you viewed as a brother, and when he abandoned you, you did everything in your power to care for your daughter, and—"

"Stop," she interrupted him, unable to listen to him extol her virtues for another second. "You make me sound so good. I am not, Felix. I am weak, and I have allowed my brother to rule me when I knew better. I failed to fight when I should have. I should have been stronger, too, with Pearl's father. I should have known better."

He stopped her with a finger pressed over her lips. "Hush.

You are good, Johanna. You are one of the most kindhearted people I have ever met. I have never met another woman as good as you, aside from one."

When he paused and clenched his jaw, he did not need to say more. She knew who he referred to. And though in a sense, she was honored he compared her to the woman he had so worshiped and loved, she was also acutely aware of what that appraisal meant for her.

"I am not her," she told him, the fear that had been slowly burning inside her for the last few days finally finding its voice. "I am not your wife, Felix."

She had no wish to be the replacement for the woman he loved. She was not a different version of his former duchess. She was herself. And she had no doubt his wife would have been perfection. Her hair would have always been neatly tamed into the most fashionable styles. Her dresses would have been the latest styles from Parisian fashion. She would have been an aristocrat. A lady. Someone who had been born and bred to be a duchess. Someone who would have brought neither shame nor scandal to his name.

Someone he could have been proud of.

"You will be my wife," he countered. "When you marry me."

"No." She shook her head, steeling herself against a bitter flood of tears that threatened to consume her. The fear of inadequacy was beginning to steal her breath. "That is not what I meant. You misunderstand me. And you do so intentionally, I think."

His gaze searched hers, unfathomable. "What would you have me say, Johanna?"

"The truth," she whispered. "Tell me the truth, Felix. Do not insult my intelligence by expecting me to blindly believe you want to make an American actress who once bore a child out of wedlock your wife."

His expression hardened, becoming impassive. "I do not scorn your past. I, too, have a past. Just as we all have."

But that was not the point.

"We all have pasts, yes, but not all of our pasts are as scandalous as mine," she reminded him gently. "You are a nobleman. You are held to different, higher standards. I am a lowly American girl. I am a no one. A nothing."

"There is nothing," he said, his voice vibrating with quiet fury, "not one single thing about you that is lowly, Johanna. Nor are you no one or a nothing. You are the most gifted actress I have ever seen tread the boards. You are the great Rose Beaumont. You have worked so hard to be who you are, to attain what you have. There is no shame in that, only pride."

How easy it was for a man to say that. For a duke. There was shame in who she was. In what she had done. And that same shame had followed her here, to London. She was still the same woman he had invited only to the home he had shared with his paramours.

And while she had accepted it before, in the maelstrom surrounding them, she could not forget it now. Not when she needed to remember it most. And use it like a shield. A protective shield.

"And was it pride in my abilities that led you to want to take me to bed?" she asked, finding the courage to ask the question. "Was it pride that kept you from inviting me to your true home? Was it pride that relegated me to this townhome, with its remembrances of all your former paramours?"

She loved Felix. She knew she did. But she could not accept being his wife, his duchess, because she did not belong to his world. He was infatuated with her, she was sure of it, and he was allowing those feelings to rule his common sense.

There was no other reason why a man like the Duke of Winchelsea would ask Johanna McKenna—or even Rose Beaumont, for that matter—to become his wife.

"No," he said, his voice low, the lone word sounding as if it had been torn from him. "It was not."

"You were ashamed of me, then?" she asked.

It was a necessary question, but she did not relish the asking. Nor the response.

"I was not ashamed of you," he denied. "But I was looking to protect Verity. My daughter is everything to me, and you know that."

Of course she knew how much his daughter meant to him.

"It is because of Verity and how much I care for the both of you that I cannot possibly marry you," she said brokenly. "Can you not see that?"

"I have fallen in love with you, Johanna," he told her then. "Against my better judgment, it is true. I never thought my heart would find another woman I was capable of loving after Hattie died. But then I met you, and you proved otherwise. You brought me back to life again. In the past two days, you have brought more joy and laughter to Verity and me than we have had in the past five years. And I am a greedy, selfish man. I want that lightness, that happiness. I want you for myself."

She searched his gaze, his countenance, for some sign he was jesting. That he was toying with her. Because surely he could not have just said he loved her.

Surely not.

Unless…

Could it be?

"Felix," she said softly. "What can you be thinking? Did

you not listen to any of the things I have said? You do not love me. You cannot love me."

Although there was nothing she wanted more in this world than Felix's love—and to become his wife—she knew she could not. His proposal, and indeed, even his confession, were rash and rushed. Quite unlike the man she had come to know.

"I can," he assured her, "and I do. But I will be honest with you now, Johanna. There is another reason why I have asked you to marry me today, aside from the way I feel for you."

Ah, there it was. Another reason. The true motive behind his abrupt proposal. She had not been wrong in her assessments, then.

She stiffened, preparing for whatever it was he had to say, certain it would not be anything she wanted to hear. "What reason could you possibly have for wanting to marry me, Felix?"

"To protect you." His jaw tightened, a grim note she had not heard before underlying his words. "I received word this morning that the Special Investigative Unit of Scotland Yard intends to arrest you."

Shock hit her, and she felt, for a beat, as if all the air had been stolen from her lungs. Her knees went weak as one of her greatest fears washed over her.

"Arrest me," she repeated, her lips numb, coldness seeping into her marrow.

"Yes." Felix paused, closing his eyes for a moment as if he, too, were struggling to compose himself. "It is not the sole reason why I wish to make you my duchess, Johanna. But it is the reason why I must do so imminently."

"You must marry me imminently," she said, struggling to comprehend everything he had just revealed to her. "Why?"

She had already been in shock from his unexpected proposal. She had begun their interview believing she would be telling him goodbye, believing these precious few minutes were the last she could ever allow herself to have with him.

But now, he had told her he loved her.

That he wanted to marry her.

Still, any incipient joy she experienced because of the first two was crushed beneath the gripping weight of the next, undeniable fact.

It was all because she was going to be arrested.

"Scotland Yard intends to arrest you soon," he said. "Perhaps today. We have not much time to tarry. When I was gone this morning, I was securing the license we need to marry. Fortunately, I was able to procure it in time."

The weakest part of her was tempted to accept Felix's proposal. But neither her pride nor her heart would allow her to do so.

"How will marrying me keep me from being arrested?" she asked, still struggling to make sense of everything.

Fearing there was no possible way to make sense of it.

"I will not be able to testify against you," he answered swiftly, "regarding the trunk and the explosives you smuggled into England. From what I understand, Scotland Yard intends to use one of your brother's men as Queen's Evidence against you."

Before Johanna could offer a response, there was a commotion at the door to the study. She heard the familiar voice of the butler raised in alarm, mingling with other male voices.

He was too late, she realized. They were already coming for her.

Stricken, her gaze searched Felix's.

The door burst open.

A handful of men stormed over the threshold.

"Johanna McKenna," one of them said.

Her eyes slid closed, all the fight draining from her. "I will go with you. You need not say anything more."

"Johanna," Felix cried.

Rough hands took her by the arms, dragging her from Felix's comforting embrace. She allowed it, her resistance gone. Like always, the sins of the past had a way of inevitably returning to the present, and it would seem the time had come for her to face her fate.

"Step aside, your Grace," ordered another of the men. "We are under orders to arrest her on suspicion of conspiracy."

"By whose authority, damn you?" Felix demanded.

"The Criminal Investigation Department of Scotland Yard," answered another as manacles were placed on Johanna's wrists.

They closed with the snap of grim finality.

Chapter Fourteen

JOHANNA WAS SEATED across from a detective. After she had been taken from Felix's home, she had been driven to the Scotland Yard offices where, she had been informed, all Fenian investigations were conducted. She had been handled quite roughly by the men who had taken her into custody despite Felix's protestations. Her hands had been shackled, and she had been treated much in the manner of a prisoner. Pushed and prodded. Spoken to in short sentences. Reviled.

It only occurred to her as she settled into the small and windowless room where she had been taken to await her fate that she was a prisoner. The questioning was a formality. She would be going to prison.

The realization left her chilled. Almost numb. She attempted to distract herself with details. To forget about what was to come and to protect herself as best she could. For Felix could not save her from the tangled web in which she now found herself. No one could.

The table at which they sat was bare. The chair was stiff-backed and hard. The man facing her was, she judged, ten years or so her senior. Dark whiskers covered his jaw, and he was dour and unsmiling. He possessed the air of a man who had found great disappointment in his life and was determined to make everyone around him pay for his displeasure.

He pinned her with his flinty gaze.

"Miss McKenna," he said, his tone almost conversational, "I am Mr. Ravenhurst, and quite pleased to make your acquaintance. Would you care for a cup of tea before we begin?"

His query was not what she had expected. But tea was the last thing on her mind. And she recognized the false cheer in his tone for what it was, an attempt to get her to warm to him. A means of facilitating his questions.

"No, thank you," she said. "I would prefer to face whatever is in store for me rather than delay."

"A woman of decision," he observed, flashing her a grim smile. "I admire your eagerness to arrive at the reason for your presence here."

"Yes," she agreed, swallowing down a knot of fear.

"You are an actress by trade, are you not, Miss McKenna?" he asked, almost lazily.

"I am." Her shackles had been removed, and her hands were now in her lap. Belatedly, she realized she was clutching at her gown with such desperation, her fingers were biting into her thighs. Later, she would probably find bruises.

She forced herself to exhale.

"And your name for the stage," he added. "It is Miss Rose Beaumont. Is that correct?"

"It is," she acknowledged.

"Do you deny being the sister of Mr. Drummond McKenna?" he asked next.

"No," she said quietly. "I do not deny that. He is my brother."

He had also been her curse. Her bane. Her tormentor.

And, it would seem, her ultimate downfall.

"Your brother, Drummond McKenna, provided you with a trunk for your journey from New York City to Liverpool, is that accurate, Miss McKenna?" he queried.

The words Felix had whispered in her ear returned to her then.

Admit nothing.

It occurred to her that perhaps her best chance at fighting for her freedom was not to acknowledge the truth. The truth was damning. She would have to think of this as yet another role. She was playing a part.

"I am not aware of such a trunk," she told the detective.

"The Duke of Winchelsea contacted the Special League with information concerning a trunk in your possession," he countered, his false smile once more in place. "A trunk which had been given to you by Mr. Drummond McKenna. The trunk was said to contain lignin dynamite, nitroglycerin, and a packet of correspondence. Do you now deny its existence?"

Had there been nitroglycerin? She had only known of the dynamite and the letters. She wondered if the man before her was adding to the information he possessed to scare her, or if he had been provided with false information.

Her heart was beating fast. Her mouth was dry. Everything within her screamed to tell the truth. To admit to the trunk, to explain how it had come into her possession. To reveal the full extent of her brother's campaign of torture.

But again, she heard Felix's voice.

Admit nothing.

And she believed in him. Because if she did not believe in the man she had come to love, what else had she to believe in?

"I do not know of the trunk you speak of, sir," she said, forcing herself to be calm. "Nor am I familiar with such contents. I never was in possession of such an item."

"You are lying, madam," he accused.

She met his gaze without flinching or looking away. "I do not recall such a trunk, sir. I would think I should know if I had dynamite in my possession. Do you not think so?"

His lips thinned. "Do you think because you are warming the bed of the Duke of Winchelsea that you are above reproach, Miss McKenna?"

"I do not presume to think I am above anything, sir," she said, for this was the truth, regardless of how badly his words had stung.

She did not want to think of herself in those terms, as if she were a mistress. A lightskirt. As if she ought to be ashamed of herself. She was not ashamed. She would never be ashamed of what she had shared with Felix. Nor would she ever be ashamed of the love she felt for him.

"You are aware, Miss McKenna, that Winchelsea was initially charged with watching you," Mr. Ravenhurst said. "That is the reason you exerted your wiles upon him, is it not?"

She frowned, attempting to make sense of what he had just said.

"Winchelsea was charged with watching me," she repeated.

"In the course of his work for the Home Office, yes," agreed her captor. "You were aware of Winchelsea's position, and that is why you chose him as your target."

"I had no target." Confusion warred with dread, deep within her. "Nor had I any knowledge of the Duke of Winchelsea's work for the Home Office. Indeed, I do not know what the Home Office is."

Ravenhurst's eyes narrowed. "Of course you do, Miss McKenna. You may have easily influenced Winchelsea with your beautiful face, but I am not a man so diverted by the female form. You know very well that Winchelsea was tasked with investigating your involvement with Mr. Drummond McKenna. You knew Winchelsea was attempting to use you to lure Mr. McKenna to London."

His words sent another chill through her.

Because either he was lying to manipulate her, or there was some truth to his words. And if there was truth to his words, it sounded as if Felix was somehow involved in all of this.

But, of course, he could not be. He had never breathed a word of such involvement to her. The man before her was prevaricating. That was the only truth she could believe. Her heart told her anything else was wrong.

"I am not familiar with anything you have just said, Mr. Ravenhurst," she said.

"But of course you are," he countered, before pausing and studying her. "The Duke of Winchelsea was using you, my dear, in much the same way you are using him."

"Which way is that, sir?" she asked, feeling as if the ground had been pulled from beneath her. "I confess, I do not follow your reasoning."

One moment, she had been certain.

And now, she was...

Dear God, she could not bear to contemplate the way she felt. But the doubt was everywhere, infectious. Filling her with trepidation and dread.

Shaking her.

Shaking everything she thought she had known...

"Winchelsea was using you to further the investigation into your brother," Ravenhurst said smoothly. "Just as you were using him to keep from being arrested. And yet, here you are. Your plans did not come to fruition in the manner you had hoped."

Felix had been investigating Drummond?

But how could that be? When she had laid bare all the painful details of her past, he had never for one moment suggested he was already familiar with her brother's name. Or with her. Or with any detail remotely connected to herself, her brother, or the Fenians.

"Winchelsea was not investigating me," she denied.

Felix, her Felix, would never betray her in such a fashion. She was sure of it.

"Of course he was," Mr. Ravenhurst said. "Winchelsea himself was responsible for bringing you here to London."

"Explain yourself, if you please," she demanded. "How can His Grace have been responsible for my time here? I was hired by the Crown and Thorn."

Her entire being was cold, as if she had just plunged into the waters of a frozen winter's lake.

"By Mr. Theo Saville," the detective agreed. "Saville is a close friend of Winchelsea's. He was willing to accommodate Winchelsea's request. Surely His Grace mentioned all this to you in the course of your…relationship with him. Did he not?"

No, he most certainly had not. He had mentioned nothing of the sort.

Felix was friends with Mr. Saville. She knew that much herself without having to ask.

"His Grace is a very private man," she said, attempting to deflect any further attention upon her relationship with Felix to another matter.

To anything else.

For her own sake as well as for her wellbeing and future freedom.

She could not afford any more mistakes. She had already lived a life of so many. From the time she had run away from her father and the life she had detested, she had been fleeing. Too fearful to settle down and find a home anywhere, with anyone.

Felix had changed that for her.

For the first time, she had wanted to stay with him. To remain with him, wherever he was. She wanted him to be her home.

"Winchelsea is indeed a private man," Ravenhurst agreed. "He has always been a bastion of honor, which is why I am perplexed by the manner in which he has attempted to protect you. His instinct to keep you safe, I can only put down to your seductress ways. You have brought a great man low, and for that you must be well-pleased with yourself."

She would never be happy with herself for bringing Felix low.

"I am no seductress, sir," she denied.

"There is no need to lie, Miss McKenna. The evidence speaks for itself. Why else would a dignified member of the Home Office, a man charged with overseeing the operations of the Special League, be so determined to protect you?" he asked.

She struggled to understand what Ravenhurst had just revealed to her. She understood that the Special League was a force tasked with attempting to curtail Fenian activities throughout England and Ireland. But as for who that man might be, or what it had to do with the Home Office, she was at a loss.

"Forgive me," she began hesitantly, "but I am afraid you will have to explain yourself further. I do not know who you speak of or what these charges are which you have presumed to level against me."

He smiled slowly. "I speak of the Duke of Winchelsea, of course. Do not play the actress with me, my dear. I know you are entirely aware of the role His Grace plays in Her Majesty's government."

Felix was involved in counter-Fenian enforcement? Involved in the government?

Everything inside her went cold. He had never said a word. Not in all the time they had spent together. Not when she had confessed everything to him. Not when she had told him she was in possession of dynamite. Not when he had kissed her or held her. Most definitely not when he had shared her bed.

"You are telling me that His Grace is the reason I am under arrest?" she asked, a sick sense of betrayal brewing inside her, filling her stomach with a churning sea of nausea.

"You are under arrest because you admitted to brining lignin dynamite into England with the express purpose of delivering it to known Fenians," Ravenhurst countered. "Fortunately, that information was given to us by Winchelsea before you were able to sufficiently work your wiles upon him."

"I asked him to give that information to the proper authorities," she said, still struggling to make sense of the situation.

"The Duke of Winchelsea was the proper authority," Ravenhurst informed her. "But of course, you knew that when you fabricated your plan to seduce him. Do not think for a moment that your naïve innocence act is deceiving me. Was it your brother's idea, or was it yours, Miss McKenna, to infiltrate counter-Fenian operations? It was a clever notion, I will admit."

She stared at Ravenhurst, the betrayal merging with anguish. If what he was telling her was true, that meant Felix had deceived her. That Felix had used her. That perhaps everything he had told her, everything he had shared with her, had been a lie.

That he had been manipulating her all along.

"I had no such plan," she defended herself, finding her voice at last. "My only plan was to thwart my brother using whatever means I could. I want his men to be arrested. I want him to be brought to justice."

"Ah, and now you will act the part of the martyr."

"I am not a martyr," she denied, tears burning her eyes. Tears of frustration. Of rage. Of confusion. "I am just a woman who was trying to escape a desperate situation. A woman who was trying to do what was right and protect myself at the same time."

And Felix had taken her trust and abused it. He had lied to her.

Dear God, he had been in her bed. Had told her he had tender feelings for her. He had offered to make her his wife, had delivered such a pretty speech. He had made her believe him. Had made her believe *in* him. Had made her love him.

How dare he?

"What you are, Miss McKenna," said Ravenhurst calmly and coldly, "is a Fenian viper. An excellent actress and seductress. But your games have ended. Give me all the information you possess on your brother, and I will consider reducing the charges which will be laid against you."

Charges.

She was going to go to prison.

This was it, then. The end. For once she reached prison, surely Drummond's foot soldiers would find her. She was as good as dead.

She inhaled slowly, trying to decide what her next course of action should be.

But before she could speak, the world exploded around her.

And then, everything went black.

FELIX WAS DESPERATE.

Desperate to find a way to save the woman he loved from being incarcerated for a crime she had not committed. Watching her being taken away by Scotland Yard detectives earlier that day, knowing there was nothing he could do to stop them, had been akin to a dagger in the heart.

After seeing to Verity's safety and making certain she would be well looked after and guarded, he had gone immediately to Arden. It required every shred of control he possessed to walk calmly behind Arden's butler as he showed him to the study. Everything within him was crying out and raging to chase after Johanna. To save her.

But he knew he had to proceed with caution. He needed to approach Johanna's arrest with as clear and untroubled a mind as he could manage. Because she needed him now more than she ever had before.

Guilt skewered him as the butler announced him and he stalked into Arden's study. If he had procured the license quicker, if he had not bungled his proposal, they would have been wed. As his duchess and a peeress, her standing would have been much greater. His position with the Home Office would have benefited her in a way it could not now.

Arden stood at his entrance. "Winchelsea."

"Arden," he greeted in turn. "Scotland Yard detectives forced their way into my home a mere hour ago. They took Johanna and are charging her with conspiracy."

"Damn Ravenhurst," Arden swore. "He is overstepping his bounds."

"Yes," Felix agreed angrily. "He most certainly is. The Home Office and the Special League have been directing all inquiries into Fenian operations for the past three years. The establishment of this new arm of Scotland Yard does not give them the power to make arrests without our consent."

"I am afraid he and his cronies believe it does," Arden said, his tone grim. "I have suspected them of keeping the League and the Home Office out of their circle of information, but this move confirms it."

The insubordination of Ravenhurst and Scotland Yard's Criminal Investigation Department was a matter he would be forced to address, but it would have to wait until later. For now, Felix's chief concern was Johanna and how he could best procure the means to see her freed.

The mere thought of her confined in prison was enough to rob him of breath. It was not to be borne.

"We will pursue that matter as we must," Felix said. "For now, I am most worried about what we can do for Johanna."

"Your feelings for her run deeper than you previously suggested," Arden observed shrewdly.

"I am in love with her," he said baldly. "There is no point in denying it. If loving her means I must step down from my position in the Home Office, I will. But not before doing everything in my power to see her released and freed of any charges the CID is attempting to lay against her."

"Damn it all, Winchelsea," Arden said, releasing a weary-sounding sigh. "I thought no one could muck up matters more than I could, first with the Duke of Strathmore, then with the duchess. A fine pair we make, do we not?"

"I suppose love will do that to a man." He paused, still acquainting himself to the notion that he had fallen hopelessly in love with Johanna. "I confess, I do not recall being so tied up in knots the first time."

"Undoubtedly, that is because you did not fall in love with an American actress with ties to the Fenian cause," Arden observed wryly. "I cannot say I blame you, however, having fallen prey to an American woman myself. Albeit, not one with a violent criminal for a brother. Or one who smuggled lignin dynamite into England."

"Enough," Felix bit out. "Johanna is an innocent pawn in her brother's games."

"Time will tell," Arden quipped.

Felix could not blame him, for he had been hard on the duke in the wake of the scandal he had created by nearly having a League agent wrongly incarcerated on charges of treason. By his own admission, Johanna's story sounded damning indeed. Part of him could not fault anyone for thinking her guilty.

But he knew her.

He knew her heart.

He had been closer to her than anyone. Inside her, for God's sake.

"Time can sod off," he told Arden. "I am telling you now. Johanna is innocent of all charges. She did not commit conspiracy and nor did she willingly smuggle the dynamite. She was forced to by McKenna, who has been waging a private campaign of terror upon her for years."

"We can agree upon one fact, at least," Arden observed. "McKenna must be stopped."

But not at the expense of Johanna. Felix would not allow her to become a casualty in the war on Fenians.

He was about to say as much when a quick rap sounded on the study door.

"Enter," Arden called.

"This just arrived for Your Grace," said his butler, bearing a missive Felix instantly recognized as being a League communication.

"Thank you," Arden said, striding forward and accepting the message from his butler. "That will be all."

He scarcely waited for the door to close before tearing open the missive and hastily scanning the contents. Felix's stomach was weighed with dread as he watched Arden's expression change.

"What is it?" he demanded, praying silently that the message was not somehow about Johanna.

"Explosions are being reported," Arden said grimly. "One in St. James's Square, another at the home of an MP, another at Scotland Yard."

"Scotland Yard," he repeated, everything inside him freezing.

One word, one face filled his desperate thoughts.

Johanna.

Dear God, Johanna.

"Johanna was taken there," he said. "My God, Arden. Is there word of the damages? Are there injuries?"

Arden's face was ashen, his mouth drawn tight. "The report only says that severe damage and injuries are confirmed. There is another suspected device which was found in Trafalgar Square, at the base of Nelson's Column. It did not explode."

Bloody, bloody hell.

"I have to get to her," he said, even as the same old panic assailed him.

It was visceral. Like a hand closing on his throat. His chest hurt. He felt hot and dizzy. A cold sweat beaded on his forehead. The signs were undeniable, the fear, the pounding of his heart, as if it were about to burst free of his chest. He was about to suffer one of his fits.

He clenched his fists, denial roaring through him as he attempted to ward it off. He could not afford to be laid low now. But his vision was darkening, and he could not seem to drag in a breath.

The last fit to claim him had been when Verity had been lost after the fire. And Johanna had been there with a calming hand, a reassuring voice. But she was not here this time.

Indeed, she may never be again...

The explosions. Injuries. Arden's pallor. Johanna's tear-stained face as she had been led away. She was alone. Without anyone to protect her. Without anyone to save her. And there had been dynamite.

All the facts swirled together in a sickening sea of dread. If something had happened to her, he did not know how he would make it through such a loss. Especially when he had only just found her.

It was terrifying. He attempted to drag in a breath, but his lungs were burning. The walls around him seemed close. Too close.

"Winchelsea?"

From far away, the concerned voice of Arden reached him, pricking through the haze of panic infecting his mind. Laying him low. Making him weak.

Think of Johanna, he told himself.

You must be strong for her.

You must find her. Make sure she is safe.

At last, he inhaled. The breath was a struggle. But after it followed another, and then another. And Arden was there at his side, pressing a whisky into his hand.

"Drink this to calm yourself," he ordered. "We will go to Scotland Yard posthaste and find out what has happened."

With great effort, he unclenched his fist, his hand trembling as he accepted the tumbler from Arden. He blew out another unsteady breath and tilted his head back, downing the contents of the glass in one gulp. It burned a path of fire straight to his gut.

But with it came a return to lucidity. He fought back against the panic. Pushed it back down where it belonged, in the dark recesses of his mind. Decisiveness returned to him, and he was able to think. To breathe.

"Thank you," he managed to tell Arden, grateful for the man's calming presence at his side. "Let us go now. We have not a moment to spare or waste."

Arden nodded. "Time is of the essence, more now than ever."

Truer words, Felix was sure, had never been uttered.

Chapter Fifteen

J OHANNA WAS LOST at sea, alone in the darkness. The waves were storm-tossed. Lightning bolts shot across the sky. Ominous thunder boomed, the crack of it so loud, she could feel the reverberation in her chest. Her heart was thumping wildly, her mouth dry.

She was in a boat, but the vessel was taking on water as rain poured from the angry skies overhead. She was cold—colder than she had ever been—and drenched. Her skirts were sodden, her hair matted to her face. That was when she saw the hole in the bottom of the boat. Water was rushing up from the sea beneath her, threatening to fill the boat and sink her.

She scrambled to find something to plug the hole, but the boat was slippery. She fell headlong into the water, and for a moment she feared she would drown then and there. But somehow, she found the power to rise to her knees. Thinking she might use it to cover the hole, she clawed at a piece of wooden trim on the boat until her fingers bled. Until the fleshy pads felt as if they were on fire and the pain of a hundred tiny splinters embedded in her skin left her screaming.

The rain turned to hail, pelting her. Hitting her head, her face. Her head began to ache abominably. There was a white light searing her eyes from seemingly nowhere, and a voice she had never before heard was calling her name…

"Miss McKenna, can you hear me?"

The unfamiliar female voice cut through the nightmare, gradually chasing it from Johanna's mind. The light was still there, however. Bright and painful. Everything seemed painful, actually. Her body felt as if it had been run over by a team of carriage horses.

"Miss McKenna?"

With great difficulty, Johanna opened her eyes, blinking slowly as her blurred vision settled and became clear. Why were her eyelids so heavy? And why did she feel so strange, almost as if she were removed from her body, aside from the throbbing pain in her head.

A brunette woman, finely dressed in a smart periwinkle blue gown, hovered over her, her expression one of concern. "Miss McKenna?"

"Yes," she managed to rasp past a tongue that seemed to have gone unbearably dry. Confusion washed over her. "Who are you, and where am I?"

The woman offered her a kind smile. "I am the Duchess of Arden, and you are at my home. But I would be pleased if you would call me Hazel."

Johanna was more confused than ever. "Forgive me, but how did I come to be at your home?"

She struggled to remember what had happened, but her head hurt with a devilish ferocity. She could recall Felix's proposal, followed by her arrest. Then, the interview with Ravenhurst. Then nothing more.

"You were at the Scotland Yard offices yesterday, being questioned by Mr. Ravenhurst," said the woman—Hazel, she supposed, for Johanna had already forgotten what manner of duchess she had called herself.

"I recall," she said, still searching her mind, desperate for answers. It was as if a great, gaping hole had been blown into her memory...

And then, suddenly, remembrance hit her.

All the discoveries she had made about Felix. Every word Ravenhurst had said, all the revelations. The painful truths she had learned. The slicing pain of his betrayal.

The explosion.

Yes, she remembered it now, all at once. There had been a roaring in her ears, the very world had seemed to shake, and then a driving pain had radiated through her skull. She had fallen, headlong, into oblivion.

"A bomb exploded outside the offices," Hazel said slowly. "You were injured when the ceiling of the room you were being questioned in collapsed. Fortunately, you were not in a chamber with windows, or the damage could have been far worse."

Dear God, it *had* been a bomb. Likely planted by one of her brother's men.

She hesitated as that devastating information settled into her mind. "How did I come to be at your home?"

"Winchelsea felt the risk of taking you to a hospital was too great," Hazel told her gently. "Returning you to his home would have also put you in danger."

Winchelsea.

Felix.

A far greater pain sliced through her then at the thought of him. At the thought of all his lies and betrayals. His manipulation of her. Despite everything, her heart still ached for him. She still loved him. Longing slid through her—the need to see him, to touch him—before she could quell it.

"He is not here now, is he?" she asked, praying the answer would be no.

"Of course he is," confirmed Hazel. "Do you wish to see him, my dear?"

"No." The answer left her like the blast of a shotgun: a

quick, angry report.

"Forgive me, my dear." Hazel's countenance turned troubled. "He has been here by your side since you were brought here last night. I finally forced him to try to get some rest...I assumed you would be eager to see him as his fiancée."

As his fiancée.

The word left her cold.

Yet another lie in a sea of so many. Perhaps that was what her nightmare had signified—the water she had been adrift in, the water rushing in and filling her boat, threatening to drown her. She felt a myriad of emotions, all of them so much the same, though she was lucid.

"I am not his fiancée," she denied. "Nor do I have any wish to see the duke."

Hazel's brow furrowed. "Winchelsea was quite adamant you are. Your status as his betrothed, along with the fact you are a woman and you suffered a grievous injury, was enough to keep Scotland Yard from formally charging you for now."

If he expected her to be thankful to him for the lies he had told on her behalf, he would discover soon enough how little gratitude she possessed when it came to him. Her body was still in pain from the aftermath of the explosion, but her heart fared far worse.

"Since His Grace is the reason I was arrested by Scotland Yard in the first place, I can only presume he felt enough guilt to lie to attempt to keep me from prison while I am an invalid," she said, anger making her voice tremble.

She was weak, she was tired, and her heart was broken.

And then, quite belatedly, something else occurred to her.

She had trusted this woman because she seemed kind. Because she was at her bedside. Because she was a woman, a duchess.

But she clearly knew Felix well.

"Who are you to Winchelsea?" she asked, suspicion blossoming within her. "And why am I any safer here with you than I would be somewhere else?"

"I am Winchelsea's friend, you might say," Hazel told her quietly. "But I am also a detective myself who has aided in the investigations of the Special League alongside my husband, the Duke of Arden. In New York City, I was a Pinkerton agent. I infiltrated the Emerald Club to investigate your brother. Winchelsea hired me to help with investigations into your brother's men here in London. That is how I met my husband. Now that I am expecting a child, however, I have stepped down from my role, and the Duke of Westmorland will be taking my place."

Dread enveloped her. Was there no one here she could trust? How prophetic her dream was, for she was alone, in a sinking boat, in the midst of a vast and angry ocean. No one to save her. There was only one way this story could end, and it was with her sinking to the bottom of the sea.

"Perhaps you wish to arrest me then," she bit out, doing her best to stare down the duchess, even from her sickbed, weak as she felt.

"I wish for no such thing," Hazel told her softly, giving her hand a gentle pat where it was fisted in the bedclothes. "What I want is for you to get well, my dear, so this mess in which you have found yourself can be sorted out properly."

Johanna did not dare believe it. She had been manipulated enough. "Thank you for your hospitality, Duchess, but I cannot remain here beneath your roof a moment longer."

With her left hand, she attempted to flip back the bedclothes, only to cry out in anguish as a sharp pain exploded in her shoulder.

"Remain still, Miss McKenna," Hazel chastised. "You were quite badly bruised in the explosion. Indeed, you are lucky to be alive. You will be going nowhere until you are healed and until your brother is no longer a threat to your safety."

"Or until Scotland Yard decides to shackle me and cast me into prison," she countered bitterly. "I will not remain here."

"Yes," the duchess argued firmly, "you will. As your fellow countrywoman, I insist upon it. You must trust me to look after you on that count alone. But if nothing else, let me assure you we have a good deal more in common than you might suppose. I am your ally, Miss McKenna, like it or not."

"Not," she decided. "I cannot trust anyone after all the lies I have been told."

Hazel grasped her hand then, meeting Johanna's gaze. "I know of three people you can trust with your life, Miss McKenna. Myself, my husband, and most of all, Winchelsea. Believe what you may of him, but know that I have never met a finer gentleman than he. He is honorable, noble, and good."

She did not want to believe this.

Could not.

For she had the evidence to suggest otherwise.

"Do you deny he works for the Home Office?" she demanded.

Hazel shook her head. "No."

"And do you deny that he was watching me?" she asked. "That he knew about my connections to Drummond before he ever met me?"

"No," Hazel said gently. "But I also cannot deny the way he has been protecting you, tending to you, and worrying over you since yesterday. Actions do not lie even when words may seem to deceive and confuse us, Miss McKenna. Winchelsea is in love with you, and he is doing his best to keep you safe."

She could not bear to believe it.

Did not dare.

Her heart could not sustain one more blow from him. Already, she had given him so much. Indeed, she had given him *everything*. Her heart, her body, her trust.

"I wish I could believe you," she whispered, lost in pain—physical warring with emotional. "But I cannot."

"You cannot or you will not?" Hazel asked her shrewdly. "Whatever happened between you and Winchelsea, no one knows but the two of you. And that must be sorted out by you both accordingly. All I know is that I have an exhausted duke down the hall who will have my hide if I do not alert him to the fact that you are awake."

"Do not tell him," she begged, desperation eclipsing every other emotion.

Because if she had to face him now, after everything, she was not certain she could be strong enough. She was not sure she could resist him as she must.

"One way or another, you must see him, Miss McKenna," Hazel said, giving her a sympathetic smile. "But please know you are safe and welcome here at Lark House. If you will excuse me, I must send for the doctor so he can have a look at you now that you are awake."

With those parting words, the duchess rose to her commanding height and swept from the room with a regal elegance that belied her dress. For once she had stood, Johanna noted Hazel was wearing billowing trousers beneath her bodice. It had not been a gown she wore after all.

Here was another lesson that, like so many other things in life, all was not always as it seemed. But the fear inside her would not abate. And Johanna was not willing to give Felix the benefit of her doubt.

Instead, she would cling to her rage.

"How dare you come in here, Your Grace?" Johanna demanded, her voice vibrating with quiet fury.

The Duchess of Arden had warned him, of course, that the woman he loved had no wish to see him. That she had accused him of lying to her, which he had. That she had said he was responsible for her arrest by the CID, which he was. That she claimed she was not his betrothed at all.

Which she most decidedly—and to his great consternation—was not.

Thankfully, the clout he possessed within the Home Office had been enough to grant her a reprieve in the wake of the bombing and to keep her from the dank walls of a prison cell. He would do everything in his power to see that she remained free. And safe.

Everything.

Because he loved her.

God, how he loved the woman before him, the one spitting rancor and fire from her lips and her eyes. The one looking upon him now as if he were a lowly worm who had dared to cross her path.

She was not wrong in that assessment. For he felt like a worm for keeping the truth from her. He had not left her side from the time she had been pulled from the rubble of the Scotland Yard offices, bleeding from the head and insensate, and a few hours before when the duchess had demanded he seek a respite.

It had only been the need to stay strong for Johanna which had prompted him to retire to a guest chamber and attempt to nap. But sleep had not been forthcoming. He had lain in the bed, thinking of her, worrying over her.

Wondering when she would wake.

Wondering if she would wake.

"How do you feel?" he asked her instead of answering her brutal query.

She was wan, a bandage wrapped around her head, and scratches on her cheeks. But she had never looked more beautiful to him than she did then. She was alive. Awake and alive, thank God.

She was also angry with him, it was clear. What Ravenhurst had revealed to her remained to be seen. But he suspected it was everything, and in damning detail.

"I feel as if a roof fell upon my head," she said, still cold and pale, so unlike the laughing, vibrant, openhearted woman he had come to know. "And as if the man I believed loved me betrayed me in the cruelest fashion possible."

That hit him where he deserved it. With the force of a blow. But she could not be further from the truth.

"I do love you," he said, moving closer, drawn to her as a magnet though she was furious with him.

He needed to touch her. To prove to himself that she was real. The fear of losing her had been so tremendous, it had almost broken him. It had only been thoughts of Verity and of needing to see Johanna through this time of trial which had kept him going.

"Do not dare to mock me with more of your lies," she said, her voice bearing the lash and sting of a whip.

"I would never lie to you about the way I feel for you, Johanna," he said, closing the rest of the distance between them and folding himself into the chair at her bedside where he had spent so many listless, worried hours.

"What *would* you lie to me about?" she asked, her tone tart. Unforgiving and icy. "Everything else?"

"No," he denied, clenching his fists to keep from touching her. Seeing her alive, her face etched with pain, her complexion ashen, filled him with such an immense sense of relief, that it was all he could do to keep from taking her in his arms. Simply holding her to him, feeling the reassuring beat of her heart against his chest.

"Then you deny lying to me about who you were from the moment we met?"

Her voice was weakening, and he could plainly see the strain in her countenance. She had suffered a blow to the head when the Scotland Yard offices had come crashing down in the wake of the bombing. And numerous other injuries as well.

"You are unwell, Johanna," he said, hoping she would let the matter rest until she was at least somewhat healed. "Let us speak about this another day. For now, the most important thing is that you are awake. The doctor will examine you when he arrives, and I expect he will order some broth and rest."

How he wished his only concern was her welfare and recovery from the traumatic injuries she had sustained. But in truth, it was only a small part of the battle in this massive war they fought. He needed to keep her from prison, to keep her safe from her brother's wrath, to convince her she could believe in him… The list was as daunting as it was endless.

"I am unwell, it is true," she said, "but it is because of you, Your Grace. How dare you tell anyone that I am your betrothed?"

"I proposed to you," he reminded her.

"I denied you," she countered, "and then, I was hauled off to prison."

"I am sorry for that." *God*, how very sorry he was. He blamed himself for the way everything had unfolded. "If I had possessed an inkling of how quickly it would have happened—"

"You would have made certain to cozen me into marrying you so I was well and truly trapped?" she interrupted. "Was that your plan all along, Winchelsea? To stop my brother at any cost? Did I ever mean anything to you at all? Was it all a farce? Was everything we shared a lie? Did you seduce me so you could get to him?"

"I never had a plan when it came to you," he admitted, the words torn from him. "I was meant to, Johanna, but nothing has happened the way I expected it would, from the moment I first met you. Because that night, I met a woman I admired. A woman who was not just beautiful, but daring and bold. One who looked down her nose at me and told me *no* when I had expected her to say *yes*."

"I do not believe you," she said, hurt sparkling in her brilliant-blue gaze.

He did not expect her to.

He did not deserve her trust, and he knew it.

He had let her down in so many ways.

"Here is the truth, Johanna," he said, needing to explain himself even if she had no wish to hear it and even if she still rejected him at the end. "I have spent the last few years of my life devoted to my service to the Home Office. When dynamite began to be planted throughout England and when innocent civilians were wounded and hurt, I was compelled to do my part. I became involved in plans to capture your brother, using you as a lure. At the time, it was believed you were McKenna's mistress. The supposition was that you would possess knowledge of him better than anyone."

"And that is why you approached me that first night," she guessed.

"That is why you were offered the tour at the Crown and Thorn," he added. "I asked Theo to bring you here. In truth, your talent is undeniable and renowned, and Theo would have made you an offer regardless of my request."

She seemed to shrink away from him in the bed. "You knew, all along. You do not deny it. You knew who I was, and you intended to use me."

"I knew you were connected to McKenna," he corrected her. "I had no inkling you were his sister until you divulged that information to me. Nor did I know you had smuggled dynamite and correspondence here. But from the start, before I realized you had never been McKenna's mistress and that you possessed a heart that was true and good, I was inexplicably drawn to you. My attraction to you and my admiration for you were never feigned, Johanna. Please believe that. Nor was my love. Nor *is* my love."

Her lips tightened. "I wish I could believe anything you tell me, Your Grace, but I cannot."

"Will you not call me Felix?" he asked, hating the wall she had put up between them.

A wall of formality.

A wall of his own making, it was true.

He had been wrong, so wrong, and he knew that now. He had failed her on so many fronts. It was his fault she had been arrested, his fault she had been in the offices of Scotland Yard when the Fenian bomb laid in the street outside had exploded.

"To speak so familiarly suggests a relationship we do not have, Your Grace," she denied. "Indeed, we do not have a relationship at all."

Her words filled him with a new anguish. He had not lost her in the explosion, and yet, he was losing her anyway. He felt it as surely as he felt the chair beneath him. She was slipping away before his eyes. Retreating to a place deep inside herself. A place where he could not reach her. And he had forced her into it.

"I planned to tell you everything," he told her. "I would

have told you before, but everything was happening so suddenly."

"How convenient for you to believe that," she snapped. "You had ample opportunities to tell me the truth. You had days upon days to tell me. But you knew if you had, I would have never willingly allowed you into my bed."

She was right.

He could have told her.

He *should* have told her.

"The fear of losing you kept me from telling you," he said, being bitterly honest now. "I knew I had to, but I also knew I was falling in love with you. The moment just never seemed right. The risk was too great. I am a selfish fool when it comes to you, Johanna. An utter blockhead, and that is the undeniable truth."

"You lost me anyway," she told him, the sheen of tears in her eyes. "Please go now, and leave me in peace. I am weary and in pain, and I should like to rest before your police arrive to arrest me again."

Just the thought of the manacles being slapped on her wrists, watching her be led away from him, was enough to fill him with impotent rage all over again.

"You will not be arrested again, Johanna," he vowed. "Not if I have anything to say about it."

"Any more than you had a say about it the first time?" she asked.

"I do not blame you for not trusting me," he said, "but I am determined to make this right however I can. You do not deserve to be imprisoned for your brother's sins. Do you not see, Johanna? That is why you must marry me."

A tear trailed down her cheek. "I will not marry you, Your Grace. Not even to save myself. Go now. I am tired, and I do not want to look upon you for a moment more. It hurts too much."

He could have said the same. He hated himself for the suffering she had endured. For every hurt he had caused her.

"Think of me what you will," he said then, his voice low with sentiment. "But know that there is one thing I have never lied to you about, and that is loving you."

"Just go," she whispered, looking away from him. "Leave me, Winchelsea."

Swallowing against a knot of his own tears, he rose, offering her a bow. "The Duke and Duchess of Arden will keep you safe here, for as long as you need. I suggest you remain, for your own good."

Knowing her, she would attempt to flee the moment he left the chamber.

"What I do or do not do is no longer your concern, Your Grace," she said, her voice cold with finality. "You lost that right."

He had lost so much more than that.

As he left the chamber and the woman he loved behind, he knew he had to find a way to keep her safe. No matter the cost.

Chapter Sixteen

FELIX FACED THE chief investigator of the Scotland Yard Criminal Investigation Department. Like Johanna, Commissioner Vincent Ravenhurst had been injured in the Scotland Yard office bombing. Unlike her, however, he had not suffered a blow to the head.

Felix could not help but to think it rather a pity as he faced his nemesis now.

"What are you doing here, Winchelsea?" Ravenhurst asked.

He wore his left arm in a sling, and aside from some abrasions on his face, he looked hale and hearty as ever.

"I am here to aid in the investigation," he said calmly, knowing that what he was about to do would require every bit of sangfroid he possessed.

"The investigation into your slattern?" the Commissioner asked with a smirk.

It took all his control to keep from rising and planting his fist in the man's teeth.

"I do not have a slattern, Commissioner," he corrected. "The investigation I speak of is the one concerning lignin dynamite along with papers belonging to Drummond McKenna, the American Fenian who so recently orchestrated the bombings at the Praed Street and Charing Cross stations."

"Ah, yes," Ravenhurst said. "Mr. Drummond McKenna,

who happens to also be the brother of your slattern."

"There is no need to debase Miss McKenna," he gritted, allowing the Commissioner to get beneath his skin in spite of his best efforts not to. "She has no bearing upon this conversation, aside from the fact that she was wrongfully detained by your forces."

"I am not debasing her, Winchelsea, merely speaking plainly to you." Ravenhurst's eyes were hard, gleaming. He was a man intent upon his prey.

And his prey was Johanna.

But Felix was not going to allow that to happen.

Not on his watch.

Not ever.

"You have bedded her, have you not?" Ravenhurst asked. "I cannot blame you. She is a prime piece. I thought about having a go at her myself when I arrest her next. What do you think?"

He thought he was going to kill the Commissioner of the CID. That is what he thought. He clenched his jaw so hard, pain spiked through his skull.

"I have done nothing untoward with Miss McKenna, and I will thank you to speak of her in a respectful manner," he growled. "I came to you today to do you the courtesy of informing you that I plan to go above you, directly to the Home Secretary."

"Oh? And you plan to tell him what?" The smirk was back in place now. "That you have been fucking a Fenian actress who smuggled dynamite into Liverpool? That would be rich, Winchelsea."

Looking pleased with himself, Ravenhurst lit a pipe and stuffed it into his mouth, puffing a cloud of smoke into the air. The urge to deliver a drubbing to another man had never been stronger, burning to a seething crescendo inside Felix. It was only with the greatest exertion of his rigid control that he remained calm.

"I will tell him you are subverting the authority of the Home Office," he countered. "That you are conducting witch hunts involving innocent women. That you have been planting evidence upon suspected Fenians so you have cause to arrest them."

The last was information he had obtained directly from Arden, who had himself been pursuing an investigation into Ravenhurst's conduct. The recent CID arrest of one Irishman named John Tierney had been predicated upon the planting of evidence at his home in the form of nitroglycerine and explosive Atlas powder buried in the yard.

Ravenhurst looked distinctly less smug now. "I don't know what you're speaking of."

"Does the name John Tierney mean anything to you?" Felix asked, warming to his cause now that the tables had been so distinctly turned.

"Tierney was charged with conspiracy to cause an explosion," the Commissioner clipped. "He was found to be in possession of dynamite at the time of his arrest."

"Dynamite which was given to him by your own undercover agents," Felix accused. "The evidence against Tierney was manufactured. When you cannot find dynamitards, you make them yourself, is that not true?"

"Tierney is a known Fenian," Ravenhurst argued. "The case in his possession on his arrest was his own."

"In fact, he was asked to carry the case by your informant while he was traveling." Felix paused, and it was his turn to smile, for he felt the stirrings of victory over Ravenhurst. Everything was proceeding according to plan. Johanna would be free of suspicion before he was done. "When your men arrested him, they did not even open the trunk to determine the contents, did they? Why is that, I wonder? How could Mr. Tierney have been arrested for conspiracy to cause an explosion if no one knew what was actually in the trunk?"

The Commissioner paled, because he knew Felix was right. He also knew the evidence had been planted on Tierney, just as the mole within the CID ranks had claimed to Arden.

"That is a blatant falsehood," Ravenhurst bluffed. "The trunk was opened at the time of Tierney's arrest."

"No," Felix insisted, "it was not. The Special League is in possession of a sworn statement to the opposite. A concerned CID officer approached Arden with the information. The Home Office will not be pleased to receive this information or the statement, but I am obliged to provide both."

Ravenhurst sneered. "Do you think you can bribe me into keeping your slattern free of prison? Is that what this is, Winchelsea?"

Felix's fist slammed on the desk between him and the Commissioner with so much force, the blow echoed through the room. "I told you to speak of Miss McKenna with the respect she deserves. If you call her a slattern again, so help me, I will feed you your fucking teeth. Listen to me, Ravenhurst, and listen to me well because I shan't repeat myself. When I leave here, I am going directly to the Home Secretary. I will be accompanied by the Duke of Arden, who is in possession of the statement. I will tell him everything I know. I will also tell him about your false imprisonment of Miss Johanna McKenna, who is innocent of all charges you leveled against her."

"The Home Office was happy to see Tierney arrested," Ravenhurst said, stubborn to the last. "Do you really think the Home Secretary will give a damn how his arrest was secured?"

"Yes, I do expect the Home Secretary will object to the

violation of civil liberties and the planting of evidence upon a suspect," he gritted. "If you do not see the wrong in what you have done, then you have no right to claim to be a man upholding the law."

"Go ahead and fight for Tierney if you wish," Ravenhurst said, "but there is something you are forgetting, Winchelsea. Two very big, very undeniable somethings, in fact: the dynamite and the correspondence your slattern smuggled into England. I have an informant who was willing to turn Queen's Evidence against her. He will testify that she brought the dynamite here at her brother's behest, and that she met with him at the Royal Aquarium to deliver the correspondence, which included a list of public targets for future bombings."

Felix met Ravenhurst's stare unflinchingly, for he had already known this was the man's final trump card—the dynamite and the man Johanna had met at her brother's orders at the Royal Aquarium. But he had a more powerful move to make. The only one, in fact, he could. He had thought long and hard about what he was about to do, and the only conclusion he reached every time was that he would do anything—whatever he must—for the woman he loved.

"I will inform the Home Secretary that I was conducting my own campaign without the knowledge of the Home Office, the Special League, and the CID," he said. "During the course of my investigation, I contacted Johanna McKenna in New York and paid her to act as my informant. At my orders, she brought her brother's dynamite and correspondence to England. At my orders, she met with her brother's man at the Royal Aquarium. My staff will confirm I followed Miss McKenna to the aquarium on the day in question. I also ordered Miss McKenna to copy all the correspondence contained in the trunk prior to her turning it over."

"You are lying," Ravenhurst snarled, slamming his pipe down upon his desk. "You conducted no such campaign, and you know it."

"I will be bringing to the Home Secretary the trunk in question, which has been in my possession from the moment Miss McKenna arrived in London," he continued, unmoved by the other man's rage. "In it, the Home Secretary will find the dynamite, untouched, along with the copies of the correspondence I asked Miss McKenna to make, written in her own hand. The Duke and Duchess of Arden are willing to testify on my and Miss McKenna's behalf, along with the Duke of Westmorland. I feel confident the Home Secretary will see as clearly as I do that there is no evidence against Miss McKenna at all. Indeed, she has been working for the Home Office and for me, doing everything I asked of her."

"You would go that far for an Irish whore who treads the boards for her living?" Ravenhurst asked cruelly.

"I would go to the ends of the earth to protect an innocent woman from being imprisoned for a crime she did not commit," he corrected, standing.

And to protect the woman I love, he silently added. But he did not dare say those words aloud, for he could not give Ravenhurst any ammunition against him or Johanna.

Ravenhurst stood with such force, his chair toppled backward in a noisy clatter onto the wooden floor. "You will go to hell for this, Winchelsea," he vowed.

Felix sketched him an ironic bow. "If I do, I will expect to see you there, Ravenhurst."

And with that parting shot, he took his leave, his heart pounding in his chest as if he had just run a mile. Johanna's name was going to be cleared, he vowed as he strode from the temporary CID offices. Even if it meant thrusting his into the mud.

Because he would do anything for her.

Including giving up his position in the Home Office.

Whatever it took.

JOHANNA STARED AT her reflection in the looking glass in the guest bedchamber she had been given at Lark House. Several days had passed since the explosion at Scotland Yard. She had lingered for as long as her pride would allow. But just that morning, the doctor who had been tending to her injuries had removed the bandage on her head and had proclaimed her recovered.

If only the rest of her had recovered just as well as the stitches the doctor had sewn. Fortunately, the deepest laceration she had suffered had been near her nape, and she could disguise the injury with a creative hairstyle so that it would not affect her appearance on the stage.

Ah, the stage. For so long, it had been the only home she had known. The sole joy in her life. Until for a fleeting moment, she had been given a rare glimpse of truer happiness. But that had all been a chimera, had it not?

Yes it had, a cruel jest on the part of fate.

And now, the time had come for her to return to where she belonged. She had missed far too many performances of *The Tempest* as it stood. Mr. Saville had been kind enough to visit her at Lark House and to reassure her the role of Miranda would still be hers when she was well enough. He had also apologized for the part he had played in bringing her to London, telling her he would have brought her to London for a tour regardless of her connections to Drummond.

She had forgiven him, for she had no choice in the matter. She was relying upon him for her wages. He had told her that when her tour ended, he would like her to star in a new play he had written. He had left behind the script for her to read, and the role was perfect for her style of acting. The play itself was brilliantly written. She tried to be thrilled, as she should be, at the prospect of taking on the role.

But for the first time in the eleven years she had been working as an actress, her heart was not in it.

Because her heart was broken. Mangled irrevocably.

The Duke of Winchelsea had ruined her in every way.

She closed her eyes, exhaling on a painful sigh that had nothing to do with her injuries and everything to do with him. He had not returned to her bedside, and she had been grateful. For seeing him again would have been more than she could bear, she was sure.

Her only regret was that she would not get to see Verity again. The little girl had stolen her heart just as surely as her father had. Johanna would miss her.

A subtle knock at the chamber door disrupted her miserable musings.

"Enter," she called.

Hazel swept inside with a hesitant smile, carrying a missive at her side. "Johanna, you are dressed."

"Yes," she said, smoothing a hand over the pale pink silk of her skirts. "Thank you for arranging for my trunks to arrive here from the Duke of Winchelsea's home."

"Winchelsea saw to it," Hazel said solemnly, her gaze searching.

Over the course of her stay here at Lark House, Johanna had bonded with the unusual American duchess. She liked Hazel, and she could not shake the feeling that, in another time, if the circumstances had been different, they would have been great friends.

This was the first time Hazel had mentioned Winchelsea

since that awful first day.

"Perhaps you can convey my gratitude to him on my behalf," she managed, employing all her skills as an actress to feign indifference.

To pretend as if the mere mention of Felix did not tear her apart inside.

Hazel moved closer, watching her in a contemplative fashion. "Maybe you could tell him yourself."

"No," she denied quickly. Too quickly, and she knew it. "I have no interest in seeing or speaking to the Duke of Winchelsea ever again."

That was a lie.

What she wouldn't give to see him again.

To touch him.

To kiss him.

What she wouldn't give for everything he had told her to have been real and true.

"He is a good man," Hazel said softly. "I do not think I am mistaken in believing you have feelings for him."

"He killed all the feelings I once had for him with his lies and manipulations," she said bitterly.

Another lie.

She still loved him.

She always would.

"He was in a desperate position," Hazel told her.

"As was I," she countered. "And he took advantage of that. He brought me here to England with the intent to use me. He pretended to care about me. He told me he loved me. He slipped past all my defenses in a way I have never allowed another."

In the end, that was what hurt the most.

She had trusted him. Had opened her heart. And she had been a fool.

"I know Winchelsea well enough by now," Hazel said, "and I can honestly tell you, he has feelings for you too."

"I do not believe that," she denied. Because she had to.

"Hold on to your anger for him if you must," said Hazel gently, "but know that he has done everything in his power to make certain you are safe from imprisonment. I have rarely seen another man make the kind of sacrifice he has just made for you."

Despite herself, Hazel's words found their way around her walls. "What sacrifice are you speaking of?"

"He resigned his position with the Home Office," Hazel revealed.

Felix had resigned? The news startled her, for he had always struck her as a man who took his responsibilities seriously. She did not think that part of him had been a deception. But still, she did not understand why Hazel would call his resignation a sacrifice made on her behalf.

"I fail to see how that is a concern of mine," she said coolly.

"He told the Home Secretary that he had begun his own covert campaign, subverting the authority of the Home Office," the duchess explained. "He said you were acting as his informant when you came here to England and that it was under his instruction that you smuggled the dynamite and correspondence in an effort to implicate your brother and aid the arrests of Fenians already here in London. He claimed the trunk you brought here was in his possession for the entirety of your stay in London, and that it was at his orders that you copied the contents of the packet of correspondence you had delivered at the Royal Aquarium. He surrendered the trunk over to the Home Secretary and the Special League, and then he stepped down from his post."

Felix had lied for her.

He had shouldered the responsibility for all her actions.

But how could that be? Did she dare believe it was true? She had been manipulated and turned about in so many different directions, she scarcely knew who or what to believe at this juncture.

"How do you know all this?" she asked, her emotions suddenly at war.

Part of her wanted to believe it was true, that Felix had sacrificed himself, his position, and his honor to save her. Part of her railed that it could not be.

"My husband and the Duke of Westmorland accompanied him, and they vouched for what he said," Hazel told her. "We all believe in your innocence, Johanna, and we want to see the true villain—your brother—brought to justice. You do not need to fear being imprisoned again. As long as you stay clear of all Fenians and your brother, Scotland Yard will not be able to touch you. Winchelsea saw to that."

Johanna was frozen. She could not move, could not breathe. It was as if her feet had grown roots, and she would forever be planted on this precise patch of Aubusson on the floor of her Lark House guest chamber. That was how strong the shock was, washing over her. Surely if he had no feelings for her at all, he would never have gone to such lengths on her behalf.

His words to her returned, echoing through her mind, increasing the doubt. *There is one thing I have never lied to you about, and that is loving you.* Was that not what he had said? And what if, *oh God*, what if he had meant it?

What if the actions he had taken—all for her—were proof of his love?

Or a guilty mind, cautioned a voice within her.

Would a man sacrifice all out of guilt? Would Felix?

"Thank you," she forced at last, past her numb lips. "I

cannot thank you all enough for everything you have done for me. That your husband and the Duke of Westmorland would also vouch for my innocence…it is most humbling, Your Grace."

"It is what Felix wanted," Hazel said, "and please, do not revert to formality with me. We are friends now, you and I. I like you, Johanna. I know you are a kind woman with a good heart, and I know you will do what is right."

"Thank you, Hazel," she corrected herself, still in awe. She had been nothing but a burden to the Duke and Duchess of Arden, an invalid who had arrived at their door quite unexpectedly. And yet they had treated her as if she were family. "I am honored to call you friend."

"Winchelsea asked me to give you something," Hazel added, holding out the missive for Johanna to take. "I will give you some time in private to read it."

Her first instinct was to refuse the elegant-looking envelope, closed with a seal. His seal, for he was a duke, and she must not forget the disparity between them.

"I do not want to read it," she denied, doing her best to guard what was left of her heart.

"After all he did for you today, I should think accepting a letter from him a trifling matter indeed," Hazel said, a subtle note of reproach entering her voice for the first time.

The duchess was right, of course. Regardless of his motives for doing so, Felix had made certain she would not be arrested. What harm was there in reading what he had written?

She took the envelope with a shaking hand. "I will have a look at it when I am able. I was just preparing myself to take my leave of your home when you knocked. I have been a burden upon your household for long enough, and the time has come for me to find lodging elsewhere."

Though she had not yet decided where she would go, she knew she could not return to her former hotel. Drummond had known where she was staying, and she had no doubt his men would come looking for her there. Since Scotland Yard was already in possession of the documents she had given to Drummond's man at the Royal Aquarium that day, they would likely have begun making arrests based on the information the documents contained. And if arrests were being made, that meant Johanna was in grave danger.

Drummond would be out for her blood.

"Do not be silly," Hazel interrupted the grim bent of her thoughts. "You must remain here for the duration of your stay in London. It is safest for you, and Arden and I are happy to host you."

The missive seemed to burn into her palm. She could not wait to read it, and yet she could not bear to. She was a study in contradictions, part of her wanting Felix with so much longing, every part of her ached, while part of her wanted to run as far and as fast from him as she could. Before he could hurt her again. Before he could lure her back to him with his knowing kisses and his comforting embraces, his way of always tending to her when she needed it most.

She hated him for what he had done, and she had never loved him more.

But she had also never been more convinced of their wrongness for each other, regardless. He was a duke, and she had just cost him his position. She was an actress with a Fenian brother she could not shake. One who would now want her dead.

She shook her head. "I cannot stay here, Hazel, though I do thank you. The time has come for me to do what I do best, and that is to be on my own. I have been since I was fifteen."

"Stay here just a bit longer," Hazel urged, her expression

concerned. "No one knows this is where you were taken, where you have been staying, except for a select few. You are worried your brother's men will find you. I can see it in your face. If you are here, you are in the safest place you can be."

"It matters not where I stay," she said, bitterness she could not entirely hide tingeing her voice. "I will be back on the stage. They will find me wherever I go. I will not be truly safe from him until I reach Paris because he does not have any men planted there to do his bidding. Maybe not even until I get to Berlin."

Hazel's brows rose. "You cannot truly be thinking of returning to the stage so soon, Johanna?"

"I must," she said. "The show must go on."

"The choice is, of course, yours," Hazel said, "but you would be a fool to go anywhere else."

"I would be a fool if I stayed." Sadness colored her voice. "Thank you, Hazel. I cannot begin to express my gratitude for everything you have done for me, and I will treasure our friendship always. But the time has come for me to go."

Hazel's lips tightened, her countenance a study in disapproval. "Winchelsea will not be pleased by this development. But it will be as you wish. I will take my leave of you so you can prepare yourself for whatever it is you must do."

She bit her lip as she watched Hazel go, staving off an unwanted rush of emotion. The door had scarcely clicked shut when she tore open the seal on the envelope and extracted a thick, folded sheet of paper.

The letter was written in bold, masculine scrawl, which suited him. She had never seen his hand before, but she thought she would have recognized it anywhere, without knowing it had been his. A tremble passed through her as she began to read.

Darling Johanna,

Keeping my involvement with the Home Office a secret from you will forever be one of my everlasting sorrows. I have but a few in this life. The first was losing my wife, whom I loved. My second was lying to you, whom I love.

My third was losing you.

Please accept this, the very least I owe you. Perhaps one day, you will forgive me. On that day, know that I will be waiting. I will wait for you, and I will never stop loving you.

Be safe, be happy, and be well.

Ever yours,

Winchelsea

P.S. If you will not accept this gift for yourself, perhaps you might put it to good use at the orphanage you spoke of visiting, back in New York City.

Along with the letter was a note for five thousand pounds. It fluttered to the floor from fingers that had suddenly gone nerveless. She closed her eyes against an unwanted rush of longing and a flood of tears.

He had remembered the orphanage. He claimed to love her still. That he would always love her. A great, shuddering sob wracked her. And God help her, she wanted to believe him. She wanted to believe those words, in conjunction with everything Hazel had just told her.

How difficult it was to remain strong. To keep him at bay. But she knew she must.

She folded the letter and placed it back inside the envelope, but not before tracing her finger over the words he had written. Not before tears slid from her eyes, leaving hot trails down her cheeks. Pressing a hand to her mouth to stifle her sobs, she allowed herself to sink to the floor.

Allowed herself to mourn what had been, what could never be. Allowed herself to mourn the pieces of her heart the Duke of Winchelsea would always own. She clenched the envelope, and she wept for everything she had lost.

And when her tears at last dried, she rose again, placing the five thousand pound note back in the envelope alongside Felix's letter. She had lost their wager, and she did not want his five thousand pounds. He had won the bet, through fair means or foul.

But she was going to keep the money, she decided. And she was going to send it all back to the orphanage in honor of two little girls who had stolen her heart as well.

Pearl and Verity.

Chapter Seventeen

THERE WERE NIGHTS when the crowd's energy infused Johanna with zeal.

Tonight, her fifth night back as Miranda after her unexpected absence, was one of those nights.

Beneath the glow of the limelight, she was hot and uncomfortable in her costume, and yet she felt vibrant and alive. Thankfully, Mr. Saville's theater employed electric lights rather than the hot and odorous gaslight so many theaters still used. She and the actor who played Prospero had the audience coming to life. The sound effects of thunder rolling and crashing waves had seemed heightened, and the stage had been a place of awe.

Perhaps it was everything she had endured in the last week that had changed her. Perhaps it was the magic of the evening and the crowd. Perhaps it was love, which had been so long absent from her life, that made the difference. Whatever the cause, when she made her way to her dressing room to change following her final scene, she knew she had just delivered one of the greatest performances of her life.

She also knew she would never stop loving Felix.

It had taken her some time to settle back into her routine.

The door to her dressing room clicked closed behind her, and it was as if time had not passed since the last day she had first shed her costume within its walls. And yet, everything had changed. She had changed.

It might have been a lifetime ago.

But she could not dwell upon that now. Did not dare. For if she lingered too long upon her thoughts, she would unravel faster than a ball of twine. And she could not afford to unravel now. She had come too far, had worked too hard. She was an actress by trade, and by God, she would continue carrying on, just as she always had.

Johanna set to work on the thick paints on her face, scrubbing them away with water and soap. There was a knock on her door, which she presumed to be Jenny coming to aid her with the tapes in the back of her costume.

"Enter," she called out, dabbing at her face with a towel to dry it.

Her back was to the door, but the moment it opened, the very energy around her seemed to change. The hair on the back of her neck stood up. And she knew who it was before the beautiful sound of his baritone broke the silence.

"Johanna."

It was as if something inside her cracked and broke open. She spun to face him, her heart pounding. Longing hit her with a blow forceful enough to steal her breath. He was handsome as ever, and elegant too, wearing dark evening clothes. There were dark smudges beneath his vibrant eyes, just as there had been on the last occasion she had seen him.

She wondered what kept him awake.

And then she wondered if it was the same thing that kept her awake.

The endless, aching longing for him. The love that would not seem to die, no matter how much she wished to squelch it.

She forced her emotions aside. Summoned up her strength. Her armor. "Your Grace," she said, keeping her voice cold. "What are you doing here?"

He crossed the threshold of the small, windowless room and closed the door at his back. "I could not stay away."

She wished he had, because now he was here. Four steps away. Her feet itched to move.

"You should have," she said, unable to keep the bitterness from her tone.

How impossible it was to be impervious to this man, when she loved him so.

His gaze seemed to devour her with a hunger she recognized all too well. "You were tremendous tonight as Miranda. Even better than the last time I saw you."

"You were in the audience tonight?" She gripped the damp towel, twisting it in her fingers.

For some reason, she had not imagined he would watch her again. Perhaps it had been easier for her to believe. She was not certain how well she could have performed had she known his eyes were upon her.

"I was," he confirmed.

She could not help but to note the taut manner in which he held his lips, the firm clench of his jaw. The dark stubble of whiskers shaded it, as if he had not shaved in a day or two. The urge to skim her hand there, to caress him, rose within her.

"Why?" she asked, though she knew she should not.

Though she feared the answer.

"I had to see you," he said, the admission sounding as if it had been torn from him.

"You have seen me," she said, gripping the towel harder than ever. "You may go now."

"I had to speak with you also, Johanna." He took another step nearer.

Instinctively, she took one in retreat. Her heart was thudding faster. If he touched her, she would be lost. Helpless to resist.

"We have already said everything that needs to be said," she countered.

One more step backward, and her bottom connected with the sharp corner of the table upon which the basin and bowl of water sat. She cried out at the unexpected pain.

He rushed forward, reaching for her, taking her arms in a firm grip "What is the matter?"

"I ran into the table." She wrenched herself away from him, putting some distance between them once more. "It is nothing. I was merely surprised."

His scent washed over her, familiar. Haunting. Like the ghost of a caress.

He remained where he was, his countenance solemn. "How are you?"

She summoned up a false smile. "I am well. Can you not see? But I will be better when you leave."

"I understand you are angry with me," he began.

"Anger does not begin to describe the emotions I feel for you," she interrupted, holding on to her indignation. It was all she had left.

"You have every right to feel the way you do," he said softly. "I understand, Johanna. But what I do not understand is the danger you are placing yourself in by refusing to remain at Lark House where you are safe."

So that was the reason for his visit? He must have learned from Hazel that she had left, much to the duke and duchess's dismay.

"I have no intention of doing my brother's bidding ever again, if that is what concerns you," she assured him coolly.

"That is not what concerns me," he said, stepping forward yet again.

It was rather like a dance between them. He tried to close the distance. She tried desperately to maintain it.

"To be candid, I do not care what does or does not concern you, Your Grace," she snapped. "I do not care about anything to do with you at all."

That was a desperate and terrible lie, of course, but one she needed to maintain all the same.

He flinched as if she had struck him. "Do you hate me that much?"

Quite the opposite. She *loved* him that much.

But she could not love him. Could not trust him. Because even if she allowed herself to do both of those things, she could not erase who she was. Nor could she bear to take the chance that Drummond might try to harm Verity or Felix again.

"I do not hate you," she said, doing her best to steel herself against him and to avoid falling into his verdant gaze. "I feel nothing for you."

He closed the last step between them, and there was nowhere else she could go. Nowhere to run. She had to remain where she was as he loomed, near enough to touch. Even as every part of her screamed to throw herself into his arms.

But that was not where she belonged.

He touched her then. Nothing but his fingertips on her chin, holding her still and in his thrall. "Look me in the eye when you tell me you feel nothing at all for me, Johanna."

He forgot she was an actress. And it did indeed require all the skills she had honed in her years on the stage to hold his gaze. "I care nothing for you, Your Grace."

"Kiss me," he said.

His demand had the opposite effect of what it should. Heat pooled low in her belly, an ache beginning in her core and radiating throughout her entire body.

"Why do you hesitate?" he asked. "Perhaps you are not as unaffected as you claim."

"I am," she insisted, but the words left her as little more than a whisper, and when he cupped her cheek, she closed her eyes and could not resist nuzzling his big, warm palm.

How right he still felt.

How beloved.

Damn him, and damn her heart too. Damn her foolish, traitorous body. Damn Theo Saville for allowing him into the theater. Damn her for not leaving the dressing room the moment she had turned around and seen him.

"Kiss me, Johanna," he urged, his voice a decadent rumble pouring over her like warm honey. "Kiss me and show me how unmoved you are. Show me there was never anything between us, that everything we shared, the love I have for you, is meaningless."

Her eyes flew open, and she cried out with all the misery teeming in the depths of her soul. Because she could not do it. Her skills as an actress could not carry her that far. And neither could she resist him for another moment more.

The towel she had been clutching as if it were a shield fell from her fingers, unheeded, to the floor. She stepped toward him, into him, and then her arms were wrapping around his neck, and he was holding her tighter than he had ever held her before, and his lips were hard and fast on hers. This kiss was bittersweet, their mouths clinging and melding as naturally as always.

But there was a desperation simmering beneath.

She forgot all the reasons why she should not be opening her mouth to his questing tongue. Why she should not taste him, kiss him back, why she should not hold him to her as if she feared the second she would have to let him go again. She forgot she was not supposed to love him.

In those wild, frenzied moments of unbridled passion, she was once more his, and he was hers. Nothing and no one could tear them apart. Or at least, that was what she fooled herself into believing.

HAVING JOHANNA BACK in his arms was like seeing the sun again after being trapped in a windowless dungeon all the days they had been apart. Her lips were soft and responsive beneath his, her fingers tunneling in his hair. He could taste the urgency in her kiss. Could feel her body's response through the flimsy costume she had worn as Miranda.

Her curves melted into him. The soft, breathy sound she made deep in her throat told him she was every bit as starved for him as he was for her. Gratitude unfurled within him, alongside a bolt of desire so powerful, his cock went instantly erect and his ballocks drew up tight. The need to be inside her was overwhelming.

He had not intended any of this when he had sought her out this evening.

He had told himself, of course, he should stay away from her. Give her the distance she so obviously wanted. His missive to her had gone unanswered, and he had heard not a word from her in each of the days since. Six days. He had counted them.

Almost an entire week.

The only fate worse than six days without Johanna was the prospect of a lifetime without her, which seemed increasingly likely with each day that had passed. He would have waited longer. He would have kept his distance, he told himself now as he kissed down the smooth, creamy column of her throat. He found the hollow at the base where her pulse fluttered a rapid staccato against his lips.

She was as affected as he was, and he knew it.

She knew it too, even if she despised herself for her weakness.

But then Arden had come to him, earlier that day, with word that Drummond McKenna was believed to be in London. Double agents in New York had confirmed the news to the Special League, and though Felix had resigned his position, Arden was a loyal friend who knew what the possibility of her brother being in London would mean for Johanna.

Felix had gone to the Crown and Thorn immediately, only to find the production about to begin for the evening. And so, he had watched Johanna perform once more. The pleasure he took in her undeniable talent had distracted him from his purpose.

That was his excuse for the reaction he had to sitting in the audience and witnessing her grand command of the stage. He had been, once more, in awe of her. He had never seen another actress like her.

He could still hear clearly the raw emotion in her voice when she had called out *How beauteous mankind is! O brave new world that has such people in't!* And oh, how he had yearned for the brave new world of which she spoke, one with her in it.

He still yearned for it now.

But he yearned for something else. Something deeper. Something true.

"You want me," he accused against her skin, tasting her there. Roses and sweet orange.

She swallowed. "Yes."

The susurrus of her affirmation lit a new fire within him.

He wanted her too. Needed her, in fact. Had to have her.

How he had gone six days without seeing her was a mystery to him. He was going to make up for the lost time now. It did not matter that they were in a dark, almost airless space. That anyone could interrupt them at any moment. It did not matter that she had told him to go, that she claimed to have no feelings for him. Not even his reasons for seeking her out mattered.

All that did matter was the truth of the desire they shared.

They could worry about the rest later. First, the passion between them needed to be answered. Right here, right now.

He dragged his mouth from her beautiful skin with only the greatest exertion of control. Looked down into her upturned face. She was pale, her skin flushed pink from the makeup she had scrubbed from her skin. Her lips were full and dark from their kisses, her eyes glazed, her pupils wide. Somehow, the loose chignon she had worn her hair in for the final scene had begun to come undone.

Golden tendrils curled over her forehead, framed her face.

And what he saw when he searched her face gave him hope.

"Tell me to go now," he said.

Her lips parted.

Not a sound emerged.

He slid a hand from her waist to her breast, cupping it through the layers of her costume. She was not the innocent Miranda now, but Johanna, his lover. The soft weight of her breast in his hand almost took his breath, sending a sharp arrow of lust to his groin. He squeezed gently, damning the barrier of her corset.

"You want this," he told her.

Still, she remained silent, saying nothing.

But she did not push away from him as she could have at any moment. Rather, her eyes dipped to his mouth.

"Say something," he begged.

Because he was not above begging. Not when it came to this woman.

"Stay," she said.

Not a confession. Not a lowering of her guard. But it was something.

And that lone word turned the fires inside him into an inferno.

He couldn't speak. All he could do was act. He claimed her mouth again. This kiss was not slow, not a seduction. It was a possession. He slanted his lips over hers, kissing her as he had never kissed another. He kissed her as if he could brand her with his lips and tongue alone. Kissed her so she would never forget him, as long as she lived, no matter where she roamed.

If this was to be their final goodbye, he was going to make it worth every moment.

He devoured her mouth, his hands traveling over her curves in worshipful awe. The tiny room was cramped, sparsely furnished. In his whirling mind, he decided upon the table over the lone chair.

He moved them as one, kissing her, nipping her. He used his tongue, his teeth. And she was every bit as ferocious in her reaction to him. Her nails raked at his back. Her teeth bit into his bottom lip.

Three steps, that was all it took. He was still kissing her as he waved his arm behind her, clearing the tabletop. The sound of breaking porcelain and splashing water reached his ears but had no effect upon his ardor. He didn't give a damn what he broke.

He would gladly pay Theo whatever he wanted for replacements.

It was worth it.

He would pay it a thousand times over. Ten thousand times. One hundred thousand times, easily.

Just for this one moment. This one, last chance.

He lifted her and settled her rump atop the newly cleared table.

Her arms were still looped around his neck as she jerked her head back. Her eyes were dazed and luminous. "You broke the wash basin."

"I don't give a damn," he told her. "Do you?"

Her tongue darted over the lush fullness of her lower lip.

He longed to chase it.

"No," she said.

And then, they were kissing again. He pushed up the skirts of her Miranda costume, leaving it pooled about her waist. He wanted nothing more than to tear it in two, to leave it in shreds on the floor. But he knew he needed to govern himself. He had committed enough destruction this night.

His hands found her thighs, warm and soft through her silken drawers. He parted them, stepped into her. His cock was straining against the fall of his trousers. Aching to be inside her hot, tight cunny.

But he wanted to prolong this. To make it last.

Because if it was the last time…

Nay, he refused to think it. How could this be the last time he would make love to her, kiss her, touch her?

He broke the kiss again, gazing down into her upturned face. This was not about mere passion for him. Wanting her, desiring her—it was about love. He loved her, and he still wanted her as his duchess every bit as much as he had on the day he had asked her to marry him.

"I love you, Johanna," he said.

But she did not say the words back to him. He had not expected it, of course, but he could not lie and say the omission did not hurt. She still did not trust him. He had earned her skepticism on his own.

She said nothing at all. Instead, she pulled his head back down to hers for another kiss. And this one was longer than the others which had come before. It was slow. Hungry. Deliberate. Her tongue was in his mouth first. This time, she was the one to claim.

He liked it. God, how he liked it.

He liked it too much.

When she caught his lower lip between her teeth and tugged sensuously, he could not stifle the moan she wrung from him. Nor could he stop his hips from rocking into hers. His aching cock glanced over her heated center, separated by the barrier of far too much cloth.

Too many layers keeping him from what he wanted most.

Too many walls denying him what he needed.

"Johanna."

He said her name aloud and into her lips like a prayer, rocking into her as he did so. Her legs wrapped around his waist. Every thought other than her was erased from his mind in that instant.

She was all he saw, all he felt, all he tasted. Her every little mewl of desire, the way she writhed against him, her curves and her sensuous skin, her scent, her arms around his neck. Rose petals and orange and sweet, delicious woman.

The woman who owned his heart.

This time, he did not pause to fret over the damage he might cause, the repercussions. He caught the bodice of her Miranda costume in his hands and he dragged them apart. Fabric rent. The chemise she wore beneath it ripped simultaneously, stopping only at the edge of her corset, which he removed with ease.

Thank God.

Her breasts sprang free, into his waiting, greedy hands.

She tore her mouth from his on a gasp. "Felix, what have you done?"

"I believe I may have ruined Miranda's dress," he said, unable to summon up a modicum of contrition.

He would do it again, just for the chance to hear his given name on her lips. And just to behold the glorious, erotic sight of her pale breasts, revealed by the glow of the room's electric light. Her nipples prodded the air, stiff and hungry. He wanted to suck them until she screamed.

He took one in his mouth, dragging on it. Then the other, biting the hard little bud until she moaned and arched into him. And then, he could not wait a moment longer. His right hand moved from her outer thigh to her inner, and then beyond. To the slit of her drawers.

To the seam of her sex. His fingers brushed over her, parting her curls, her flesh. She was sleek and wet and hot. So very inviting. He found her clitoris next, circling it with teasing strokes until she was gasping his name, thrusting into his hand. Until she forgot all about her ire at his willful destruction of her costume.

He would buy her another anyway. He would buy her a thousand of them. And he would tear one off her every night if she would let him.

He knew she would never let him.

But he could not allow that to intrude upon this moment. He kissed his way from her breast to her throat, all the way to her ear, his lips grazing the delicate shell.

"I will always love you," he whispered as he slid his finger through her drenched folds until he found her entrance.

He slid inside her with ease, and she made a sound of need. Her cunny gripped him, flooded him. She was ready, and he could not wait. He bit the fleshy lobe of her ear, licked the hollow behind it where she smelled of rose petals.

Her hands were on him.

She never said the words back to him.

She didn't need to. He loved her enough for the both of them.

He would have told her, but the capacity for speech was beyond him. She had undone the fall of his trousers, and her hand was on his eager cock. Stroking him. Her fingers curling around his shaft was enough to drive him over the edge. Her grip tightened. He sank another finger inside her, moving them in a slow and steady rhythm.

He lifted his head, wanting to watch her. He could not deprive himself of the sight of her pleasure rising. Her cheeks were more flushed, her kiss-darkened lips slack. Her eyes were glazed with desire. He committed her to memory this way: coming beautifully undone for him.

His.

Forever his.

Burying his hand in the silken remnants of her chignon, he tugged her head back, holding her still, trapping her with his gaze. He kissed her softly, slowly, in stark contrast to the fury of the passion blazing through him. On a sigh, she kissed him back. One of her arms was around his neck, holding him tightly to her.

If he had his way, they would never be apart.

He could not bear to lose her. To never see her again. How could he? He had already lost the woman he loved once. To do so a second time would be nigh impossible.

He would never recover.

He told her so with his lips and tongue.

She continued stroking him, making his ballocks draw up tighter. Need licked down his spine. And still he kissed her. If this was to be their goodbye, it would be a long one. A lingering one.

God, how he never wanted it to end.

But his restraint was fraying. Her caresses were driving him wild. So, too, her tongue writhing against his. She pressed her body nearer. He wanted to get lost in her. To breathe her in. Consume her. Possess her.

He broke the kiss, staring down at her, his breathing harsh.

"Enough," he bit out, removing her knowing hand. "I want inside you."

"Yes," she breathed.

He drove into her with one swift thrust. He was deep, so deep. It was a homecoming. They both gasped when he began to move, pumping his hips in a slow, deliberate rhythm. She was so slick, so tight, her heat all around him, and she felt so good, so right. He told himself to prolong this moment too, but his body would not listen to reason.

There was no reason.

There was only hunger.

Her legs wrapped around his waist. He kissed her, his hand still buried in her hair, the other on the sweet curve of her hip, holding her in place as he withdrew almost entirely, only to sink home inside her again. She arched into him, her breasts rising like offerings.

He accepted. Lowered his head. Licked over one nipple as he thrust harder.

She moaned. Her nipples were so sensitive. Her cunny so wet. He was going to lose himself and spend inside her if he was not careful. *Control*, he reminded himself. He had spent inside her once before, and he could not do so again.

He increased his pace again, fucking her so hard, the table moved across the floor with a clatter, slamming into the wall. They were going to destroy this blasted dressing room, and he did not give a damn. If he had his way, there would be nothing left. Not a stick of furniture untouched. Nothing but him and Johanna, naked and sated.

He found his way back to her mouth as he slammed inside her, and their lips fused on her cry as she tightened on him, spending. A new surge of wetness bathed his cock, and as the shudders radiated through her body, he reached the point where he could no longer hold off his own release.

He withdrew from her, gripping his cock tightly, as he came so hard, he could not suppress his own growl of release. He tore his lips from hers, breaking their kiss as he spent all over her thigh. His heart was thundering in his chest, and he could scarcely catch his breath.

The sight of her on the table, her breasts and cunny on display, all cream and pink, her legs spread, his seed on her skin, was unbearably erotic. She was breathing every bit as harshly as he, her expression dazed. He leaned against her, pressing a tender kiss to her forehead.

His love for her had never been stronger.

Nor had his need to somehow overcome the walls between them.

A knock sounded at the door.

"Mademoiselle Beaumont?" called a feminine voice.

"Yes, Jenny?" Johanna answered, eyes going wide, her voice still throaty and low with the aftereffects of the passion they had just shared.

"I heard a commotion," said the woman on the other side of the door.

"Everything is fine," Johanna reassured her, though there was a hitch in her voice that suggested the opposite.

Her stricken sky-blue eyes met his, and he saw all the doubts and shadows lingering there. He wanted to chase them away. If only he knew how to.

"Are you needing my help?" asked the woman, ever persistent.

Cursing, Felix stepped back from Johanna, adjusting himself and fastening his trousers once more. He extracted a handkerchief from within his coat and used it to wipe the traces of his seed from her thigh.

Johana clutched at the tattered ends of her costume, gathering them around her protectively. "No, Jenny," she called. "I will not be needing you tonight. Thank you, you may go."

"Johanna," he said, thinking he should apologize for the ravenous fashion in which he had taken her. *Bloody hell*, he had made a wreckage of the room and of her as well. Her hair was mostly unbound now, spilling over her shoulders. Her dress was ruined. The table had smashed into the wall, and the pitcher and basin were upended, their shards in the midst of a puddle of water.

"You may go as well," she told him, the sated glow of lovemaking gone from her countenance.

"Allow me to escort you to your carriage, at least," he said.

"No," she denied, sweeping from the table and out of his reach once more. "That was goodbye, Felix. I cannot keep doing what we are doing."

"I agree." He stepped toward her. "Marry me, Johanna. The offer still stands. There is every indication that your brother is in London. I heard from the Duke of Arden today, and it is the reason I came to see you. I will do everything in my power to keep you safe."

She stilled, her complexion going pale. "Drummond is here?"

"According to reports from double agents within the Fenian ranks, he is," Felix told her. "Please, Johanna. If you will not allow me to protect you, go back to Lark House.

Arden will see to your safety."

She pressed a shaking hand to her lips, as if to stifle a sob.

How he wanted to take her back in his arms, to comfort her. But he did not dare. She still did not trust him. That much was obvious. And he had no wish to push her further than he already had.

"I will wait for you outside and escort you to your carriage," he said grimly. "It is the least I can do."

But she shook her head, determined. "No, Felix. I will face whatever I must, as I always have. Alone."

Everything in him wanted to fight her. But he could see the determination on her beautiful face. And so he did the only thing he could do. He relented.

"I'll be damned if this was goodbye, Johanna," he told her, and then he turned on his heel and stalked from the room.

He was going to find Theo and ask that he make certain Johanna had an escort from this night onward. If she would not accept his aid, he would have to make certain she was safe by other means.

As his footsteps carried him away from her, he could not shake the feeling that he had left a part of himself behind. He despised the sadness in her eyes. And he hated himself for being the one who had put it there.

Chapter Eighteen

THREE NIGHTS HAD passed since Felix had come to Johanna in her dressing room and they had made love. She had heard not a word from him in the days since. Much to her everlasting shame, she searched the audience for his face each night.

But each night, like the one preceding it, he had not been there.

She should not have been surprised, she supposed, for she had told him to go. She had refused his marriage proposal, had told him that last, frantic encounter had been their goodbye. And though he had been adamant it was not, she had no expectations of him.

Why should she? Though she loved him, she could not trust him. And even if she could, a duke could not marry a woman like her. She could not change her past. She would always be Rose Beaumont, always Pearl's mother. And she would always be the sister of his enemy.

This was for the best, she told herself as she made her way down a dimly lit theater corridor. Tonight was no different than any of the others which had come before. They blended together, an indistinct river without end. Drummond would stay away from Felix and Verity, and Johanna would have her life as she had always known it, living on the stage.

Unable to shake the sadness permeating her ever since

their last encounter, Johanna emerged from the Crown and Thorn, into the little alley where her driver typically awaited her. The play had carried on a bit later that evening thanks to a problem with the limelight, which led to a tardy start to the show. Shivering as a wall of cool air hit her, she scanned the alley for her carriage.

Suddenly, something hard pressed into her back, and a familiar voice was at her ear. "Do not scream, Jojo, or I will shoot."

"Drummond," she said on a gasp.

Felix's warning had been correct.

Her brother was here. In London. And not only had he found her, but he was holding a pistol to her back.

The dread and the fear which had been her constant companions since the day he had reentered her life came crashing down upon her. For a moment, her knees gave out, and she would have fallen to the street had he not caught her in an unforgiving grip, holding her steady.

"Not a word," he warned.

Her heart was pounding, her mouth dry. She looked all around her, trying to find someone—anyone—who could help her.

"If you call out, I will put a bullet in you, Jojo," Drummond said.

How coldly he could call her by her hated childhood sobriquet and threaten to shoot her at the same time. She did not dare put anyone else in danger.

"Mademoiselle Beaumont," called out a voice from behind her.

She turned to see Mr. Nelson, one of the stagehands who had been markedly attentive for the last few nights, standing in the theater door. His expression was concerned.

"If you give him cause for concern, I will shoot him too,"

Drummond whispered, lodging the pistol's barrel more firmly in her back.

"Have a good evening, Mr. Nelson," she called back, keeping the tremble from her voice by calling upon all her honed skills as an actress.

She pinned a false smile to her lips.

Mr. Nelson held his hat in his hands, looking from Johanna to Drummond, then back to Johanna. "Who is your friend, Mademoiselle Beaumont?"

"Mr. Silas Walker," Drummond said smoothly, as if he were not threatening her life at that very moment. His tone was chipper, as if he had not a care. "A friend of Mademoiselle Beaumont's from New York. Have a good evening, sir."

The gun nudged her once more.

"Have a good evening, Mr. Nelson," she added. "I will see you tomorrow."

Mr. Nelson was frowning, but he jammed his hat on his head and tipped the brim to her, before disappearing back inside the Crown and Thorn once more. The door had scarcely closed when Drummond started propelling her forward.

"Where is your carriage?" he demanded.

She glanced around the alley, desperate to find some way of escaping him. But there was no one else about, except for a handful of waiting conveyances and their drivers. She could not bear to put anyone else's life at risk merely to save hers.

She had no doubt Drummond would shoot her if she tried to escape.

"It is waiting for me just over there," she managed to say, pointing in the direction where her driver awaited her.

"You will walk calmly to it," Drummond ordered. "You will smile and act as if nothing is amiss. If you alert your driver in any way, I will shoot him in the head. Do you understand?"

She swallowed down a knot of pure terror. "Yes."

"Good. You will tell the driver you are no longer in need of his services for the evening. And then you will return to me. If you attempt to communicate anything to him in any fashion, he will die. Now walk, Jojo."

Johanna did as he asked, feigning nonchalance. She approached her driver, smiling as she went, keenly aware of her brother watching her every move. She did not dare attempt to show her driver she was under duress for fear Drummond would make good on his threats. Her driver did not appear suspicious. She had already paid him for the evening, and he seemed only too happy to be on his way.

Attempting to be as calm as possible, she walked back to her brother. He grasped her elbow. "Come with me, Jojo."

He walked them hurriedly to the end of the alleyway and turned a corner to where another vehicle waited.

"Get inside," he told her, nudging her with the pistol barrel. The force he exerted sent a rush of pain through her, and she knew there would later be a bruise. But a bruise was the least of her worries as she allowed herself to be shoved into the vehicle. She tripped on her hem and sprawled to the floor as she attempted to scramble onto the bench.

"Up, you clumsy cow." Drummond caught her chignon and roughly pulled her to her feet. Tears stung her eyes as sharp pain lanced through her.

Choking back a sob, she righted herself before hastily sitting.

Drummond climbed inside and settled across from her, his gaze as hard as flint as he pointed the pistol toward her. The carriage seemed extraordinarily small. But larger still than her chances of escaping this situation alive.

She could run, but her past always found her. The carriage lurched into motion, bearing them to an unknown destination.

"I have heard a great deal about you, sister," Drummond said then, sneering. "You have been whoring yourself for the Home Office and Scotland Yard."

She flinched at his viciousness. "I was not doing anything of the kind."

"I have it on good authority you were," he said bitterly. "All I do for you, sister, and as soon as you are out of my sight, you are a slut for the enemy. I expected better from you."

"All you have done for me is terrorize me and force me to assist you in your plotting," she said, her outrage getting the best of her and making her speak too freely. "You were being watched in New York and you knew it, and that is why you used me in your schemes."

"I see being a duke's whore has given you airs," he said coolly, assessing her as one might an insect about to be squashed. "I would advise you against using them with me. You won't like the consequences."

"Where are you taking me?" she demanded.

His smile was ugly. "To a place where you will be most useful to me, *Mademoiselle Beaumont*."

"You can tell everyone who I am," she said, meeting his stare. "I won't cower to you any longer. I won't do what you want me to do. Tell the world I am Johanna McKenna. See it printed in every newspaper. I will explain the monster I was running from. Rose Beaumont is just another role."

"Ah, but you are cowering to me now, Jojo," he countered, his tone one of mock sympathy.

"You have a pistol pointed at me, Drummond," she said. "And me, your own sister. Your flesh and blood. What else am I to do?"

"You were always weak," he spat. "Just like Ma."

He was so much their father's image in that moment—the feral beast, the snarl and the rage—that she wanted to retch.

"And you were always a brutal monster, like Pa," she returned.

He gave her a cruel smile, but it did not reach his eyes. His eyes—the reflection of hers, in the same shade of deep blue as their father's—were flat. "I am who the world has made me."

She supposed he was right about that. He was the product of their father's rages, his beatings. She had escaped at a young age, while Drummond had become their father.

"Where are you taking me?" she asked again.

"I am taking you to where I have been staying during my time here in London," he said, his tone turning conversational. "Just over an apothecary's shop. I am afraid it will not be comparable to a duke's home, but you will manage well enough."

There again was the dig at Felix. She wondered how Drummond had found out about her relationship with him. Just how long had he been in London? And had he been watching her? Suddenly, everything made sense.

Her imagination had not been at work on the instances when she had been so convinced she had seen him.

"It *was* you," she said as realization hit her. "I saw you watching me. You have been here in London all along, haven't you?"

"I have," he confirmed, sounding pleased with himself. "I knew you were not to be trusted, but the dynamite was best smuggled by a woman. They are suspicious of almost all my men. The risk of having the powder confiscated, a man arrested, and the entire plot unraveled, was too great. As it turned out, you were not my only worry. Rourke, that sniveling little coward, turned Queen's Evidence the moment Scotland Yard arrested him."

She supposed Rourke was the man she had met at the Royal Aquarium. The one who had offered evidence against her.

"But I did not give the dynamite to anyone," she said, struggling to make sense of what had happened. "How were the bombs assembled?"

Drummond laughed. "How foolish you are, Jojo. You can memorize all the lines of a play, and yet you failed to realize someone had come to your hotel and replaced the dynamite in your trunk with biscuit boxes containing actual biscuits instead of powder."

The revelation chilled her.

"You sent someone into my room to obtain the dynamite?" she asked. "When?"

"During your rehearsals." He whistled lowly. "Oh, Jojo. You truly had no idea, did you? It was the dynamite you smuggled here that blew a hole in the outer wall of your duke's townhome. It was also the same dynamite that exploded outside the Scotland Yard offices the day you were being questioned. So you see, you had a part in your own downfall. Not so high and mighty now, are you?"

She felt as if she had turned to ice. She had been so certain the dynamite she had smuggled had still been in her possession, unable to harm anyone. And Drummond had outfoxed her. Not only that, but he had used that same dynamite as a weapon to harm herself and those she loved.

"You are a devil," she accused. "How could you have laid a bomb outside a home? A child could have died because of you."

"She would have died because of you as well," Drummond said. "That is what troubles you most, isn't it, Jojo? You think yourself such an angel, but you are just as soiled and fallen as all the rest of us."

"Tell me what you intend to do with me, Drummond," she said then. "I will have you remember that I am your sister. I share your blood."

His eyes narrowed upon her with lethal intent. "Fine time for you to recall that, Jojo."

And she knew her fate was sealed.

FELIX WAS READING Verity a story when word reached him, via an urgent missive sent from Theo's Crown and Thorn. And then via an urgent communication from the Duke of Arden.

The unthinkable had happened. Johanna had left the theater, escaping the watch of the stagehand who was being paid additional wages to guard her. By the time the man had noticed her exit of the building, he had discovered her with a stranger who described himself as an old friend. Johanna had reassured the man all was well, but the stagehand thought her manner had been troubled.

Arden's men had been watching the theater as well, and one of them had followed the stranger and Johanna to an apothecary's shop in the East End. It appeared to the agent as if Johanna was being controlled by the man in question. A man who was almost certainly Drummond McKenna.

Denial, rage, and despair twisted in Felix's gut. He had done everything in his power to keep Johanna safe.

And yet, it had not been enough.

Because her bastard of a brother had come for her anyway. And he had not been there to protect her. Not that she would have wanted him to. Because of the secrets he had kept from her, she still did not trust him. Perhaps she never would again. And he could not blame her for his own failures.

He could only blame himself.

But that did not mean he was about to rest on his laurels while Johanna was in danger. He had to get to her.

"What is the matter, Papa?" Verity asked, concern in her voice.

Still the picture of her mother. He hugged her to him and kissed her crown. "Nothing is wrong, poppet. It is time, however, for young ladies to go to bed. You need your rest, and I shall see you in the morning."

Though he did his best to keep his tone controlled and even, dread held him in its claws.

"Why are you sad?" Verity asked suddenly.

She was dreadfully perceptive for a child of five years.

"I am not sad at all," he lied, clutching the missives so tightly his knuckles ached with the strain.

"Papa?"

He glanced up at her. She was tucked into her bed, an innocent girl with Hattie's dark curls and his eyes. When he looked upon her now and saw the resemblance, the knife in his chest was no longer lodged quite as deep.

"Yes, poppet?" He was keenly aware of how precious every second was.

Arden had given him the address of the apothecary's shop, though he had warned him to stay away. But there was no bloody way Felix was going to sit calmly by while Drummond McKenna held Johanna captive. Still, he had no wish to alarm Verity.

"Is Miss McKenna ever going to come back to sing with me again?" she asked. "She was ever so much fun. I have not laughed so much since I met her, and neither have you."

If he had anything to say about it, she would come back

as his duchess. But he knew that was out of his hands. And Johanna was in terrible danger. Danger he could not allow himself to contemplate.

Already, he could feel one of his fits beginning. His chest hurt. His heart was pounding. He kept his eyes pinned upon Verity, forcing himself to remain clam.

"I hope she does come back one day soon, poppet," he said, his voice thick with suppressed emotion.

"I like it when you laugh, Papa," Verity said softly. "It makes my heart happy."

He smiled, grateful anew for his daughter. She had been the guiding light through all his darkness, and she would continue to remain so. "It makes my heart happy, too. Rest well, poppet. I shall see you in the morning."

He lowered the lights and made his retreat.

Just as he crossed over the threshold, her small voice stopped him once more.

"Papa?"

"Yes, Verity?" He turned back, the light from the hall slanting over her bed and illuminating nothing more than her sweet little face.

"Miss McKenna makes my heart happy, too."

A wall of emotion hit him. "Mine too, Verity," he choked out. "Mine, too."

And then, before he said anything more, he gently closed her door. He had not given up on fighting for Johanna yet.

"SIT DOWN, JOJO."

Drummond's order cracked through the air of the room where he had taken her. It was a humble abode, consisting of nothing more than a large room with a stove and sparse furniture.

She looked at the chair he had pointed to with the barrel of his pistol, and then to the ropes in her brother's hand. "No."

"Sit," he repeated. "If you do as I say, no harm will come to you."

"I do not believe you." She could not bear to be tied. To be unable to defend herself. To be unable to move.

Surely, this was the end for her. Perhaps Drummond was taking pleasure in prolonging her inevitable death. Making her suffer. When they had been but children, he had drowned a sack of puppies in the Hudson. He hurt and killed because he liked it.

He was sick. A sick man who was using a worthy cause as an excuse to hurt others.

"Do you want me to shoot you, or do you want to sit in the bleeding chair?" he asked sharply. "You have until the count of five, Jojo."

The hated name rankled.

"One. Two. Three…"

She sat. Her mind was still whirling, grasping at ways she might conceivably escape. If he shot her now, which she had no doubt he would, there would be no escape.

"What do you want from me?" she asked him.

"I want you to shut up," he snapped. "Put your feet together."

She did as he asked, suppressing a shudder when he wound the rope around her ankles. She could kick him, she realized. Use both feet at once. She wore sturdy boots tonight because the sky had been overcast and she had supposed it would rain.

One kick, perhaps to his chin…

Suddenly, the door burst open. Drummond scrambled to

his feet. His instincts were quick, far quicker than hers. Before she could attempt to flee, he was behind her, an arm pressed tightly around her throat.

The lone man standing on the threshold was painfully familiar. Painfully beloved as well.

"Felix," she cried out, though the pressure of her brother's arm on her throat was almost enough to choke her.

His gaze did not waver from Drummond. He held a gun in his hands, as naturally as if it were an extension of himself.

"McKenna," he said in a low, angry growl. "We meet at last."

"Winchelsea," Drummond greeted, training his pistol upon Felix's head. "Lower your weapon now, if you please."

Felix's jaw clenched. His gaze flitted to Johanna's before returning to her brother. "I will not drop it until you release her."

"I knew you would come," Drummond said, triumph in his voice as he ignored Felix's demand. "My whore of a sister did her job well."

Dear God.

He had planned for Felix to find them.

And there was only one reason why he would have such an aim.

Horror clawed at her.

"Felix," she called out, her mouth dry, her voice barely functioning, so great was her terror. "Go. Save yourself. Think of Verity!"

"I told her to bed you," Drummond continued, his tone taunting now. "And she did. How does it feel to know you lied to protect a traitorous whore?"

"He is lying," she denied, tears swimming in her eyes. She clawed at her brother's arm to no avail. He would not release her, and her efforts only earned her a vicious blow to the side of the head, courtesy of his pistol.

"Silence," Drummond ordered. "Stop moving, or this will go badly for you, sister."

She struggled for a breath, but his arm had tightened.

Felix looked as if he were made of stone, all his attention upon Drummond, the gun still pointed at him. He crossed the threshold slowly. "Your true quarrel is with me, is it not?" Felix asked. "Let your sister go."

"Stop right there," Drummond warned, and then the barrel of the pistol was a cold metal threat butting into her temple. "If you take another step, I will put a bullet in her brain."

Her breathing was already altered from the tightness of his hold upon her, but now she could scarcely breathe at all. "Please," she managed to croak. "Go, Felix. This is not your battle."

It was hers.

It had always been hers.

She had run, but not far enough. And she had been strong. But not strong enough.

That was going to change today. Because the man she loved was in danger, and she could not bear for anything to happen to him.

Her hands were free. Though she did not possess strength enough to tear her brother's arm from her neck, there was the possibility she could move slowly enough—stealthily enough—to attempt to hit the hand holding the pistol. If she could knock it away from him…

"I knew about your plot, you know," Drummond said to Felix. "You intended to use Jojo against me, but in the end, I used her against you. I have eyes and ears everywhere, you see. I knew I was being watched at home. I was being followed every day for weeks, even before we carried out the bombings at Praed Street and Charing Cross."

Felix took another slow step closer. "So you used your sister. Forced her into your tangled web so you could remain at your club and maintain your façade of innocence."

Drummond jammed the pistol into her temple with punishing force. "Not another step forward, Winchelsea. I needed someone who would not be watched. Someone no one would suspect. The press caught on, believed she was my mistress. It was an excellent cover. I could not have planned it all out better myself. Until you intervened."

"You orchestrated the bomb that exploded at my home," Felix said, his gaze flitting briefly to Johanna once more.

His gaze gave her comfort. Reassured her. She could do this. She must do this.

"And others," Drummond confirmed with cold triumph. "There will be more. We will never stop until Ireland is free of tyranny."

"There are other ways to achieve the ends you desire." Felix's eyes went to something over Drummond's shoulder. He appeared to give an almost imperceptible nod. "But if it is victory you want over me, then leave Johanna out of this. I will lower my weapon if you promise to remove your gun from her temple."

"No," Johanna attempted to cry out her denial. But she was still gasping for air, her throat held in such a tight grip she could not manage to project.

It felt like the nightmare which had plagued her in the months following Pearl's death. The dream where she could see Pearl about to be taken from her, and she tried so desperately to reach her, and yet she never could. Her body had been paralyzed, her voice frozen. She had wrenched herself from slumber so many nights, body covered in sweat, still trembling from the helplessness and the sheer anguish.

This moment was every bit like that nightmare, but worse.

Because it was real.

And Felix was before her, doing the unthinkable—lowering his pistol to the floor at his feet—all whilst keeping his hands on display, his eyes pinned to Drummond. Her brother would not hesitate to kill Felix. She knew it. This was what he had come here for.

Felix slowly stood, leaving his gun on the floor.

"Kick it toward me," Drummond ordered.

She attempted to cry out again, but it only made her brother's hold on her throat tighten.

Felix did as her brother asked, nudging the weapon with his shoe.

The pistol slid noisily across the floor, stopping halfway between where Felix stood and the chair where Drummond was holding Johanna captive. The pistol barrel left her temple, and it was pointed instead directly at Felix.

"Jojo, you did your job well," Drummond said. "You must be better on your back than you are on the stage. Look at how willing the mighty duke is to sacrifice himself for you."

Tears were streaming down her cheeks. Hot tears of terror. She had to do something. To act before her brother shot Felix. But she was afraid that any wrong move on her part would make him pull the trigger.

"I love her," Felix said simply.

Drummond released a bark of bitter laughter. "Love is a fiction invented by fools. But I am heartily glad you are a fool. It will make this far easier than I could have imagined."

Suddenly, the report of a gunshot echoed through the room. Everything seemed to happen all at once. Drummond's hold on her neck eased, and he slumped forward, the weight of his body slamming into her chair. Something warm and wet was all over her neck.

Felix cried out her name.

The gun fell from Drummond's limp hand, hitting the floor with a clatter.

Felix was running toward her, arms outstretched, and he was safe, unharmed, she thought. *Thank God.* Everything slammed into her all at once: sensation, emotion, air forcing its way back into her lungs, fear—that constant companion—robbing her of her ability to speak.

She was hot. Cold. Terrified. Colors blurred. Shapes became indistinct. Other shouts rose up, more voices, more footsteps, as the room was flooded with a sea of men. She gasped for breath, her vision darkening around the edges. Her heart was beating so fast in her chest. Her lungs burned. Ringing sounded in her ears. It was as if she had lost control of her body. As if she were watching from somewhere else as she pitched forward, falling into nothing but darkness.

Chapter Nineteen

FELIX HELD JOHANNA in his arms, cradling her like a babe, as he carried her down the narrow stairs leading to the flat above the apothecary where Drummond McKenna had been secreting himself, using an alias, since his arrival in London. She was breathing, *thank Christ*, and she had not suffered any wounds he had been able to see in his frantic inspection of her person.

In the wake of the tense operations between himself, Drummond McKenna, and the Duke of Westmorland, his heart was still pounding. When he had arrived at the apothecary's shop, it had been to a small gathering of Special League men. Arden had been adamant that Felix could not be the one to enter the flat and confront McKenna directly. Westmorland, who had recently inherited his dukedom and the latest addition to the League, had argued Felix was the best choice to go.

They had already learned from the apothecary belowstairs that there was a separate rear entrance to the upstairs flat, one accessed via the apothecary's shop. Westmorland and some reinforcements had quietly approached the flat in covert fashion while Felix had been the one to confront McKenna.

The sight of Johanna, her eyes wide with terror, helpless at her brother's mercy, had hit him like a blow. He had not been prepared. With the Home Office, his duties had not entailed field work. He had scarcely ever wielded a gun against another man before this night, though he was an expert marksman and more than familiar with firearms.

Her eyes fluttered open as he reached the lower floor corridor, which was lit by a lone gas lamp. "Felix?"

"I am here, darling," he said, part of him not feeling safe until they were free of this building.

Until they were as far away from Drummond McKenna's lifeless body as his feet could carry them. The bastard was dead, and thank the Lord for that. Westmorland's approach from the rear had been stealthy and silent. His timing had been impeccable. As had his aim.

The moment McKenna had turned the pistol upon Felix, Westmorland had taken his shot. His bullet had lodged in McKenna's skull before the man had known what hit him. His eyes had gone lifeless in the seconds before the pistol had fallen from his limp fingers and he had slumped forward, his dead weight falling upon Johanna.

Felix wished he could kill the bastard all over again for the ruthless force he had exerted upon her. The pressure he had been applying to Johanna's throat had been so strong that she had lost consciousness because of it. The combination of shock and her inability to breathe had led her to swoon.

He had endured the fright of his life watching her eyes flutter closed and seeing her pitch to the floor as he rushed forward in a vain attempt to catch her. At first, he had been afraid she had been hit by a bullet from either McKenna's gun or that Westmorland's shot had traveled straight through McKenna to lodge in Johanna. But the lack of blood had suggested she had simply been in shock and deprived of air.

He would give her the air she needed now.

By God, he would give her anything she wanted.

Everything she wanted. All his love, all of himself, every

single bloody thing she needed.

Forever.

Just as long as she would let him.

Gratitude was pouring over him in great waves, along with relief. They were both safe. McKenna was dead. And Johanna would forever be free from her brother's tyranny. She would never again have to fear him or be forced into doing his bidding against her will.

"Felix?" she rasped again as he reached the street and his waiting carriage.

To hell with anything and anyone else. There was no way he was taking her anywhere other than to beneath his own roof this night. He needed to know she was safe. To have her near. After what they had just gone through together… But he could not forget the contempt she held him in, the anger she had for him.

He stopped, halfway to his carriage, gathering his wits and his breath. "Johanna, are you hurt?"

"No," she said slowly. "I…Felix, what happened? You were not injured, were you?"

"No," he reassured her, pressing a kiss to her forehead. "It is all over now, thank God. McKenna can never hurt you or anyone else again."

Arden approached him then, patting him on the back. "Well done, Winchelsea. Your fearlessness is to be commended. I cannot help but to think the Home Office would have you back without hesitation after the bravery you've exhibited tonight."

"My time with the Home Office is done," Felix said, and he meant those words. The only responsibility he wanted, from this moment forward, was as a father and a husband.

But first he had to convince the woman in his arms to marry him.

Arden inclined his head. "Understood. If you will excuse me, I need to send word to the Criminal Investigation Department."

"I can walk, Felix," Johanna protested as Arden walked away.

"I do not want to let you go," he said with brutal honesty.

He had been so certain, with McKenna's pistol pressed to her temple, that he would lose her forever. It was as if he had to continue touching her to assure himself she was real.

Once he had her inside the carriage, he settled her on the squab. He seated himself opposite her as the vehicle swayed into motion, but decided it was not good enough. Instead, he joined her and hauled her into his lap.

She wrapped her arms around his neck, not protesting his commandeering of her person. For a few minutes, neither of them spoke. They held each other tightly, with the embrace of two people who had just stared death in the face and survived. The frantic cling of two people who had almost lost each other.

He buried his face in her rose-scented hair, overwhelmed by the rush of emotion.

It was not one of his fits he was suffering, but something else. Something different. Their hearts were beating against each other, visceral reminders of all they had just been through. Of how fragile were the bonds of life.

How precious.

"Marry me," he said at last into the silence. "I was wrong to lie to you, Johanna, and for that I am sorry. You can hold on to your anger for as long as you need. But please, say you will become my duchess."

"How can you want to marry me?" she asked softly. "We have been ensnared in deceptions ever since the moment we first met. We do not know each other as we truly are."

"Then we will get to know each other," Felix offered. "We will begin again. We will start over."

She looked up at him, meeting his gaze in the low light. There was such sadness in her eyes it brought a new physical ache to his chest. He wanted to kiss away the sadness, to chase away her doubts.

"How can we, Felix? We have done nothing but lie to each other, and I have only brought you danger and hurt." She paused, cupping his jaw tenderly. "Verity was almost killed because of me, and when I think what could have happened to you tonight…"

"You are not to blame for the actions of Drummond McKenna," he told her, interrupting.

He could not bear to utter the phrase *your brother* after what he had just witnessed. Johanna could not be more different from that man, and Felix could scarcely believe they shared blood.

"I am to blame for bringing you so close to danger," she argued, tears glittering in her eyes. "I am the reason you stepped down from the Home Office."

"You are the woman who stole my heart when I least expected it," he returned tenderly, unable to keep from worshiping her with his gaze. She was so lovely, so beloved. "You are the reason Verity and I found laughter again. You are the light that was missing from my life."

"Do you not see, Felix? You cannot marry me. I had a child out of wedlock. I am an actress, and I cannot hide that. My face and name are far too well-known. I am scandalous." The tears were on her cheeks now, trailing down her silken skin.

He wanted to follow them with his lips. To kiss them until there was no trace left of her sadness. To swallow it whole, take away her every pain. "If you are scandalous, my love, then I shall simply be a scandalous duke. And to the devil with anyone who turns up their noses at us. We will face them all together."

"Felix," she whispered.

He kissed her lips gently. Slowly. "I love you, Johanna."

"How can you love me after everything that has happened?" She shook her head, a sob tearing from deep within her.

She was torn, he could see, but he felt as if her tides were shifting. Just a few more nudges, and she would relent.

"Our circumstances dictated who we were, what we could reveal to each other. I propose starting fresh." He paused and kissed the tip of her nose before continuing. "As Miranda says, *How beauteous mankind is! O brave new world that has such people in't!* Let us create a brave new world together. Let us write our own story, free from all the chains that once bound us."

"Oh, Felix." Her heart was in her eyes, though she had not spoken the words yet.

He thought they were there.

He believed they were waiting to be uttered.

Because he could feel the strength of the emotion emanating between them. Theirs was a connection that was extraordinary. It surpassed everything else. Not even the dividing lines between them mattered.

"Tell me you will be mine," he urged. "Tell me you will, because I almost lost you tonight, and I cannot bear to lose you ever again."

"I love you," she said. "I love you so much, Felix, and there is nothing I want more than to be yours."

At last.

He was kissing her before she could say another word. The first three were all he needed to hear. His lips moved over hers with all the love in his heart, showing her the depth of the emotion he felt for her. It went beyond the marrow of him, all the way to his soul.

But then he realized she had not yet said the one word—the one specific, equally necessary word—he needed from her lips. He broke the kiss.

"You did not answer my question, darling," he said. "Will you marry me? Be my duchess and a mother to Verity?"

"I will never take Verity's mother's place." She caressed his jaw. "But it would be my honor to be your wife and to be a mother to your daughter. I love you both, you see, so much my heart hurts."

"Thank God." He rested his forehead against hers. "We love you too, Johanna. Every bit as much."

As the carriage rocked slowly back through the London night, they held tightly to each other. Felix had never felt so much hope for the future.

JOHANNA HAD JUST emerged from a hot, restorative bath when there was a knock at her chamber door. She had cleansed the awfulness of the night from her skin, but she knew cleansing it from her mind would not be nearly as easy. But she had time, and she had Felix and Verity. And she would survive, just as she always had.

Only, this time, she would not be alone.

A second rap at the door shook her from her musings.

"Enter," she called softly, aware of the lateness of the hour.

Much of the household—including Lady Verity—was abed.

The door opened to reveal Felix, a most welcome sight.

And looking distinctly like the scandalous duke he had claimed he would be, he was wearing nothing more than a robe and bearing a tray in his hands. It was laden with food and wine.

Her stomach growled at the sight, and the rest of her filled with heat and awareness.

She had missed him. *Dear God*, how she had missed his hands on her, his lips on her. The way he looked at her with those vibrant green eyes. The way he smelled, the quiet strength of his big body, the way he held her in his arms.

"How are you feeling, darling?" he asked her, his concerned gaze searching hers as he crossed the threshold and closed the door at his back.

"Much better now that you are here," she told him, for it was true.

Just him being in the chamber with her was enough to calm her. How she had ever supposed she could spend the rest of her life loving him from afar was beyond her now as she drank in his presence.

"I thought you might be hungry," he said, laying the tray on a writing desk.

It was laden with meat and cheeses and tarts. Her stomach rumbled again.

She pressed a hand over her midriff, heat prickling her cheeks. "You are always taking care of me."

He smiled, and Lord, but he was beautiful when he smiled. "Someone should have been, all this time."

"I took care of myself," she protested lightly.

But he was walking toward her now, his arms open, and she could not deny the rightness of walking into them and feeling his embrace close around her. She pressed her cheek over his heart, listening to the steady, reassuring thumps, and slid her arms around his lean waist.

He kissed her crown. "You do not need to take care of yourself any longer, my love."

Gratitude and love washed over her. "This feels as if it must be a dream."

"If it is a dream, let me sleep, for I don't want to wake." The deep rumble of his baritone infused her with warmth.

"Nor do I," she said.

And then she could not resist sliding her fingers around to his side and lightly tickling him. He emitted a squeak that was not at all ducal.

"Why did you do that?" he asked, sounding perplexed.

She tilted her head back to gaze up at him, allowing all the love she had for him to show in her eyes. "I wanted to make certain you were real, and that this is not a dream after all. It would seem scandalous dukes are ticklish."

"Saucy wench," he said, smiling softly back at her. "Perhaps I shall have to see where scandalous duchesses are ticklish."

How necessary it was, to share this brief moment of lightness after all they had endured that evening. After her brother's death. After his attempt on her life and Felix's. She still felt quite sure he had meant to kill them both.

That part still seemed like a nightmare in itself. But although she was relieved she would never again need to fear Drummond, she could not be happy he had been killed. Nor would she soon forget the sound of the gunfire echoing in the room, the horror clawing at her throat, the heavy weight of his body falling against hers as the life drained from him.

"I am not a duchess," she pointed out to Felix at last, forcing her mind from her turbulent thoughts.

She knew from past experience that it was no good to dwell in the darkness. *The people that walked in darkness have seen a great light*, the Bible told her, and she believed it. She had lived it. And the light she had seen was shining above her and standing before her. That light was an innocent child sleeping soundly down the hall. That light was love and happiness and laughter, and everything that was good.

Everything that was necessary.

"I have a license at the ready," Felix told her then, his countenance growing somber once more. "Marry me tomorrow."

"Tomorrow?" She searched his expression, but all she could find was intent.

He was serious. "I would marry you tonight, this very second, if I could."

What else could she say to that? There seemed only one rational response. Her heart knew it. Her tongue knew it before her mind had even reached a decision.

"Yes," she said, "I will marry you tomorrow."

She would marry him now if she could as well, and it was that realization which propelled her forward. Following her head had never been difficult for her. Following her heart, however, was something new.

Worth it for the chance at happiness. For the chance at forever with Felix and his daughter.

His grin widened, with relief, she thought, and something else—perhaps sheer, unadulterated joy. "You will not regret it, Johanna. I swear to you. From this moment forward, I will do everything in my power to love you and to keep you safe. I promise I will never let anything or anyone come between us."

She fell headlong into his gaze, and she forgot all about her stomach. There was only one hunger she sought to abate now. "I promise the same, Felix. There is nothing I want more than a life with you and your daughter. I am ready to move forward, into that brave new world with you."

"You have made me so happy. Happier than I could have

ever imagined being again, before you came into my life." He kissed her forehead with a reverence that stole her breath. "I love you, Johanna. I feel all the way to my soul that I was always meant to love you. That we were meant to find our way to each other. That this love of ours was meant to be."

Tears pricked her eyes, studding her lashes. "That is how I feel, too. I was afraid to acknowledge it before, because I feared Drummond and what he would try to do to you and Verity. I didn't want you to be in danger because of me. At first, I was too afraid to trust you—"

"You can trust me, darling," he broke in. "I have been telling you all this time. If given the choice between duty and love, I choose love. I choose you."

"I know that now." She swallowed against a lump of intense emotion. "In truth, I think I have known it always, deep in my heart. But I was so afraid, after the bomb that was planted at your home and the fire…"

"It is in the past now," he said. "Tonight, we move forward. Together."

"Together," she echoed, liking the sound of that.

Loving the sound of that lone word and all it encompassed.

"Now let me take care of you. I am certain you must be starving."

"I am," she said, blinking away her tears, feeling reckless and bold. She was searching for the light. Reaching for love. For *Felix*. "But not for food."

He raised a brow, his eyes dipping to her lips and then returning to her gaze. "Oh? What is it you are hungry for, my future scandalous duchess?"

"You," she confessed.

"That is scandalous indeed," he told her, and then he smiled.

It was one of his truly mesmerizing smiles, the kind that made little crinkles bracket his eyes. She wanted to kiss them. In fact, she was suddenly beset by the urge to kiss every inch of him. He was so beloved to her, and every part of him was perfect, from the blade of his nose to the breadth of his shoulders. To his well-formed calves, the muscles of his chest, his strong arms, his wonderful lips.

If she had not already been in love with him, she fancied she would have fallen in love with him all over again for this night. He had saved her life. And then he had held her in his arms the whole way home. He had come to her with food. With his warmth and his love.

Emotion seized her at the same moment as his mouth claimed hers.

Love.

Such raw, undeniable, frenzied love. His lips were open, hungry. One of his hands found her hair, his fingers tightening in the chignon she had fashioned herself when she had emerged from her bath. Pins were falling. She didn't care.

Tonight was a celebration of life and love.

They were alive. They were together.

Tomorrow, she would worry about everything else. Tomorrow, she would think about how a scandalous duke and duchess would be received. Tomorrow, she would fret over all the details of today. The pain, the terror, the anguish, the death.

All of the darkness could wait.

She was alight and alive, on fire for this man she loved. This man who loved her in return, against all odds, and despite what it had already cost him. Despite what it would potentially cost him still. They would not have an easy road to travel as husband and wife. She knew that, of course. Her past could not be changed, and neither would she hide it. She was an actress. Some part of her life would always be in the theater.

The thought gave her pause.

She pulled her head back, gazing up at him as her lips tingled and every part of her cried out for more. "I am an actress," she told him.

He stared at her. "I am aware, darling. And a very fine one. The finest I have ever seen."

"Being an actress has been my life for the last eleven years. It is all I have known," she added.

A frown creased his forehead. "Of course it has. I have no wish to stifle you."

Did his goodness and his love for her know no bounds?

"But you must," she argued. "For your own good—for your sake, and for Lady Verity's I must stop being an actress. I cannot be both."

"Of course you can." He cupped her cheek, his gaze plumbing the depths of hers. "I am not going to ask you to stop being an actress when you wed me, if that is your fear."

No, he would not, would he? Because he was Felix, and his love was so unbelievably pure and strong. As she searched his handsome face, she could see the truth for what it was.

A weight lifted from her heart. If he had demanded she cease acting, she could not have borne it, regardless of how much she loved him. But here he was, being selfless, telling her she could continue acting at great peril to his reputation.

And it was her concern for his reputation and Verity's that told her what she must do.

"You need not ask me, Felix," she said. "I will stop acting. It is what is best for everyone, and I know it."

"What would you say if I told you I was planning upon building a new theater with Theo Saville, and that it would be yours to run as you saw fit?" he asked then.

She stilled, so taken aback by his question, she did not know what to say at first. "Truly?"

"Truly," he said. "After the night I went to you in your dressing room, I knew you still had feelings for me, merely that you were doing your damnedest to thrust them aside and ignore them. For the past few days, I have been doing everything in my power to both see to it that you were safe and that I might have something to offer you as my wife."

"Felix." She stared at him, caressing his jaw. "The last thing I want is for you to make concessions for me. Please do not give up anything on my behalf. You, Verity, and your love are all I need. I promise you."

"Along with Theo, I have invested in a new theater, to be named as you choose. We will own two thirds of the theater, and he will own one third." he continued, ignoring her protestations.

"Why would Mr. Saville accept such a disparate partnership?" she asked.

She had seen the way in which Mr. Saville had run the Crown and Thorn. He was a perceptive man, quite canny, adept at marketing himself and his theater to those around him. Surely he had no need of an additional theater, especially one where he would only own a third, when he had such a thriving venture all to himself.

"Because he has seen you in action, Johanna," Felix said. "He knows how talented and perspicacious you are. Running another theater from afar will suit him. He can fill his pockets without all the work."

"The work will be mine," she guessed, rather warming to the notion. One of her dreams—far-flung, she had supposed—had been to run her own theater one day. The inevitable end to every actress and actor was that their roles became more difficult as they aged. She had not yet reached that point, but she had reached the point of understanding what lay ahead of her.

She was a career-minded lady. A new woman, after all. And she would not feel ashamed or deny that part of herself. Nor would Felix want that, she was sure.

"If you want the work," Felix elaborated carefully, "it will be yours. I make no expectations or demands of you. If this is not what you want, we shall not do it. If it is what you want, the stage will be yours to do with as you wish. If you want to continue acting, you may. I will admit I have my own best interest at heart, hoping that you would choose to act here in London rather than traveling the Continent as you had originally planned."

He still wanted her to act?

Her heart was pounding.

And aching. With love. So much love.

"You do not mind if I continue as an actress," she said slowly.

"Of course I do not mind," he said, his voice wry now. "How dare I deprive the world of such an impeccable talent?"

"What if I want to stop acting?" she asked.

She loved acting, it was true. But she was not averse to making a change. She had been pursuing the same vocation for almost half her life. The notion of running her own theater held untold appeal.

"Do you want to stop acting?" he asked, searching her face.

"If I can run my own theater, I would like nothing better." She paused, working through her thoughts as the notion settled in. "I could direct, perhaps teach others. But Felix, you have already given up so much for me. I cannot ask you to make any more sacrifices."

"For you, there is no sacrifice too great to make," he told

her intently. "All I want is to make you happy. I promise you, here and now, that I do not care what society thinks. I do not give a damn about what is proper and what is not. I lived my life for duty alone these past few years, and I will be damned if I continue."

"You make me happy." She caressed the proud line of his jaw. "Happier than I ever imagined it was possible to be."

"Christ." He cupped her face in his hands, his expression tender. "I love you so much. When I thought I would lose you…"

She pressed a finger to his lips, stilling the words. "You will never lose me, Felix. I am yours now. Forever."

"Forever," he echoed against her fingertip, and then he kissed it.

They stared at each other, gazes holding, exchanging so much heavy sentiment with that lone look. And then, they were kissing. Their lips moving, tongues chasing each other. It was a kiss of life, of promise, of hope. A kiss of the future.

Of beginnings.

Of light after darkness.

Of happiness after so much bitter sadness.

He tasted sweet and sinful, like wine and Felix. She never wanted to stop kissing him. She wanted his lips on hers forever, branding her, giving her strength. They were moving, the tray of food forgotten. She was only starved for his touch, his claiming. That was all she needed, all she craved.

Their hands were on each other, traveling. Knots came undone. Robes slid to the floor. Naked skin met her questing touch. Strong, smooth shoulders. The broad plane of his back. Sinews of his muscled arms.

They were still kissing when they fell into the bed together. Felix cushioned their fall by catching his weight on his forearms. She was on her back with him atop her, her thighs spread naturally to accept him. His cock was a rigid temptation prodding her belly. His desire for her inspired an answering throb in her core.

She was wet and aching for him.

Desperate for him.

He broke the kiss first, dragging his mouth down her neck to a place that drove her mad. Then to her ear. He tongued the hollow, his breath hot and decadent, sending a new frisson of desire through her.

"I want you inside me," she said, half plea, half command.

"Patience," he murmured against her skin.

And then he kissed his way lower still.

FELIX FOUND HIS way to the beauty mark on her right breast. Her skin was so soft, scented delicately of the floral soap from her bath. Tonight, she smelled like a summer's garden in full bloom, rich and exotic. He took a nipple in his mouth and sucked.

She made the breathy sound he loved and arched her back, offering her breast to him. He flicked his tongue over the distended bud, then blew on it. She made another sweet sigh of surrender. What a sight she was, all creamy curves, her golden hair damp from her bath and fanned out around her. He lowered his head to her other nipple, sucking it slowly, using his fingers to pluck at the other one, tugging and rolling it between thumb and forefinger.

He wished he had all night to worship her, but the truth was, his hold on his control was slipping. He had gone from fearing he would watch her die before his eyes to hearing her tell him she loved him and would be his duchess in the span of one night. His body was raging with the need to claim her, to possess her.

He kissed down her belly, all the way to her hip bone, where he teased her by delivering an open-mouthed kiss. She shimmied against him, as eager as he was. He parted her thighs wider. There she was, the very center of her, pink and glistening and all his.

He could do nothing but lower his head. He swiped his tongue up her seam before lingering on her clitoris. He laved the swollen bud with slow, savoring licks. The taste of her on his tongue was nothing short of delicious, a blend of sweet floral notes and Johanna. Her hips shifted restlessly, telling him she wanted more as her fingers slid into his hair.

So he gave her more. He drew her into his mouth and sucked until she cried out and her body trembled beneath him with the force of a great, rushing release. But he was not finished with her yet. He had only just begun.

He licked into her, using his tongue on her as he would his cock. Penetrating thrusts, as deep as he could go. She made another mewl, writhing beneath him, her fingers tightening on his hair. He went back to her pearl, flicking his tongue over it, then sucking once more as he thrust a finger into her channel.

She gripped him, body bowing from the bed. He added a second finger, beginning a rhythm. The tight grasp of her slick cunny on his fingers was delicious. His cock hardened, his ballocks drawing tight. And then he caught her bud in his teeth, biting gently.

She came on a moan, contracting on him as her entire body stiffened. He remained where he was, fucking her with his fingers, biting and sucking, until the last of her spend. He could not wait any longer to be inside her. He had tortured them both enough.

Felix rose over her, guiding his cock to her entrance. One

surge of his hips, and he was inside her. He kissed her, his lips still wet with her essence, and ran his tongue against hers so she could taste herself. She moaned into his mouth. He pumped into her again and again, his pace turning frenzied, almost savage. All the care was gone from him. There was only raw, all-consuming need.

She milked his cock, bringing him deeper into her depths, her hips slamming against his as she caught his rhythm. It was so good. Too good. This was not just a mere joining but an affirmation of life, of love, of them.

Felix and Johanna. In her, he had found himself again. And he told her with his body. As he whispered the words. As he kissed her everywhere, every patch of delectable skin he could find. As he thrust in and out of her slippery cunny. He reached between them, finding her pearl and stroking it.

She came again on a scream he silenced with his lips. As she tightened on him with such delicious, slick strength, he knew he could not last a second longer. He slammed deep into her one last time before pleasure exploded. His release was potent and sudden. He spilled into her hot, wet depths, filling her with his seed because he could. Because tomorrow, she would be his duchess, and they would never again spend another night apart.

When the last pulse of his pinnacle faded, he collapsed against her, holding her tight. Their hearts matched a frantic pace, beating almost as one.

"I love you, Felix," she whispered, clutching him every bit as tightly as he did her.

He kissed her swollen lips once more, emotion cracking open inside him, the sweetest release of all. "And I love you."

Safe in each other's arms, they fell asleep at last.

Epilogue

New York City, 1883—Their Graces, the Duke and Duchess of Winchelsea, of London, England, have today announced the opening of a well-appointed new orphanage called the Pearl-Verity House. Her Grace, more famously known by her former stage name, Mademoiselle Rose Beaumont, previously presented a generous donation of five thousand pounds to the New York Foundling Hospital in honor of His Grace.

The Duchess, who has retired from the stage and is now an expatriate, has also recently taken on the management of a three thousand seat capacity theater in the West End of London called The Pearl. His Grace, the Duke of Winchelsea, purchased and restored the theater along with renowned theater owner Mr. Theodore Saville, to tremendous opulence…
reported in The New York Times

JOHANNA WAS SEATED at the piano in the grand music room she and Felix had designed as part of the restorations to Halford House in the wake of the explosion and fire. Tucked to each side were her two favorite people in the world: Felix on her left and Verity on her right.

Felix's long fingers worked nimbly over the keys as the melody of a familiar ditty filled the chamber. Verity's little hands joined in seamlessly. Johanna looked from father to daughter, love filling her so full she could do nothing but radiate pure, unadulterated joy.

She had never been happier. Nor had she ever loved more, or been more loved. It seemed she had found her brave new world, and it was here and now.

"I walked past a spruce," sang Felix then in his beautiful, deep voice, "and found a goose on the loose who was pecking the feet of a man named Pete."

Verity giggled. "Good one, Papa!"

"Thank you, poppet." He cast a wink in his daughter's direction before glancing back to Johanna. "Your turn, my dear."

He sang the words to her. Sang them. The man would have won her heart all over again had it not already belonged to him, for that alone. He was such a good father. And soon, their little family would grow. She cradled her burgeoning belly, just beginning to be noticeable beneath her gown.

Fortunately, she had been working up her rhymes and had one at the ready.

"There once was a man from New York," she sang, "who refused to use his fork. He said when I dine, I shall eat like a swine."

She ended her verse by mimicking the snorting oinks of a pig.

She was an unconventional duchess, it was true. Fortunately, Felix was an unconventional duke, and Verity was an unconventional little lady. She had no doubt that the daughter or son in her womb would emerge quite unconventional as well. They were a family, and that was all that mattered.

Verity and Felix both collapsed in peals of laughter at her pig impression, Felix wiping tears of hilarity from the corners of his eyes. "My favorite part was the bit where you made the pig sound. Your nose scrunched up adorably."

"The naughty goose was terribly funny," Verity added as

her giggles subsided, "but I must admit Mama outperformed you once more. It seems to be a going concern, Papa."

Mama. No matter how many times she heard Verity say that precious word, it would always find its way inside her heart. She had become the Duchess of Winchelsea when she had wed Felix, but *Mama* was the greatest title she could ever possess. And Mama to Verity—that was a title which had been earned. A title she had been reluctant to usurp. She had never asked for it. But when Verity had chosen to call her Mama for the first time, it had been one of the best days of Johanna's life.

"A going concern, is it?" Felix asked, repeating Verity's words as he raised a brow at his daughter. "I cannot argue with you on the matter, poppet. She is my better in every way."

"I am not," Johanna denied, another rush of love washing over her, this time so strong, it made her eyes sting.

She sniffled.

Being in a delicate condition had turned her into a veritable watering pot.

"You are," Felix insisted.

"She is certainly better at silly songs," Verity said.

"Papa is the best," she argued, sniffling some more. "Who else can think of a goose and a spruce and the feet of a man named Pete?"

And more to the point, who else could be so handsome, so charming, so silly, and so wonderful, all at once? She swore that with each day that passed, as she watched the man he was, the father he was, the husband he was, she loved him more.

"Mama needs a handkerchief," Verity decreed.

"I keep no less than five tucked about my person at all times," Felix said, extracting one with a flourish and offering it to Johanna. "One never knows when Mama will have need of one."

Smiling, she accepted it and used it to dab gingerly at her tears. It seemed happy tears were becoming a habit.

"I am just so very content," she said, rather tremulously.

"If you are any more content, I shall have to buy a handkerchief factory," Felix teased, but his eyes were glistening into hers.

The Pearl Theater had seen its opening night earlier that evening and had boasted a sold-out crowd. She had presided over the triumph from a private box with Felix and Verity. Johanna could not have been more pleased or proud. The play she had chosen was one of her favorite Shakespearean works, *Twelfth Night*.

"I scarcely wept at all today," she defended herself.

"Twice at breakfast," Verity said.

"Once on the way to the theater," Felix added. "Again when the curtain fell. Just now. I dare say that was my last handkerchief of the day. No more happy tears, darling, or I will need to replenish my stock."

"Perhaps you could use the sleeve of Papa's coat," Verity suggested cheekily.

"Volunteer your own sleeves, poppet," he said with mock outrage.

Johanna smiled, looking fondly from father to daughter. "Happy tears are a good thing."

Felix drew her into his side, and Johanna put her arm around Verity's little shoulders, drawing her into her side in turn.

"Happy tears are the best," he told her.

"I think cocoa biscuits are the best," Verity offered.

Johanna just laughed, heart content as she sat there with her family. "I think the two of *you* are the best."

"If you insist," Felix and Verity said in unison.

Her smile grew, and the prickle of happy tears returned. She sniffled. "I do."

It was indeed a brave new world. *Their* brave new world.

The End

Author's Note

Dear Reader,

Thank you for reading Felix and Johanna's story! I hope you enjoyed this fifth book in the League of Dukes series and that it made you sniffle over a few happy tears of your own. Felix and Johanna's happily ever after was fraught with danger and roadblocks, and complicated by their past losses, but in the end, love triumphed. Just as it always should.

Please consider leaving an honest review of *Scandalous Duke*. Reviews are greatly appreciated! If you'd like to keep up to date with my latest releases and series news, sign up for my newsletter here or follow me on Amazon or BookBub. Join my reader's group on Facebook for bonus content, early excerpts, giveaways, and more.

If you'd like a preview of *Fearless Duke*, Book Six, and the final installment of the League of Dukes series, featuring the newest member of the Special League, the Duke of Westmorland, and the independent lady who clashes with him in a delicious battle of wits and wills, do read on.

Until next time,
Scarlett

Author's Note on Historical Accuracy

The bombing of the Scotland Yard offices, in conjunction with bombings at St. James's Square, and the home of Sir Watkin Williams-Wynn MP, along with the unexploded dynamite in Trafalgar Square occurred on May 30, 1884. The Criminal Investigation Department of Scotland Yard (or the CID) was founded in 1878. I took some creative license and tweaked the timelines of these events to fit in with my fictional timeline where necessary.

Drummond McKenna is a purely fictional character. In truth, a number of different men—many of whom were indeed Irish-American in origin—were engaged in Fenian plotting and bombings during the 1880s. John Tierney, while a character I invented for this book, is loosely based on Irishman John Daly, who was arrested in 1883 with suspect evidence found upon his person.

Johanna McKenna's life as an actress was inspired by actress of the time Ada Rehan, who was born in Limerick, Ireland, and immigrated to America when she was five. She first appeared onstage when she was just fourteen and went on to a long and storied career as a lead actress that included tours of England and Europe.

Irish Home Rule was an incredibly divisive part of English, Irish, and American history. While much of this series has focused on my fictional Special League's efforts to capture Fenian bombers, I've also tried, whenever possible, to represent both sides of the matter. The Fenians who launched dynamite campaigns were the minority. Most Irish and Irish-Americans believed violence was not the answer to achieving

Home Rule.

Finally, a note on historical accuracy in terms of language and sexual content. Not only did people of the nineteenth century curse, use lewd words, and enjoy sex—and this is richly documented in literature, art, photographs, diaries, and letters—but people have been doing all those things for centuries. One of my literary heroes, Geoffrey Chaucer, was writing quite naughty things back in the 1300s. Use of the word *fuck* has been documented since at least the 1500s. As for sex, there are centuries' worth of erotic literature and other forms of art to attest to its role in the lives of everyday people throughout history. And good for them, I say!

Now, on to that preview I promised…

Fearless Duke

By
Scarlett Scott

Miss Isabella Hilgrove, proprietress of the Ladies' Typewriting School, prides herself on the quality of her staff. After the Duke of Westmorland sacks the third typist she has sent him in as many days, she's not just outraged, she's determined to put the arrogant bully in his place.

Benedict Manning, Duke of Westmorland, is having the worst week of his life. A bomb has exploded on London Bridge, the Special League is unraveling, and he cannot seem to find a secretary who is not a spineless watering pot. When the prim and proper Miss Hilgrove arrives on his doorstep, calling him everything but a gentleman, he can't resist toying with her.

Their mutual attempts to teach each other a lesson quickly turn into something more. But danger is in the air, and the brooding duke and the self-avowed spinster are about to become targets of the most lethal menace London has faced...

Chapter One

London, 1884

"I BEG YOUR pardon, Your Grace, but there is a Miss Isabella Hilgrove demanding an audience."

Benedict looked up from the reports of Scotland Yard's Criminal Investigation Department he had been poring over. It would appear the only good thing about the attempt to bomb London Bridge was that the dynamitards responsible had unintentionally detonated their infernal machine too soon.

They had blown themselves to bits in the process.

He frowned at his butler, the grim subject matter he had been reading infecting him like an ailment. "I am not at home."

Young's countenance was implacable as ever. "I informed Miss Hilgrove as much. However, she claims she has been sent by the Ladies' Typewriting School."

"Not another one," he grumbled.

Three typists had been sent to him by the school. Since he had undertaken the duty of managing the Special League, he required a seemingly endless amount of reports for the Home Office. Hiring a typist had seemed an excellent decision, especially since the Home Secretary himself had suggested it and recommended the school.

The decision had proved a dreadful error of judgment on

Benedict's part.

The first had hummed to herself as she completed a task. When he had pointed out how disturbing such a habit was, she burst into tears and fled.

The second had been dreadfully slow, her fingers hunting about the keys in plodding fashion so that she had accomplished frightfully little in the course of three hours. He had told her to leave and not return.

The third had been sniffling and coughing. He had taken one look at her red nose and watery eyes and sent her on her merry way. Illness aggrieved him mightily. Indeed, he could not afford to contract something catching in his current position.

There was far too much at stake.

But he became aware that Young was still lingering at the threshold of Benedict's study, looming like a wraith.

"What is it?" he snapped at the butler.

"I am afraid the lady in question has informed me she will not be denied an audience with Your Grace. She has indicated she will remain all day if necessary."

Devil take it.

He had no doubt the fourth offering from the school would not be any better than her three predecessors had been.

"Tell the lady in question her services are no longer required, if you please," he informed his butler.

His butler's countenance had never been more aggrieved. "I will try, Your Grace."

"Try?" he asked, for Young was ordinarily an exemplary domestic.

Benedict had expectations of his staff. Obeying his edicts and performing their tasks well and promptly were strict requirements. In addition to not being an irritant or a walking ailment, of course. He was not too stern, he felt certain. He merely expected from all those in his employ the same standards to which he held himself.

Namely, excellence.

Young cleared his throat, apparently seeing his mistake. "I will explain it as you require, Your Grace. Thank you."

He bowed and then took his leave.

Benedict exhaled slowly as the door clicked closed. He listened for the staccato of the butler's shoes on the marble hall. Solitude pleased him. Disruption irked him. He was a beast of habit, it was certain. But upon his shoulders, he bore a great weight of responsibility.

He bowed his head and resumed reading the reports awaiting him, assured Young would dismiss the creature at the front door and he would be done with the Ladies' Typewriting School for eternity.

He had scarcely even read two sentences when the indignant squawking began.

Truly, there was no other means of describing the sound reaching his hears. It was feminine and outraged. Followed by two sets of footsteps echoing down the marble hall.

"Madam, I beg you," said Young.

"Beg as you wish," responded the angry hen who had caused the initial squawking and unrest, "but I shall see the Duke of Westmorland, and I shall see him now."

What cheek.

What daring.

The effrontery of the baggage…why, it was unprecedented.

The fourth would not last any longer than the prior three, it was certain. Nettled, he rose from his desk, before skirting it and stalking toward the door. The door opened. And there stood a female.

The female.

Behind her hovered an anxious-looking Young, eyebrows raised. A waterfall of protestations rained down upon the moment.

"Miss Hilgrove, I must insist you go. This is quite improper. You cannot disrupt His Grace."

The last assertion appeared to spur the creature hovering on the threshold into action. She swept forward, small of stature and yet all womanly curves. She was golden-haired, pale of visage, and delectable of form. Her gown was dour: ebony and gray, conservative silk bereft of ornamentation.

But beneath it all hid the lush body of a woman. Her breasts were large and full. Her curves were plentiful, the sort that could not be hidden by plain dress. She was, all of her, from head to toe, woman.

And his cock sprang to life.

Feminine curves were his sole weakness, and he knew it.

Want more? Get *Fearless Duke*!

Don't miss Scarlett's other romances!
(Listed by Series)

Complete Book List
scarlettscottauthor.com/books

HISTORICAL ROMANCE

Heart's Temptation
A Mad Passion (Book One)
Rebel Love (Book Two)
Reckless Need (Book Three)
Sweet Scandal (Book Four)
Restless Rake (Book Five)
Darling Duke (Book Six)
The Night Before Scandal (Book Seven)

Wicked Husbands
Her Errant Earl (Book One)
Her Lovestruck Lord (Book Two)
Her Reformed Rake (Book Three)
Her Deceptive Duke (Book Four)
Her Missing Marquess (Book Five)

League of Dukes
Nobody's Duke (Book One)
Heartless Duke (Book Two)
Dangerous Duke (Book Three)
Shameless Duke (Book Four)
Scandalous Duke (Book Five)
Fearless Duke (Book Six)

Sins and Scoundrels
Duke of Depravity (Book One)

Prince of Persuasion (Book Two)
Marquess of Mayhem (Book Three)
Earl of Every Sin (Book Four)

The Wicked Winters
Wicked in Winter (Book One)
Wedded in Winter (Book Two)
Wanton in Winter (Book Three)
Willful in Winter (Book Four)
Wagered in Winter (Book Five)
Wild in Winter (Book Six)

Stand-alone Novella
Lord of Pirates

CONTEMPORARY ROMANCE

Love's Second Chance
Reprieve (Book One)
Perfect Persuasion (Book Two)
Win My Love (Book Three)

Coastal Heat
Loved Up (Book One)

About the Author

USA Today and Amazon bestselling author Scarlett Scott writes steamy Victorian and Regency romance with strong, intelligent heroines and sexy alpha heroes. She lives in Pennsylvania with her Canadian husband, adorable identical twins, and one TV-loving dog.

A self-professed literary junkie and nerd, she loves reading anything, but especially romance novels, poetry, and Middle English verse. Catch up with her on her website www.scarlettscottauthor.com. Hearing from readers never fails to make her day.

Scarlett's complete book list and information about upcoming releases can be found at www.scarlettscottauthor.com.

Connect with Scarlett! You can find her here:
Join Scarlett Scott's reader's group on Facebook for early excerpts, giveaways, and a whole lot of fun!
Sign up for her newsletter here.
scarlettscottauthor.com/contact
Follow Scarlett on Amazon
Follow Scarlett on BookBub
www.instagram.com/scarlettscottauthor
www.twitter.com/scarscoromance
www.pinterest.com/scarlettscott
www.facebook.com/AuthorScarlettScott
Join the Historical Harlots on Facebook

Made in the USA
Middletown, DE
04 December 2021

54196852R00203